ABRAM AND SARAI

ABRAM and SARAI

by
J. SerVaas Williams

Corinth House

ABRAM AND SARAI

Copyright © 1981 by Corinth House Publishers

Library of Congress Cataloging in Publication Data

Williams, J. SerVaas
  Abram and Sarai.

  1. Abraham, the Patriarch—Fiction.   2. Sarah
(Biblical character)—Fiction.   I. Title.
PS3573.I44932A64   813'.54   80-69805
ISBN 0938280-01-5

Dedicated to Rod—and all others who
know the mystery and the power of genuine
faith and pure love.

THE FERTILE CRESCENT

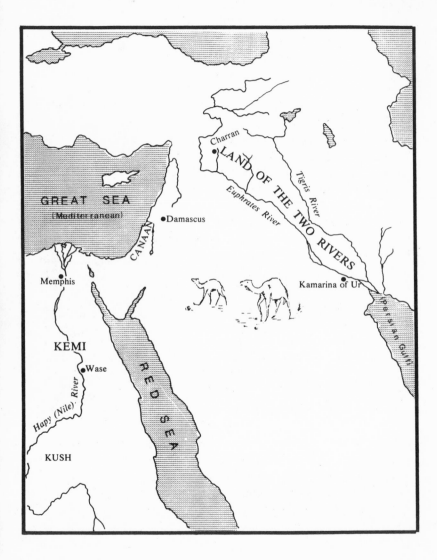

Chapter I
PAGANISM IN UR
c. 2615 BC

"Your fathers lived of old beyond the Euphrates, Terah, the father of Abraham and of Nahor; and they served other gods." Joshua 24:2

In the study of ancient history and archeology, traces of paganism—the worship of strange gods and idols—begin to appear in the middle of the third millennium BC. There is little evidence of any systematized paganism occurring earlier. Rather what is being discovered more and more is that people of that time and before held two strong universal beliefs: 1) that there is one God—hidden, powerful and without name—and 2) that this same God caused a devastating flood to cover the earth during which only one man and his family were spared.

Uniquely, the Tigris-Euphrates valley holds vast stores of man's earliest written documents. Inscribed on clay tablets, these recently discovered libraries are the archives of city-states, city-states that attained unbelievably advanced civilizations—almost all established between 4500 and 5000 years ago.

The most cultured of these city-states was Ur in the region of Sumer, the lower river valley near the sea which is now called the Persian Gulf. Out of Ur grew and spread the first insidious paganism. It was in Ur that a man made his own god, assigned him a shape and gave him a name: the moon was proclaimed god, the god Nannar-Sin.

Akalamdu clasped the priest's shoulders. "Ipali, I am trusting you," he whispered hoarsely, bitterly. Akalamdu's eyes unblinkingly fixed upon the young man. "Add the poison immediately. But you must not be detected! Be sure that all are watching me when I move to leave the tomb."

"I understand, sir," Ipali answered solemnly. The ritual robes which he was unaccustomed to wearing caused him to squirm slightly.

"On the morrow," Akalamdu continued, "I will bring Artatappi and other witnesses to declare that all are dead." Then he cautioned, "You must not attempt to escape until Puabi's tomb is sealed."

Akalamdu heaved a sigh of relief. The planning was done, and he was weary with it. The young priest looked affectionately at Akalamdu. "I shall try to make you proud of me, my king," he smiled nervously.

The funeral of the young woman, Puabi, halted the city's activities and commerce for three days. Two of these days were set aside for fasting and preparation with times for tribute and public mourning.

The last day found thousands of the citizenry of Kamarina filing through the great towered gate of the royal grounds. They crowded into the forecourt and up the steps to the Temenos, the raised inner court that surrounded the massive Ziggurat.

The Ziggurat dwarfed the people below. The giant stepped pyramid was a succession of three broad tiers. Lacing each of the Ziggurat's levels were green rows of manicured trees. From high balcony gardens, masses of brilliant flowers and wall vines hung profusely down the sloping sides. Water was supplied through deep wells whose shafts opened on each level. Though the core of the monolith was made of mud bricks covered with bitumen, the outer layer was an intricate mosaic of shining colored tiles. A free-standing monumental staircase jutted out from the eastern side of the Ziggurat. It was joined by two wall-flanking cases at a high, beautifully adorned portico on the first tier. Smaller stairs led up to the second and third levels. Atop the third tier was a small glistening structure, the royal chambers.

Although revered by most as a sacred symbol of divine salvation from the Great Flood, the Ziggurat had more than once been a refuge to the kingdom of Ur in present times of disaster. Beneath the very pavement where the people were assembling lay vast storerooms of grain, jugs of oil and ale, and basket upon basket of dried meat, fish and fruits. There were enough provisions for the whole area to wait out the storms of nature—or of man.

Kamarina was the capital of the city-state of Ur which covered the western delta of the Tigris and Euphrates rivers. Kamarina was at the height of its power and influence. The elevated city, built on a mound, was protected by thick high buttressed walls. A wide canal half circled the city, extending to the east and linking Kamarina with the broad Euphrates. Though the sea was still some distance away, Kamarina with its canal docks was the great port of the land of the rivers. Boats harbored there from distant lands, as far away as India, Kemi—the name used for Egypt throughout ancient times— and beyond.

The countryside of Ur surrounding the city was a beautiful array of verdant fields of wheat, barley and flax, rows of vegetables, orchards of fruit trees, and large stretches of pasture for cattle, sheep and goats. Date palms lined the many waterways that criss-crossed the farmlands. This was once all marshland of the Tigris and Euphrates delta area. The rich land had been drained by a complicated system of canals and dikes. Near the great rivers, high gray seawalls restrained and diverted the seasonal floodwater. An extensive untamed section of marsh with palm jungles and giant

11

bullrushes still existed and bordered Ur to the far east and south. Barren desert stretched to the distant north and west.

While a large part of the population of Ur was engaged in occupations relative to farm and pasture, Kamarina as a port city and capital was busy in trade and commerce from land and river traffic as well as from sea. Talented craftsmen that were drawn to the city flourished and excelled. With comforts and luxuries easily provided, a civilization evolved in Ur that made remarkable advances in accounting and banking, mathematics and astronomy, botany, geology, medicine and literature. Law, justice and moral standards were kept and honored.

For this expansive growth, two men were basically responsible: the incredible king, Akalamdu, who was adored with obsession by most of his people—and who hungered for such adulation; and a wise unpretentious chancellor who was usually capable of adjusting any adverse situation into something that would provide a favorable advantage for all concerned. Under this joint leadership, the borders of the city-state continuously expanded and Ur held dominant control over all water access to the upper rivers and even the land caravan routes that served the sea trade. Cargo and dock tax levies flowed amply into Ur's treasury and allowed for the flowering of culture and for extensive building projects. Slave labor was cheaply imported as it was needed.

King Akalamdu was quick and smart, but ponderous advisory council meetings or any tedious study bored him. In the same way, he highly respected the Academy with its resident scholars and system of schools, relishing the prestige the cultural institution had brought to Ur. But other than taking credit for its existence, the king generally shunned the Academy and left its control to the chancellor, Gimil, and others.

Akalamdu preferred being out with the people. His short muscular frame was a familiar sight in the streets of the city. Covering the countryside, he often rode on horseback or took a canal boat just to greet and visit with the farmers and herders. He knew most of his people by sight if not by name. He was especially loved by the older people in his kingdom and by the little children. Many youth, however, held him in contempt and mocked him—usually privately—with jokes and parodies. Rebellion in the schools of the Academy had recently flared up against the king but was quieted by cautious professors.

The Urians were descendants of Noah through Shem, and their early families were called Shemerians, or later Sumerians.[1] They believed in the God of Noah and the event of the Great Flood, but over the years many superstitions and myths had crept into their religious beliefs. This brought about a bondage of fear for the ignorant and an indifference to religion among most of the tradesmen and intellectuals. In ruling and influencing his people, Akalamdu adroitly used fervent piety when it would be effective. And if not effective, he could easily set his theology and spirituality aside.

The queen, Beltani, was the king's junior by several years. Her beauty had faded early, but because of her sharp wit and tongue she was jokingly known as Akalamdu's leash. He seemed to feel more secure when she was with him. Often Beltani retired from public view for many months, however, to be in the city of Nippur with her aged and dying mother. During these times Puabi, the couple's only child, would accompany her father on his tours.

Perhaps it was Akalamdu's early impotency that made him so idolize his daughter, seeing in her the fulfillment of all the children he could never have. He refused to view her intelligent but plain appearance as anything but pure beauty and his own reflection.

Princess Puabi was not so deceived. She was now at the age of eighteen and inwardly desired to be genuinely loved and to be married. To her deepening agony this yearning had become centered on her father's advisor and her own former tutor, the chancellor Gimil. Puabi had known and loved Gimil since her childhood. When playing in his courtyard with his daughter, Azuani, or when the two girls were together for lessons, Gimil would treat them with equal affection. Possibly because of the loss of his beautiful wife who died bearing Azuani, Gimil

1. For this and all other footnotes, see Appendix on page 356.

had taken extra time and pleasure in nurturing the two girls in their studies.

Gimil loved and appreciated Puabi as he did Azuani. His own daughter had none of his wife's beauty. Like Puabi she had learned to treat life honestly and with humor. Gimil enjoyed watching the two mature while he was their tutor. But in his fatherly love toward the princess, he neglected to notice the problems that were evolving.

Puabi was a woman at twelve and even more so at eighteen—a woman who had sense enough to know her lack of any great physical attractiveness and pride enough to be repulsed by shallow attention of palace suitors. Gimil became for years the intimate lover of her hidden fantasy world.

The tragedy of Princess Puabi began on the night of the king's fiftieth birthday. After a long day of festivities, banqueting and much ale drinking, Akalamdu went to his bedroom suite in the palace, dismissed his attendants and began pacing back and forth. The events of the day had not tired him, but he felt suddenly old, unfulfilled and anxious. He had never been plagued by sickness or ill health, but somehow this day brought a fear of death and a feeling of futility. Akalamdu also sensed a thread of rebellion beginning to weave itself into the fabric of his government.

Up to this time the king had not encouraged Puabi to marry. He feared any competition to his throne or to his daughter's affection. However, he now suddenly wanted to assure his royal line.

"I must have an heir. She must give me a son!" he convinced himself. His eyes flashing, Akalamdu impulsively dashed to the window balcony and called down to the guards, "One of you! Go fetch Princess Puabi . . . immediately!"

A guard retreated through the lower hall and inner courtyard to the princess' quarters. A maid received the message and hurried to tell the princess. Soon Puabi came into her father's presence. On seeing her, Akalamdu assumed a relaxed mood.

"Puabi, my lovely daughter," he greeted her. His broad smile and twinkling eyes sought for her attention. Embracing her, the king kissed her forehead.

"Sit down, my dear, we have an important matter to discuss."

Puabi smiled lovingly at her father. "I know, sweet father, you are an old, old man of fifty. Do you want to decide what to do during the next fifty years yet tonight?" Puabi teased, clasping Akalamdu's hands. "My, what a lot of rings you wear, Father. Is this a new one?" She twisted the unfamiliar stone between her fingers.

"Just a gift from that wily lawyer, Artatappi. He would like to run the country for me if he could," the king replied. His smile remained, but his eyes had sobered.

"Puabi," he began, and the girl watched him carefully. Puabi enjoyed her father, but she, more than any other except the queen, knew his ways. She knew he was up to something and was about to begin a lengthy prologue to win her interest.

"Kamarina as you know is one of the centers of the civilized world," he began. "It *could* become the greatest! There are few to compare with us from Ebla to Kemi or anywhere to the east. Our scholars are being sought after everywhere. People from high courts of every known city come here to Ur to study. And nowhere are our artisans and craftsmen being excelled.

"And it is *my* people who have done it; *my people* have done it for *me!*" he said emphatically. "I have the great ideas, and it is *I* who inspire them to build, to produce, to make the state of Ur stand high above the others!"

Puabi interrupted and chided, "Now, Father. Many brilliant men have helped build Ur. You would not want to claim credit for the Academy and all that Gimil and the others have done."

"But it is *I* who give them the freedom and the funds to do it all," he retorted sharply. "*I* am the one who can persuade the people, make them proud enough of their scholars, their beautiful city, their Ziggurat, to work their heads off so that those professors and lawyers can sit around all day playing

15

with their 'idea toys,' their 'pretty laws' that even try to fence me in a corner!"

"I have not noticed any fence you have not jumped over . . . or dug under," his daughter smilingly replied as she settled herself on the large cushions.

"Puabi," the king spoke directly. "I am fifty years old. Kamarina and Ur are *mine*! I *must* have my stamp on them forever!"

He paused before going on. "I speak of a god in my talks with the people—how he saved the ancient father, Noah, from the Great Flood, and how I likewise built the Ziggurat as a symbol and reality of those times. But do you really believe in such a god, Puabi? Do you believe in the God of Noah?"

"I think so," replied the girl. "I have prayed to him. There is too much order in the world and the heavens not to believe in some great power. Gimil says it is ridiculous to worship anything created and not the creator. He says that the orbits of the sun and the moon, the planets and stars are too determined and must be in the divine plan. Certainly those heavenly bodies have no control over us. . . ."

Akalamdu stopped her, "But what if we took the emblem of Kamarina, the moon. And what if I told the people that God who *made* the moon *was also the moon?* What if I told them that to see the moon is to see the God of Noah?" The king's groin suddenly reminded him of the quantity of ale he had consumed, and he hastily excused himself.

Puabi sat in perplexed silence. Her father's circular discussion was nonsense, but coming from him it could lead to trouble. She knew he would probably never stop this type of scheming until he tried it out on some group somewhere. And if it went too far, he would not back down without at least a compromise—which could be just as bad. Gimil, the civil officials and all the others would have to object in unity. Even then. . . .

Akalamdu must have been doing much thinking while he was gone, for he rushed back into the room shouting, "You, my daughter, will marry a god! What a plan I have!" The king was trembling with excitement. "You will have *divine* sons.

16

The god of the moon will husband you, and you shall bear me sons! Sons who will reign for me! Sons to keep my possessions in *my* power, under *my* name!" There, he had said it. Now to believe it.

Such blatant talk made Puabi's conscious thoughts long for Gimil. Whatever her father was planning, she could desire no other man than Gimil.

As if Akalamdu entertained her thoughts, the king bent down and lifted her chin until their eyes met. "I know you are in love with Gimil." The daughter gasped. With unaccustomed openness the king went on, "But he *cannot* be the next king of Ur! Gimil is too old, too wise, and too respected by the people. I know I act foolishly, even rashly at times. But as long as no one else is even close to me in power, I can cover over my mistakes, and even change my actions if the occasion calls for it."

Puabi tried to regain her control. "You want an heir from me . . . a *divine* heir even . . . but you want me to have a weak and stupid husband?" She had replied with some humor although she was still stunned by her father's directness and his knowledge of her love for Gimil.

"I am getting a plan," said the king, his tired eyes lighting up, his bottom lip puffed out in a proud and smiling pout. "We could dominate the world, you and I, if Kamarina were declared the holy city of a god . . . a god as we see him in the pure white form of the moon. *Nannar,* the moon name of the Sumerians, will be our god! *'Sin'* is the name for the moon in the lands of the north . . . so not just a god of the Sumerians of Ur, but Nannar-Sin he will be called, a god of all peoples!"

Akalamdu paused to enjoy his eloquence, his eyes closed and his nostrils stretching. "Can you not see the allegiances we could form? Your sons, Puabi, would be sent out to rule with divine power as high priests of every city-state. It would take little persuasion after some time to declare that the god of the moon desired they become kings as well."

The daughter broke into laughter, "Father, and how many sons do you have in mind? My womb is aching already!"

Akalamdu became more enthusiastic than ever as his sensible daughter seemed caught up in his visions. As if to summarize and congeal his myth into reality, he stated elatedly, "We will win over the world! All kingdoms will pay homage to Ur and to me the high priest of Nannar-Sin, the moon god." And gazing strongly at Puabi he said commandingly, "And *you* must be the one to see that my dream continues . . . forever!"

It was late. This interchange between father and daughter was to change the known world—but not in the way Akalamdu imagined.

Puabi returned to her quarters. The women who waited on her had retired, leaving her bed turned down. On a small table lay a plate with fruit cakes and a wedge of curd cheese. Gimil's daughter, Azuani, was reclining on an adjacent bed brought in for her during her frequent visits at the palace.

The two friends smiled sleepily. "What did your father want?" Azuani inquired. "You were gone long enough to settle all the problems of Ur."

Puabi began to laugh. "I do think you must have been listening. That is just what we did." She sat down on the edge of her bed. "My dear father," she said jokingly, "wants me to produce heirs for his kingdom."

"Oh," teased Azuani. "The king's baby girl has just come of age?"

"Ah, yes, but there is more. He wants to proclaim that the *moon* is a god, Nannar-Sin, by name. 'Sin', to double the name of the moon into a title and to play up to the dialect in the north." Puabi, still smiling, bit her lip and tears swelled in her eyes. "Somehow he has a plan to marry me off to this figment of his fancy, and I will bear offspring to be priests— priests first and then rulers of the world!" She paused and sighed, "I just hope he forgets the whole thing in the morning. . . ."

Azuani was quiet. Her large eyes stared, but she saw nothing. Her bright mind was absorbed in what might be the consequences of Akalamdu's plan if he really followed through on it. How would he try to introduce it? How would her father, Gimil, manage to keep the king from destroying all that has been built up through the years? Pushing such a foolish myth on the people would not be too difficult for

18

Akalamdu. When he was possessed with an idea he would try all kinds of schemes. How persuasive he was! The people would nearly make themselves slaves to fulfill his dreams. Up to this time most of his ideas were for the betterment of Ur, for it was *his* kingdom, and he wanted it to be the best. Also, Gimil and the other leaders had always been able before to redirect Akalamdu's follies into something beneficial.

Like the Ziggurat. When Azuani and Puabi were but small girls, Akalamdu announced that he would build the great tower to heaven that other cities had failed to accomplish. He mobilized the entire area into volunteer work teams and spread ideas about climbing the tower to reach the stars, to see the God of Noah, and more. It was Puabi who had led Gimil to her father to show Akalamdu a model of the tower he was proposing, and the impossible building problems it would present. It was Gimil who brought forth the compromise plan of a broad-based tower that could be used as a fortress and flood refuge. The king was relieved for he had soon tired of the high tower project and was fearful of failure when he realized the structural problems. But Akalamdu needed a potent and indisputable reason for the change. His quick mind found a ready answer in an old but prevalent superstition. It was the story found in many of the Flood accounts that the God of Noah first appeared to the survivors of the Flood in the form of a mountain—a smooth, cone-like pyramid that projected up alone among the waters. "We will build such a mountain!" exclaimed the delighted king at the time. "We will call it the 'Mountain of God' . . . the *Ziggurat!*" This appealed especially to the common people. They appreciated their king even more, knowing that the Ziggurat was also for their protection.

Azuani could imagine in her mind Akalamdu's strategy. She could almost hear him saying, "You, O Kamarinians, are those set apart by Nannar-Sin. He chose us and gave us the name Kamarina . . . city of moon light . . . because in our beautiful white walls and buildings he saw his own image. Now he wants to shine in his complete fulness here in his city. As the God of Noah once came to man as a mountain, now he comes to us in his 'Watching Over' form—the moon. He will bless you and send you out to tell others about his chosen dwelling place, the city of Kamarina of Ur. Here will come the great kings of the cities of the fertile crescent to pay the 'god of the crescent' honor. Pilgrimages to Kamarina will bring wealth to Ur, the land of the moon-god. . . ."

Yes, he could do it, Azuani thought.

Speaking aloud, Azuani tried to be jovial, "And when will the heavenly wedding be? Do I have time to dress?"

"Oh, yes, my friend," Puabi answered. "I presume this newly fashioned god will find himself incarnated in a young Urian male of my choosing."

The princess then stood, closed her eyes and stretched out her arm. Pointing her finger she turned slowly in place. "I must find my young white bull first. Who shall it be, Azuani? My little cousin, Kapi? Or that new, nice-looking guard you like? Or maybe your dear father Gimil?" Puabi kept her act in high motion but looked for a reaction from Azuani at the mention of Gimil. There was no reaction. What Akalamdu had sensed about Puabi's attraction for Gimil had been missed over the years by the usually perceptive Azuani.

Puabi continued, "If I would put on a flaxen country dress and walk the pasture paths even the shepherd boys would turn away. But as Princess Puabi, searching for a man to sire priests and kings, I ought to excite every man within my father's voice."

"You already have your choice," laughed Azuani. "Neither of us will ever be called beautiful except by liars! But you *are* the princess, and that *does* make a difference. You might as well enjoy having your pick!"

Puabi was tiring but continued the farce. "Well," she said, "let's line up the whole male population after breakfast, and I will let you help me choose."

With this the two girls readied themselves for bed, and the oil lamps were put out. The darkness was not gone, for the full moon cut shafts of light through the latticed windows. Both lay in apprehensive thought for some time before sleep came.

As the days passed, no more word of that late evening episode was spoken by the king to his daughter. Puabi kept

20

watching her father. "Was it all just a passing idea brought on by over-indulgence on a royal birthday?" she pondered, afraid to question him if he had forgotten it.

But her concerns remained and perplexed her. "Is it for more power and control? Does he really want to dominate people through religious fear of something he knows does not exist? Would he go so far as to use even me to achieve his ends? If I bore even one son, would his affections not be turned from me to this new heir—especially if the boy were called the son of Akalamdu, the son of Nannar-Sin?"

A suspicious fear began to emerge that should Akalamdu's plan begin to materialize, all the very best things in Kamarina might be sacrificed to fulfill it—even the love she knew from her father and her own desires to please him. Would the Academy be forced to back up these new religious decrees? Would not everyone have to be subservient to the new doctrine?

"And Gimil," Puabi shuddered. "Would he find a way out?"

Gimil had maintained his home near the Academy since he first began as tutor to Princess Puabi. The king had enjoyed the idea of his daughter being instructed with Azuani. Puabi's enthusiasm about her teacher had brought Gimil to the king's attention, and the tutor advanced quickly in prestige and position in the Academy. It was not long before he was appointed royal advisor and then chancellor.

Gimil was a tall and gaunt man. His balding head had a hawkish face that continually surprised the beholder by breaking into an infectious smile, eyes glowing with merriment—or compassion. As advisor, he had maneuvered Akalamdu out of many of the king's follies, but Gimil had also been trapped by some of them. It was Gimil's wisdom, however, that had used the king's dual desires for popularity and power to spread and expand Urian culture. Gimil had learned to steer a course of freedom and intellectual growth by always allowing any major achievement to be acclaimed as the king's own design.

21

It was only through such deceptive tactics that professors in the Academy had been free to rise to intellectual heights. The library and archives bulged with clay tablets of their writings and records. But it was a difficult balance to maintain. Gimil grew to depend on the help of the king's wife and daughter.

Because of Puabi's trust in him, Gimil had kept much of the Academy's fascinating intellectual progress hidden from the king until such time as the princess had more power. The fact that Puabi showed no desire to marry concerned Gimil. He was also beginning to notice Puabi's covert glances, and her strong attachment to him was making him uneasy. A girl of eighteen was unpredictable, and he wondered about the result should her affection be more than he imagined. He loved Puabi almost as much as his own daughter. The idea of marrying her himself did cross his mind, but he always shut it out like an incestuous thought.

The affairs of state seemed calm. Akalamdu had been preoccupied with something of late, so Gimil had turned his mind to a difficult trading problem. Azuani had told her father what had happened the night she spent with Puabi. Gimil thought it was all too preposterous, even for Akalamdu, and assumed the king had been drunk. Gimil therefore was not to be prepared for the explosive events that would begin at the next new moon.

Because of its rounded shape and its white painted walls and buildings, Kamarina had long been referred to by travelers as "the moon city." It was an appropriate artistic symbol, and new moon days were often chosen for special occasions. So it was that at the new moon Akalamdu sent messengers proclaiming a holiday and asking all citizens to appear at the Temenos for a "most happy announcement." Some rumors spread that perhaps the king might announce the betrothal of Puabi, and other speculations abounded.

An unexpected holiday always stirred up a jovial excitement throughout Ur. Men, women and children thronged eagerly between the Temenos gates. Though the setting sun's rays were still bright, the heat of the day was passing and a

22

light breeze was refreshing. It was a favorite time for celebration.

Just being in the great Temenos courtyard elated the citizens. They would mingle among their fellow Urians, exchanging greetings and enjoying the fellowship. Being so close to the majestic Ziggurat caused them to intersperse their conversations with awed looks up the heavy slope of steps and the mounting tiers.

Suddenly blasts from a dozen horns were blown and there was some quieting down. Eyes began to focus on the portico of the Ziggurat where the lower stairs converged. The portico was Akalamdu's pulpit. Its three vivid blue walls were plastered smooth and adorned with frescoed pictures with appliqués of gold, silver and gleaming stones. Guards arrayed in brilliant regalia were stationed on the steps leading up to the portico. They seemed miniature in size compared to the mammoth backdrop.

Akalamdu was intentionally late. While the people waited below, he paced around a cloistered walkway on the first Ziggurat tier. Occasionally he would dash across the court of that level and peer between the vines and shrubbery, looking for people he thought were missing. Addressing a messenger he would say, "I do not see Nanip-tilla. Go to his home. Tell him the king hopes he is not ill and that I desire his presence . . . I *must* have his presence! Good news is to be announced!"

Akalamdu knew that the words he would soon say would be divisive. It was important that every one of his strong supporters be present—but that suspicions not be raised. He must completely sway enough people to counteract any backlash. And he must be able to deal quickly with those who rose to oppose him.

"Akalamdu! What are you up to?" a familiar voice whispered behind him.

The king wheeled nervously around to see his wife, the queen. Her searching eyes were analyzing his every move. Beltani was heavily jeweled with intricately wrought necklaces and numerous bracelets binding her upper arms and wrists. Her gleaming gold tiara was studded with huge gems

23

and rested becomingly on the black curls of her highly styled wig. A beautifully draped white gown bared her smooth plumpish arms. It fell gently toward the floor in graceful folds, covering all except her gold ribboned sandals.

Akalamdu looked like a desperate animal that had been suddenly caught. To escape her question he quickly embraced her with unaccustomed gusto. Her body stiffened and for a moment halted his spirit.

Although his face remained flushed, Akalamdu released her enough to meet her gaze. "You have been gone too long, Beltani," he tried to sound affectionate. "I *had* to send for you. I am glad that you dressed so elegantly. This is our greatest hour!"

The king's voice trembled as he spoke on, "In the future we must bring your mother here to the palace. I need you at my side *all* the time."

"Akalamdu, I want to know what you are conniving!" demanded the queen. "You do something rash and all the good that has been done may come crashing around you! The young people in Ur are beginning to lose respect for you!"

The king was cautious. He knew her reproofs had kept him from many awkward blunders. But even when he had failed to heed her warnings, Beltani would always support him. If she had not been gone so long this time, perhaps the enormity of his plot would not have developed.

Almost in panic he decided to protect his project from her completely. There was little time and should she attack with criticism he might waver. He could ill afford any loss of confidence.

"You must trust me, Beltani," he said firmly. "You must have *absolute* faith in whatever I say. It is not my words, but . . . I speak the words of Nannar-Sin." Akalamdu amazed himself by what he was saying. Pride began to swell within him. "I have been *told* what to say. Nannar-Sin, the moon, is my god and speaks through me as his high priest!"

Beltani grew pale. She could not grasp what Akalamdu was saying, but somehow she realized it was too late, and she was afraid. For the first time she sensed that the control she held over her husband was breaking and perhaps gone forever.

Whatever he was doing, even *she* would be dispensable. Sensing this marital victory, Akalamdu loftily turned away from her with a determined step and went to the portico.

At Akalamdu's signal another even louder fanfare of horns and trumpets blared forth. The jumbled crowd jockeyed to get good views of their king. "What new glory for Ur this time? Another trade route opened up? A scientific discovery or a new medicine? More roads and canals? A wedding?" Always the king's announcements involved time and money for the citizens, but as the city grew the people prospered. Whatever the king announced it would usually end up to be for their advantage. Most enjoyed the excitement of such occasions. For others like Gimil, the event brought only anxiety. When Akalamdu had a large audience before him, he was very unpredictable.

Akalamdu delayed, standing solidly and erect in the center of the portico. The cloudless sky still glowed overhead but was darkening beyond the far walls of the city. Above and behind the people, glimmered the thin fingernail of the new moon. All was going as the king had planned.

The silence was prolonged, and there was some shifting here and there. Akalamdu's eyes focused on the horizon as he listened for the sound. Then all heard it.

Coming from a distance was an unfamiliar cadence of marching feet and a muffled jangle of armor. The air became heavy with the crescendoing sounds. Children began wiggling through the crowd and, joined by others, raced up the various outer wall steps of the Temenos. Stretching and leaning over the edge of the walls, they saw platoon after platoon of Urian soldiers. Soon uniformed men filled the street that circled the large inner city area of the Ziggurat, the palace, the Academy, and other civic buildings.

Close scrutiny would have revealed that this appearance was organized on short notice. The army of Ur was an extensive border guard. After serving an initial year of duty and training, male citizens would return to their station ten days of each season. Many were excused from this duty, but most enjoyed the companionship and change of pace. Except for the colorful palace and Ziggurat guards, uniforms were seldom seen in the city. Such a military mass as was now gathered could only mean that all borders had been vacated. In anyone's memory, such an inexplicable deployment of troops had never before occurred.

The word was passed quickly, "The whole border brigade is here!" A strange chill of fear invaded the celebration. Confusion mixed with a fading merriment. Only upon seeing the king's gracious smile and welcoming outstretched arms did the apprehension relax. The psychological effect was just as Akalamdu had hoped.

"My wonderful people! My fellow Urians!" Akalamdu's words floated down from the portico. He paused to get their attention. A baby's piercing cry annoyed him, changing his wide smile to a grimace.

As he began to speak again there was a stridency in his voice despite the pleasantness of the words. "What a joy to have you all gathered here! For this special occasion I even sent for our troops to join us. This is going to be a great and memorable night!"

The king spoke with more mellow tones as he recalled the mighty feats that had built Ur from a disease-infested swamp surrounded by flat reaches of desert to a gleaming city with rich farmlands and sparkling canals. "We are like a magnificent white pearl set in a mosaic of the finest jade and lazuli.

"Now I want to share with you, my friends, a strange and wonderful thing," said Akalamdu, looking intently at the staring faces below. "Since the last full moon, I have spent the darkness of the nights praying. During this time it was *revealed* to me that the one we worship, that saved our forefathers from the Great Flood, can be seen and known. He can be *seen* and *known* . . . because he is the *moon*. Nannar-Sin is his name. Nannar-Sin the moon god . . . is our god!

"My people, it is not some hidden shadow that we worship. We worship a god that is high in the heavens, who holds the sun at bay so we are not scorched off the earth. It is Nannar-Sin who pushes back the seas with his tides so that we are not deluged.

26

"When we do not see him, when the moon is dark and absent, our god roams the earth looking for a city to be his own, for a resting place, for love.

"And now, I must tell you! Nannar-Sin has revealed himself to me! He is our god, and he has chosen *us* to be his people. We have found *favor* in his eyes and *here* shall be his holy temple, *here* his holy worship!"

The childlike were beginning to be caught up in the king's tale, but hundreds scattered among the assemblage were obviously confused or else stunned by what they sensed was happening. Beltani had joined her daughter and other women of the court on the right balcony, one of two podiums built between the lower Ziggurat staircases, about halfway down from the portico. Gimil and other officials were on the left balcony. All had been caught by surprise.

Akalamdu began to press in. "Look behind you and see your god!" he proclaimed triumphantly. "See him beginning his journey, ever guarding and keeping you. Speak to him! Give him your praise! Behold, Nannar-Sin is our god! We are his chosen city! It is here he will dwell in his darkness and give blessing during his time of light!"

Akalamdu stopped. His mind raced with power as he willed his words to become creed. In hushed tones he drew back their attention. "We must prepare for the next coming of Nannar-Sin. By the time his light comes to fulness and wanes, we must complete rooms for his holy habitation, garments and food.

"No sacrifice can be too great. Remember, my dear ones, Nannar-Sin is coming to dwell *here—here in Kamarina,* city of the moon!

"I will give the most, for I am his high priest! My royal rooms of the Ziggurat are his. My largest jewels, my finest gold. I will keep nothing back from him!"

He waited, lifting his head toward the moon. Then he said deliberately, "Even my only child, my precious daughter . . . I will give for his pleasure!"

All eyes went toward Puabi. She remained motionless and the approaching darkness hid the terror in her face.

27

The king became nervous. There was little response to his declarations. Usually the people cheered and clapped. Now what applause was given was sparse and forced.

Akalamdu went on talking, repeating much of what he had just said. Torches were lit and the crowd became restless. As some with young ones tried to slip out, Akalamdu halted his speech abruptly and shouted to the guards at the outer gate, "Stop those people! They dishonor our god! Cut them down!"

The shaken guards looked puzzled at their king, then scurried off only to retrieve a lad and his mother.

"Bring them here!" Akalamdu demanded. The guards gently led the two to the steps.

"I . . . I am sorry, my king," stammered the woman. "My son has a fever. I thought it best to get him home."

Taking a sword from a guard near him, the king pointed with it to the step beneath him. "Come up here, boy!" he said sternly.

The child stretched his small legs and slowly climbed the height, kneeling down before the gleaming sword. With a swift, deadly blow the king swung the sword slicing the boy's neck and tumbling his young body down the steps to sprawl in front of his mother. She screamed and then fainted beside her son.

The suddenness and the madness of the event caused a panic. Many in the crowd sought to flee only to be wedged in by the platoons of soldiers in the street.

Shouting out over the tumult, the king raised the bloody sword, "Your sacrifice, Nannar-Sin! Your sacrifice, god of Kamarina, lord of Ur!" Retreating through the portico Akalamdu climbed the higher stairs until he breathlessly arrived at the top Ziggurat level.

Opening the door of the royal chambers, he staggered across the room and spread himself on his couch, then rolled off of it and flung himself on the floor. "I went too far!" he cried bitterly. "I went too far! Why did I go that far?"

Rising, Akalamdu ran out the door to the terrace wall. Far below through the smoke of the torchlights he saw the chaos and heard the sounds of confusion and screams of those being crushed by the pushing mob. Fear and remorse brought forth sobs that shook his heavy body.

His eyes scanned the lower steps. He could see two guards wrapping the dead boy in a dark cloak. The mother was now conscious and weeping. Gimil stood a few feet away from her, somber but directing the activity.

Akalamdu could not bear to look longer. His growing terror was not due just to his ruthless act, but he knew that the murder of the boy was irrevocable. The deed would prematurely set his plans in motion, and there would be no way to recant.

Lifting his eyes Akalamdu caught sight of the moon. The sheer crescent seemed high and aloof from the din beneath. Suddenly the tenseness left Akalamdu's body and a quick smile lightened his face. Addressing the moon he said slyly and with relief, "You may be just a floating rock to Gimil and his colleagues. But I, Akalamdu, king of Ur, have now made you a god!"

Akalamdu felt the weight of the evening's happenings gone, and his mind began to surge with ideas. He must move quickly—and carefully. He returned to his chambers speaking aloud to himself, "The boy's death . . . it must not be *just* a sacrifice. No . . . the lad was pure! Nannar-Sin *told* me he desired a *pure* sacrifice . . . the fever and the mother's leaving with the child . . . it was a foretold *sign* to me . . . yes, a sign that Nannar-Sin was choosing his sacrifice. The sacrifice had been chosen by the moon god himself to celebrate his rising." The king began to chuckle softly.

Familiar voices and rushing footsteps broke in upon his imaginings. With an explanation to cover the debacle of less than an hour before, Akalamdu was calm and gracious as he opened the door to the now frantic poundings of Beltani. The queen was overwrought and tears streaked her face. Puabi stood pale and shaken beside her. Gimil, tall and erect behind them, riveted his piercing eyes upon the king. To comprehend the ways of a fool is the unbearable pain of the wise. Though they had loved Akalamdu, honored him and humored him, these three were bitterly wise and frightened.

29

"You've gone mad!" declared Beltani. "How can you ever explain such an atrocity?"

"My dear three advisors," soothed the king. "Come, enter the portals of the future holy rooms of Nannar-Sin. For it is here he shall abide...."

The sing-songish monologue went on as the three were ushered into the royal chambers. Akalamdu took a lighting cane and touched its rope tip to one of the burning entry lamps. It was quite dark now as he lit the wicks of the heavy brass oil pots that rested in ornate niches of the interior walls.

"We have a happy god tonight, my loved ones. The sacrifice pleased him. Nannar-Sin will dwell in these very rooms," he continued, pointing to a center spot. "Here will his statue rest. Here the dear people of Ur will bring their tribute . . . and the dear people, I might add, of every thriving city upon his crescent . . . from here to the land of Kemi." The listeners kept silent.

"On special occasions, of course, we will bring his statue down . . . times of great festivals when all the faithful in each city will come to pay homage. Yes, just special occasions! Between times. . . ." He wandered about the room as a new thought began to excite him, and he pointed to Gimil, "Between times, we will have our famous tile makers reproduce the god's statue. Think what a price we could get for each one!"

"Father, do not go on," pleaded Puabi. "You will begin to believe yourself! Please, Father, stop now. Let us think together of a way out of this awful night!"

Akalamdu sobered. He looked at the daughter he had loved so much and at his wife—hard but loyal and always tolerant of his many weaknesses. Then he turned to his long-time counselor Gimil who had propelled him to popularity and credibility.

The sanity of Puabi's cry and the presence of the three who could pull Akalamdu back from his actions forced him to the inevitable decision. Either he backed away and withdrew in disgrace from what he had instigated, or else he must cut himself off from his former support and use those whom he could easily deceive or coerce to establish his new position.

"I have gone too far to stop now," he spoke sharply. He then looked at each one in turn and said resolutely, "Either you believe what I have proclaimed . . . or you must leave." An unspeakable depression weighed in the air.

Breaking the stillness, Gimil spoke, "Akalamdu, the events of this terrible night can be covered over. Somehow we will do it. But you cannot ruin all that we have built by this devilish scheme!"

Akalamdu reared up and smashed his fist against the large table that separated them. "*We* have built nothing! It is *my* city, *my* state, and now *my* god!

"And you, Gimil," he snarled, glaring at the chancellor accusingly, "protector of the intellectuals and the rebellious, promoter of justice and freedom! *You,* who would keep me from having sons through my daughter because of her mad lust for your bony old frame! Her desire for you will *not* be fulfilled! She will wed the god Nannar-Sin. And if you value your life, you will not get in my way!"

Changing his mood quickly, Akalamdu went to Puabi. As if to charm her away from the other two, he put his arm around her shoulder and tenderly led her to a slitted window. The moon had risen high in the sky and the delicate curve was brighter. "There is your husband, Puabi. For his pleasure, we will pick the most handsome man of Ur to lie with you in his behalf. You shall know passion right here in these rooms— these holy rooms of Nannar-Sin. And you shall conceive gods to rule the world!"

The embarrassment of her love for Gimil so crudely exposed by her father, and now this vile talk was too much after all else that had happened. Puabi pulled away and turned on her father. "I detest you!" she burst out, screaming. "I will not be your holy harlot nor kiss the feet of your stupid god!" She began to cry and fled the room. Her footsteps and sobs could be heard as she made the long descent down the torchlit stairs of the Ziggurat. Gimil nodded to the queen and the two left Akalamdu standing defiantly alone.

It did not take many days for Akalamdu to surround himself with new counselors and to promote willing officials

31

to higher places. Gimil and others who might be in opposition to the king were left uninformed or simply discharged.

Akalamdu maintained much of the army in the city, dispatching only the barest few to watch the borders. The military presence strengthened his nerve, and he seldom went out in the streets without flanks of uniformed men around him.

Less than a week after their last encounter at the Ziggurat, Gimil received a message from the king. It was a notice to move the Academy and its libraries to other quarters in the city in order that those buildings might be converted into a temple for Nannar-Sin. Akalamdu also sent along a statement of doctrines concerning Nannar-Sin. Gimil was requested to dismiss any teacher from the Academy or its schools that could not agree to the statement. A report on the two matters was to be sent to Artatappi, the lawyer, by the next new moon.

"And why should I send it to that scoundrel, Artatappi?" Gimil inquired with contempt.

The young messenger replied haltingly, "At the next new moon, King Akalamdu is going to announce Artatappi as the new chancellor. He is to replace you immediately, however. . . . Forgive me, sir, but it is a horrible life at the palace now. I only hope you can do something!"

Gimil looked at the frightened young man. "I will do what I can," he replied with a faint smile that hid the hopelessness he was feeling.

The messenger left. As Gimil watched the boy depart, his mind recoiled at the thoughts of what lay ahead. He feared for Puabi. If the princess continued to balk, her father the king would be forced to do something. Akalamdu's defenses were delicately triggered.

As Gimil thought of Puabi he remembered the king's words, ". . . her mad lust for your bony old frame. . . ." The words filled him with pity. "Would that she had wanted a common herd boy. Akalamdu would have granted that," he reasoned. Then he winced at his next thought, "To get his divine heir, would he prostitute his own daughter?"

32

His thoughts were broken by noises in the street. He climbed the courtyard steps of his home to the roof. Below was a decorated chariot pulled by palace horses and carrying the mother of Katiri, the small boy who had been killed. The woman was a mixture of sadness and pride as she smiled and meekly waved. The chariot was surrounded by soldiers and led by street dancers, tambourine and cymbal players. Following in the parade was a donkey cart full of clay images. Hawkers were selling the teraphim, shouting, "Blessed be the mother of Katiri. Blessed be the people of Kamarina, for a pure sacrifice has been made. Nannar-Sin grants blessing to every home that is adorned with the figure of Katiri. Come, buy your Katiri! Buy blessings and safety!"

As the nights progressed, the moon grew full and then waned until at last its light could not be seen. It was the dark of the moon, and the time for Akalamdu's next move. After long pleadings and arguments with her husband, Beltani had left the palace to be with her mother once again. Puabi had stayed in her quarters and avoided seeing her father. Now Akalamdu sent for his daughter. When Puabi entered his room Akalamdu was shocked by her appearance. Her hair was uncombed and matted, and her dark eyes sunken and defiant. She had grown quite thin from fasting.

On seeing her, Akalamdu choked with emotion and tears. He wanted to embrace his daughter, to comfort her and do away with whomever had offended her. He immediately stopped himself. "How could I console her?" he reflected grimly. It was he who had caused the grief and shame. He had brought evil upon the one he had always shielded from harm. And now he was devising to do more. No, he dare not think that way! He must believe what he was doing was best for Puabi. She was not a pretty girl. She should really appreciate what he was going to do!

"Puabi," he said gently. "I am ordering your women to prepare you for your slumber with Nannar-Sin. It will be his first night to walk the earth since choosing Kamarina of Ur to be his city. Should he want to lie with you tonight, I want you to be ready."

"I find your round moon a strange thing to sleep with," Puabi replied faintly, biting her lip to keep from saying more.

"But his crescent! What a symbol of fertility! Think of his crescent, Puabi!" Akalamdu spoke loftily.

The girl was repulsed and turned to leave.

"Do not dare leave my presence!" Akalamdu shouted, his face growing hard and calculating. Now he knew he must use the tactic he had planned should she resist. "Sit down! Sit down, and do as I say," her father commanded. "Or else Gimil and Azuani will be tried for treason!" Puabi's eyes showed the terror she felt. Was this really her father? Would he threaten her this way if she refused to cooperate with him? Her weakened body gave way, and she collapsed on the floor in front of Akalamdu, weeping.

Akalamdu was learning to steel himself against the compassionate emotions that welled up within him. His voice remained harsh as he charged her, "You will go this night to Nannar-Sin's holy sanctuary. I have refurbished the royal chambers for his use and have made the sleeping area especially attractive. I am sure you will be most pleased." He lifted her up, but she would not look at him.

"At sunset," he continued, "you will be escorted by three handsome young Urian men that I have selected with great care. As you mount the stairway to the top of the Ziggurat, you must choose the man you wish to join you. The other two will then stand guard until such time as you decide to descend—which, I might add, should be *after all* has been accomplished."

Puabi at last looked up at her father, "And what is *all?*" she asked contemptuously.

"*All* is when the young man of your choice shall act for Nannar-Sin and impregnate you with . . . shall we say . . . holy seed." For all of Akalamdu's matter-of-factness, the words were increasingly difficult for him to say. His daughter's sorrowful eyes made him feel unclean. Waves of self-hatred began to blur his determined plans, and his heart ached for the love of his daughter and his estranged wife, for the fellowship and wise words of Gimil. The loneliness of being a deceiver oppressed him. He despised what he was doing and detested the lackeys and flatterers that now surrounded him. But he could not turn back. To admit a hoax would be to surrender a crown.

34

"Go willingly, Puabi," he spoke lovingly, but firmly. "I do not want to force you with threats, for I do not wish to harm Gimil. But I will execute both Gimil and Azuani if that is what it takes to convince you!"

Puabi turned and walked away. "I will be ready," she said quietly as she departed.

In late afternoon Puabi was led by five of her attendants to the palace entryway. Her black hair fell in long curls. Gold ribbons crossed between her breasts and tied around her waist, holding her sheer flowing gown in place. She was regally arrayed in fine jewelry that the king had sent for her to wear. Her tiara was made of intricately wrought leaves of gold with jewelled, star-like flowers stemming out to form a glittering halo. Gold also shimmered in the thick crescents that hung from each ear and the dangling necklace of overlapping medallions. Beautiful bracelets encircled her wrists and ankles. Puabi walked with assurance and her strong character was evident in her countenance. Despite the marks of her fasting and distress, she was a royal looking princess.

Three young men about Puabi's own age waited for her. She faintly remembered seeing them in the Academy schools. They were not from Kamarina but from the farmlands, perhaps they were even herders. "Father did not want any family in the city to claim the heir to the throne," she thought intuitively.

Suddenly Puabi turned to her attendants, "Wait here, I must get something." Quickly she was gone, leaving the three men and the women to stare anxiously after her. Almost immediately she returned, carrying a tapestry-covered box. They were relieved, for the king had commanded that his daughter be constantly watched. "I am sorry," she said lightly, smiling up at the young men. "I forgot my perfumes."

One of the men reached out and offered to carry the box, but Puabi held it tightly. "Oh, no," she refused him. "Only the one I choose may know of the hidden odors of my little box. I alone will carry it!"

In an act of pretended gaity Puabi walked ahead of the three men who fell in behind her. The women remained in the palace. Puabi was momentarily shaken when the guards

35

opened up the palace gates, and she saw the broad expanse of the Temenos empty of people. Her eyes slowly traced the Ziggurat steps to the summit, and she allowed a defiant smile to hide her thoughts. "I shall never come back down," Puabi said to herself painfully. "How short my life has been."

When the four reached the top chambers, Puabi was breathless. She spoke with as much calmness as possible, "Let me rest a bit inside. I will come back soon with my decision."

After the princess closed the doors of the high chambers, the three men looked at each other. "Is this really happening?" asked the youngest. "A few days ago we were out in the fields, and now here we are on the royal level of the Ziggurat waiting like bulls for a heifer!"

"What is the matter, Ipali?" asked one named Nikazi. "Are you afraid you will not be able to produce if she chooses you?"

"No," he replied nervously. "I do not know . . . I really have never had such experience, I guess. . . ."

"Well, do not worry," Nikazi laughed knowingly. "She will probably pick old Maristar here anyway. Think, Maristar, if she chooses you, you will become a priest of Nannar-Sin! No more field work or dirty sheep to tend!"

Maristar stared out across the city at the fading sun's glow. Then he spoke carefully, "Just what *will* happen to the one she chooses? King Akalamdu said that Nannar-Sin would tell the princess which one of us was worthy." He glanced at each one.

"The boy Katiri was *also* worthy. Akalamdu *murdered* him!" Nikazi interjected.

"What if," Maristar mused, "we were *all* worthy? What if this Nannar-Sin came to us right now, and told us we were all *three* chosen?"

"You mean all of us have a . . . a time with her?" Nikazi's eyes lit up as he spoke.

"The princess," objected Ipali, "what would she do if we suggested such a thing?"

"She need not have much time to think about it!" Nikazi retorted, chuckling.

"Should she get pregnant, who will know who fathered the next heir," declared Maristar, becoming more enthusiastic. "And the king will have no way to hurt us if we say that his made-up god spoke to us. He's had a hard enough time convincing the people of his stories. Why, we might even make a believer out of old King Akalamdu himself!"

"I think we have waited long enough," Nikazi almost shouted. "Let us go in and see what that little perfume box smells like!"

Maristar and Nikazi went for the doors, opened them and entered the first chamber. Akalamdu's furniture had been removed. The niche lamps were lit causing flickering shadows on the thick carpet and the gold statue that dominated the room. The statue of Nannar-Sin looked much like a stylized and idealized Akalamdu. The gold body was clothed with a skirt of leather armor plates. A triple necklace of luminous blue stones and silver moons lay flat across the broad chest.

Maristar and Nikazi were aroused. They rushed for the bedroom entrance while Ipali, who had followed them, stayed behind to study the statue. "Come on, little calf," Maristar called to Ipali. "Watch us and you will learn how it is done!"

Nikazi was the first to enter. The floor of one side of the sleeping chamber was elegantly tiled with a round sunken bath and couches against the wall for dressing. On the other side, half hidden by long fringed draperies, was a large, carved wooden bed with high down mattresses covered with fresh linen sheets. Bright-colored cushions and pillows were piled back against the headboard. Puabi lay quietly on the bed. Her perfume box had been opened and was empty beside her.

"I am first!" Nikazi yelled as Maristar followed him to the bed. "Princess Puabi, we are *all* here to enjoy you!" He reached for her body, pulling off her tiara and tearing her dress down off her shoulders, but Puabi had made no response. Her eyes were alive, her body warm, but she was rigid and paralyzed. Nikazi shrieked, "Maristar! There on the pillows! A horned asp!"

Quickly, Maristar reached for the empty box and deftly clamped it over the small coiled snake and closed it with the lid. He stared into Puabi's eyes, "She does not have much time."

"Nor have we . . ." smirked Nikazi.

"True," Maristar replied calmly.

As the two ravished the dying princess, Ipali watched from the doorway of the bedchamber, nauseated.

Puabi's body lay cold and disheveled among the pillows. Nikazi poured wine into golden goblets and began eating of the food that had been laid out on a side table. Maristar called to Ipali, and they emptied the prepared jars of warm water into the bath. Maristar splashed and soaked his stripped body, but Ipali retired behind a screen that hid a commode. He was sick and vomiting.

This was the scene that met Akalamdu's eyes when he silently entered the bedchamber. Guilt had haunted him since he had watched the princess climb the long steps. Great fear for her safety consumed him. As darkness fell he waited at the palace window. The torchlights of the Ziggurat made deceiving shadows on the summit level. He strained to see who was guarding the doors and if one had entered the chambers. Yet he could see no one. He knew he must find out for himself if all was well.

Now before him his premonitions of danger were realized. He wanted to lash out his feelings on the men and rip his nails through their flesh, to squeeze their very blood into the bath. But he was alone and vulnerable. Their punishment must wait. He turned to leave but Maristar called, standing in the bath, insolently exposing himself to the king. "You missed the visit from Nannar-Sin. Your god does enjoy lovemaking! He used us with Princess Puabi. It was such good sport that Nannar-Sin took her spirit off with him!"

Akalamdu's eyes fastened on the girl's still form. Maristar spoke on, "You *drove* her to kill herself, King Akalamdu. Her body is quite dead from snake bite. She brought a horned asp up here herself, in that perfume box of hers. The maids will tell you that she went to get it. But I am sure we will see her again, riding Nannar-Sin's crescent at the next moon. My king, think what a great story you will have to tell everyone.

When they gather here tomorrow, you must ordain all three of us priests of Nannar-Sin. We will back up your fables, and the stupid people will have no choice but to believe. Puabi is no longer a princess but a consort of the god, bride of Nannar-Sin!"

Maristar stepped out of the bath and toward the king. Akalamdu's face reddened with fear and rage. Maristar's words sounded so much like his own that he knew he was being mocked. He backed through the door and left with haste, hearing the laughter that followed.

Maristar went after him and shouted down the steps, "Do not send any guards up here, old fox, or we will cut up her body and throw it down to the dogs! Do as I have said, and the people will believe your lies!"

By the time Akalamdu reached the palace his grief and anger turned to merciless scheming. He must have revenge for this night. And he would combine that revenge with the elimination of those who might soon instigate rebellion.

Earlier Akalamdu had ordered priestly garments made. At dawn he sent three of these with his attendants to the summit of the Ziggurat. The attendants also took a litter to carry Puabi's body. Soon Maristar, Nikazi and Ipali were before the king looking rather boyish in the impressive priestly attire. Their white tunics were mostly covered by full black cloaks which were fastened to their heads with golden mitres.

The king began the conversation, "You gentlemen were honored last night with the presence of Nannar-Sin as he walked the earth. Your story of the god's love for Puabi has moved me greatly and eases my sorrow from her death. I shall send messengers to announce your holy visitation with Nannar-Sin and also the funeral. You, as I promised earlier, will be priests and serve in the temple of Nannar-Sin, and I want you to participate in the funeral. Until that time you may stay in the former Academy living quarters.

"Publicly, you must confirm all that is proclaimed," he commanded. "If Nannar-Sin's coming last night and choosing Puabi as his consort is thought by any to be a fraud, *you,* of course, will pay with your lives!" Akalamdu had held his bitterness in check until his last words. He turned to hide his hatred. "Leave me now," he said abruptly. "I mourn my daughter."

"You will find us very convincing," smiled Maristar haughtily. "Let us go examine our temple, priests of Nannar-Sin!" he added triumphantly to Nikazi and Ipali as they departed.

Moments later Ipali returned to the king. He knelt before Akalamdu, pleading, "Please, my king, hear me! I did no harm to your daughter. I have never had anything but respect and honor for you and the princess. Since I was a small boy," he wept, "I have watched you ride through the farmlands. Many times you waved to me. You, my king, became the father I never knew. On rest days, I have walked around these palace walls looking for sight of you or your family, wishing I could talk to you or could serve you in some way. Now that I do serve you, you detest me. Please believe me, I had no part in what they did to Princess Puabi! If Nannar-Sin is a god, and he took her spirit away, it must have been to save her from that horrible attack. Believe me, King Akalamdu, I hate what those two did as much as you do! I hate anyone who would offend my king!"

Akalamdu studied Ipali's sad eyes and strained face. He was moved by the youth's professed devotion. A desire darted through his mind that someone like Ipali might have been his son. "Can I really trust you, Ipali?"

"I will do *anything* for you, my king!" he promised.

A large burial room beneath the southeast palace wall was designated for Princess Puabi's tomb. During the third day of public mourning, Akalamdu addressed the gathered citizens at the Ziggurat. Once again the king stood on the high portico. Closing his speech, he asked Gimil and the leading professors of the Academy, the three newly-appointed priests, and Puabi's women attendants to join him for a period of time within Puabi's tomb chamber that they might mourn for her together. He also requested Gimil to have Azuani play on the harp during this wake.

Beltani, the queen, was at the king's side, but she kept her veiled head lowered. The king called for a guard to escort his wife back to the palace. "She can endure no more. See that the Queen is taken care of by her women," he ordered sternly.

A procession formed of soldiers and those who were to accompany the king. The crowd respectfully followed the procession down the Temenos steps and through the forecourt and its gates. There a large cart waited with Puabi's bier. The embalmed princess was clothed in a beautiful red gown and the tiara and jewels that she wore the night of her death. She was a light burden for the ox-drawn cart. The wheels rolled over the flagstone street to the distant wall tomb entrance. The people, dressed mostly in traditional green mourning clothes, made a long path behind.

King Akalamdu led the selected group of Gimil and the others down the shaft of stairs to the burial room. Guards carried Puabi's body. Burning oil lamps revealed costly appointments, most of which had furnished Puabi's palace quarters. There were her beautiful game table with its inlays of pearl and shell, exquisite chests full of her jewelry and clothes, soft couches and carved tables. Shelves lined the walls with glistening gold, silver and copper ornaments and objects.

Azuani took a place near the bier and began strumming the lovely gold harp she had played so often with Puabi. Her tears would not stop, but she ignored them. Hour after hour she played until her fingers ached, and she dropped her exhausted arms. By then the sun had set. The mourners had returned to their homes except for those chosen few who sat silently within the tomb and the guards stationed at the entrance.

Goblets had been set out on one of the tables. Akalamdu rose and poured wine into one, lifted a toast to his daughter and drained the cup. "I leave now, my friends. I ask that after I go, you drink a similar toast together to honor my daughter before you depart. I wish her to have your final blessing."

All eyes were on the king as he left the tomb chamber. They heard him ascend the steps and repeat his last command about drinking a toast to the guards as well. No one noticed Ipali as he slipped behind the table and dropped a poisonous mixture into the flask of wine from which Akalamdu had recently poured.

The next morning a trembling gardener reported to the king, "They are all dead, my king! All who watched at the tomb! They are all dead—the guards, the priests, the women, Master Gimil and the professors!"

"No, no! You lie!" Akalamdu refuted the man. "You must be mad! They are but sleeping off the wine!"

"They are all dead, my king!" the gardener repeated. "They are all stiff . . . strangely sitting and lying on the couches. Master Gimil's daughter . . . she . . . she is still at the harp . . . leaning over it like she had just finished playing!"

Akalamdu called for Artatappi, the new chancellor, and others to witness the scene with him. As they crowded down the steps and into the musty tomb chamber, they saw what the gardener had described.

"Nannar-Sin has done this," Akalamdu cried out plaintively. "I do not know why! He must have wanted these dead to be company for his queen. Why didn't he choose *me* to go with her?"

"You must remain here to lead us," consoled one of his new counselors. "You are the one who speaks for the god."

"Yes," Akalamdu replied, looking forlorn. "But why then would Nannar-Sin not let the three young priests he had ordained remain behind?"

"We cannot understand the ways of a god," another replied.

The same day King Akalamdu had the oxen slaughtered that had drawn Puabi's bier. Their sacrificed carcasses were placed at the entrance of the tomb along with the two chariots used in the funeral. Then Akalamdu ordered the tomb to be sealed.

One of the chests set against the side wall of the tomb chamber covered a large hole that had been earlier chipped away. The hole opened into an adjacent empty tomb. Ipali, who had feigned death when the gardener and the other witnesses came to the tomb, easily escaped as had been planned. Akalamdu later announced that as he lay prostrate before Nannar-Sin's statue in

42

the royal chambers of the Ziggurat that Ipali suddenly appeared. Nannar-Sin had answered the king's prayers by returning the young priest from death so that Ipali could serve in the moon god's temple and be useful to the king. Ipali allowed his doubts in the midst of this deceit to be covered over by his gratefulness and love for the king. The king's trust in him blinded him to the treacherous reality in which he had played such a crucial part.[2]

As Ipali matured, he enjoyed the ways of power. He began to use subtle methods to threaten the king with exposure of the past. Before Ipali was thirty, he was appointed chancellor, and when Akalamdu was mysteriously killed during a wild boar hunt, Ipali quickly usurped the throne and became king of Ur. Methodically, as the new king, Ipali entrenched the religion of Nannar-Sin into Ur, reminding the people how Nannar-Sin had returned him from death to be their priest and now their king. All who traded in Ur were pressured to convert to the pagan beliefs, and the worship of Nannar-Sin spread to every city on the rivers.

Historical Interlude

King Sargon I, of the city-state of Akkad, came to power in 2334 BC. From his mid-river capital he waged war against Ur and the other city-states of Sumer, trying to establish himself king over all the southern river valley. The Akkadian armies periodically wasted parts of Ur, for Sargon's sworn devotion to Nannar-Sin instilled in him a savage jealousy toward the temple city of Kamarina. During his raids on Ur, Sargon and his men broke down vital dikes, swamping the fields and turning much of the precious land back into marsh. Only his fear of the moon god kept Sargon from destroying the Urian state altogether.

But the independent rebellious people of Ur would not tolerate the Akkadians ruling over them. In a begrudging compromise, Sargon allowed Ur some semblance of self rule. But in return, he demanded high tribute to be sent to Akkad, and had his daughter, known to be both devious and brilliant, ceremoniously installed as high priestess of Nannar-Sin in Kamarina.

Enkheduana was the name Sargon's daughter chose for her role as high priestess. On arriving in Ur, she immediately assessed a temple tax on all the male citizens. In return she granted each man a night's sleeping privilege in the temple. During such an experience, Nannar-Sin was said to appear in dreams and reveal wisdom, grant healing, or give blessings of wealth and good fortune.

With this new tax money Enkheduana established a convent called the Gagûm. Young women from the city's leading families were chosen or coerced to reside in the spacious buildings built for the Gagûm near the temple. The women were never allowed to marry and were required to bring with them at their initiation their dowries of lands, gold, and silver for the convent's use. Many in the convent became active business-women, running lively and remunerative operations by making low interest loans and leasing out their properties. Others prostituted themselves for the overnight visitors in the temple.

To extend her control, Enkheduana promulgated the idea that the stars made manifest the divine will of Nannar-Sin and that the planets themselves were powerful deities. She began to issue prophecies and omens whenever lunar phenomena occurred in conjunction with various fixed stars or the planets. The dire edicts, she insisted, could only be tempered by supplication and sacred rites for divine intervention of the moon god.

To establish Nannar-Sin's approval of Akkad and her father's capital, Enkheduana announced the birth of a goddess—the goddess Ishtar. Ishtar, the people were told, was the offspring of Nannar-Sin and his consort. The temple of the new goddess was built in Akkad where Ishtar was to be worshipped and her rites performed. Enkheduana declared Ishtar to be a goddess who delighted in bodily love and one who, if worshipped, would lead armies into battle and to victory. The high priestess knew this would appeal to her rough, military-minded homeland. She sent the most beautiful women of the Gagûm of Ur to be prostitutes in the new temple at Akkad. They were to be Ishtar's incarnations. To pay for a temple prostitute was to have pleasure with the goddess her-self. Under these conditions the temple of Ishtar became a renowned center of activity, and its accumulation of wealth gave it wide influence and degrading power.

Thus the evil genius of Sargon's daughter built on the paganism of Nannar-Sin. The worship of her goddess, Ishtar, was perpetuated over the centuries throughout the Tigris-Euphrates valley, into Canaan, and as far away as Kemi (Egypt).

When Abram and Sarai appear in history, the knowledge and worship of the holy God of Noah had dimmed, overshadowed by idolatry. Yet the awareness of the one God could never be suppressed. Then as now, all people had experiences of the overwhelming reality of their creator, if sometimes only fleetingly. To those who continued to worship him and became obedient, God revealed the mystery and the power of genuine faith—and pure love.

Chapter II
THE MOUNTAINS OF ARARAT
2045 BC

"You are hungry, Sarai?" the old woman asked.

"Not yet," replied the girl.

The two continued to pull at the spikelets of wheat, putting the seeds from the high grasses in leather pouches tied around their waists. The warm sun fought off the chill wind from the lake. The deep blue glacial waters of Lake Aratta lay sparkling beneath the high slope where Hosani and Sarai gathered grain. It was a beautiful morning, and the two chatted like close friends.

Parting the tall slender leaves, Hosani walked over to a well-used spiral coiled basket. Its sides bulged with wheat. She called to Sarai and each gripped one of the side handles. Leaning away from the basket to bear the weight, they walked down a nearby path toward a distant thatched-roof log cottage.

Hosani and Sarai carried their basket through the small orchard of apricot, olive and walnut trees. Ripening fruit shone from under the green leafy canopies. The path became sets of worn stone steps as it led down the center of an ancient terraced vineyard. The split rail supports of the vines had given way in most places, and the vineyard was unkempt and overgrown with weeds. Here and there hardy grapes grew in reddish clusters.

Hosani sighed and smiled as they paused to rest. "No wine for this old woman next winter," she said with resignation.

Sarai studied Hosani's deeply lined face. "Is no one coming back, Hosani?" she inquired hesitantly.

"A year we have waited, little one," Hosani responded. "We will wait a while longer, then we too must leave."

"But can we leave? We are the last ones."

"The Lord knows we are here. He will provide," Hosani smiled again, sorry that she had momentarily broken their light mood. They carried their burden on in silence until they reached the cottage. Their home was an old but well-built structure. Each log had been carefully hollowed out enough to be the resting place for the one above it. Soft green moss grew from the mud-filled cracks. The windows had leather awning flaps that could be securely clamped down against the cold or else propped up as they were now to let in air and sunshine.

Hosani and Sarai placed the heavy basket on a bench outside the door and then sat down on either side of it. "Praise you, my Lord!" shouted Hosani, lifting her worn hands high above her head. "You have supplied us again, dear friend and God! We thank you! We praise you!"

Sarai's hands were clasped in her lap. Her face was lifted upward, and her eyes were closed. A faint but radiant smile separated her young lips as she softly sang. Her delicate hymn accompanied the fervent prayers of Hosani. Then, as if by command, both stopped. Looking across the basket at each other they began to laugh. Tears rolled down their cheeks.

"We have a good time with the Lord, Sarai!"

Sarai's beautiful dark eyes glowed with joy. Though her voice was still child-like, she spoke as one who had known the God of Noah for many years. "He was with us!" she responded happily.

Beyond Hosani's cottage and the cultivated hills rose dense forests of pine and oak. Looming above those treetops were the rugged mountains and plateaus of the Ararats. Even in these summer months, many of the tall peaks were still

THE LAND OF THE TWO RIVERS

crusted with snow. In the mountains, wedged in a high crevice and glacier ice of a tall massif called the Great Ararat, lay the remains of an enormous boat—the ark of Noah. The hulk had rested in frozen preservation for hundreds of years ever since the remnant of life it once held had departed from it.

Stories of the past, the Flood and the ark were vividly real to Hosani, and each day at this time she would begin to tell them in great detail to her companion.

"You must remember these things," insisted the old woman, as she thought back in her mind for something she might have forgotten to disclose. Usually the discourse would continue while the two prepared their mid-day meal and conclude by the fire at night.

To Sarai, who had lived all of her life on the very ground that Noah had tilled, none of the things Hosani said were unbelievable. They were reality that others had forgotten—or feared to remember.

Hosani had risen from the bench. "Let us bring our meal outside today," she suggested. "The warm sun feels so good and the lake. . . ." She halted abruptly, her eyes focusing some distance from the shore. "Sarai, is that a boat coming?"

The girl leapt to her feet and stood on the bench. "It is Satuke, the boatman, and another!"

"The other one . . . who is he?"

Sarai watched as Satuke steered the boat toward shore. At the right moment, he pivoted the ponderous steering oar at the stern, turning the bow into the wind. The square brown sail flapped and fluttered from horizontal spars that held it to the mast. The other man lowered the halyards, and the boat drifted and rocked in the waves until it reached the stone-piled landing pier.

"I do not know him. He is a young man," the girl replied.

Satuke led his passenger up the bank. The visitor had black tousled hair and was wearing finely sewn chamois clothing. His open, friendly smile contrasted with his searching dark eyes. He was not as tall or as muscular as Satuke, but his body was well proportioned and his movements extremely agile.

"Satuke," greeted Hosani. "Welcome to you. Welcome to you also, young stranger. You are an answer to our prayers!"

Satuke bowed before her. "It is my good fortune to see you, my sister Hosani." He turned to the girl, his broad grin revealing several missing front teeth, "And the God of Noah's richest blessings on you, Sarai."

"We have prayed to see your boat coming," Sarai spoke shyly. "No one has been here since last summer."

"I, too, am alone, my sisters," replied Satuke. "The lake is big and too strong for me now. But look here! Look at this fine young man I have brought. He knows much about boats. Even I, who have sailed this lake so many years, even I have learned from him.

"His name is Abirami. His line is from Shem through Terrakki and Nakkur . . . that is, through Terah and Nahor."

"We women, keepers of the land of Noah, greet you, Abirami," said Hosani. "Do you speak the language of your fathers?"

Abirami had been watching Hosani and Sarai with amazement as they spoke a language that was new to him, yet he knew each word from different languages he had learned. He greeted them, speaking slowly and with care, "It is my honor to meet you, dear lady Hosani, and you, my child Sarai.

"I have studied many languages," he went on. "I am surprised that I can understand you and what you say. It is as if each word that you speak is from a different tongue."

Hosani and Sarai stared at him blankly.

"But you do not understand *me*, do you?" Abirami asked disappointedly.

Satuke interrupted, "Watch their hands, Abirami. If either raises her hand, you will know the word is foreign to her. Their tongue is the tongue of Noah. It has few words," he explained, "but those words were the beginning of all speech and language."

Satuke and Abirami spoke to each other in the northern dialect of Charran,[3] a trading center from which Abirami had recently come. The city was a difficult ten day journey away from Lake Aratta and Hosani's cottage. Located on the

51

Balikh, an upper tributary of the Euphrates, Charran had long been the mid-point on many north-south caravan routes as well as all of the east-west ones. The boisterous city was like a second home to those who travelled, and its dialect had become an international language. Herders also came to Charran from Ur, migrating with their flocks after the late winter rains. Some herders from Ur had homes in Charran. The wealthiest owners established small villages nearby for themselves and their people. This was the case of Abirami's father and grandfather.

"I will prepare something to eat for us," Hosani said, dismissing herself to the cottage.

Satuke thanked her jovially, then in exhaustion stretched himself out on the soft grass. His tall burly body ached from the long day and night sail. "My last trip," he groaned, "my last trip across that cold spring of youth!"

"An odd description, Satuke," commented Abirami as he took Hosani's place on the bench. "Why do you call the lake that?"

"Sarai can tell you better than I, once you two can understand each other," Satuke said. "But people used to come here to find the secret of youth and long life. Many who once dwelled in this area lived four, five and six hundred years. They were all close descendants of Noah. Now they have either gone or died, except for Hosani and Sarai.

"There were two old men left when I moved here from Charran," he patiently continued. "I settled where you first met me on the far side, fishing and carrying passengers when they needed me. Hosani was wife to one of the men, and the other took a young bride from Ebla and sired Sarai. It was a bitter cold winter and all died but Hosani and the girl." Heaving a long sigh, he added, "Ah, but the ground is a better place to lie than that boat!"

Abirami looked across the basket at Sarai. Once again he was aware of her large, dark eyes that held their gaze on his lips. He knew she was straining to know what was being said. He spoke to her slowly, "Why does Satuke call you Sarai? In my country. . . ." Sarai's hand went up and Abirami tried other translations of the word. The Akkadian word for

52

"country" she understood. It took until the time that Hosani brought food for Abirami to finish his one sentence. Sometimes he could supply the right word. Sometimes Sarai knew what he meant and told him the word—one that had been lost from the languages he had studied.

"In my country a girl is called Sarai only if she is the daughter of the king," Abirami repeated the finished statement.

"Very good! You learn quickly!" Hosani said to Abirami as she served bowls of steaming porridge stew and flat bread.

In answer to Abirami, Sarai explained, "All men and women are sons and daughters of Noah. But Noah's son Shem was my father's grandfather. . . ."

"That is impossible, Sarai!" Abirami interposed quietly, but firmly.

Sarai looked to Satuke to interpret.

"He does not believe you," the old man uttered. Satuke was still stretched out on the grass, his elbow supporting his head as he enjoyed the hot stew. He paused to finish a rather large bite of the flat bread. Then he addressed Abirami, "Sarai's father was well over five hundred years old when she was born. He was the last son born to his father, who was the last son born to Shem, the son of the righteous Noah. Her father named her Sarai as a reminder of her royal birth line."

"My line is of Shem also," said Abirami defensively. "For hundreds of years my fathers have not lived but a few years beyond two hundred, most not nearly that long. Are you positive that the method of counting was as it is today?"

Satuke shook his head thoughtfully. "Many things I do not understand—maybe I do not believe," he answered. "But I *knew* Sarai's father!"

"And he really lived to be over five hundred?" the young man asked incredulously.

"He was a student in Ur during the reign of King Akalamdu!" the old man replied emphatically. "He told me that the whole worship of Nannar-Sin was a hoax, for he was there when it happened. King Akalamdu ended in destroying his family and all his friends before he was finished."

"That is not so!" Abirami argued. "The very best men in Ur willingly sacrificed themselves to Nannar-Sin. . . ."

"You believe that pagan story, then?"

"To me," Abirami conceded, "the moon is a symbol of . . . of the unknown God . . . the God of Noah. The sacrifice of brilliant men like Chancellor Gimil shows that the God of Noah must have revealed himself somehow in all that happened!"

"This time I am glad that they do not understand you," murmured Satuke, wanting to end the conversation.

Abirami turned to Sarai and spoke slowly, "You must teach me more words. Then we can talk of these things."

The girl's smile was fresh and innocent. It lighted up her face, and Abirami suddenly realized that he had never before seen such a beautiful child. Nor had he ever seen one so young look so wise.

More stew and bread were served, and Sarai brought cups of hot milk sweetened with honey. Satuke shared with Hosani and Sarai the reason for their visit to the north shores where they lived. He told them more about Abirami, how he desired to study their language and to chart and map the area. He told them that Abirami had great knowledge about astronomy and mathematics and other matters studied in the cities. If Hosani approved, they would like to stay in one of the abandoned cottages.

"You are most welcome to all we possess," Hosani genuinely declared. "Does he not seek the secrets of life like the others?"

"Sometimes those who know so much are too full to swallow the truth," Satuke replied enigmatically.

Abirami's face reddened. "I am sorry if I have offended, Satuke," he apologized.

"Learn from these two, my son," said Satuke. "They *know* the God of Noah."

After the meal was over the men unloaded the boat. Abirami brought small wooden chests full of gifts into the cottage for Hosani and Sarai. Laid out on the table were boxes of dried meat and spices, gold ornaments, and lengths of colorful cloth and woven wools.

54

"Let us rejoice and give praise," sang Hosani as she and the girl fell to their knees and began worshipping God. Abirami was startled and backed away toward the door.

Sarai, too, prayed saying, "Thank you, precious Lord. Thank you for Abirami and his gifts. Thank you for bringing him here. Fill him with your wisdom, that he may bow to no other god except you!"

The small room was filled with a calm but joyous presence. Abirami felt a gentle warmth sweep over him as he continued to listen to the unembarrassed prayers. Sarai began to sing. The melody was delicate and haunting and the words completely foreign to Abirami. But he knew they were words of honor and adoration.

Suddenly Hosani stood and lifting both hands, began to prophesy, "Abram, son of Shem, you are chosen by the God of Noah. Forsake all evil, and you will be blessed and your name will be great!"

In the silence that followed Abirami sensed that he was in the presence of the real God—a presence he was to know often in the days ahead.

"Why did you call me Abram?" he asked, carefully choosing words he thought known. "That is my Sumerian name. I only use Abirami when I speak Akkadian or the dialect of Charran."

He was understood this time, and Hosani answered, "It is your name in our language as well. Abram means 'the Father is exalted.' "

Abirami, or Abram as he preferred them to call him, had brought rolls of papyrus and an ample supply of reed pens. During the weeks of his stay, he planned to keep a journal of his studies and discoveries and also make maps for his personal records.

After several days of exploring the area around the northern shores of Lake Aratta, Abram asked Satuke, since the oarsman was in his employ, if he would help Hosani. Abram wanted to go farther distances and take the young girl, Sarai, with him. He liked her name, Sarai. She certainly fit the part of a princess, he thought, in this beautiful but forsaken land. Abrám was especially impressed that Sarai knew much about the animals and the flora as well as every path through the dense forests and the mountain passes.

Hosani was pleased with the arrangement. She and Sarai prepared food for the trips, then early each morning Sarai led Abram a new direction. By nightfall they arrived back to enjoy a warm fire and hot porridge.

The Noachian language came quickly for Abram, and Sarai wanted to learn Sumerian, the language of Ur, as well. Never had Abram seen such a quick and able student as Sarai proved to be.

The countryside was active with many animals, but the two explorers were not bothered by them. Nevertheless, Abram kept his two hunting knives close to him. Occasionally in the forests they would see a bear grubbing in the thicket. There were small packs of wolves and hyenas, a few peering foxes and wildcats, cautious beavers, and many fleet-footed deer. Gazelles and wild goats roamed the plateaus in large herds.

As the summer was waning, Abram and Sarai packed for a longer journey to see the highest of the mountains of Ararat, the mountain of Noah and the resting place of his ark. It would take ten to twelve days to get there, so they had to depend on gathering some food as they went. To carry other supplies and tent equipment, they loaded Hosani's two asses.

Sarai had become like a young sister to Abram. Besides being a guide, she was a very good assistant in his work as well. Though she was only a child, he found that she was capable of handling every situation with ease.

They had not gone far on the trip to the Great Ararat when Abram mentioned the fact, saying, "You are the best helper I have ever worked with, Sarai. How did you learn so much?"

"I am not a child in years, Abram," she said hesitantly. "I am twenty years old."

Her answer so surprised him that at first he could find nothing to say. Instead he kept staring at her, examining her youthful stature with his eyes. She appeared to him no more than nine or ten, although perhaps a little tall for that age. Her boyish body was slender with long arms and legs. Her dark hair was pulled back and tied so that it fell in a single length, like that of most young girls.

"Do you want to explain what you mean," he finally asked her. She smiled embarrassedly and shrugged her shoulders at his question. "Perhaps later tonight," she answered, looking away from him.

This happened on their second day as they were unloading and setting up the tent. Abram had to quell some of the thoughts that came to his mind as he was suddenly aware that he was preparing to spend the night with a child who just said that she was twenty years old. He had been a bachelor long enough to know that those thoughts have to be dealt with soon, or they are quick to multiply.

It was true that the age of puberty had drastically lowered from the time of Abram's father and grandfather. Abram himself matured later than most of his colleagues, being nearly twenty before his beard grew. For many years he had enjoyed the company of women; however, he found his studies more important to him, and he had never sought involvement or marriage.

When the camp was set up and they had finished their meal, Abram firmly demanded an answer. "What did you mean, Sarai, about being twenty years old?"

Moments passed before she looked up and responded. "Abram, I am still a child. I do not feel like a woman . . . or think like a woman . . . yet." Then she added carefully, "Although if I did, I would certainly fall in love with you!"

Abram's disciplined mind suppressed what he was feeling. "I am sure that when you do become a woman," he said objectively, "I would never be so fortunate."

"Will you wait for me?" Sarai asked seriously and guilelessly.

Abram had never felt so tongue-tied. Earlier that day he had been completely absorbed by the work he was doing with the help of his capable young friend. Now to his surprise he wanted to shout out, "Yes, I will wait for you! I will wait! I shall never know another!"

Instead he forced a laugh and replied flatly, "Your God will find you a husband when the times comes."

"As the God of Noah is my witness, I will wait for *you,* Abram," she promised. While she said the words, Abram sensed again the strange but comforting presence of the holy God. It was as if the God of Noah himself were there in the forest witnessing Sarai's vow.

Abram was to remember that incident for many years. It would flash into his consciousness every time he had any desire for another woman.

During the next days of their travel, Sarai explained what Hosani had told her concerning those born in a close, direct line to Noah; namely, that the growing processes of the body continue for them twenty-five to thirty years before adult maturity is reached. When Abram looked unbelievingly, Sarai began to relate what she had been taught.

"Before the days of the Flood," she said earnestly, "the climate of the earth knew little change. There were few days of hot or cold. The summers were moderate and the winters mild. Winds were slight and always from the west. A thick cloudy mist covered the sky. It caused the rays of the sun to fan out and evenly warm all but the farthest places to the north and to the south."

"With so little sunlight did plants grow well?" Abram interrupted her with one of the many questions her story posed for him.

"They grew very slowly due to the mist," she answered with assurance. "But the slow growth brought forth rich and heavy fruit and grains, much better than what we have now."[4]

Abram was dubious. "And you think that is what increased the length of the life span?"

Sarai thought for a moment and then replied, "God blessed man by these conditions, and men did live long lives. Some, before the Great Flood, produced hundreds of offspring, even having children by younger wives when they were eight and nine hundred years old."

"Do you mean then," he pointedly quizzed her, "that because of inferior food and the direct rays of the sun, present day man has a shorter life each generation he is removed from Noah?"

58

Sarai nodded. "At least up to a certain point," she answered seriously, "the seed of man becomes weaker from father to son."

It was the time of the autumn equinox. After a few more days of travel, Abram and Sarai would have their first unobstructed view of the Great Ararat. It had been a strenuous but pleasant trip. Abram had been fascinated by the stories Sarai related. During rest stops, he in turn had discussed his theories in mathematics and science. Abram was again amazed by Sarai's intuition and alacrity in these matters. She seemed to grasp even the more difficult explanations of calculation and measurement.

He discoursed at length on the advantages of the sexagesimal system versus the centesimal. "Both have their place," he acknowledged. "It is certainly easier to teach young children a system based on their ten fingers and ten toes. But the multiple divisibility of the number sixty is so much superior to the awkward divisions that are made into one hundred. By what can you divide one hundred? One, two, four, five, ten—then nothing until twenty. But look at the number sixty, Sarai! How easily and evenly it divides itself by one, two, three, four, five, six, ten, twelve, fifteen, and twenty. . . ."

Sarai quickly interjected, "Also its base number of six is smaller and easier to work with than ten. It is the only low number to divide evenly in half and thirds. Its double, twelve, is still a low number, too, but can divide in half, thirds, fourths and sixths. I think for common use it is much better than ten!"

"True!" he shouted, excited by her understanding. Mathematics and its related fields could completely absorb Abram's interest. Base number theories were issues of heated controversy in the Academies of cities like Kamarina in Ur.

Abram had long been a strong proponent for the instruction of sexagesimal arithmetic. He enjoyed demonstrating to Sarai his own development of a place value and decimal system, tabulating sums of six according to their placement from right to left. In this way, addition, subtraction, multiplication, division, squaring, cubing, and extracting roots were easily recorded. His plan suggested the use of a special zero symbol to relieve the confusion caused by previous place value systems.

Such a system based on six and sixty had been established centuries before at Ur during Akalamdu's reign. But other scholars now argued for the centesimal change. It was not just the simple mathematical beauty of the sexagesimal system Abram preferred that made him support it. It was in part the obvious orderliness of the twelve month year, dividing evenly into four seasons, the day and night each of twelve hours, and the hour of sixty minutes. These and other base-six axioms had long been well tested. Also, and of more importance to him personally, was the use of the system as applied to the measurement of the circle, the computation of angles and distances in such areas as astronomy, map-making, surveying and even military planning.

On the day they would see the Great Ararat, Abram and Sarai departed before sunrise. They left their equipment and donkeys at their campsite. The path that they followed became steeper and more barren. The austerity was broken only by the bright blue flowers of the gentian that grew along the way. Their trail led them to a high plain. The tall trees were left behind. Only an occasional juniper and a few groves of birch grew on the parched land. Cold unobstructed winds blew, causing the two travelers to pull their cloaks tightly around them. Two griffon vultures swung past them, disappearing to feed on carrion in the high dry grass. It was still early morning. The sun's rising rays silhouetted a panorama of great mountain ranges beyond the plain.

The two stood in silence. In front of them towered the majestic, snow-capped mountain of Noah—the Great Ararat. Light, misty clouds hovered about its summit, revealing through their sheer veil the dazzling white peak.

"Where is the ark supposed to be, Sarai?"

"The top of the mountain is divided," she replied, shivering from the cold winds. "There is a lower peak a short distance behind the one you see. The ark lies in a shallow place of snow and ice between the two peaks. If we move quickly we can climb up to the first ridge on the south slope. The clouds will cover the top of the mountain by noontime. Usually the only clear views of the ark can be had in the morning."

Sarai walked on ahead, talking as she went, "Look at that mountain over there, Abram. It is called the Lesser Ararat. Of what does it remind you?" She pointed to a somewhat lower mountain immediately adjacent but a bit behind and to the right of the Great Ararat.

The cold, breathtaking beauty and the mystery of the Great Ararat had seized Abram's attention. He only reluctantly shifted his gaze to study the other mountain. In contrast to the Great Ararat's ruggedness, the Lesser Ararat rose as a bare, steep, perfectly symmetrical cone. It was reddish-gray and draped low on one side by the foliage of dark green trees.

Abram looked for a moment and gasped, "The Ziggurat! And the Pyramids of Kemi!"

Sarai nodded in affirmation and stopped a moment to explain, "Besides the summit on which the ark came to rest, the first thing Noah's family saw as the waters went down was that strange peak rising out of the sea. Noah's daughters-in-law were afraid of it and thought in this strange shape they were seeing the shape of God himself. Later, these women still feared the Lesser Ararat, even prayed to it. In different ways, this superstition was passed on to many generations."

Abram and Sarai trudged on quietly, carefully picking their way over the plain to avoid the sharp lava and basalt rocks. Crossing several low foothills, they came upon a wet marshy area that, moat-like, encircled the great mountain. Sarai led, skirting the soggy strip until she found a stone path that bridged it.

"Who laid these stones, Sarai?" he asked.

"Noah, or one of his descendants who stayed here," she told him. "There used to be villages on the plain as in all the area we have travelled. Stones were cut here and metals were mined. Trees were also felled and sold. Flocks and herds were pastured in the summer on the grass ahead of us."

They continued to hike up from the west toward the southern slope, going through some of the grassy pastures that separated the Greater from the Lesser Ararat. The climb became difficult as they ascended toward the first ridge. Loose unstable rocks gave way easily if each foot were not carefully placed. Deep holes and crevices gaped in the black mountainside and large tumbled boulders, some of them two to eight cubits in diameter, often stood precipitously in the way.

The winds had ceased, and the sun burned down through the rarefied air. They paused but a moment on the ridge, a rocky level some three thousand cubits above the pastures. The steeper slope still ascended before them, but Sarai directed Abram to continue on the ridge until they reached the far south side of the Greater Ararat.

It was not long before Sarai suddenly stopped and pointed excitedly, "There! There it is! There is Noah's ark, Abram!"

Abram craned his neck back and looked up the ponderous mountain heights. He saw the saddle of glacier ice and heavy snow that capped the twin peaks and extended down the mountain fissures in drifts and chalky streaks. But his eyes riveted on the magnificent square-ended prow of the giant boat that jutted seventy-five cubits or more out of the whiteness. The black pitch-covered hulk was tilted slightly upward. Abram's trained eyes surveyed every detail until, to his consternation, thick clouds moved to cover the ark completely from view.

"Sarai!" he exclaimed. "That boat is gigantic! It must be fifty cubits wide and thirty high. Resting at that angle, it would have to be three hundred cubits at least in length! What masterful proportions and how excellently it must be designed. . . . At last, I am beginning to understand your answers."

"You just need to know the Great Answer, Abram," she responded softly.

Clouds continued to form, blocking out the sun and bringing back the bitter, mountain coldness. Thunder rumbled from above them and chilling rains began falling.

The time had passed quickly, and to reach their former campsite before dark, Abram knew they must leave immediately. Questions pounded his mind. His logical thought patterns were being assailed and torn apart by this strange adventure. He longed for the time that night when they would share together. He, Abram, who had always felt so intellectually confident, now yearned for more answers from this unusual young girl.

He watched Sarai descend the path ahead of him. At one stony difficult place she reached back for his support. As he held her hand he noticed how long and slender were all her fingers and how soft her touch.

Before nightfall they arrived at their former campsite. Sarai went to tend the donkeys they had left behind along with their other supplies. Abram made a fire with dry brush and wood which quickly ignited from the sparks of his flints. He filled a clay pot with glacial water from the tumbling rivulet a short distance away.

When the water boiled, Sarai added dried meat and meal. She stirred the mixture slowly until it thickened and the meat was tender. It was not long before their cold, tired bodies were warmed by the fire and the savory gruel.

"I thought we had the finest foods in Ur, but I shall never allow that anything could taste better than this!" Abram commented, appreciatively smiling at his cook. Sarai made a slight bow in his direction.

Before Abram questioned her, he described some of the fraudulent religions that he had encountered. "You cannot imagine the garbled stories that have come down through the years about the Great Flood. Names, places, all have changed. Noah and the ark is just one story among many now, and has been identified with false gods of every sort.

"The people of Ur mainly worship Nannar-Sin, the moon god. Charran and its neighboring villages, under Urian influence, still do the same. Priests in other cities, however, have devised stories creating gods so numerous that the people can scarcely remember them all.

"I have studied the sky and the stars," he continued. "I am convinced of the orderliness of the universe. I know that the sun, the moon, the stars are all under control—and, if controlled, they have no power of their own. A floating, magnetic rock like the moon could never be a god. . . . But, at

63

times, I did believe that the moon was a unique symbol of God . . . perhaps I even let myself believe more. But until I came on this trip, I never felt the presence of God . . . like I do when you or Hosani are praying."

"The God of Noah knows that you have not really given yourself to a false god," Sarai said thoughtfully. "He is choosing you. He is revealing himself to you while you are here. He is choosing you to be. . . ."

Without warning Sarai suddenly broke into tears. Abram gently held her in his arms, supporting her until the deep sobbing ceased. At last she lifted her face from his shoulder. "Let us speak to him, Sarai," he said solemnly, "to this great God that you know."

She nodded, and still holding her he hesitantly began, "O God of Noah, who created Sarai . . . and me . . . and all that we see and know, come make yourself known to us. I want to know you, the *real* and *living* God!"

The warm glow of the fire contrasted with the dark towering trees surrounding the campsite. Stars were sparkling and the forest night sounds had commenced an accompaniment with the distant rushing waters. No breeze was blowing now, but the air was chilled.

As Abram and Sarai prayed, the holy presence of God enveloped them. Abram was awed and overwhelmed. He looked at Sarai and, to her surprise, he began to laugh. He laughed with the bursting joy he felt all through his being. "There is a *real* God! There is a God! Sarai, I know I heard the God of Noah speak to me!"

He released the girl and fell prostrate on the ground, still laughing. "Praise you, my Lord!" he continued to worship. "Praise you! I have found you, the living and holy God. O, how I praise you!" he shouted, his vibrant voice resounding through the tall trees.

After much time in searching prayer and in long silence, Abram sat again beside Sarai and told her, "It was as if I were speaking to a man, a friend, or. . . . It was a mighty presence of love . . . and joy . . . and peace."

Abram was amazed with himself. After such an emotional and exhilarating experience, he had not expected to feel

64

totally rational and alert. His mind was hungry and eager to seek infinite answers to his finite puzzlement.

"I feel so new . . . and clean. . . . Sarai, I feel completely new!"

Sarai's beautiful dark eyes shone from her dusty, tear-streaked face. How exquisite she appeared to him!

"Now, my young and beautiful friend," he said. "I have even more questions to ask you. But praise the God of Noah, I already have the greatest answer!"

The sun was fully risen when Abram woke Sarai the next morning. They packed quickly and were soon on the trail. As they made their way back to Lake Aratta by a different route, Sarai related many of the details she had learned about Noah and the Great Flood.

"Noah was asked by God to build an ark and was told exactly how to make it," she began as she gently prodded the asses ahead of her through some heavy brush. Then as the path cleared she went on with the story. "This took much time, for the ark, as you know, was to be large, and Noah had only the help of his sons. The women, Noah's wife and his son's wives, gathered food and dried and stored it. This was the food of those ancient days when a very small amount was so rich and healthful that it was enough for a whole meal."

"That would have made it easier for us to pack for a journey like this one, Sarai," Abram jokingly remarked.

"It must have made many things easier," she agreed as she readjusted the pack she was carrying. "After the ark was completed and the dried food stored inside, Noah and his family began to collect pairs of animals as God had commanded.

"Then the rains began and the water rose around the boat. Thunder and lightning frightened the people and the animals in the ark. Noah and his family lowered the wooden deck awnings and closed themselves in."

Abram shook his head and smiled. "Sarai, if I had not seen that magnificent ark just yesterday I could never believe the story you are telling me. But go on. . . ."

She paused. Sarai knew that what she would tell Abram next would be even more difficult for him. "The animals were restless and noisy, and the food supply was going quickly," she began hesitantly.

"Now that part I *can* believe!" Abram laughed and Sarai smiled back at him.

With more confidence she started again. "As the rains continued, the ark kept rising higher and the temperature became very cold. The animals went into a deep sleep, like bears do in winter. They needed no attention or food for the rest of the time of the Flood.

"The heavy layer of mist and clouds that had so long covered the earth began to disappear as day after day the rains fell. Forty days it rained. As the weight of water from the rain pushed into and beneath the ground, great layers of earth began to slide and shift. Whole mountain ranges were lifted up, and there were many eruptions from the deep parts of the earth.[5] Some lands rose as others sank. With the heavy mist gone, the winds began to blow strongly."

Abram was fascinated. He motioned to Sarai to stop for a moment and pointed to a place where they could sit and rest. It was near one of the many mountain streams, and they unburdened the asses so that the animals could graze and get water.

"That was quite a calamity for even the big ark to survive," Abram commented as his mind tried to comprehend what she had been telling him.

"Only the ark remained from all that was before the Flood," she replied slowly. "The ark and those that were in it. As it floated on the water everything else of those ancient days was buried in the clay."[6]

There was silence as both meditated on what the almost total destruction must have been like.

"Hosani told me," Sarai resumed once again, "that at the end of the forty days, Noah and his family walked out on the upper deck. A light rain was still falling and the bright sun shone through the clouds. Suddenly a great rainbow crossed the sky. Noah prayed, asking what the beautiful colors meant. God told Noah that it was a sign of the promise which he was making with him and every living creature that was with him. It was a promise that the waters would never again become a flood to destroy all flesh."

"Strange," Abram interrupted her. "Our family ensign is the rainbow. I had never thought much about the reason for it." He nodded for her to continue.

"Some time after seeing the rainbow, the ark anchored on the top of the Great Ararat," she explained. "As the waters lowered they washed through the newly made mountains and the old hills, cutting out canyons and broad valleys and making many other kinds of changes on the earth. Oceans were formed in the large sunken places of land. During the Flood the waters which flowed far to the north and south froze. When other waters drained away, the giant ice slabs slid and shoved toward warmer areas, moving and changing things that were in their path.

Abram looked sceptical. He was determined to listen and tried not be critical. "What did Noah and the others do for food after the Flood?" he asked instead.

"Seeds of plants that had taken months and sometimes years to grow sprang up because of the direct sun," she answered. "But with the fast growth came poorer grains and fruit. Even the amount of grass that once fed an animal would not begin to fill its appetite after the Flood."

Abram plied Sarai with more questions, and he was amazed that she had extraordinary answers for each one of them. Hosani had taught her well, he thought. It was only when he asked her about the sin that divided Noah's family after the deluge that Sarai found the discussion difficult.

Perhaps Hosani herself never knew the details. All that Abram could put together from Sarai's sparse account was that Noah drank wine in excess from his vineyard, the same one that was behind Hosani's cottage. When Noah lay down in his tent, he was naked. Some unnatural act was done, probably by Canaan, Sarai believed, since he was the one who was later exiled and cursed. Ham, Noah's son and the father of Canaan, witnessed his father's disgrace and told his brothers. The brothers, Shem and Japheth, covered their father, taking pains not to observe him.

As they picked up their journey again, Sarai confided to Abram, "I have been very happy during these days with you. What will you do after you leave us?"

Abram smiled warmly at her and put his arm around her shoulder. "I will probably go somewhere and wish I were back here with you and Hosani."

"Do you have plans?"

"My plan *was* to go to Damascus," he answered. "The city has suffered many attacks from the sea people. These are people from islands in the Great Sea that have been landing raiding parties on the beaches. At first they attacked only coastal cities, but they have become bolder and are moving inland. I have some strategies that could help the ensi of Damascus. We studied together at Ur and were close friends."

"Will you stay long?" she asked.

"I will have to go some place and stay long enough to rethink everything. I have learned and experienced much these past days. Now all my ambitions have been blown up into the sky like feathers in the wind. And I am not sure that I really want to go chasing after them."

Sarai looked puzzled. "Have you asked God what he wants you to do?" she inquired hesitantly.

Abram paused. "No, I guess I am not used to doing that,' he replied soberly.

The next days went by quickly as they made their return. They arrived late in the afternoon. Walking down the vineyard steps, they spied Satuke tying up the vines. The supports had been repaired, and the weeds were cleared.

"Well, my friend," called Abram gaily. "I see Hosani kept you busy while we were gone."

Satuke had not heard them coming, and the surprise obviously startled him. His dark eyes looked up sharply, but he kept his large back bent over his work.

"Satuke," laughed Sarai. "We are back! Where is Hosani?"

As Abram and Sarai approached him, Satuke turned his head away.

"What is the matter with you?" Abram asked loudly. "Satuke! What is wrong?"

The big man slowly stood erect and faced them. "Hosani is dead," he stated mournfully.

"Oh, no," cried Sarai. "No, Satuke. Please . . . no!"

"Two days ago as we were repairing the vineyard, she just fell to the ground," Satuke explained, his words halting and difficult to express. "I waited for your return. I felt I had to bury her today. I finished but an hour ago."

Abram turned to comfort Sarai. He was surprised to see how noticeably her grief and shock had changed. Tears were falling, but her face was uplifted as were her arms. Her radiant smile set her face aglow.

"She is with God, Abram! She is with the God of Noah!" she rejoiced. "Hosani is with God! What a lovely way to meet him!"

Satuke led them to the sloping burial field that lay beyond the vineyard. They walked through the rows of pillared stones. Each hillock of stones marked the remains of one of Noah's descendants. The freshly-dug earth that covered Hosani's body lay ahead of them. Satuke had carefully set up a pillar of stones and had cleared away the nearby brush and tall grasses.

The three knelt by the grave. Abram and Sarai prayed while Satuke sang laments with his hoarse, deep voice.

The warm rays of the sun were gone and Lake Aratta's cold breezes sprang up. Satuke and Abram went for wood and Sarai returned to the cottage. As they sat around the fire that evening, Abram suggested a plan to the others. "I think it best if we close things here and leave as soon as possible. Sarai, I feel I must go on to Damascus. I want you to come with me as far as Charran. My father will still be there. He sent his herds back to Ur early and planned to stay and trade until I returned. He is a very wealthy man. You could 'grow up'," he continued, with an amused smile, "and be tutored in all the wisdom of Ur."

Satuke spat loudly into the fire. "Ur!" he ejaculated disgustedly. "You would destroy her?"

69

"I do not think Sarai is that fragile," Abram said emphatically. "Her mind has had many years to develop. She must learn the world if she is to serve it. And the studies will fill her time . . . until she is a woman."

Abram took Sarai with him to Terrakki near Charran. Terrakki, his family village, had always seemed more like Abram's home to him than his father's large villa in Ur. He had spent his happiest days there as a youth and had many friends in the area.

When Terah, Abram's father, learned of Sarai's background and her precocious mind, he quickly agreed to sponsor her. Shortly thereafter Terah took Sarai to Kamarina and according to the customs and laws of Ur, Abram's father legally adopted her. The arrangement worked well until Terah found himself having to spend more and more time in Charran. Abram received a message while in Damascus that his father had asked Haran, Abram's older brother in Kamarina, to provide for Sarai, and Sarai joined Haran and his children, the two daughters, Milcah and Ishcah, and the youngest, Haran's only son, Lot.

Haran, being alone since his wife died, was pleased to have Sarai, for although she appeared no older than his daughters, she easily took over and managed the household affairs for him. From other messages, Abram learned that Sarai shared with Haran and his children much of what she had told Abram in the mountains about the God of Noah and the Great Flood. Milcah and Lot yearned to believe in God the way Sarai did, and soon knew what it was to worship him. However, Haran and his daughter, Ishcah, never broke away from the traditions of the city and the pagan worship of Nannar-Sin. Abram also heard that Sarai had become very adept at weaving, and her goods of bright colors and unique intricate designs were sought after by the Urian merchants.

It had been almost two years since Abram had any further word of his family or of Sarai. His mind had become almost totally involved in Damascus' affairs, and the vividness of the period he spent in the Ararats had faded. Occasionally,

70

however, Abram thought about Sarai and wondered what it would be like to see her.

Altogether, he had remained in Damascus for nearly ten years, and at last felt his commitment was finished. The city was well-armed, and the sea people had taken their raiding parties southward after losing many of their finest warriors.[7]

Mikhail, the ensi of Damascus, had been quite ill when Abram first arrived in the city. Damu, king of Ebla, to whom Damascus paid tribute, requested Abram to replace Mikhail. To avoid making such a decision which might offend his friend or the king, Abram asked that he serve temporarily until Mikhail recovered. In effect, Abram ruled Damascus the whole time he remained there.

When he first came to Damascus, Abram brought with him over two hundred men. They had been trained by him at Terrakki even before he had visited the Ararats. Some of these men were his long-time friends, some servants of his father, and many young drifters and migrants. A young boy named Eliezer, who was the son of one of Terah's servants, came along as mascot. He had been born in Damascus, and his widowed mother wished to have him grow up in the city of his father.

Abram enjoyed the hearty camaraderie of this kind of military life. Even more, he relished the opportunity to apply his knowledge of mathematics and surveying to military tactics and to civil expansion in Damascus.

Mikhail never became well and finally died of his ailment. King Damu appointed someone else as ensi since Abram wished to be relieved and return to Kamarina of Ur. With forty of his original brigade and Eliezer, now a handsome young man, Abram departed, leaving first for Charran.

Upon arriving in the trading city, Eliezer asked Abram if he would legally adopt him. To this Abram agreed, seeing Eliezer's grief on learning of his mother's death. When the two had ring-sealed the adoption document, a haunting question came to Abram's mind, "Should I never have children or perhaps never even marry, would Eliezer be legal heir to my name and my fortune?"

71

For the first time in many years, Hosani's prophecy surged through his head, ". . . and you will be blessed and your name will be great!"

Abram was most anxious to see his father after so many years away. It was by then late spring. Discovering that Terah was not at their family village of Terrakki but had wintered in Ur, Abram left with his men by boat from Charran. The trip down the Balikh and into the Euphrates would carry them to the area of migration for this time of year. Abram hoped that Terah would be coming along with the herds.

Chapter III
TRIP DOWN THE
EUPHRATES

The great rush of waters from the winter rains and the melting snows had abated. The rivers coursed full and steady. It was the perfect time of year for speedy passage to Ur. Such a trip should take only six or seven travel days. Also it was still spring, that brief respite before the intense heat of summer began.

Abram had been paid substantially while serving in Damascus. He invested most of his wealth in silver and gold. On this voyage he purchased and loaded a third commodity that would be of extreme value in Ur—good timber.

Six kalaks were assembled to carry the wood for Abram by the boatmakers in Charran. These large rafts of tightly fitted logs and brushwood were supported on numerous inflated skins. Each kalak could carry well over a thousand talents, about thirty tons, without a dangerous draft. The boats themselves would later be dismantled and profitably sold to carpenters in Ur. The special skins were usually returned by land to Charran to be used again.

Abram assigned seven men to each boat, with Eliezer, five others and himself in the lead. Tents were pitched on the deck covering the cargo. Shifts at the sculling oar were divided as

73

were the simple chores. It began as a pleasant and relaxing voyage. The men occupied their time with long stories, games and fishing. The latter was most rewarding as the river carp and catfish were large and provided good sport.

Not since those weeks in the Ararats had Abram been so free from responsibility. After several days he sat in the prow of the boat watching the Euphrates slowly widen before him. The spring grasslands spread out on either side, having been enriched by the silt and water of the river's overflow. Flocks and herds were fattening themselves as herders gently prodded them on their slow migration. Small clumps of poplar, willow and tamarisk trees broke the flatness of the landscape. Soft green licorice bushes edged the river banks. Abram kept watching for sign of his father's entourage.

Far off from the shores, cities and villages would now and then appear. River entry canals from these communities greatly increased the river traffic. The heavy-laden kalaks kept to the deeper right bank. Ferry boats called guffahs crossed the river before Abram's rafts, making steering quite challenging. Guffahs, which could carry twenty passengers or more, were large circular coracles made of basketwork coated with bitumen. Odd-shaped sails were rigged to keep the boats on course against the downstream currents.

There was usually much waving and calling back and forth between boats. Abram unselfconsciously enjoyed this for he was of a friendly nature. The bantering between his and a passing boat would continue until the shimmering distance between them hushed the voices.

Abram had traversed this area many times, both when he was a youth helping with the herds and later during several years of surveying. There were few dialects along the river that he had not mastered. Such familiarity made him at home wherever he went.

During the fourth day of the trip, there came into view the distant rose-colored buildings of Akkad. The sight usually provoked a disgusted spit over the side of the boat and a curse by the average Urian. Abram directed his oarsman to head up the wide Akkad canal.

"Sir, are we to stay long in Akkad?" Eliezer asked hopefully.

Abram returned a stern look, for he could read the young man's thoughts. "The idea of being in Akkad interests you? I hope you have no idea about going to the temple!"

Eliezer flushed. Abram had always seemed so worldly, so much a part of life. "Was he now being prudish about a night in the temple?" he thought. "Surely he has done it himself . . . all those years in this area." Eliezer had long heard the stories of the caravaners. A night at the temple with a lovely priestess was considered part of the river trip.

"What do you think it will cost me?" Eliezer questioned, somewhat insolently.

"It will probably cost you a disgusting night with a well-used whore!" Abram retorted sharply.

"But it is my religious duty," Eliezer pleaded whimsically.

"Your religious duty is not to Ishtar or Nannar-Sin. They are not God."

"Then why do people worship them?" Eliezer asked, his eyes looking intently ahead at the city.

"Because fools have made it seem wise to worship something created instead of the creator. Only a fool, a stupid fool, can look at the order and the miracle of this earth and all its life and not believe it was created by a powerful, holy God. In our hearts we *know* that the real God *is,* but we like to shield ourselves from him. . . ." Abram's voice was distant. His words brought back to him the scene in the Ararats when he was with Sarai, when he had felt God's presence so vividly.

Eliezer did not seem to notice the pause, for he was barely listening as Abram went on, "We shield ourselves from him . . . because not to do so would mean we must become obedient, to honor and give thanks to the God that is invisible, the God of Noah. So instead we become obedient to lesser things . . . ourselves, our own lusts, our fears . . . and things that we can see that other men say are our gods."

"But Abram, I like to believe in Nannar-Sin," Eliezer broke his gaze on Akkad and tried to pick up the conversation. "I can see the moon, but how real is a god that I *feel* in my heart?"

They could talk no more for the boats were docking. Abram found his heart heavy from the discussion.

The wharves of Akkad were busy and crowded. After Abram left his boat he went to each kalak in turn, checking on his men and inspecting the boats and their loads. All had gone quite well, and he was thankful. He called his five captains aside while the other men worked with dock crews to batten down cargo and tie up the kalaks to the wharf pilings.

"We will spend the night here and enjoy a good meal. One thing an Akkadian *can* do is cook! Tomorrow I will pay the cargo safety tax, that bribery to Ishtar to protect us from her pirates, and perhaps we can be off by sunrise.

"Until then, rotate the guard duty between the men. Other than that you are all free. I shall be visiting with my old friend, Ibalu."

Abram turned to face Milkusa, his chief assistant among his men. "Will you take Eliezer with you?" Abram asked him. "And keep him out of trouble if you can!"

"That I will try, sir. But this is not an easy city for such a task," Milkusa replied frankly.

Abram located his friend, Ibalu, at his government office and together they went to eat at the inn where Abram was a guest. Bowls of buttermilk, steaming vegetable stews, platters of smoked partridge, grilled lamb, rich custards, and fresh flat bread were set before them. It was a long and delicious feast, but Abram noted his friend's uneasiness. He began to ply Ibalu with questions about himself and his work as royal surveyor to Akkad's King Sin Bani.

"Well, I have not been surveying any captured lands of conquest," Ibalu tried to respond humorously. "The king keeps his army busy fighting off the pesky Gutians and Martu. Usually if you just feed a Gutian, he will turn around and fight with you rather than against you. But the Martu! They are stealing us bare!"

76

"Is the confederacy of Sumer and Akkad holding together?" Abram questioned.

"You know the Sumerians, especially Urians! They never want to fight until someone is on their back. King Sin Bani is always threatening to keep them in line, but they just ignore him as much as possible.

"Language," Ibalu added, "is still the sore spot. Sin Bani insists that all legal, religious and trade communications be in Akkadian, whether it be temple omens or cargo receipts. That really offends the Academy at Kamarina!"

"Has anything been done in Ur to oppose Sin Bani?" Abram asked.

"Yes . . . and it is bound to bring trouble!" Cautiously whispering, Ibalu related what had been burdening him, "The leading men of Ur, including your father and your brother, Haran, pushed King Shulgi of Ur into banishing the Akkadian high priestess and the whole cult of Ishtar."

"I should think that would be suicide!" Abram exclaimed, trying to control the alarm in his voice. "Nearly a third of the people in Ur now are Akkadians. What has King Sin Bani done about it?"

"Outwardly, nothing. He is bound by treaty to stay out of internal affairs, if he wants his protection tribute. A prosperous Ur still means money for Akkad.

"No," Ibalu resumed guardedly, "he doesn't want to stir up civil war in Ur."

"What then?" Abram pressed him for an answer.

The clamorous noise of the inn almost obliterated Ibalu's words. Cupping his hand so that only Abram could hear, he said, "Gutians were hired to raid the homes of those opposed to Ishtar. They were to vandalize and abduct any daughters. The Gutians could do as they wish with the women; however, King Sin Bani said he would secretly buy any of them, depending on their beauty, for the temple in Akkad."

Abram's face drained of color. "O my God, my Lord . . . no!" he cried out. Then quietly he began to pray, ignoring his friend, "My God, most high. God and Lord of all the world and everything that is made, please spare them! Please spare my family and Haran's daughters. Please, my God, spare Sarai—precious Sarai. Lord, please spare her!''

"You believe in the one God?" Ibalu asked hopefully. "Abram, are you too a friend of God? Noah's God?"

Abram stared disbelievingly at his friend. "You . . . you worship the God of Noah, Ibalu?"

"There is no other God, Abram."

"Yes, I know," he answered slowly, the pain and fear still pounding in his heart.

"There are a group of us here in Akkad," Ibalu informed him. "We meet together and pray for this evil city. Many believers have come from Ur recently to join with us. People are getting weary of the constant sin and debauchery, and some yearn for the reality of the righteous God."

"Will you have your friends pray for the safety of my family . . . and for Sarai?" Abram implored.

"Of course, my brother Abram. There is a good chance that the Gutians would refuse to do anything for Sin Bani. And the Urian border guard is not about to let those ruffians in if they can prevent it. By the way, who is Sarai? Are you taking a wife?"

"No . . . she . . . she is just a young girl who was adopted by Haran," he answered, the memory of Sarai's young face vividly appearing before his eyes.

Abram spent the night in agony and prayer. But he failed to feel God's presence, and his words seemed only to resound off the walls of his room.

At dawn the men gathered on the docks, loading new supplies and preparing the equipment and tents. Abram did not divulge his knowledge of the plot against Ur for fear of jeopardizing Ibalu. Hiding his impatience, he hurried the men at their tasks as pleasantly as possible.

"You have many men to care for your load," the head inspector said suspiciously. "Are you sure you are not out pirating?"

"I am Abram of Ur, son of Terah from Nakkur and Kamarina. I have no need to pirate from any man. Have you heard anything of my father's herds? He must have started late from Ur as we have not sighted him yet."

The inspector smirked and said, "I'm sure your father had *some* good reason for being late!" With that he motioned to his assistants and left Abram to stare questioningly after him. Premonitions burdened Abram as he boarded his boat.

It took all the men to push the six kalaks with long poles through the urban canal. Boats of varying shapes and sizes were already crowding the passage. Some were laden with fresh fruits and vegetables or flowers, and some with stacks of flat bread. Others were empty save for the oarsmen who were en route to make purchases or to fish.

Shops and markets perched on either side of the waterway. The merchants called out for customers and exchanged greetings and curses with the boatmen. Strong pungent odors of fish, onions, garlic and refuse mixed with fragrant smells of baking bread, coriander and cassia, frankincense and perfumes. Lengths of bright-colored materials hung like draped banners from the balconies of the cloth merchants. Gossamer ribbons of smoke drifted skyward from the burning coals of countless braziers.

The crews maneuvered the kalaks out of the canal and over to the current of the right bank. The powerful brown flow was widening its channel and becoming heavy with silt. Men and women busily worked on the alluvial farmlands that stretched out on both sides of the river. Tall, wooden waterwheels were spaced along the shorelines. Earthenware jars attached to their rims were filled and raised by the force of the water, emptying themselves into elevated irrigation troughs. Work had to begin early. The cool of the morning would soon be replaced by the burning desert sun, and the humidity of the river valley would be intense by afternoon.

Eliezer looked tired and somewhat sick. He lay under the protection of the tent. Abram left his watch at the front of the boat to see about him. "You are not well, Eliezer?" he asked compassionately.

The young man lay stretched out on a soft mat. He turned his face away from Abram's gaze. "The food," he answered faintly. "I ate too much and drank too much ale."

"Where did you sleep?"

There was an awkward silence. Then Eliezer turned toward Abram and smiled sheepishly, answering, "One doesn't get much sleep in the temple." He lifted himself on his elbows, his eyes bloodshot and squinting. "I really was going to take your advice, Abram," he said, still smiling, "but I've heard about Akkad for so long. I had to see those women!"

Eliezer's words made Abram recoil. He ached inwardly from Ibalu's disclosure the previous evening and thoughts burned in his mind of Sarai and Haran's daughters being abused and sold for temple prostitutes. His fists clenched, crushing his nails into his palms. He fought to control his desire to lash out at the young man.

Eliezer sobered, aware of the rising fury in Abram's face. Abram was exacting and could be demanding on occasion, but Eliezer had never seen him angry. "I am sorry," Eliezer apologized nervously. "I did not know it would offend you this much. It really was a miserable experience. I hated it, and I hated myself afterward! . . . Can you imagine, I had to wait in line to have my time with some tired, crying little girl!"

Abram studied the remorse and humiliation on his adopted son's face, and Abram's anger turned to compassion and frustration. "I am . . . very burdened, Eliezer, by news I was told last night," he said brokenly. "Akkad's king has hired some Gutians to attack my family and others in Ur who have opposed the worship of Ishtar. He offered to buy any unmarried young women they might capture. Haran, my brother, has . . . three grown daughters."

Before Abram could explain more, Papeni, one of the servants, shouted out, "Master Abram, I see your father's ensign!" Abram hastily left the tent, followed by Eliezer.

Across the broad river, beyond the left bank and still some distance to the south, grazed flock after flock of Terah's sheep and goats. Each group of fifty or so was led by its own hireling shepherd. Herds of oxen fed nearer the bank. Pack asses and camels—several hundred of them—arranged ahead and behind the migration, were laden with tents, supplies and belongings. Servants with long staffed spears kept watch over them. Ensign bearers carried the Urian blue banner with its white crescent as well as Terah's ensign, a flag brightly striped like a rainbow.

"Terah must be with the lead men," Abram said to the others on the boat, his mixed emotions surging within him. "I must go to him!"

"The left bank is too rough and shallow for the kalaks at this point, Abram," Sukri, the oarsman, stated. "The flotations would burst with the load."

"Signal the others to group, Sukri," Abram called urgently as he went back into the tent. "Tell them that I will go on by land and rejoin all of you at the Marad canal docks."

Abram stripped himself and put on a brief loincloth. Taking a spare inflated skin from the rear of the craft, he slipped his strong, supple body into the muddy waters. Buoyed up by the ballooned skin, he fought his way through the dangerous current. The waters on the left of the wide river were more sluggish, and he floated on them toward a clump of willow trees. Finding a footing was difficult. The thick silt oozed and gave way under his feet as he tried to stand near the shore. Floating once again he came closer to the drooping limbs until he could grasp them. Holding onto the branches with one hand, he discarded his flotation skin. Then hand over hand he pulled himself by the branches around the trees and up on firm land.

Gerbils and jerboas scurried and jumped away among the trees and grasses. A few herons were disturbed and reluctantly flapped farther downstream. The croaking and splashing of departing frogs and the buzzing of river insects were all familiar sounds of his long-ago boyhood.

Abram was quickly joined by a detachment of servants who welcomed him and brought him to his father. Terah was dismounting from the padded wooden seat of his well-groomed riding camel. He reached out his long arms and they clasped one another.

"My son, my beloved son. The God of Noah has surely sent you!" he sighed heavily. Terah's tall lean body was advanced in age but his appearance manifested strong authority and dignity.

"What has happened, Father!" Abram asked anxiously. "The Gutian barbarians? I heard they were hired to do you harm!"

"What more harm could they do than murder my eldest son and rape his daughter before my eyes!" Terah said bitterly, gritting his square jaw to check his feelings.

"They killed Haran? Oh, my father. . . ." Abram grieved, overwhelmed by Terah's words. "And . . . Sarai? Ishcah? Milcah? Which one?"

"Ishcah," Terah replied. "The other two had gone with Nahor and Lot to help with the spring shearing."

"Did no border guard try to stop those insane murderers?"

"There were at least sixty Gutians," Terah answered bitterly. "They came late in the day, hiding themselves in the cargo of several pirated kalaks. Before anyone knew it, they lunged out of the boats and murdered the custom guards and duty collectors.

"They waved those sickening knives, screaming wild yells. The crowds in the streets panicked, causing just the confusion they needed to do their assignment. Every home of those who were resisting Akkad was attacked. At each stop one or more was murdered, and the women abused and kidnapped.

"When they returned to their boats, they threatened to kill their hostages if they were not granted safe conduct through the canal. We could do nothing but let them escape."

"Ishcah, what will they do to her?"

Terah winced at the terrible memory. "They tortured her, pulling out her hair and burning her feet."

"Why? Why would they. . . ."

"They wanted Sarai. They thought we were hiding her somewhere in the house."

"Sarai. . . ." Abram questioned.

"Sarai is known throughout Ur. She is a very beautiful woman. Men cannot take their eyes off her. It has been very difficult at times to protect her. It has been her own wisdom and strength that have been able to do it."

"And then, what happened to Ishcah?"

"They took her, still threatening her to find out about Sarai. We found her mutilated body in the canal."

82

"Oh, no . . ." Abram gasped unbelievingly.

The hot noon-day sun beat down upon the father and son as they stood in silence for some time. Shepherds and servants were pitching shade tents and pausing to rest. The women and stewards passed out flat bread, long smoked sausages, and diluted ale. Terah and Abram partook of the meal under one of the open air tents.

"Are Nahor and the others with you?" Abram finally inquired.

"No, they wanted to stay. Because of the Gutians' threat to return, Nahor has recently married Haran's daughter, Milcah. To get away from the tragedy they took Lot and went to Sarai's house in the marsh for a few days."

"Sarai's house in the marsh! With the reed people?" Abram almost shouted in his alarm. "That could be more dangerous than the Gutians for the women!"

For the first time during their reunion, Terah's strong aged face broke into a smile as he spoke, "Not with wise Sarai to protect them. She has lived there secretly most of the time since she . . . since she matured."

"Lived in the swamps?"

"Nahor and Lot helped her build a house. She was more comfortable away from the city. She had openly spoken against Nannar-Sin, even preached to the women of the Gagûm. If every guard had not been overwhelmed by her beauty, she would probably be in bonds by now."

Abram persisted, "But how could she survive in the swamps with those runaway slaves and criminals?"

"She became a leper," Terah said obtusely.

"A leper!" Abram cried out. His mind and emotions, usually steady and under control, were being strained as never before.

Terah quickly interjected, "No, I do not mean that she *had* leprosy—only that she *feigned* having the disease. Her faultless beauty may have saved her many times, but it has been a burden for her. As a leper, she dressed in rags and bandages. At a distance, she could talk freely and openly with the reed people. Even if the men desired her, they would never touch her, you can be sure. Many of the people grew to love her, especially the poor women who must spend their miserables lives there. They love her not because she is beautiful but because she cares about them, and teaches them . . . and prays for them."

"How could she teach them? They would not come within six rods of a leper."

"She goes up and down those canals by boat and just talks to them," Terah explained patiently. "She never really lied and told them she had leprosy, and they never asked. Many times she would come by night down the canals to Kamarina and stay a week or so at Haran's or with me. . . ."

"Does she have plans for marriage?" Abram inquired with concern.

"Only to you!" Terah answered bluntly. Abram could say nothing in response, but his heart began to pound. Marriage was something he planned carefully to avoid.

"If you find her," his father continued, smiling wisely, "and have desire for her, then you have my blessing if you marry. It would protect her from being sought after by Akkad. But be prepared to defend yourself for the rest of your life from other men who will try to steal her away from you.

"And remember this as well," he warned his son. "Sarai is only four generations away from those who lived before the Flood. Her great beauty will continue to increase. She will be full of years before it ever begins to fade."

"It has been ten years since I brought her to you," Abram said somewhat defensively. "Her memory has always haunted me, but she was . . . such a young girl then."

"She is not a young girl now!" Terah said emphatically.

Terah pulled himself up. He was a commanding figure, and Abram had always admired and respected him. Terah looked directly down into Abram's eyes as he spoke, "My son, I am old and getting weary of the years I have spent in these pagan cities. I have served other gods. I wish to repent and worship the God of my fathers, the God of Noah. Knowing Sarai and witnessing her strong faith has convinced me."

He stopped, then continued, "Old Nahor, my father, believed like Sarai, although his faith in the God of Noah was why I stayed away in Ur most of the time. I was afraid of a

84

God who might ask of me something I would not want, like build an ark or something else I could not understand. I wanted wealth. And I wanted my sons to be educated and be part of the world...."

Then Terah's flint-like eyes, dark but still clear like his son's, looked pleadingly at Abram, "When I return in autumn, will you depart these lands with me—the lands of Ur and Akkad and Charran and all the rest with their evil practices? Will you and Sarai and Lot, the son of my eldest, leave with me? Together we would have enough men and servants and wealth to be our own city!"

"Where . . . where would we go, Father?" Abram asked in amazement, wondering how far ahead Terah had planned.

"Perhaps the land south of Damascus. It is not heavily settled. We could migrate the herds between Damascus and the Lake of Gomorrah and establish trade relationships with the cities there. But we would be our own city . . . a city without foundations, whose king will be the God of Noah."

Abram was slow to answer. He had been independent and free of family responsibilities and concerns these many years. It was difficult for him to imagine constantly living in tents with the herds, being isolated from people and the stimulation of city life. Hesitantly he responded, "I am not sure, Father...."

"You do not need to decide until I return. But do this for me: trade off all of Haran's properties in Lot's name for gold, silver or herds. Otherwise, they will revert to the temple. I have already given Nahor his inheritance when he married Milcah. You may stay at the villa, of course, but see if you can find a trade for it, as well as my pastures and farmlands by my return. Perhaps you and I might even want to make a scouting trip to Canaan before the spring."

Abram rejoiced to see the spark and determination that rose in Terah. Some of the enthusiasm and excitement began to course through him as well. It was a new idea to him—to live in a land as a wandering city, free to determine life as God would have it.

The two men left the tent and walked out among the others. Abram greeted them warmly, embracing various relatives and

85

familiar servants and friends and meeting new additions of men and maidservants.

Terah ordered two swift camels to be brought, and a servant accompanied Abram on the overland journey to the river bank opposite Marad. The servant then left to return with the camels, and Abram ferried to Marad and found his men waiting for him. There he shared with them about the murders and tragedy brought forth by the Gutians in Kamarina.

The rest of the trip to Ur was outwardly uneventful. During the time Abram struggled to free himself of the waves of indignant grief and impatience that swept over him. Mixed desires grew almost unbearable—the desire for revenge, the desire to know of the safety of the four in Ur, the desire to see Sarai—but even more, a hungering desire to be once again in the presence of the living God.

The kalaks turned into the canal that led to Kamarina. Urian customs officials signaled to the boats to stop for inspection. Nervous guards kept their shields and sharp spears alerted. When they were satisfied that the kalaks carried only cargo and not Gutians, the boats were allowed to be attached to a waiting oxen team. The six boats were tied together, and the oxen pulled the procession from the canal bank path toward the city.

Abram watched as they passed by the well-known lands on either side of the canal. Ur had deteriorated after the centuries of aggressive campaigns by Sargon's Akkadians. Added now were the erratic hostilities by the Gutians and other bands from the east. The marsh had reclaimed much of the ancient kingdom of Akalamdu. So many precious dikes had been destroyed during the skirmishes that it had been deemed easier to give the lands back to the swamps and to import food than to rebuild.

"It is good that Terah wants to leave Ur," Abram thought. "Winter fodder will soon be hard to secure."

Eliezer was seated beside him. The young man was raptly watching the imposing city that loomed ahead. It was his first time to see the high, white-washed walls and buildings of Kamarina or the gardened terraces of the massive gleaming

Ziggurat, the gold overlay of its summit chambers glittering in the bright sunlight. Abram himself was always impressed by the majestic skyline that rose out of the flat desert. On seeing the Ziggurat he was startled as the image of the Lesser Ararat flashed in his mind. A sudden change came over him. Something caused him to be repulsed by the scene that lay before him. He felt strangely unclean as his boats were being dragged toward it.

After settling his duty accounts, Abram quartered his people in Terah's large and commodious home. Terah's servants who had remained there were relieved to have Abram and his strong retinue of men in the villa. The servants' fears of the Gutians' return were quite evident.

Abram sent the servant, Papeni, out to make some special arrangements and assigned duties to his other servants. He then called together his remaining brigade of twenty-four men. These were versatile, well-trained soldiers. They had long been in Abram's employ and were strongly devoted to him. Most had gone to Damascus with Abram from Charran and were part of the strategy that had routed out the sea peoples. Some were married and had left their wives and families in the north until they returned next spring.

"I must look for my brother and the others tomorrow," Abram spoke seriously. "The villa may be watched by Gutian spies, so I have devised a plan that will require four of you to help me—Arzikari, Taizu, Kapuli, and Suani. I wish that the rest of you remain here under Milkusa's authority. See if you can find out what the situation really is in Ur. A drunk Akkadian will tell you everything he knows. Someone here was well informed of the attack.

"Also, Milkusa," Abram added. "Train Eliezer. He should make a good soldier in time."

Before dawn of the next day Abram and his four men quietly entered the dark streets of Kamarina, avoiding the light of the occasional street lanterns. Carrying packs of supplies on their backs, they found their way to the city canal docks. There a large tarada and a small canoe, for which

Abram had sent Papeni to make purchases the previous day, awaited them.

Both types of boats were in common use throughout Ur. The tarada was over twenty cubits long and about two cubits at its widest beam. Its high slender prow rose in a long thin tapering curve which allowed the craft to weave through intricate canals and ditches or force its way through the water paths of the giant reedbeds. The beautiful taradas were the pride of Ur. Their wooden plank sides were smoothly covered on the outside with bitumen, and their interiors were decorated with metal studs and medallions—iron, bronze, silver or gold, depending on the owner's position and wealth. The flat bottom taradas could carry heavy loads with a shallow draught of only a handspan.

With the coming of the morning light, the dock gates were unlocked and the canal traffic opened. Arzikari and the other three men loaded the larger boat while Abram stood some distance away. The docks soon became crowded with crewmen and early morning traders, but no one dared come near Abram. He stood isolated, his body clothed in the bandages of leprosy. His plan to find Sarai included using her own devices.

"Beware, unclean," he wailed, following the ancient warning law. Not to call out when people were near was punishable by a death of fire. The cry of a leper was an unnerving call that made even a coarse oarsman shrink in fear.

When the men were ready, Abram stepped into the waiting canoe and Taizu tied the two boats together. Then the four took their places in the tarada and pushed off, pulling the canoe a short distance behind. Abram sat alone and quiet in the rear boat.

The men punted the tarada, two in the stern and two in the bow. In turn they drove long poles in the water, first on one side and then on the other.

They detoured off the main channel into the canal that led through the countryside and would eventually flow into the marsh. The morning was fresh and clear. Vibrant textured patchworks of green farmlands lay on either side. At even intervals along the canal the sentry-like waterwheels rotated their water jars, incessantly spilling their contents to irrigate the rich fields.

Already workers were busy cultivating the wheat and barley and tending to the vineyards and orchards. Cattle, sheep and goats, not migrated toward Charran, were pastured in rich areas of grass that bordered the irrigation ditches. Their young ones freely played beside them, sometimes slipping on the muddy banks only to scramble up again.

As the boats neared the marsh, the sides of the canal became steeper. Along the top of the drab bank grew the sharp cutting leaves of the sedge grass, its tall clumps mixed with brambles and willow bushes. Large soft-shelled terrapins, slithering and flopping off the banks, were joined by smaller tortoises. Leaping frogs splashed, hitting the water like so many large raindrops. Pied fly-catchers and kites circled overhead and sometimes a flock of rooks flapped away almost vertically ahead of the tarada.

The boats next entered a thick grove of untended palms. The tall forest was made impenetrable by a thick undergrowth of matted thorn bushes. Beyond the palms began the great reedbeds. The giant, bamboo-like grass grew to heights of fifteen cubits or more. The long stems, ending in tasselled, buff-colored heads, formed a high hedge on either side of the canal. The colors varied from the pale gold and grey of the older growth to the light greens of the new.

Other canoes, similar to the one Abram was in, began crowding into the canal from the interior of the marsh. The young men and boys who manned the boats each wielded sharp saw-edged sickles. They were cutting and gathering the young green reeds and piling them in their boats for cattle fodder. There was much calling to one another, laughter and singing.

The tarada, its long graceful body gliding through the curtain of reeds, at last turned into a small lake. The sparkling blue waters were a change from the brown opaque flow of the canals.

At the far side of the lake stood a picturesque village of barrel-vaulted reed houses and buildings.[8] Arzikari directed the men to pull ashore. Canoes and other assorted boats, some just rafts made from tied together reeds, clustered about the small sandy harbor. This was a trading post area. The marshlanders had brought and laid out their products. There were piles of palm lumber and reed poles, stacks of reed mats, skins of water buffalo butter, jars of milk and yogurt, and the most valuable trade item—neatly formed cakes of water buffalo dung, Urian fuel.

Women did most of the bartering. It was they, too, who sat in the midst of buzzing flies patting the dung cakes into shape. Others were busy churning butter in airtight skins which they vigorously shook on tripod cradles made from thick reed poles. Taradas from the Kamarina business district were unloading sacks of grain, bolts of cloth, and stacks of leather.

Finished dung cakes were stacked along shore in beehive-shaped piles. Each cake was identified with the imprint of its maker's left hand. The plain cakes could be burned, but generally they were dipped in bitumen for a hotter and longer burning fire—and to bring a better price.

Arzikari left the others in the boats and wandered through the small lively market, finally approaching a squatting old man. The almost toothless figure sat naked in the warm morning sun except for a dirty cloth tied between his legs and wrapped carelessly around his hips. His thin, weather-beaten body was well scarred from lashings and perhaps torture.

"You know where to come," the old man cackled knowingly, his broken laughter causing him to heave deep, hoarse coughs. "My name in the swamp is Jaraizi, Little Rat—a good name! You want to buy little girls or little boys?" His nervous eyes squinted in the bright light as he restlessly waited for Arzikari's response. "Cheaper here than in the city, and you pay no filthy tax!" he added.

Arzikari stared at him impassively. He dropped a silver shekel in front of the old man. The gnarled hands hastily grabbed for it, but Arzikari covered the coin quickly with his foot. "So . . . what *are* you buying?" Jaraizi asked suspiciously.

With a nod in the direction of the shore, Arzikari said flatly, "The man alone in the canoe . . . where are others like him?"

"Oh, you want to dump a leper, is it? Why not turn his canoe upside down and be done with him? We do not want any more of those rotting dogs! Why are they sending their garbage to us? We have one now contaminating the place and she is bringing in more. A woman she is—and she is always *preaching* to me! *She,* a *leper,* telling *me* my trade is dirty!"

Arzikari threw down another shekel and said, "If you direct us to her, they are both yours."

The old man scooped up the second shekel and unsteadily teetered to his feet. He looked down at Arzikari's foot then back at his unexpressive face. "And that one! I suppose I get that one when you see the other vermin?" he said disgustedly.

Arzikari picked up the coin and led Jaraizi to the waiting boats, regretfully wishing he had chosen someone else for this errand.

Jaraizi waved his head back and forth emphatically, "No! I will lead you in my own boat. I do not want to get near your bag of rags," he exclaimed brusquely, pulling off his slipping loincloth and throwing it in the prow of his battered canoe. The sun was getting hot, a time when few clothes were tolerated by those who lived in the humid and sweltering heat of the swamp.

They departed, following Jaraizi's canoe as he punted into a canal that led away from the lake and deeper into the marsh. Small, scrubby farms bordered the waterway, separated from each other by low mud walls and water-filled ditches. Barking, snapping dogs guarded with frenzy each small plot's boundaries.

Part of every farm wall facing the canal was broadened into a water buffalo platform. Most of the ponderous animals, who belonged to the farmers, had retreated to distant reed beds to graze on the new green shoots. Some, however, were lazily swimming in the canal, submerged except for their heads and curving horns. They moaned from the effort of swimming and breathed heavily, their eyes rolling erratically as they watched the passing boats. The big, phlegmatic beasts would eat all day and come loyally back to their platforms at night to devour piles of green shoots cut by their masters. The more they ate the more rich milk they produced, and even more important for their owners, the more dung they expelled when they returned to their platforms.

The farms stopped abruptly, and the high reeds began once again. The canal divided and parted many times. Sometimes Jaraizi went left, sometimes right. Abram remained almost motionless during his solitary voyage behind the tarada. He carefully memorized the route they were taking, his heart beginning to beat faster in uneasy apprehension.

The four men in the tarada pushed in silence while the old man yelled back terse directions. "They are around the next bend!" he called finally. "There are four of them. We never had lepers until that young one came. Why do they want to come to this infested swamp? They should stay and beg in the city!"

The boats swung around the narrow bend. High reeds grew on either side except for a single clearing that was sequestered from the encroaching reeds by mud walls and bordering deep ditches. On the wild sides of the ditches the reeds had been cut back several cubits for more sunlight. A large reed house stood on a raised area in the middle of the remote land.

"Give me my money!" Jaraizi demanded, swinging his canoe back and alongside the tarada. "I want to go back before those filthy dogs think I am one of them!" Arzikari threw him the other shekel, and the old man and his canoe were quickly lost from sight after he turned the bend.

Arzikari and Taizu shoved the prow of the tarada up the slippery mud ramp that was part of a water buffalo platform. Kapuli and Suani pulled the canoe alongside by the rope. Abram and the four men remained motionless in the boats looking cautiously at what lay before them. Except for the incessant buzzing of flies, the other swamp noises were hushed. Then from the reed house, shattering the stillness, came the shrill, disconcerting words, "Unclean, unclean! Beware, unclean!"

Chapter IV
THE REED HOUSE

The house was fronted with tall entrance pillars of smooth reed canes bound tightly together. Rows of similar pillars, each over a cubit in thickness, had been bent over at the top and bound together to form a series of arches. To this framework long bundles of reeds were lashed together forming thin logs which were laid and strapped to the arches for siding. Layers of honey-colored reed mats covered the roof. The doorway was a tall narrow slit covered by a flap of gauze-like netting.

To the right a waist-high fence of sharp pointed poles shielded a well and a garden of lentils and onions. On the other side of the house neat piles of dung cakes posed in regimental order. Freshly cut fodder lay in wet heaps by the platform.

The flap of the doorway was slightly drawn back and a rag-bandaged figure peer out. The voice of a young woman repeated, "Unclean, unclean! Beware, unclean!"

The voice was strangely familiar to Abram. It was definitely the dialect of someone from the aristocracy of Ur. "Could it possibly be Milcah?" he thought. Abram had hardly known his brother's children. His only memories of them were when they were slumbering infants and light-hearted toddlers.

The girl spied Abram's wrappings. Her eyes widened in panic as she cried out, "No, go away! We have no more room here!"

Arzikari stepped out to moor the boat, and the girl became more frightened and pulled back into the house. Almost immediately she returned, her hands gripping two funnel shaped clappers. She wildly clanged the cymbals. "Nahor! Nahor! Na-a-hor!" she screamed frantically.

Abram quickly pulled off his leprosy rags and leapt to the bank, agilely keeping his balance on the slippery mud. "Milcah, Milcah!" he shouted, smiling warmly to fend off her fears. "I am Abram, your father's brother!"

Milcah stopped. Her hands still held the clappers in position, either to strike together or use as a weapon on the strange man approaching her.

"I am Abram, Milcah!" he repeated loudly.

Milcah paused warily, fears of the ruthless Gutians still haunting her. "How do I know that you tell me the truth?" she asked cautiously. "Tell me, if you are Abram, who is my mother?"

Abram looked at her trembling form with compassion. He remembered how recently it was that her father and sister had been murdered, and she and Sarai hunted down by the marauders. Softly he spoke to her, "Your mother, Hasim-nati, died shortly after Lot was born. She was a beautiful woman, Milcah, with a halo of brown curls which I see you have inherited."

"You are my uncle?" she asked, tears now streaming freely.

"I am," he assured her, gently taking the cymbals from her hands. "Will these have called the others?" he asked her.

Milcah's mood changed completely. "Oh yes, my uncle. Oh yes, Abram!" she laughed almost hysterically. "I am so glad it is you! Clang them hard, Abram! Nahor, Lot and Sarai . . . they are all gathering reeds for the buffalo. They will be so happy to see you!"

Looking toward the tarada, Milcah called to the other men, "Please, please, come into the house! I was just baking bread when you came." The girl nervously trembled from excitement and her past fears. "I am so glad it is you, Abram!" she repeated over and over.

The men had just gotten out of the tarada and Taizu was about to pull the boat up on the mud platform when two men in canoes charged toward the long boat. "Get back in that tarada all of you," shouted the older of the two attackers, whom Abram quickly recognized as his brother Nahor.

Nahor and Lot punted their canoes with formidable-looking fishing spears using the blunt end in the water. The thick reed shafts were eight or nine cubits long with five barbed prongs at the head. These they aimed at the tarada as they approached.

"Nahor!" Abram hailed his brother, bursting into laughter. "Please do not spear my tarada!"

Nahor was the middle son with many years separating him from Haran and only a few from Abram. Whereas Haran had received the honor and prestige as Terah's eldest son, Nahor was not known in the city and did not mind being relegated to the care of his father's farms and livestock. Abram, on the other hand, had taken little interest or responsibility in the family business affairs and had gone after his own pursuits. Nahor admired Abram's brilliance, and Abram had always enjoyed and sought out Nahor's humble, good-natured company during his years of study and research in Kamarina.

Abram's shout and laughter caused Nahor to look up. In his surprise he lost his balance, vaulting awkwardly on his spear into the water with a noisy splash. The men joined Abram in helping Nahor up the slick ramp. In doing so they began shaking with laughter so much that one after another slid down the slippery bank. Young Lot watched bewildered and cautious from his canoe, his fishing spear resolutely aimed at the comic group.

Eventually all climbed up the slick platform and the six mud-coated men continued to laugh uproariously at one another. They sat on the thick piles of soft green rushes that Nahor and Lot had labored that morning to cut.

Nahor was the first to compose himself, and he called out to his nephew, "Come in, Lot. It is just your hopelessly wayward uncle, Abram." Then turning to Abram he exclaimed, "See, Abram, how nervous I am trying to protect Milcah and that beautiful woman, Sarai, for you!"

The mention of her name abruptly ended Abram's hilarity. "Sarai? Nahor, where is she?" he anxiously questioned his brother.

"She should return soon," Nahor quickly assured him. Then pointing up the canal he added, "She went into that narrow waterway that winds deeper into the marsh. She has some claptraps set there to catch swamp ducks and also some fish weirs. Maybe she didn't hear Milcah's signals."

"I would like to go find her," Abram said, his heart strangely pounding again as it did when Terah first talked about Sarai.

Now it was Nahor's turn to laugh uncontrollably. Finally he managed to say, "All . . . all of these years . . . she has refused every eligible man in Ur . . . waiting for you!" More laughter convulsed him before he could finish. "And now you come to her . . . like a mud hen! You had better clean yourself up, my brother."

Abram was somewhat annoyed by the remark. Perhaps it was because in every city where he had stayed he had been pursued by the leading families to marry their daughters. He had never experienced the thought of a woman disapproving of him, and never had he gone out of his way to win any woman's approval. If he had ever been attracted by a woman, she always seemed too eager to return his attentions, and he quickly lost interest.

"I will go as I am!" Abram retorted, aware that his four men would be watching his response. "I am interested only in her welfare and safety. As far as I am concerned, there is nothing else!"

"Yes, Abram. I shall remember those words," Nahor said gleefully. "I shall remember those words, indeed!"

Not looking back, Abram put one foot in the canoe and shoved off with the other. The five men, Lot and Milcah watched his departure. "What a surprise he has in store for him!" Nahor commented, trying hard to control his laughter. "Sarai is one problem my brother's mathematics can't solve."

Abram punted the canoe into the passageway. His mind was marshalling his thoughts while his heart continued to pound inexplicably. "I am *not* going to let this woman talk me into marriage just because I helped her when she was a little girl—or *looked* like a little girl. I must keep her at a distance! No matter how beautiful she is supposed to be, I do not want to be tied down. I have always had my freedom. I always *want* my freedom! I like people. I love to be with different kinds of people . . . not just taking care of some demanding woman. I simply do not want to be married to anybody. . . . And that is what I will tell her. 'I do not want to be married to anybody!' "

The canoe had gone some distance from the house when Abram found Sarai. Her back was to him. She was busily tying together the legs of the swamp ducks that she had caught in the traps. There was much flapping and squawking as she dropped the birds in a net bag and placed it in the prow of her canoe. Then she stood in the boat and began to punt it around.

Abram gulped at what he beheld. When she did not look up he managed to say, "Sarai, it is I, Abram."

It was humid and hot in the marsh tunnel. Sarai had on a soft short tunic of brightly printed cloth that bared her right shoulder and fell loosely over her full rounded breasts. Her dark finespun hair curled in soft ringlets about her face and flowed in cascading waves down her back to her waist. A narrow white band held her hair in place at her crown.

As she turned, Abram saw that the large brown eyes he had so often remembered had become even more captivating and lovely. Those enchanting eyes, her delicate nose, and the comely shape of her face had all heightened to great beauty and radiated with a lustrous glow. Sarai's tall, smooth lean body was tanned from the sun and perfect in form and complexion.

His canoe almost adjacent to hers, Abram leaned on the punting stick and stared at her. His eyes followed down her shoulders and arms and the exquisite beauty of her hands and her long slender fingers. Her thighs and calves of her long legs were well rounded and he found even her sandaled feet were shapely and alluring.[9]

97

"Sarai . . . you are . . . beautiful," he stumbled out the words.

"I knew you were here, Abram," Sarai said directly and calmly. "I watched you arrive with Jaraizi."

"Why . . . why did you hide back here?"

"I was not hiding, Abram. I was waiting for you. I wanted to see you alone first. It . . . it has been a long time," she said seriously. "I wanted to pray . . . and be ready."

"Now look, Sarai," Abram replied, recovering himself and remembering his plan. "I did not tell you I would marry you. You are lovely—completely beautiful! But I do not want to get married to anyone!"

Sarai looked at him intensely and then broke into a wide full smile, her even teeth white and gleaming. "Oh, Abram," she responded joyfully. "You came to *release* me of my promise then? Oh, I thank you, my dear sweet friend!"

Abram was taken aback. He was suddenly conscious of his rags and mud-smeared body and the cakes of mud that clung to his hair. He wished he had cleansed himself as Nahor had suggested. He felt very uncomfortable and out of control of things.

"What do you mean, 'release' you, Sarai?"

"My dear Abram, our God has been so good to me! He has confirmed to me over and over that I am to bear a child that will carry on the faith of Noah. Because of Hosani's prophecy . . . you remember it, do you not?"

Abram nodded dejectedly.

"Because of her prophecy," she continued, her dark eyes sparkling, "I thought *you* must be the one to father such a child, for I had promised you I would wait for you."

Abram looked again at her ravishing body. His heart pounded and a sudden desire for her completely swept over him. He clenched his fists around his punting stick to repress it. Never had he felt so awkward, he thought.

"How I long to know the man God would have me marry," Sarai beamed, tears beginning to swell in her eyes. "And how I yearn to bear his child! Oh, Abram, there have been many fine men in Kamarina who have listened to me. They have forsaken Nannar-Sin for the real and wonderful God of Noah.

And they have desired me. I was not displeased with them, but I felt I *must* wait for your decision."

Sarai changed and began quietly praying, "Praise you, my Lord! Thank you for this freedom! Thank you for so kindly sending Abram to release me. Show me, my Lord. Direct me in your perfect will and desire for me!" It was as if they were back in the mountains. Sarai lifted her arms and began to sing praises in that same enchanting and mysterious melody Abram had heard in the Ararats. The presence of God suddenly seemed to pervade the tunnel and surround their two floating canoes.

It was intense, and Abram slumped down in his boat, overtaken once again as he had been in the Ararats by the awesomeness of the experience. Simultaneously he realized that in a few short poignant moments he had fallen hopelessly and lastingly in love with Sarai. Holding the frame of Abram's canoe close to her own, Sarai reached over to him. "Forgive me, my brother Abram. You mourn for your brother and niece. Did Nahor just tell you? I am sorry to speak only of myself. Please forgive me."

Abram was afraid to look up. The touch of her arm on his shoulder so stimulated him that he covered his face with his hands and mumbled, "No, Sarai. I have known about Haran and Ishcah for some time. I met my father beyond Marad."

"Then what concerns you, Abram? We will take it before the Lord. Look how the God of Noah has answered my prayers. He will answer anything you ask! Do you not remember how close you were to him in the mountains?"

"I am close to God when I am with you, Sarai," he finally sighed and looked up into the breathtakingly beautiful face so close to his own.

"Sarai!" he cried out. "I am sitting here covered with mud in a tottering canoe! And I am looking at you and falling completely in love with you . . . while you . . . you are singing and praising the Lord because you do not have to marry me!"

Sarai withdrew her arm and pushed her canoe slightly away. "You have not sought the God of Noah in all these years, have you, Abram?" she reproached him quietly.

99

"At first I thought a great deal about the things you told me. But as the years passed, my experience in the Ararats seemed as strange and remote as the myths of Gilgamesh."[10]

"And you were no different after being there?" she asked gravely.

Abram thought back. "Yes, I did change, Sarai. I believe in the God of Noah . . . in your God . . . and mine. There is no other God," he replied firmly. "But I have not sought him. I have tried to be righteous as best I knew how. But I have not asked God what righteousness really is or what he wants of me." As Abram talked, his inner feelings were calming.

Once again he looked at her—now several feet away—and confessed, "Sarai, I love you! I want you for my wife! I want you to bear *our* child to continue the faith of Noah . . . *our* faith!"

"You will seek the God of Noah and do his will—always?" she asked, glistening tears filling her eyes.

"Always, Sarai, . . . whether you marry me or not. I promise I will seek the God of Noah and do his will!" he pledged solemnly.

Sarai smiled disarmingly. "May I wait and make my final decision after I see what you look like?" she asked. "It is rather hard to tell under all that mud."

The swamp ducks had wiggled enough to have room to flap their wings within Sarai's net. They set up a clatter, and Sarai had to tend to them. Abram became aware for the first time of the attack made upon him by a swarm of persistent mosquitoes.

Sarai led the way in her canoe as they returned toward the house. Abram called ahead, "Should you not be wearing your leprosy bandaging?"

"I have many friends in the marsh," she answered back confidently. "I knew you were coming before you left the lake market."

"How?"

"The women. If anyone enters that canal off the lake one of the women drums the message."

"But Nahor? He didn't know."

"The swamp women allow few men to know their code!" Sarai explained as she guided her canoe through the narrow waterway.

When the channel widened somewhat, she allowed her canoe to drift until Abram was alongside. "Abram," Sarai spoke seriously. "We must pray more about whether we are to marry. I have caused your family great grief and trouble."

"Sarai, we will be our own family! The two of us will just have to be clever enough to keep you safe. You know," he continued, "after seeing you for the first time as a . . . woman, I now have sympathy for all the other men in the world. But our life together must grow as it did in the mountains, sharing the things we love . . . and walking with God.

"In other words, my devastatingly lovely woman, I want to love you for who you are . . . and I want you to love me for more than the mud hen that I am!"

Sarai laughed and her face glowed as she said, "I love you, Abram. I have never stopped loving you since you left me with Terah. For years I dreamed of you. I memorized the way you spoke and walked. My mind recalled nearly every word you ever said to me. But you never returned. I only knew I could not marry anyone else unless I was positive that you would not have me."

Abram decisively straightened up. "Sarai, I want you to wait here. I'm going to send the others back to Kamarina. I want to be alone with you. Can you cover yourself with something to keep from getting stung?"

"Yes . . . but we cannot just send them back. . . ."

"Sarai, if I am to be your husband. . . ."

Abram held the canoes together as they drifted quietly between the high walls of reeds. Sarai looked up at him at last and replied clearly, "I will wait."

As Abram began to push his canoe away she stopped him. "If you tell Nahor to leave a few shekels with the butter women at the market, their sons will cut fodder for us. They can leave it by the canal entrance." Then suddenly looking embarrassed she added shyly, "That way we will not have to spend our time doing it."

101

Abram smiled at her proudly, "I am going to have a *practical* wife!"

Finding his way back, Abram turned into the larger canal that passed Sarai's house. To his pleasant but complete surprise he saw the long tarada about to leave the platform. Aboard were his four men, Nahor, Milcah and Lot.

Seeing Abram, Nahor jokingly called out, "My brother, I just thought you might be coming out alone to chase us away. We leave you two for a few days. I must tend to my work. Now, don't you wish you had cleaned the mud off your face?"

Abram felt an overwhelming joy as he watched them depart. Remembering to pass on Sarai's message, he punted rapidly up to the tarada. "I promise you, my wise brother, always to listen in the future to your gems of advice." Then he announced firmly, "Before the God of Noah, Sarai will be my wife."

"That was quite an hour in the reed tunnel!" Nahor yelped loudly.

"Nahor," Abram tried to be serious but was having difficulty. All in the boat, Arzikari, Taizu, Kapuli, Suani and even Milcah, were enjoying teasing him. "Nahor!" he shouted trying to suppress his own amusement and elated feelings. "Please get a written marriage judgment for us. Announce it all over Kamarina. The Gutians will lose interest in finding Sarai if they know she is married, for they could never sell her in Akkad."

"Milcah and I will return in three or four days. I will take care of everything," Nahor promised, obviously delighted to be of help to his brother.

"Oh, by the way," Abram appended. "As you pass the market, pay the butter women a few shekels so their sons will give us some help with the fodder."

"I had planned to do just that," Nahor replied knowingly.

"The masterful bachelor has finally been caught, all right!" Suani yelled out. "Caught like a fish in the swamps of Ur!"

The joking and laughter in the tarada could be heard until the boat disappeared around the bend.

Abram beached his canoe and nimbly darted up the ramp and over the garden fence to the mud-brick well. Quickly he doused buckets of water over his body and lathered with the soft soap from a nearby jar. He wrapped a clean linen kilt around his waist and returned to get Sarai.

His strong arms eagerly plunged the pole into the water pushing the canoe quickly into the marsh channel. His mind had thoughts of only one thing, to see Sarai again. To his concern when he found her she was completely covered with netting. A thick dark cloud of mosquitoes swarmed around her canoe.

Abram rapidly tied the canoes together with the prow rope and ferried the two boats to the sunlight of the wider waterway.

Sarai peered out from under the netting, her eyes meeting his. "Oh, Abram, you are just as handsome now as you were in the Ararats . . . more handsome even than I remembered you."

"Sarai! Sarai! Let us get out of these impossible canoes!" he grimaced, yearning for her.

Once back in front of the house, Sarai picked up the net of ducks and Abram helped her from her canoe. "Now I am the dirty one," she said blithely. "Perhaps you would like to rest in the house while I prepare these birds and take my bath."

The feel of the soft palm of her hand intoxicated him, and Abram only reluctantly released her. "I will wait for you, but not very patiently," he admitted and went toward the house.

The flap of the narrow doorway was tied back. As Abram entered he noticed the airiness of the structure. The pale gold of woven reeds formed walls that rose and then rounded to a high vaulted roof. The end walls were straight and made of thick reeds woven to form a lacy latticework. The light that filtered through the diamond-shaped apertures of the lattice gave the large room a softly ethereal effect.

Except for near the firepit, the rest of the floor was covered with several layers of reed mats spread over with various many-colored rugs and cushions. Dividing off the rear of the room was a curtain of sheer netting that hung down from the concaved ceiling. The light drapery was pulled back for the daytime to allow the air to flow freely. Behind it lay a large bed of soft rushes and matting that had been neatly covered with a soft mattress of down. The bright print ticking of the mattress reminded Abram of Sarai's talent with fabrics. There were also several small wooden chests in the sleeping area—the same ones he had given, full of gifts, to Hosani and Sarai long before—and a small golden harp stood nearby.

From a rack of plates and other pottery, Abram took a mug and filled it from a hanging ale skin. He sat down cross-legged on one of the rugs. Slowly drinking the ale, he let his eyes wander, enjoying each thing that was Sarai's. When he noticed the wooden mortar and its long pestle propped against the wall, he began to imagine her rhythmically and gracefully pounding the grain. Abram continued to amuse himself this way seeing her at the butter churn, wondering how she would look working among the pots and cauldrons and at the circular grindstone.

Time passed so slowly that he was certain Sarai must be finished. Wandering out of the door he turned the corner of the house. There beside the well he could see Sarai completing her bath. She was toweling dry her soft dark hair and did not notice him. Abram gazed long and silently at her bare shapely body. His surging erotic feelings were gradually overcome by a powerful sense of awe and humility. He slowly fell to his knees and began to pray, "Holy God, what do you require of me to deserve a woman like Sarai. Please, my God, make me worthy!"

Abram returned to the house to wait for her. When Sarai came through the door sometime later she was carrying a flat basket containing the dressed birds and vegetables she had picked from the garden. Her fresh clean dress was of vivid pinks and reds, similar in style to the one she had worn before. Her only other adornment were delicate sandals made of woven reeds and red ribbons.

Abram stood to greet her, and several moments of time seemed hung in suspension before either could move or break the silence. Abram took her basket and set it by the churn. Coming close to her he studied the beautiful way her dark curls framed her lovely face, "I cannot believe it!" he smiled, knowing that the face he now adored was the same one he had known years before in the Ararats. "I am in love with a woman who understands the virtues of the sexagesimal system!"

Sarai responded, her eyes glistening with happiness, "And I am in love with a man who laughs for joy in the presence of the Lord!"

Abram gently took her hands in his and led her to where he had been sitting. "May I bring my promised wife some ale and cheese? You will soon see how useful I can be around your house!"

Sarai smiled and nodded. "I shall be honored," she replied, not able to stop looking at him.

"I have a plan, Sarai," he related as he poured the ale into a cup. His eyes twinkled with the thought. "Let us spend ten days in courtship, one for each year we have been apart."

"I would like that," Sarai replied somewhat shyly.

"Each day," Abram continued, "we will spend part of the time praying together. I must learn more from you how to walk in God's presence."

He sat beside her and handed her the cup, and they ate and drank together. "Also," he resumed, "we must spend time just talking to each other. I would like to have a marriage that was more than just physical or even just spiritual. If we had not experienced such a relationship as we did in the Ararats, I would not imagine it possible. But I want a marriage where we can be close friends and do things together!"

"Perhaps that is why the God of Noah allowed me to be adopted by Terah," Sarai replied brightly. "You are my brother . . . and you will also be my husband."

Abram sensed that she desired him to kiss her, and he yearned to do so. Instead, he set down his cup and held her left hand in his. He examined each delicate long finger and gently caressed and kissed her palm. Hesitantly he said, "I want us to gradually love and learn about each other. Sarai, every fibre of my being wants to know you completely, even at this moment. But if God gives me the endurance, I pray that we not rush too fast in the pleasures of lovers."

Sarai looked quizzical. Then her eyes lighted with amusement. "Men are not the only ones who need to pray for endurance," she informed him.

"You see! I am learning things about you already!" Abram laughed and then he spoke tenderly, "Let us say that after ten days, if we still feel committed as we do today and our love has grown and developed, we will consummate our marriage."

"It will be ten wonderful days . . . just to be with you, Abram!" Sarai beamed with anticipation.

He reached over to kiss her lightly on the lips when abruptly outside the door resounded loud grunts and splashes. Leaping to his feet, Abram pulled his knife and raced to the door.

"It is not an attack, my darling, but only Alpuia and Wagar-beli!" Saria called out.

Feeling a bit foolish, Abram lifted the door flap and saw two big dark-hided water buffalo struggling to climb up the slippery mud ramp of the platform. They had spent the day since early morning lumberingly swimming among the canals in search of green reed shoots. Now they hungrily clamored up the platform for more from the piles of cut fodder that awaited them.

"Do we have to do anything for them?" Abram asked, hoping the annoying beasts would soon depart.

"It is not a very romantic thought," Sarai confessed. "But in about an hour they will have relieved themselves. Then they will need milking and cakes must be made of the dung before it dries or they will step in it."

"Oh, Sarai. . . ." Abram moaned. "There go my near perfect plans!"

Sarai rose and went to the doorway. She put her arms gently on his shoulders, her hands clasped behind his neck. He felt the soft roundness of her breasts against the bareness of his chest.

Forgetting the buffalo, Abram pulled her to him, his arms wrapping around her slim waist. Their lips met and their kiss was long and tender. Then, still holding her close, he whispered softly with amused resignation, "I think that was what I planned for 'day three'!"

"I love you, Abram!" Sarah said warmly. "I will not tempt you or myself again. I *do* like your schedule. And I appreciate your wanting to pray and talk together. We will have a lifetime for embracing. These are important days!"

Abram nodded in agreement although he found it very difficult.

As they prayed and talked and worked together, the time passed far more quickly than they realized. They cultivated the garden and took the canoes on trips through the canals, sometimes fishing, other times just drifting alongside one another absorbed in deep conversations and sharing thoughts on many topics. In the evenings after their meal, Sarai played her harp, and they spent the hours together until the last coals in the fire pit stopped glowing. Sarai then retired to her bed and Abram slept on bedding near the door.

Nahor returned after several days. He stayed only long enough to leave supplies and the marriage papers.

At the end of the tenth day Abram entered Sarai's sleeping chamber with her. They knelt beside the bed and after a time of prayer made their vows of marriage.

"I, Abram, son of Terah, descendant of Noah, before you, my God, take Sarai to be my wife," Abram began.

Then Sarai repeated, "I, Sarai, daughter of Terah, descendant of Noah, before you, my God, take Abram to be my husband."

An oil lamp had been left burning near the fire pit. It cast a soft flickering glow that faded as it reached the darkness of the high roof.

As it happened his first day in the marsh, Abram found himself gazing upon Sarai's unadorned beauty. Once again he felt unworthy as he kissed her and held her close to him. Abram felt the warmth of her response as Sarai tenderly embraced his body and totally gave herself to him. The pleasure was exquisite.

Chapter V
THE COMMAND

"You may have just become a woman during the past years," Abram confessed hours later, softly holding her as they lay together. "But I feel I know now what it is to be a real man."

Sarai tenderly nestled her head under his chin, lightly kissing his neck with each movement. "A very wonderful man. . . ." she responded.

He looked down at her, loving her. "Being one with you has been the richest physical manhood I could ever know. But my spirit has also found what I think every man's spirit yearns after. . . . Sarai, my darling, I know at last where I am going, and what I am doing . . . and with whom. Together, you and I are going where the God of Noah directs us and do what he commands. Nothing else!"

He could say no more for Sarai's mouth had reached his, and her ardent embrace was enough to express the fulness of her joy and exuberance.

That evening the stars shone brightly reflecting like rippling silver coins in the water. Sarai knelt beside her two munching water buffalo and alternately stroked their heads. They responded by lifting and shaking their heavy faces while placidly devouring green shoots from the stacks piled on the platform.

"Alpuia, you are a hungry ox tonight . . . Wagar-beli, you are more beautiful than ever," Sarai spoke fondly. "Abram, do you not think these two are noble beasts?"

Abram was loading their canoes. He turned and pondered the cumbrous peaceable animals. "Yes," he conceded. "Noble, productive and a bit tedious. Will they be all right for a few days?"

"Alpuia and Wagar-beli are very independent in the daytime, but they will always return here at night," Sarai answered proudly. "I have a red cord that I tie to the reeds by the farm canal. The boys will know that I am away and will come and care for them."

Abram and Sarai donned their leprosy disguises and put on veils of netting. The covering would keep them safe from marsh thieves and from the gorging attacks of the mosquitoes that waited in the reed tunnels. Each got into one of the canoes and pushed off. Alpuia and Wagar-beli bade them farewell by expiring deep buffalo groans.

The giant reed beds were like high black walls at night. For some time Abram and Sarai punted and paddled the canoes through the darkness amid an orchestrated chorus of frogs. Only the twinkling starlight guided them.

They passed through the canal of farms. The small patches resembled lighted boats anchored side by side. Dark silhouettes of feeding water buffalo fronted each moated plot. Abram and Sarai paddled their way soundlessly over the quiet waters. Looking through the tall narrow doorways of the houses they could see families and animals gathered in the firelight.

By the time they reached the lake village, a half moon had risen above the thick palm forests. Crossing the lake they lifted their veils to enjoy the cool breeze and the absence of the droning mosquitoes.

It was nearly midnight when they arrived in Kamarina, and Abram awakened a servant at Terah's villa. The man brought jugs of warm water for bathing to their rooms, and also some cool ale and a plate of bread and cheese.

The walls of the master bedrooms were frescoed with pastoral scenes in soft colors. Dark imported wood beams crossed the ceiling from which hung ornate gold lamps. On the floor lay thick wool carpets woven in symmetrical floral designs.

The bed had been readied, as Nahor had anticipated their early return and forewarned the household servants. "My considerate brother must be reading my thoughts again," Abram said, smiling as he remembered Nahor's remarks during their first meeting in the marsh.

Both Abram and Sarai bathed and enjoyed the light meal in bed. As Abram rose to extinguish the lamps, Sarai looked puzzled and questioned him, "Did you and Nahor and Haran all have the same mother? Terah never spoke of his wife . . . or wives."

"I am not surprised that he would not speak of them," Abram answered as he sat by her on the edge of the bed. "Terah always feared making comparisons since we three brothers each had different mothers.

"My father's first wife was the daughter of Sukkal-makh, King Ur-Nammu's chancellor. She was Akkadian, and her name was Sin-Balti. She was a strong believer in the omens of the stars and Nannar-Sin practices. Terah was indifferent to her pagan zeal, since I think he loved her and enjoyed the wealth and prestige their marriage brought to him. Terah's own father, old Nahor, really despised their union, however, and refused to see his son or even allow Sin-Balti and Terah to name their only child after him. That child was Haran. Years later Sin-Balti died during a plague.

"Soon after Sin-Balti's death, old Nahor took courage and made the river trip to Ur bringing with him a young farm girl, Leah, from his village of Nakkur, near Charran. He insisted that Terah marry the girl or at least take her as a servant and have a son by her. Old Nahor greatly desired a namesake through his eldest son, but he wanted the heir by a woman who believed in the God of Noah. Leah, I was told by many, was a sweet and warm-natured girl who dearly loved my father immediately.

They did marry. They had a daughter who died in infancy and then came Nahor whose birth complications caused Leah's death.

"My father had to seek for someone to care for Nahor. Friends of his at the Academy recommended a pretty girl who was studying for a royal tutorship, a position that had just become popular at that time. Bright young women were trained in special Academy classes and then employed by the wealthy and those in government to teach the daughters of their families."

"Those are the studies I pursued when I first came to Ur," Sarai interjected.

Abram nodded appreciatively. "I thought you would probably be one of their best pupils!"

He continued with his story. "The girl's name was Ilmika. She was an energetic and outgoing person who soon won my father's heart. Terah married her, and I was their one child. For a long time, this was a very happy home. However, Ilmika, my mother, became ill and for many years suffered severe pain. It was especially difficult for my father. He had to leave her here for long periods of time when he took the herds on the migration. When he returned she would always be weaker. At last she died, and my father never married again. He once said he felt her death was God's judgment on him."

"And now the murder of Haran and Ishcah. . . ." Sarai murmured compassionately. "But how good it is, Abram, that Terah is seeking God now and not living in bitterness."

"My father wants us to leave Ur with him and live in the wilderness of Canaan where we can worship God freely. Did you know that? Charran, like Ur, has also become such a center for the worship of Nannar-Sin and Ishtar that he wants to be as far away from any city as possible."

"No," Sarai answered, her eyes pensive as she recalled the day of the Gutian attack on Kamarina. "I never saw him after the murders. Did he say the God of Noah spoke to him?"

"He did not put it that way. He is just convinced that he must leave."

Quickly tears came to Sarai's eyes. She reached for Abram's hand and began to pray, "We praise you and thank you, our God. We thank you for leading Terah. Thank you for helping him to seek after you."

She slipped out of the bed and knelt before Abram. "God of Noah," she prayed ardently, "I make Abram my guide. However you speak to him, I will follow. Direct us, I pray, through Abram. May I serve you, my God, as I am obedient and serve my husband."

Abram stroked the bowed head of his devout wife. His heart knew the conviction Terah had felt. If he were to lead Sarai and himself in the ways of a righteous God, then he, Abram, must hear from the God of Noah or not move at all.

Several days later, an official messenger arrived at the villa with a summons for Abram to meet with King Shulgi. Through Nahor and the information Abram's own men had discovered Abram had a general knowledge of the new king's difficult situation. But Abram also had other knowledge of Shulgi, the present king of Ur.

King Shulgi had risen rapidly in government officialdom. He had learned how to work diplomatically for freedom and the favors from Akkad that the Urians coveted. And in return, Shulgi made efforts to please King Sin-Bani of the Akkadians by finding new ways to levy taxes in Ur for Akkad's treasuries.

It had become the custom under Shulgi's predecessor, Ur-Nammu, to call the head of state the king when in Ur, but in Akkad he was referred to as the ensi, or governor. Early in his reign, Ur-Nammu defiantly attempted to build up the armed strength of Ur in order eventually to break from Akkad, but it proved too difficult a task. Therefore, with no strong army in Ur to force a decisive military clash, Akkad kept its tight control over the mid-river section and, hence, over Ur's freedom. King Ur-Nammu gave up resisting Akkad and turned to other projects, concentrating on the improvement of the city and rebuilding and enlarging the Ziggurat.

When King Ur-Nammu was first appointed to govern Ur, Abram had been twenty-one. Shulgi was then a young student in the Academy and a strong admirer of Abram, so much so that to please Abram Shulgi would run errands and do any kind of menial work for him. Abram in turn tutored Shulgi in his studies and allowed the boy to accompany him on some of his surveying trips. Now nearly twenty years had passed, and it was the same Shulgi who, as king, was requesting Abram at the palace.

A royal chariot brought Abram through the city streets and into the palace grounds. Shulgi was waiting for him and rushed down the palace steps to embrace his friend.

"Abram! Abram!" he called happily, his royal attire glittering in the sunlight. "How I have wished for your return. Do come in! You are just the person I have needed to talk to! It is excellent of you to have arrived at this time!"

They mounted the palace steps passing by a series of red and gold uniformed guards that stood stoically at attention. "It is good to see you again, my old friend," Abram said genuinely. "You look much the same!"

"Well," laughed Shulgi whose short, lithe stature made his crown and regal garments look outsized. "I never started out a handsome man like you did. So no change is no improvement."

Shulgi led Abram into an elegantly furnished dining room where numerous servants arranged platters of rich seasoned meats, steaming vegetables, breads and a rose colored Canaanite wine.

As they ate together they spoke only of the past, but when the meal was over Abram said with concern to his friend, "You have heavy responsibilities, Shulgi. I do not envy you."

"Nor do I envy myself, Abram," Shulgi admitted. The king rose and motioned to some chairs at the far end of the long room, out of hearing distance of the servants. "Others more capable than I wanted this governorship. King Sin-Bani only approved me because he thinks he can control me. He kept vetoing everyone else the Council put forward."

"Perhaps you will prove just the right person to rule Ur, Shulgi," Abram said thoughtfully. The two men pulled the chairs closer together and sat down.

"Me? Look what happened when I defied Sin-Bani and sided with the majority of the Council about abolishing the Ishtar cult!" Shulgi exclaimed but kept his voice low. "You know that Sin-Bani was behind that Gutian attack!"

"Yes, I do know," he replied tensely. The hatred Abram held for the Gutians and Sin-Bani rose up within him at the mention of their names.

"Abram," Shulgi began earnestly. "I heard how you helped Mikhail in Damascus. It was your men who drove the sea raiders out of that whole area. If Damascus had fallen, so would the whole string of northern cities, one by one."

Abram noticed Shulgi's left eye twitch. It occurred years ago, Abram remembered, whenever Shulgi was worried about his studies or when he was deeply concerned about something. The king unconsciously covered his eye with his hand as he spoke further, "We are in the same plight. Only it seems more complicated in Ur. Akkad does not have a large army, but Sin-Bani would have little to do to conquer us completely."

Abram smiled understandingly. "Break down the sea walls, you mean?"

Shulgi nodded.

"But Ur would be wasted and of no value to him then."

"It is his constant threat, though," Shulgi said dejectedly. "It is not that the walls could not be rebuilt, just like the dikes that have been destroyed could have been rebuilt. It is more a ruination of the soil that will eventually starve Ur out of existence. The salt content in the river silt is getting heavier. When lands are flooded by the broken dikes, little grows there again. That is the main reason Ur-Nammu did not rebuild, although the people were told otherwise."

"How do you think I could help you?" Abram questioned him.

"My friend, Ur cannot go alone anymore. We need a confederacy of the Sumerian cities. After all, the whole delta area was settled by one people. We speak the same language, have the same concerns. . . ."

Abram interrupted him, "What about the same gods? Look how ridiculously Sumerians are separated by their fabricated gods! A group of Urians say they do not believe in Nannar-Sin, so they settle up the river and rebuild Nippur. Then to show they are superior to Ur, and just as stupid as the Akkadians, they make up the god, Enlil, and claim he is greater than Nannar-Sin because they claim Enlil is Nannar-Sin's father."

Shulgi's face showed sad amusement. "Now Akkad, I hear, Abram, is going to claim another god, a new god Sin-Bali calls An. The king claims An is the father of Enlil. How can we men do such foolish things? Why do the people believe it? Did you know that Ur-Nammu, just before he died, declared Nannar-Sin to be the father of any and all sun gods?"

"You do not really believe any of it, Shulgi?" Abram asked him directly.

"I love this city, Abram. I love Kamarina and the countryside of Ur. If I have a god it is my country. If gods make the people happy they can stay. But I would gladly tear down the temple tomorrow if no one cared."

"And the God of Noah," Abram pressed him. "Do you believe the same about him?"

"If the gods have any power to do good then that power must be from the God of Noah," Shulgi acknowledged. "But I cannot see the filthy practices of Nannar-Sin and Ishtar and the rest being anything but an abomination to Noah's God. Unfortunately, Noah and the Great Flood have been so woven into the stories of the gods that I get confused!"

"There is but one God, Shulgi," Abram professed. "If Ur could be led back to the worship of the one real God, I know we could win over Akkad.

"Shulgi, I have some men with me and many more in Charran. Within a year I could train a small army at my father's village, Terrakki. We could repulse attacks from any enemy, whether Akkad or the Gutians."

"Abram, what you say is just what I wanted to request of you. But I do not worship or know *any* god. And if I did, my position is too weak to change the religious views of the people of Ur."

"King Akalamdu did it!" Abram retorted. "He polluted Ur with his myths! Shulgi, if Ur returned to the worship of the God of Noah. . . ."

"I wish I were strong like you, Abram. I wish I knew the God of Noah about whom you speak. But I am Shulgi. I know how to compromise, to play one favor against another, to win approval by flattery. I want peace and prosperity for Ur . . . that is all."

There was a long silence before Abram stood to leave. "Shulgi, I will be here until spring. I have married Sarai whom both my father and brother adopted."

Shulgi laughed, relieved to have the subject changed. "Everyone in Ur knows you have taken the heart of the renowned Sarai. But I have waited for you to tell me about it. For some time I feared she had been captured by the Gutians after her last disappearance. What a gorgeous, mysterious creature she is!"

"How did you know her?" Abram asked.

"She was brought before the Council by the Gagûm. Many of the young initiates had left the convent after Sarai talked with them. The others were furious with Sarai, as well as being consumed with jealousy, to my mind. When she defended herself before the Council, she was so beautiful and chaste compared to her accusers that the Council decided then and there to cleanse the Gagûm of all its illicit practices. I, too, was persuaded by Sarai and even ordered the Akkadian priestesses back to Akkad."

Shulgi paused and then added sorrowfully, "I have eight daughters, Abram. A message was delivered to me that they would not be harmed during the last attack. But should I oppose Akkad again, my family would be the next target for the Gutians.

"No one blames Sarai for what happened," Shulgi quickly added. "She led us to do something that was good and right . . . but it was terribly costly to those on the Council who voted for it. Look how your own family has suffered."

Abram thought for some time. Then he suggested, "If you wish, I will bring my captains to meet you. Even now I believe we could strengthen your guard against the Gutians. That other attack need never to have happened. If nothing else, Shulgi, I will be glad to help you plan your defenses."

"I will bring it before the Council immediately," Shulgi promised eagerly. "If they agree, we will pay you well for your services. Would you also teach for us at the Academy?"

"I would like that," Abram answered pleasantly as he departed from the palace.

Abram and Sarai spent hours together in retreat and prayer, often going to the house in the reeds for several days. More and more Abram found that he could be alone with the God of Noah, his divine presence like that of a father, or an honored and close friend.

Lot stayed with Abram and Sarai, attending the Academy with Eliezer. He was a quiet, studious boy who could not hide the deep grief he carried because of his father's and sister's murders. Abram and Sarai found him very respectful and obedient and loved him as they would a son.

Abram's men were pleased with their work and enjoyed the assignment in Ur. Together with Abram they organized the Urian guard as had been done in Damascus to make it effective in offense as well as defense. Three bands of Gutians and one of Martu were sighted by scouts. By infiltrating the enemy tribes, ambushes were set up in time before each planned attack against Ur. The Gutians suffered losses and began to feel that the king of Akkad had deceived them. In turn, they lashed out their fury against him.

Abram and Sarai both taught at the Academy. Sarai instructed young women, some who came from the cities on the rivers and some from as far away as Kemi, in basic mathematics as well as in practical fields of textile design and garment making. Her native Noachian language was a perfect base for learning to speak other dialects and foreign languages fluently.

Shulgi was elated with Abram's help and urged him to remain in Ur in almost any capacity, as head of the Urian guards, Master Professor of the Academy, or even Chancellor— a position Shulgi had never filled since his appointment as king.[11]

The Akkadian members on Shulgi's Council, however, were not so enthusiastic. They sensed with Abram's coming a

117

weakening hold of Akkad over Ur and feared for their own loss of influence.

Abram knew he must continue to pray, for he had no direction yet from God. These were extremely happy months for him and for Sarai as well. "Perhaps," he thought, "I am even now fulfilling Hosani's prophecy. I am certainly a blessed man!"

After writing late one night, Abram laid down his reed pen and put his papyrus in a ceramic holder. Most of his writing he kept on clay sheets as was the general custom. However, for his journal and surveying work Abram preferred the more costly papyrus.

He walked over to the bed and gazed at the lovely sleeping form of Sarai. Seeing how beautiful she looked he wished that he had not written quite so long.

It was a quiet night. Abram strolled out to the balcony of the inner courtyard and climbed the steps to the flat roof of the villa. It was late winter, and the air was brisk. He pulled his warm cloak around him and stood in contentment letting his eyes scan the innumerable stars.

Suddenly, without any unusual emotion or premonition, Abram heard the God of Noah speak to him. Abram heard himself say the words, but he knew God had inspired them. They were words of command and prophecy, "Depart from your land, from your country, and from your father's house and go into the land I will show you!"

Abram was stunned, frightened not only by the command but by the urgency of it. "You spoke to me? God, the Almighty God of Noah? You spoke to me?" he exclaimed loudly. Abram fell to his knees. Joy flowed through him and poured over him like gentle warm oil. "Oh, my God! Yes! You spoke to me!" he shouted, laughter and tears mixing in his words. "You have *answered!*"

Sarai had awakened and ascended the stairway. "Has something happened, my husband?" she asked quietly, as she approached him.

"Sarai!" Abram called. "God spoke to me! Did you hear?"

"I woke when I heard you, Abram," she replied with deep love in her voice. "When you laugh like that I know God is very present with you."

He went to her and threw his arms about her, holding her close and swinging her around and around on the rooftop. "Oh, my darling," he said, kissing her fervently. "He spoke to me!"

"Abram!" she exclaimed in the darkness, the only light a small lantern on the stairway. "Your face! Your face . . . glows as if the sun were shining upon it! . . . What did the Lord say? What did he say?"

" 'Depart,' the word began, 'Depart from your land, from your country, and from your father's house and go into the land I will show you.' Sarai, I had not been but a moment in prayer! All these months I have sought him, now suddenly he comes and. . . ."

With tears and deep tremors of feeling Abram dropped to his knees and as he reached his arms up toward the heavens he experienced again the ecstasy of the divine presence of God. Sarai stood beside him. Her arms too were lifted and her prayers joined his as if they were both before the holy throne of God.

Later, as Abram rose, he suddenly realized how keenly alert his senses were. The stars shone in bright cold clear lights, and everything in the darkness was distinguishable. His nose detected faint odors and perfumes to which he had never before been sensitive. Distant noises were distinct and easily identifiable. Every nerve of his body felt alive and pulsating with sensitivity.

As Abram went to Sarai he clutched her to himself, wrapping his cloak around her. "When I have been in the presence of God," he declared as he lifted her long soft hair, freeing it so that it was not bound by his cloak, "I know what it means to be alive . . . to be *really* alive!"

Terah's shepherds had returned from the north with the flocks. They had brought the animals back by river on kalaks as was the tradition, stopping to graze them along the way wherever grass still could be found. Terah himself remained

119

and wintered in his village, doing trade in Charran. In early spring, he had his camels and asses packed with precious stores and began the trip toward Ur by the caravan route. His closest servants accompanied him.

In anticipation of Terah's return, Abram began a series of transactions that would convert all of Terah's wealth and Lot's inheritance into gold. Until that night on the rooftop, he had hesitated to trade off Terah's villa and lands, although he had made some plans for Haran's property. Lot was enthusiastic, as he had tired of the Academy and wanted to accompany his grandfather and his uncle and Sarai.

Sarai had found a small group of lepers that worshipped the God of Noah and despised the cults of the country. No one had bothered to criticize them as they met to worship outside the city walls. With Abram's consent she gave the lepers her house in the reeds and the two devoted buffalo, Alpuia and Wagar-beli.

Nahor and Abram met often to discuss their futures. Nahor was greatly concerned about Abram and Sarai going with Terah to the land of the Canaanites. Rumors of the obscene and violent nature of the Canaanite towns abounded.

Nahor and Milcah wanted to move eventually to Nakkur, where old Nahor had willed them his property. But it would take them many years to build up enough wealth to do so. Winter fodder was still cheaper in Ur, and the arid lands around Charran were not easy to cultivate.

Knowing that this might be his last opportunity, Abram went before the Council and the Academy. He pleaded and argued with them concerning the only holy God, the God of Noah. He rebuked the evil worship of idols and pleaded with the people to forsake Nannar-Sin and Ishtar and all other gods. Shulgi allowed him this freedom, but it was at the king's own personal risk.

It was not long before the Akkadians in the city were agitated. They secretly organized and virulently demanded the king to expel Abram, his household, and his men from Ur. Shulgi became nervous and alarmed. He urged Abram to depart soon, fearing for Abram's life as well as his own.

It was only a few days later that a haggard and exhausted servant of Terah's, named Simika, found Abram and crumbled in despair before him, crying out, "Master Abram, I bring ill tidings, ill tidings . . . ill tidings!" Simika's words broke as he trembled.

Abram was aware of his own calmness, although everything in him knew that Simika's message held tragedy. A faith he had not known before surged up to encounter the news. Whatever it was, God was in authority. "Simika, unburden yourself," he encouraged the servant kindly. "You have had to carry an evil word too long. Let me bear it now!"

Simika looked up with great sadness. Years ago Abram had taught him and his whole family to read and to write. He had instructed Simika in mathematics to such an extent that Terah made the humble servant his chief trade accountant. Simika knew more than anyone else the serious impact of his message. "Master Abram," he began with difficulty. "Terah's caravan was attacked above Akkad. Hateful men surrounded us saying they were Gutians, but they all spoke clear Akkadian. And what is more, the Akkadian guards, whom we must pay to watch that area, had abandoned their posts. No one was there to help us."

"What has happened to my father and the rest? Take courage, Simika. Tell me quickly," Abram exhorted him.

"They are being held hostage! The leader of the horde has detailed knowledge of your affairs, Master Abram. He has exact figures of the gold you have received from Terah's properties as well as Haran's and your own accounts. He wants all of it in exchange for the safe return of your father and the other servants."

Simika breathed an aching sigh. "It will financially destroy both you and your father," he added dismally.

Abram nodded his head in agreement. He was piercingly aware of the inevitable effect the loss would create and the change it would make in his present plans. "We will have nothing left but Terrakki and the dry lands near Charran," he said slowly.

His thoughts reverted quickly to his father. "Was Terah treated well?" he asked urgently.

"He fought with the wrath of a lion. Even at his age it took many men to bind him. As they forced me to leave, Terah strained at his tethers and cursed the thieves."

"How quickly can we take the gold to them?"

"In three days," Simika answered. "There is a marked position on the west fork of the river above the city of Larsa. They will have two boats there, one on either side. We are to load the gold in the presence of one of their men. Two of our men will take the gold and their overseer to the middle of the river. Their oarsmen will bring Terah and the others to midstream. The oarsmen will then exchange places."

"A clever scheme," Abram conceded bitterly. "We have no choice, Simika. The Akkadians on the Urian Council must have instigated this."

Abram returned to the villa where Sarai was packing to move to their temporary quarters. He rapidly unfolded the story told to him by Simika. "Does God want us to go no farther than Charran, Sarai? After I pay the ransom we will have no place to go but to my father's winter quarters. Between us, Nahor and I could work the herds and build up a trade again, but it will take years to have enough to move as I had hoped. With Terah's and my wealth plus Lot's inheritance we might have left with hundreds of trained men and many servants."

"God has given you the gift of faith. To make that faith become yours, Abram, he must test the faith that is in you. He has told you what we are to do. We must now wait for the right time to do it. He will give us a sign. He will speak again to you."

As she spoke he was reminded of the Sarai he knew as a girl in the Ararats. Now her lovely dark eyes drew his attention. Once again, he saw in them the hidden wisdom and faith of another age.

"I have you, my treasure," he said confidently. "And God has been good to spare my father. May God also give me the patience to wait . . . and I believe it will be a *long* wait."

122

Abram took six men with him along with Simika. They arrived by camel at the place designated on the river. In a boat waited a nervous elderly man. On the other side of the water a band of thirty or more men held Terah and his eight servants in bonds.

"Did they send you to take custody of this blood money?" Abram brusquely asked the man in the boat.

"Forgive me, sir," the man pleaded, his face tense and trembling. "I am a gold merchant in Akkad. These men came to my home early this morning and forced me to accompany them. Please have mercy on me! I am only to count the gold and see if it is authentic. They have threatened to drown me if I make a mistake."

Abram ordered Simika to bring the gold to the boat and the transaction was made. In less than an hour it was over. Abram and Terah mounted their camels and rode in front of the others back to Ur. Terah's face remained defiant, but his eyes stared blankly ahead. He had said little until they were out of sight of the river tryst.

"If it had been only me, my son," he said, his words labored and dry, "I would have taken death rather than cause you this suffering. You and I, we have almost nothing left . . . and Lot has lost his inheritance."

"You wanted to leave Ur, Father. We have enough funds to get as far as Charran. We will wait on the Lord there. Perhaps that is where we should be."

The two fell into deep thought and silence until they reached the Urian canals.

While they remained in Kamarina, Terah was more grieved than he or Abram had anticipated. All of the wealth and position Terah had known were gone. Haran, whom he would have leaned on during such a time, was dead. The hideous murders rose up to haunt him at every turn. He became reclusive and despondent.

The hard overland trip in the heat of summer to Charran did not improve Terah's condition. His proud spirit was broken, and he seldom would speak. The caravan included Terah, Abram, Sarai and Lot. They were accompanied by

123

some of Terah's and Abram's personal servants and about half of the men Abram had originally brought with him. The other servants had been released and the remaining soldiers of Abram took positions with Shulgi's forces, for which the king was grateful. Eliezer stayed in Kamarina. Abram made arrangements for him to live with Nahor and attend the Academy.

Chapter VI
WAIT IN TERRAKKI

Terah's village was called Terrakki in the northern dialect or language. It was located south of Charran on the Balikh River, a tributary of the Euphrates, which during half of the year was filled to overflowing from the runoff of the rains and snows. The rest of the year the river was only a small stream and sometimes almost dry. Terrakki, like Nakkur, was one of many communities that were summer camping grounds for wealthy herders. The villages were usually uninhabited in winter except for a few watchmen and servants.

Fortunately Terah had been spending more winters in Terrakki and had built a few winterized dwellings. The thick stone and clay brick walls of the structures held in the precious heat against the cold and penetrating winds of the often barren steppe land.

This area around Charran had once been covered with beautiful forests of oak, beech and conifers. However, the demand for wood promoted unwise stripping of the land, allowing the winds and water to inflict constant damage. For those who dwelled there, finding fuel for cooking and heating was a constant concern. All animal dung was carefully saved, and nothing that would burn was ever discarded.

When the exhausted caravan arrived in Terrakki, there was little water in the river bed and the wells were low. Food supplies were so sparse that Abram was forced to release all but four of the servants, allowing the others to seek work in Charran.

Abram knew the lands of his father well. He had once surveyed every section. With determination he began to lay out plans for Terrakki's development, designs to plant windbreak rows of trees, sink storage wells, and convert the dry but fertile land into pasture and productive fields.

But the ground was stubborn. Until the first rains came to loosen it, nothing could be started. When the early winter rains did come they brought cold winds that swept over the flatland. The little fuel supply was used for cooking and none could be spared for heating the cold damp buildings. The hard field work and then sickness took its toll. Two of the servants died during the winter, leaving two others and Abram and Lot to clear the rocks and till a small part of the land. Sarai worked with them until she fell ill and for months could do little more than the cooking. By the time Nahor arrived with the flocks and herds that spring, the first early grain had been harvested. It was a pitifully small yield.

"Abram, you have worked hard," Nahor sympathized, for he saw by looking at the worn and tired faces of Abram, Lot and Sarai what a strain and agonizing effort it had taken. "But the best of written plans make poor plows. I doubt if we should leave more than five flocks and some goats next fall. Most of those you will need for meat to survive."

"My plans were adequate," Abram replied thoughtfully. "But we just didn't have the men or supplies to carry through! Sarai and I have done much praying. If God is humbling us in this way, he must have something yet for us to do here before we search for the promised land."

"Which is . . . ?"

"I plan to leave Lot and Terah here during part of the year. There will be enough provisions and housing for them and the servants. Sarai and I will go to one of the river cities. I should be able to teach or do surveying there, and Sarai has many useful skills."

"She is not with child yet? Is she barren?" Nahor asked bluntly.

"A midwife examined her and said it will be difficult for her to conceive but not impossible. The Lord has promised Sarai a child to carry on the beliefs and faith of Noah . . . a child to whom Sarai could teach all the things she learned when she was a girl."

As the two brothers talked by the one small field that had been cultivated, they could hear the voices of Sarai and Milcah and smell the sweet aromas of their meal being prepared. Abram looked appreciatively at Nahor and thought how fortunate he was to have a brother with whom to share.

"It looks like you *both* are being asked to wait for the God of Noah's promises," Nahor remarked kindly.

"God promised me a land, but I do not believe this is the land. We will just have to wait as you say. We have faith in the promises. If that faith is to be tested for a long time, we will have only one kind of righteousness to offer. *We waited!*"

"I think God knew what he was doing when he chose you, Abram," Nahor laughed. "He knows how you like to lay out extensive plans and think through complicated problems. You like a challenge, my brother! And you have one!"

"You are good medicine, Nahor. It has been a very hard winter, but it *is* a challenge! I may even learn to enjoy it. By the way, is Milcah pregnant yet?"

"Yes!" Nahor replied happily. "Our first child should be born shortly after we return to Ur. Milcah is a good wife for me, Abram."

"Does she know about Reumah?" Abram asked in a lowered voice.

Nahor blushed and smiled, "Those four boys I fathered by Reumah were to bless our grandfather, old Nahor. He was ancient, but he still felt he should *'multiply'*, as he put it. 'Multiply, the God of Noah commanded!' he used to shout at me. So I helped him 'multiply.' I do not feel that Milcah needs to know that little bit of family arithmetic!"

"Do you see the boys?"

"They are all grown. When old Nahor died they went to different cities."

"And Reumah?"

"She works as a servant in Charran. I have not wanted to see her now that I am married to Milcah. But I do send her provisions," he responded. Then sniffing the fragrant cooking he exclaimed, "I am hungry! I am glad it was not *dinner* that the God of Noah promised you. I don't think I can wait any longer!" With that Nahor went quickly to finish his chores with the herdsmen.

Nahor and his shepherds grazed the flocks for several weeks near Terrakki and Nakkur. After that they led the sheep and goats up into the mountain pastures for the summer, leaving the women and children in the two villages of Nakkur and Terrakki.

So began a pattern of life that was to continue for the next thirty-five years. Eventually Abram organized the village of Terrakki so that permanent homes were added. With persistant hard labor Abram and Lot cleared more and more farmland and pastures. Orchards and windbreak trees were planted and sluices were built to capture the draining waters of the winter rains into deep cisterns. Gradually more servants and shepherds, most of them indentured, were added. The village grew as these men, women and families settled to work the land and care for the growing flocks. Abram and Lot began to buy oxen, camels and asses in larger and larger numbers until Abram was able to keep many of his men employed part of the year in a caravaning trade between Charran and Ur.

During the off seasons, Abram would take Sarai and stay in one of the thriving cities on the rivers. They seldom had difficulty winning the attention of the leaders of each community. The ease with which they both could speak the different languages and dialects brought trust and friendship readily. Fortunately, the laws concerning adultery and the abuse of another man's wife were strict with a quick and swift death penalty. This allowed Sarai even more freedom than she had before her marriage.

It was Abram's strategy that he and Sarai would teach and work among the people. Then when he felt they had respect and confidence, they would speak out boldly about the one holy God. Many listened and believed, although strong reactions and controversies usually arose. Often violent threats were issued by those whose wealth and station in life were enmeshed in idolatry or by those who had grown dependent on false worship. But there was no city where Abram and Sarai went that the pagan strongholds were not weakened. For the God of Noah was lifted up and the hearts of the people who heard felt his presence and his reality.

Lot matured, but remained unmarried. He cared for Terah and oversaw the village while Abram was absent. Nahor continued to migrate the herds and flocks from Ur.

During those passing thirty-five years, Terah's bitterness and grief finally faded, but the chilling winters had weakened his old body and his mind. He yearned to be strong again and to set out with Abram as they had planned. In his last years Terah could talk of only one thing, leaving the land of the rivers and finding a new land.

Sarai longed to leave as well. The promise of a child had not been fulfilled, and she sometimes grew deeply depressed. Milcah had borne eight children who were grown and having children of their own. Although Sarai rejoiced when in each city where they had stayed many people turned away from false gods, she still hungered for God's special promise to her.

Terah died while Abram and Sarai were in the city-state of Mari. They received a message from Lot and returned to Terrakki. A large stone pillar had been raised over Terah's tomb in a field outside the village. As Abram, Sarai and Lot stood before it Abram said soberly, "It will be a grave marker for all of us."

"Do you plan to die here, my husband?" Sarai asked, her hauntingly beautiful eyes responding wide with anxiety.

"Now that my father is dead, the land belongs to Lot and me," he replied flatly.

"But the God of Noah has not given us a child here!" Sarai cried out. "I am barren! Abram, I am barren because we have not gone where God has told us to go!"

"No, Sarai," he rebuked her gently. "We have not gone because the God of Noah has not given a sign. I thought

Terah's death might be the sign, but we don't have enough gold set aside to be able to dwell by ourselves in a strange land."

"But God will supply what we need, Abram," Sarai pleaded. "If Lot goes with us we could trade Terrakki to Nahor. He could send us some payment each year."

"It would not be enough, Sarai. If anything went wrong, within less than five years, we would be as poor as we were when we left Ur."

"God *promised* me I would bear a child," she beseeched him, tears flooding down her cheeks.

Abram looked compassionately at his wife. True to Terah's prediction, she was even more lovely than when he saw her years before in Ur. No lines traced her face and her skin was fresh and clear. Her slim body as it matured had only become more alluring. Though her walk was more full of grace and dignity, her heart and mind had not changed from the precious girl Abram first met with Satuke at Lake Aratta. He put his arm around her and led her back to their private rooms.

After they had dined there on hot broth and warm bread, Sarai broached a subject that was difficult for her. For many months Abram had been bothered by an infection, common at that time, of the foreskin. It caused a slight irritation when water was passed but sharp pains with any sexual stimulation. In itself the disease was little more than a rash, but its effects left its bearer impotent as long as the infection remained.

"Is not your disease but another sign that we should cut ourselves away from our covering and security here and let God protect us?" Sarai asked hesitantly.

"Are you trying to say that I need to circumcise myself?" he asked in astonishment.

"It is a method often used to stop the infection," she answered, her emotions causing her words to stumble. "To cut away . . . your foreskin would be a sign. It would leave you . . . exposed to God's care and protection."

"You do not know what a painful thing it is you are suggesting. Infections of the foreskin such as I have come and go. With proper care. . . ."

130

"It has been almost a year . . . since you have come to me!"
Sarai lamented tearfully.

Her words quickly moved him, and desire for her rushed
through his body. As he reached to embrace her, he felt a
tightness and a familiar pain. It grew in sharpness causing him
to draw back from her until the passion he had felt subsided.
He winced saying, "I wish I could be a man for you. When
this infection leaves, we may still have a child here."

Sarai fell into his arms and wept.

"Is something else wrong, Sarai?"

She lifted her face and explained heartbrokenly, "I fear
that soon I will not have the way of women. God may close
my womb forever!"

"No, my darling," Abram tried to comfort her. "No, Sarai,
he promised us. He promised . . . to give us a land . . . and a
child."

Releasing her, Abram bent over dejectedly, his head
covered by his hands. "God!" he cried out. "What are you
doing to us! Why do you remain silent and test us year after
year after year! Answer us, Lord! What is your will?"

Unlike Sarai, Abram's appearance had aged during the
harsh years since they had come to Terrakki. His hair had
become streaked with gray, and his face was weathered and
lined. Yet the hard labors he endured had strengthened his
body, and he was a stronger man physically than in his youth.

Abram rose and began pacing the floor. With arms uplifted,
he clenched his fists in his agony. "Speak again, Lord! Speak
to us!" he shouted, his voice ringing out in the small room.

Sarai sat bowed motionless on a bench before the fire. The
air was heavy with silence. Even the bright flames of the
charcoals caused no noise.

Suddenly a light fragrant mist filled the room. Abram and
Sarai felt as if an aura of enchanting brightness of light were
about them.

All the quick thoughts of Abram's mind bowed to the
majesty that confronted him. He knew that he stood before
the radiancy of the throne of God—a moment of time in
eternity that seemed almost endless because of its intensity,
its infinite intensity.

131

And then the voice of God spoke. This time the words vibrated through Abram's being and Abram's spirit listened as the Spirit of God communed with him:

"Go from your country and your kindred and your father's house to the land that I will show you. And I will make you a great nation, and I will bless you, and make your name great, so that you will be a blessing. I will bless those who bless you, and him who curses you I will curse; and by you all the families of the earth shall be blessed."

When the poignant immediacy of the experience was gone, Abran realized that he was back in the quiet darkening room with Sarai. But the refreshing after-effects came as they had on the rooftop in Ur, the heightening awareness of his senses and a clean freshness of his mind.

An hour went by before he could speak. Only a few warm coals remained to glow in the brazier. Sarai began singing, softly at first and then rising in strength, the melody floating in the air like the smoke of incense. Abram started to join her but was soon overcome by joy. He lay flat on the wool rugs and poured out his abundant thankfulness and love mixed with gales of delighted laughter, sharing intermittently with Sarai the wondrous encounter and the words God had spoken.

Lot had been concerned by Abram and Sarai's long absence and went to their quarters to join them. When Terah had died, the burden of responsibility and grief had been difficult for Lot. Depression had almost consumed him until Abram and Sarai returned. Now as he entered the room and witnessed their rejoicing the sorrow of his heart broke loose. Lot knelt by the door and wept.

"The time has come, Lot," Abram called and beckoned to his nephew to join them. "The Lord has just spoken, and we must leave Terrakki and look for the land God has promised! I had hoped to have more gold set aside, but at least we have enough people and flocks. God's mercy will have to provide for the rest."

"You *will* let me go with you, Abram," Lot pleaded. "I want to leave this place, and I want to stay with you and Sarai always. I am nearly fifty years old. You are my only family."

"Of course, you will come with us," Abram reassured him. "By the time we get in the provisions and have things here at Terrakki in order we will leave."

"And Nahor?"

"His large herds and flocks are cramped in Ur. If we take only the men and servants we need, the animals and what gold we have, we can lease him the land of Terrakki and the houses. It will assure us a yearly stipend, and Nahor could at last settle down in this area."

Abram and Sarai immediately began the careful planning needed for their journey. They sensed that God was leading them to go toward the land settled by the Canaanites. Special supplies were secured in Charran nearby, where every need of the caravanner could be found.

Abram called together the younger men of his servants. Nearly four hundred gathered in the large courtyard of the village. As was required in the village of Terrakki, each man had been taught the way of the God of Noah.

Abram began by embracing and praying over the men one by one. As he did so he asked for their dedication and loyalty. "The God of Noah has called me to leave this place for a land that he has promised. Until we find the land and it is ours we will dwell in tents, being a city to ourselves and under God. You will be like stones in the foundation of that city which the God of Noah alone will build. He has promised to bless me and curse my enemies. It is yet a mystery, but by what we will do, all the families of the earth, now and in the future, will be blessed."

He paused and laughter broke his composure as the joy returned that he had felt when God first spoke those words. He burst into shouts of praises to the Lord. His exuberance was infectiously caught by the young men in the assembly, and God in the heavens received a prolonged offering of praise and thanksgiving.

These men, the young families of those who were married, and about sixty maidservants would be leaving Terrakki with Abram, Sarai and Lot. The older servants and other maidservants would remain behind for Nahor's employ when he arrived.

Chapter VII
ATTACK AT CARCHEMISH

On the day of departure the village bells of Terrakki were rung three hours before sunrise. Adventurous excitement prevailed as the men, women and children aroused and busied themselves with carefully rehearsed duties.

Abram supervised the skilled watchmen. He sent out a patrol of fifty on young riding camels. They scouted the designated path and side areas. Those in the lead blew blasts on their shofars. The noise from the ram horn bugles was to frighten off predatory animals and any bands of wandering thieves. Other watchmen came behind the first and set aflame fire pots, clay jars of bitumen and dung, to mark out the cleared trail. Smaller pots alerted shepherds of dangerous ruts and thorn patches. Two foot patrols were readied to guard the flanks and rear of the procession.

The shepherds and the care of the sheep, goats and oxen were Lot's responsibility. Aided by the light of the moon in its final quarter, herders led more than two hundred oxen from the corrals of Terrakki. Then followed flock after flock of sheep and goats until five thousand of them were released. Each flock or herd had its own shepherd who carefully prodded his animals into the dark expanse between the fire pots. It was essential that the flocks have the early morning hours for eating while the heavy drops of dew clung to the lush spring grasses. It would be their food and water for the day. Eliezer was in charge of the packing. After marrying, he had settled down in Terrakki and Abram had made him his chief steward. For many years Eliezer had been the overseer of the household servants, goods and finances. He was an able and clever man and had a good wife and four strong sons who helped him.

The pack camels carried the heaviest loads. There were about one hundred of these camels, including several newborn that were tied by range ropes to their mothers. The gangling beasts knelt while being loaded, resting on the thick callused pads formed on their chests and knees. Their drooping eyes watched mournfully, and they groaned and wailed. It was their temperament to complain loudly whether their packs were light or heavy. The camels' grumbling continued until the loading was completed. With a pretense of strain and great effort they struggled to stand on their long legs. After more final protests, they loped one after another almost carefree of their burdens. As they passed by, most of the camels affectionately nuzzled their drivers.

The women and children packed the asses with personal belongings. Each man in the company had one or more asses according to the size of his family. A few of the beasts were reserved for those who were ill and for the smallest children to ride.

Except for the infants, everyone had to wait until the first rest stop to eat. That would be the time when the dew was gone, and the sheep and other animals needed to lie and ruminate on what they had devoured. Sarai walked with the other women and children. She led them in songs to ease away any fears of the darkness and assuage the hunger of the youngest.

Abram had allowed six days to reach the bridge over the Euphrates at Carchemish. By then everyone's walking muscles would be toughened and a faster pace could be set.

About ten in the morning a heavy breakfast was prepared of buttered porridge, hot milk, balls of leben cheese, dates, and delicious warm fresh bread. After eating, the children who had complained of exhaustion romped like the young lambs.

The foreguards pastured their camels with the other burden-bearing animals. Packs were removed so that the camels and asses could move freely to feed. The other guards circled the entourage and ate in small groups, keeping constant watch. Herders were joined by their wives and children for the rest time as they kept their vigil over the flocks and herds.

As the sun continued to rise, the men and boys discarded and packed away their heavy wrap-around tunics and donned short sheepskin kilts. The women and girls changed into comfortable loose-fitting sheaths of light wool. As the movement began again it followed the lone ensign of Terah's rainbow, carried by one of the front guards.

The hunger of all was sated and for the rest of the day a steady gait was kept. When there were still a few hours of sunlight left, the foreguards led the company to a place of spring waters for encampment. There the animals were watered and corralled.

Eliezer directed the menservants and the women to set up the tents. The large dark goat hair tents were ones Abram had purchased in Charran. Groups of women worked together, spreading the tent material smoothly on the ground and straightening the ropes. The menservants drove the tent pegs into the ground with large mallets. Then the men and women crawled under the tenting and lifted each tent up on nine poles. The poles were arranged in three rows with the middle poles about five cubits in height and the outside rows four cubits. Wooden rings sewed to the top of the tent were tied to tent pins on the poles. The outside ropes were tightened to the ground pegs. Lastly, straw mats were spread and lambswool mattresses stretched out in the sleeping areas.

Fires were started in the many braziers needed for the large number of people. Bags of dung had been collected during the day by the maidservants and children. Each had been given certain stations behind the herds and flocks so that none of the valuable droppings would be missed.

Eliezer called for lambs to be slaughtered. The bleating woolly animals were stunned and then bled by severing one of the large veins. Each body was then submerged in a cauldron of hot water for several minutes to loosen the wool. The wet hair was brushed from the skin, and the carcass suspended from a rail crossed between forked poles. A flaming brazier set underneath the carcass singed off the remaining fuzz. The menservants performing the butchering deftly removed the skin, opening it by a straight cut down the center of the belly. The viscera were removed, each part to be carefully utilized, and the body split down the backbone.

Pieces of lamb along with rich garlic-seasoned sausage were grilled over the dung coals. Pots of thick lentil soup simmered over other fires. Young girls patted wheat flour and water into pale dough disks. They baked the disks into the familiar flat bread on clay baking sheets laid on the hot coals.

The evening meal was a pleasant repast. It was a time of hearty fellowship and exchange of experiences that had happened during the day's trek. It was also a time of calm beauty as the setting sun bathed in golden hues the land they would traverse on the morrow. Prayers of thanksgiving and songs of worship ended the day. Herders slept with their flocks. Alternating guards watched over the camp. Others slept in the tents or the open fields.

Carchemish was on a time-worn trade route from Charran to Damascus. Its wide limestone bridge, supported by a series of thick arches, spanned the Euphrates River. The massive quarried stone pillars of the arches had been laid over a century before on a series of stone piles. During the dry season fording the river was not difficult; however, this was the high time for the river. All overland travelers sought out the city's sturdy crossover. The center sections of the bridge were not stone but made of portable wooden planks that could be lifted, cutting off traffic at night and during times of enemy threats.

It would take a full day to make the bridge crossing and trade for supplies. Abram was aware that the large size of his company might alarm the city. While his people were still out of sight of the bridge, he gathered a small regiment of men. Taking the fastest riding camels they went ahead to make negotiations with the civic officials and to bargain on the toll fees for crossing the bridge.

Shortly after leaving they came across a frightened young man who crouched, terrified, before them. "Please do not kill me," he pleaded. "I have nothing. You've already murdered most of my people and stolen everything!"

Abram spoke kindly, "Peace, my son. We are men of peace and travelers with families. Do not fear us!"

The boy looked distrustingly at each of Abram's men, then his tense face relaxed with relief. "The Amorites! They attacked us as we began to cross the bridge," he related haltingly. "The Carchemish bridge guards were afraid and drew up the wooden crossboards. We were caught there and they . . . they took. . . ." He broke into bitter weeping.

Abram studied the boy for a moment. "This could be a trap set for us, should he be lying," he cautioned his men. "I will go on ahead and see if it's as he had said. The rest of you return and prepare the people for a possible attack. Lot should arm the herders and the menservants. Tell Eliezer to encamp. We will be able to leave only part of the rear watchmen with the animals and supplies."

Pointing out one of his men, Abram commanded the boy, "Mount with Haniku!"

Abram sharply prodded his camel as did the other men their mounts, and their camels took off in fast strides.

When Abram first saw the distant bridge and the skyline of Carchemish, he knew that the boy had not lied. Corpses and wounded men lay strewn about the broad river's edge, and women, some stripped naked, were huddled and tied together. Loot was spread in disarray and clutter.

The Amorites were bands of drifters, outlaws, wayward adolescents, and men who were just restless or sought adventure. The first Amorite bands originated out of Mari and were soon outlawed by their own countrymen. They began roaming the area, spreading south and east—where they were called Martu—and north and west—where they were called Amurru. They wandered, supporting themselves by raids and thievery. As their numbers grew and the men took wives, they broke into tribes. The tribes were loosely confederated, respecting one another's territories. It was a hard and difficult life for the initiate, and only the strong, daring or foolhardy persevered. For this reason most Amorites were tall and husky, even fabled as giants.

The more audacious tribes were those original ones who began to settle in nomadic villages between Mari and Charran. Some of these had visions of overtaking Mari and all the cities from Ur to Kemi to form an Amorite empire. The weaker Amorites and those who tired of the fierce life often found refuge in the old towns of Canaan.

Abram saw that there was little time to waste. He raced his camel to rejoin his men. After arriving in camp, he called out orders. All camels and asses were to be mounted. Those that rode were to cover themselves with dark cloaks and carry shofars and spears. They were to saddle on bed padding in order to appear taller. "We must use their ways to frighten them. We too will appear as giants!" he quickly explained. "We will spread out in a single front line. When I give the signal, blow the horns and race your animals. We must count on enough dust and noise to startle them. When you see the ensign raised, all of you but the watchmen slow your mounts. But do not turn as if you were retreating. Wait until the dust from the watchmen's camels gives you cover. Then return quickly! The God of Noah be praised and be the victor!"

The guards of Carchemish stood on the far projecting bridge section. Their bows were drawn as they watched the Amorites pack the spoils of their attack on camels and pack asses. One old woman had been stabbed and several big Amorites held knives at the throats of other women, threatening to kill them if any more arrows were shot from the bridge.

Suddenly they heard the blare of shofars. The penetrating blasts seemed to come from all directions. Out of a cloud of dust in the east rode a battle line of tall dark mounted

140

warriors. In their alarmed reaction, the Amorites sought for weapons and fighting positions. By the time Abram's standard bearer raised the ensign the bridge guards had seized the opportunity to release their arrows and the Amorites found themselves trapped and being wounded and killed. They sought the water for safety and in panic swam downstream, easy prey for the reinforcements from Carchemish on one side and Abram and his watchmen on the other. Many of the Amorites willingly surrendered. Others suffered the consequences.

When Abram and his men returned to the group that had been attacked, the bridge beams had been relaid and the Carchemish guards were caring for the wounded and helping the women with their possessions.

One of the men who had been attacked by the Amorites called out to Abram. Abram dismounted his camel and went to him. The man had been speared several times and blood stained his tunic and had seeped into the ground around him. "He is a strong man to still be alive," Abram thought grimly as he knelt beside the dying body and gently lifted the man's head.

"I am Arnawar, son of Ennasaku," he said weakly. "We are Hurrians from east of the upper Tigris. We were going to the mountains of Seir. Other Hurrians, the Perrizites, have settled there. These wild Amorites ... they. ..." With a final effort to raise himself, Arnawar collapsed, giving way to deep coughs. Abram's arms held him until, after a few moments, he died.

Behind him Abram heard a woman's voice. "Those monsters demanded that we pay the extortion money owed them by the Hurrians of Seir!" Abram looked around to see three almost identical-looking women. Dark green cloaks were pulled around them to cover their torn clothes and nakedness. Each smooth oval face had the same small tilted nose and dark gazelle-like eyes. Their shining black hair was slightly disheveled but still intricately coiled and curled.

"Is he dead?" asked the oldest one, her mature voice rich and resonant.

141

"Yes," replied Abram softly. "Was Arnawar your husband, good lady?"

"I am Salanna," she said with determined dignity. "These are my daughters, Minusa and Pukuli. Yes, that wonderful but unwise man was my husband." Salanna's words were loving but bitter. Tears filled her eyes. They rested in pools on her long lashes as if she willed them not to fall. "We left our lovely home in Nuzu . . . and all our family and friends. He wanted his own village in the Seir mountains," she explained.

"My name is Abram of Terrakki. We, too, are looking for a new land. If you wish to continue your journey with us, you are most welcome."

"You are kind," Salanna replied stoically. "We would be honored. Our watchmen were almost all killed or badly wounded. But we have many flocks corralled just north of here."

Salanna allowed herself to look away from Abram and into the ashen face of the man he was still holding. She hesitated and her composure gave way enough for her to kneel beside his body and gently kiss his still warm face. Her gesture released her daughters, and they fell down beside her, sorrowfully weeping. "Come back, Father! Please come back!" cried Pukuli.

"He has left us, Mother," wept Minusa. "Oh, Mother, we are alone." Minusa turned for comfort to her mother who embraced both girls.

"Hush, my daughters!" Salanna numbly gave solace, those held-back tears now wetting her round cheeks. "We have herdsmen and servants. And we will travel with this good man. We will fulfill your father's dream and go to Seir . . . somehow."

Lot had been making arrangements with the Carchemish guard captain for the care of the wounded and the burial of the dead. He approached the place where Abram was with the woman and her daughters in their mourning. Lot watched Salanna's quiet restraint and her noble bearing with admiration and compassion. His heart felt suddenly drawn to

142

the woman. She had such obvious strength but also such great need.

Abram called to Lot. "This is my nephew, Lot," he began, and made quick introductions. "Salanna desires to travel with us. I will see that her husband's body is prepared for burial. Would you take her and some watchmen and go to her flocks. Her herders must know they will be under your authority or they may take leadership themselves and make it difficult for us."

"Should I give them opportunity to return to Nuzu if they prefer?" Lot questioned, his mind quickly sensing Abram's logic. Lot's eyes, however, were on Salanna and his heart was warmed at the prospect of looking after her.

"Very good idea," Abram confirmed. "Some of the Amorites escaped. They may seek revenge and retaliate. The sooner our two groups merge the better. If possible we should be here at the bridge before dawn tomorrow for crossing."

Lot nodded in agreement and then addressed Salanna. "I am sorry to hurry you at this time, but we should leave immediately." He offered her his hand which she accepted without looking up or seeing him.

As she rose, she quietly commanded her daughters, "Go. I want you to stay with the other women."

And then to Abram she asked, "When will I be able to bury my husband?" Salanna's attention followed the Carchemish guards who had come and were taking Arnawar's body away on a litter.

"Tomorrow, Salanna," Abram assured her. "We will bury him after the crossing. Go, now. Tend to your men. Afterward, Lot will take you to our tents. Sarai, my wife, will see that you have accommodations."

Salanna mounted Lot's camel with him, and five other watchmen joined their party. They rode off to the north.

Only three of the twenty men of Arnawar's group survived. Their wounds were severe, and they would have to remain in Carchemish. Minusa and Pukuli, along with their maid-servants, began walking beside loaded asses and camels eastward to Abram's encampment. Abram's other watchmen mounted their camels and rode before and behind them. As

Abram was about to leave, a Carchemish guard reported that two of the captured Amorites were now imprisoned in the city and begged to speak with him. He willingly accepted since he was eager to get any information they might be offering.

It was mid-afternoon and the warm springtime sun shone on the bloody massacre that had just taken place. Travelers, who had espied the brief battle from a distance and had retreated, were cautiously approaching the reopened bridge. They came in tight little clumps with their bows and spears in readiness.

The amiable guard escorted Abram across the broad expanse of the bridge and through the strong towered gates. The gate towers joined together a set of two thick walls that surrounded the fascinating city.

Carchemish had been slowly edging ahead of Charran in size and prosperity. Wood was plentiful in contrast with Charran's dwindling resources of the commodity. Evidences of the lumber trade were everywhere present as Abram threaded his way with the guard through the busy, narrow commercial streets. Noisy taps and pounds of carpenters and woodcraftsmen filled the air. Abram enjoyed the astringent tangy smell of pine and cedar and the hauntingly mellow fragrance of sawed oak.

Ink makers were rendering the galls of the oak twigs into tannin. This they mixed with iron salt to produce the distinguished blue-black ink of Carchemish. Beside the ink shops were the red dye makers. The brilliant Kermes red dye was famous everywhere and especially prized. It was obtained by crushing out the body fluids of a certain insect that harbored in the bark of the nearby Kermes oak trees.

Abram paused with his escort long enough to purchase a packet of the dye and some ink sticks. The ink sticks were wooden writing points that were heavily saturated with ink and needed only to be moistened in order to write. Also, he bought Sarai a cedar box covered with detailed designs of inlaid woods and shell pearl.

A short distance from the shops was the civic building where the Amorite captives were being held. Abram was taken to the prison room of the two who had pleaded to see him. He found them tied to stakes after having received severe floggings. Their sentence had come quickly. They were to be executed the next morning.

As Abram came near them, their beaten bodies straightened and their dull half-closed eyes lightened with hope. "Abram, Abram of Terrakki," called out the older of the two in a husky voice. "Please help us!"

Abram stood a few feet from them. Through high windows, beams of light from the afternoon sun cut broad shafts in the darkness of the room. Dust and the distinctive smells of dried blood, sweat and urine caused Abram to consciously control himself against retching.

"And why should I help you?" Abram replied dryly. "You showed no mercy to the people at the bridge."

"We are believers in the God of Noah!" cried out the other. "We heard you and Sarai, your wife, when you spoke before the crowds in Mari. We were against those who wanted you to leave!"

"If you believe in the God of Noah, why are you part of the Amorites and the Martu?"

"My name is Eshcol. This is my younger brother, Aner. Over four years ago we left Mari with Mamre, another brother and the oldest. We went as a scouting party with a few other friends to search out a land where we could freely settle.

"At that time," Eshcol continued, "many others we knew were leaving from Mari as well as all the other river cities. We formed a large band and went in the direction of Canaan. We were rather wild and wandered around together several years. Then we three brothers found an open place we felt we could manage, while some others settled and became part of the Canaanite towns along the caravan routes or near the river and lakes. But the rest were dissatisfied and returned."

"Just long enough to gather up all the ruffians they could find!" interjected Aner. "They decided 'why settle the land when we can control it?'"

"What do you mean?" Abram asked sharply.

Eshcol answered, "When they came back they attacked and plundered nearly every town south of the Sea of Chinne-

145

reth . . . except those who agreed to pay them tribute. Chedorlaomer, that wild Martu from the east that has been sacking the Akkadians for years, took over the leadership of all the loose bands of the Amorites. Since then, the people of the towns, and even people like us who live in the open, pay tribute money to the Amorite confederation."

"The other leaders, who are they?"

The pain from the lashes he had received had intensified under the strain of talking Eshcol motioned to Aner to reply.

"Tidal is the shakana, or chief, of the Amurru, the Amorites who come from the valley between the mountains west of Damascus and far to the north of Carchemish. Amraphel leads the tribe that controls everything from Mari south to Ur. He was one of our band when we first went to Canaan. It was he who leagued up with Chedorlaomer in the first raids."

"And who controls this territory?" Abram persisted. "Who was responsible for the raid this morning?"

"Arioch," Aner replied quickly. "He is the weakest shakana of the tribes and lives in fear of Chedorlaomer and the other two. Many Hurrians, like those attacked today, are moving through Canaan and forming villages in the mountains of Seir. Although Chedorlaomer has sent envoys to demand tribute, they have refused to be extorted. Arioch was told by Chedorlaomer to attack the next Hurrian movement for retaliation."

"It was a crude attack," Abram commented disgustedly. "Massacring people and stupidly leaving yourselves open to a simpler pincer offense."

"Arioch is a simple-minded man," Aner acknowledged sarcastically. "He was forced by Chedorlaomer, but his heart was not in it. He is a Hurrian himself and did not relish attacking his own people. He suddenly became quite ill, and he let one of his ruthless underlings take over the raid."

"Let us get to the issue," Abram stated flatly. "Why did you want to see me? If you were part of the attack, why do you expect me to help you?"

Eshcol's face writhed in agony as he tried to speak. "But we were not!" he cried out. "We were returning from paying our tribute money and from spending the year in Mari where we sought wives."

"How do I know you are not lying?"

"Our new wives!" Aner explained anxiously. "We four were hoping to join some traveling group at Carchemish. Arioch's men came upon us just before their attack. They forced us to carry their extra weapons. They bound our wives and carried them along. We have been praying that they are with the other Hurrian women even now."

"By the God of Noah, we speak the truth, Abram," Eshcol desperately vowed. "Find the women, Yadida and Tasuba. They will confirm our story. And your own wife, Sarai. She taught Yadida and Tasuba in the Academy of Mari. Because of your wife, they forsook the cult of Ishtar where they were to be candidates for initiation."

"We also have renounced all pagan worship of Ishtar and Hadad, her male counterpart in Mari!" Aner announced. "Especially Hadad, Abram! In Canaan, Hadad is called Baal, the fertility god of rain and harvest. Male prostitutes vie for men's attention with Ishtar's priestesses. They say they must excite Baal to give crops. The cult teaches that Baal dies in the autumn, but through sexual excitement he revives and returns to his earthly duties. It becomes worse each year!"

Abram no longer doubted the sincerity of Eshcol and Aner. He called the guards and asked to be taken to the overseeing judge. "I will get you released as soon as possible," he said to the two prisoners as he departed. "You and your wives may join our company. Somehow I feel that the God of Noah may use us to bless one another in the future!"

"Thank you, Abram!" Aner shouted out appreciatively. "Thank you!" Then Aner turned to comfort his brother who had collapsed from the strain of the conversation and the aching punishment he had endured.

Eshcol and Aner were soon released to Abram's custody, although the judge required a substantial fee for his inconvenience. The stripe wounds were cared for, and the three of them returned to Abram's encampment.

147

Lot arrived with Salanna. The distant hills were covered with flocks and herds led by her shepherds as they came to join Abram's people. With their addition, the combined group became large and formidable.

The few Amorites who escaped reported to their shakana, Arioch, describing Abram's forces as an army of giant black-hooded warriors. They labeled Abram with the epithet *Habiru*. The name meant a wandering band of people, but to the Amorites it had become a notoriously slanderous term of contempt. One advantage to their exaggerations was that it kept the Amorites from ever planning a future attack on Abram directly.

The next day the Carchemish guards let Abram's entourage pass quickly across the bridge and around the city on a by-pass route. Just beyond Carchemish all waited while the Hurrians buried and mourned their dead. There was good grazing along the low hills. Somehow crossing the bridge seemed to mark the real beginning of the adventure to find God's promised land.

It took nearly a month of slow travel to reach Damascus. Skirting the many smaller villages on the way, the large company camped near the famous cities of Khalab, Ebla and Hamath. In those places time was spent refurbishing supplies in trade for surplus butter, cheese, wool and slaughtered newborn lambs that had been dropped by ewes during the trip.

Abram and Eliezer had especially looked forward to their visit to Damascus. Eliezer wanted to show his family where he had once lived and to repeat for his sons all of the stories of the military campaigns against the sea people.

Damascus had been free to prosper since those days. The cosmopolitan city gleamed against Mount Ube, the great rounded mountain that protected it on the west. The mount received its name from the surrounding state, Ube, which was under Damascene authority. The city's river, the Abana, flowed through stone irrigation walls. Its water made the plain to the east like a rich well-kept garden. One first arriving in the city of Damascus went through rows of olive and nut trees with lentils and herbs grown in their shade. Nearer the city grew orchards of mulberry, apricot, apple and peach trees followed by terraced vineyards that circled the city and backed up on the mountain side. An abundant crop of wheat and barley thrived farther away on the plains to the south.

While in Damascus, Abram went to see the present governor, Ensi Akhiezer, and was surprised to be given special honor as the hero who had saved Damascus years before from destruction. The ensi explained that he had been a young Damascene soldier at that time and well remembered what Abram had accomplished.

Later that day Sarai went with Abram, and they climbed the trail that led to the summit of Mount Ube. Occasionally they stopped and looked back at the way they had come. Damascus lay spread out in descending levels before them with its encompassing walls, its limestone buildings and the many roads and paths that led into its gates. Delicate aspen and poplars grew throughout the city courtyards and parks and bordered the steams and the river courseway. The fruitful Abana valley reached out far into the desert until the river itself came to a stop and disappeared in the sands.

Nearing the summit of Ube they saw the breathtakingly beautiful Mount Hermon. Gleaming white snow lay heavily on its three distant peaks contrasting with its dark barren lower sides and the rounded foothills which were glowingly alive with spring greenery.

Abram took Sarai's hand and together they turned toward Canaan to the southwest. The hills of Hermon tapered off and the waters that would later feed the Jordan River flowed through a large swampland forming first a small lake and then the larger pear-shaped Lake Chinnereth.

It was a clear day. In the panorama of land that stretched far beyond the lakes they began to sense the fulfillment of God's words.

Abram and Sarai meditated and talked for some time. Before descending Mount Ube, they walked the ridge to the north, and he showed Sarai a narrow hidden pass that cut through the mountain. It had become overgrown by bushes at its entryways.

"I surveyed the state of Ube when I stayed in the city," Abram told Sarai. "I came across this large crack by accident. It gave my spies secret access to the back side of the mountain where the sea people usually hid in the brush. Even Damascus sentries didn't know of the pass, and the sea people as well as the Damascenes were amazed how quickly we discovered the enemy's raiding plans. I doubt if any in Damascus today know of its existence."

Abram could not realize then how important that secret pass would be to him again in the future.

The trade route from Damascus led to a bridge over the Jordan River just south of the Lake of Chinnereth. Abram allowed extra days for the flocks to feed on the eastern hills above the lake before making the crossing. The fishing in Lake Chinnereth was excellent, and everyone enjoyed the fresh clear lake water. The view of Mount Hermon from the lake was even more spectacular than the one from Mount Ube in Damascus. Hermon's majestic white form towered in the bright blue skies, high above the sparkling blue lake and the soft green shores and hills that surrounded it.

Abram and Sarai would have liked to stay longer, but the people of the cities around the lake were suspicious and inhospitable. So for two days the large company travelled on into the land of Canaan.

Early on the third day Abram scouted ahead of the front lines of watchmen. Near two mountains, not far from the ruins of the city of Shechem, he came upon a large oak tree where he paused to rest. Leaning against the trunk of the oak, he was enjoying the sweet fragrances of the spring morning. Instantaneously he had an awareness of the Lord's presence and heard the divine voice say, "To your descendants I will give this land."

It was a definite encounter with the God of Noah, but Abram felt none of the usual elation. To his surprise, he even wanted to cry out in rebellion. "Thirty-five years, thirty-five years, I waited to come here, my Lord! Over and over you have promised me a land for my descendants. But now that we have come and you declare this is my land, the wife you gave me is barren!"

Then it was as if the Lord brought Sarai's words ringing into Abram's mind, the words that she spoke long ago in Kamarina, "God has given you the gift of faith. To make that gift become yours, Abram, he must test the faith that is in you."

Abram took some stones and made an altar under the oak tree. He had no offering to give but dedicated his life again and prayed that God would forgive him and bless him with patience.

"This land with its unfriendly villages and its raiding Amorite tribes is to belong to *my* heir and his children throughout the rest of history," Abram declared. "I *will* have a son by my wife, Sarai. You gave her to me, my Lord. It was with Sarai that I first came to believe, and it was Sarai who first worshipped you. You have promised to bless us and give us this land for *our* descendants. *I do believe, Lord!*"

The altar that Abram built under the oak tree was his first claim on the land. He called the place the Oak of Moreh, the "Oak of Holiness."

Chapter VIII
THE LAND OF PROMISE

As Abram returned from the Oak of Moreh, he saw a familiar figure riding toward him. He spurred his camel to meet his nephew Lot.

When they had drawn together, Abram was concerned and called out, "What causes you to leave the flocks this early, Lot? Is there trouble?"

"I am having difficulties with our herders and Salanna's. They refuse to join us in worship each morning. They complain of our food, the way we tend our animals, and everything else. Mainly, they want to leave us and go on separately to Seir."

Abram was puzzled by Lot's words and replied, "They will be departing for Seir soon enough. Why should they be restless?"

Though Lot was a mature man, he often seemed more to Abram like an earnest but insecure boy. Even now he reminded Abram of the lad who once aimed a fishing spear at Abram's tarada back in the marshlands of Ur. Lot was about Abram's height. His dark hair was neatly cut below his ears and his beard was well trimmed. His countenance was usually serious, but when he relaxed his smile was lighthearted and genuine.

Abram had been preoccupied with the divine significance of his entering into the land of Canaan. Had it not been so, he would have noticed what had been occurring, and Lot's reply would not have come as such a surprise.

"I am in love with Salanna!" Lot said, as if he would explode if he did not make this confession.

"Salanna? The Hurrian?"

"Abram!" Lot cried out in frustration. "I am so in love with her that I am making a fool of myself!"

"Her husband, Lot. He was just killed," Abram interjected, halting his mount and nodding to Lot to do likewise.

They tied ranging tethers to the camels and allowed them to eat the clumps of tall grasses. The two men spread their cloaks on the ground and sat down.

Now that he had begun the conversation, Lot had difficulty continuing. Abram gave him time to gather up his courage. With their minds elsewhere, they watched their tall humped beasts. Amid grunts and groans, the camels' strong lower teeth bit off the grasses. They chewed the forage against hard upper gum plates that for camels peculiarly replace front teeth. Split upper lips opened and closed, and the animals seemingly unattached lower jaws flopped rhythmically.

"Sometimes I wish I were just like one of those camels," Lot lamented. "They do their work and do not expect much in return but the privilege to grunt and growl."

Abram could not keep from laughing and reminded Lot, "Remember, they can be most difficult when a doe is in heat!"

Lot smiled, and he felt some of the strain leave him. "After all of these years, Abram, I do feel like an old excited buck! I can think of nothing else but that woman. If I do not see her, then usually one of her daughters comes to visit the herds. They look so much like her. Again I am reminded of Salanna and become consumed with passion for her.

"What can I do?" Lot asked plaintively. "Her herdsmen fear I will somehow force her to marry me, and they will have to stay with us!"

"And Salanna? How is she reacting?"

153

"Like I am some dumb sheep she keeps stumbling over and who keeps getting in her way!" Lot admitted dejectedly.

"Perhaps it is just too soon." Abram replied. "Why not tell her how you feel? Then let her go and find a place in the mountains of the Hurrian settlements. When we find our location, you can visit her before the rains come."

"I burn like hot coals, Abram! I have never quite felt this way. What can I do?" Lot implored again.

Abram looked intently at his nephew and seriously cautioned, "Pray for God's help and guidance."

Then he added lightly, "And work even harder . . . it helps!"

They pulled their reluctant camels away from their feeding. Abram motioned to the south, "We will continue on the west slopes of those hills. According to my maps of this area, there are good camping places between the cities of Bethel and Ai. There is a Mount Seir farther on, but the range of mountains called Seir is south of the Gomorrah Lake. Salanna and her people should probably leave us and take the route from Ai that goes east of the lake."

"That means she might leave us in less than a week?" Lot inquired anxiously.

Abram nodded. "It would be best for her and for you. Let her grief know healing, and let her feel she has completed her husband's mission."

"You are wise, Abram," Lot conceded, his face a picture of forlorn resignation.

As they returned, the flocks were spread out and grazing on the hillsides in a magnificently beautiful pastoral scene. The dew-wet grasses were lavishly decorated with bright yellows and whites of wild daffodils, lilies and asphodel. These were intermingled with vivid red splashes of anemone, tulips and cyclamen. Here and there stood erect lavender spikes of lovely perfumed hyacinths. The air was still and quiet as the late morning sea breeze had not yet begun.

Once again Abram noticed how recently being in God's presence had alerted his senses. His heart was full of joy and thankfulness, while his mind raced with excitement and anticipation. God had confirmed him again! All was well! "Except for my lovesick nephew," he thought sympathetically.

At mealtime Abram sought out Aner and Eschol. Their lashing stripes had healed, and they were proving to be excellent watchmen and advisors. Abram had brought his maps. He laid them out, commenting, "These are poorly made, I have discovered. Some day I want to do an accurate survey and map this land. The trade routes are well marked, but they are not always best for grazing or even for travel."

Eshcol nodded in agreement and said, "For one small area, this land has great variety. Mountains, hills, steppes, plains, desert, jungles, lakes, ocean, rivers. It is as if God put a sample of each part of the earth in the land of Canaan."

"My wife Sarai was taught that the city of Jericho and the Lake of Gomorrah remain at the same level as before the Great Flood. The rest of the earth's lands have either risen into higher plains, hills and mountains or lowered into the ocean basins," Abram related.

"That is an interesting thought to ponder," Eshcol replied. "Jericho and the lake are certainly far below the level of the Great Sea."

"How far south are you planning to go, Abram?" Aner broke in, as he studied the rolled-out papyrus maps.

Abram pulled his knife from its sheath and using it as a pointer directed as he spoke, "I hope to find a place for winter lodging either here, between Bethel and Ai, or else further on, between the mountain ridges. That valley should have good springs."

"You had best settle near Bethel," Eshcol advised. "There are no cities or villages near the other place."

"The king of Salem lives there!" laughed Aner. Then his smile quickly left his face and he apologized, "I should not laugh at the man. Now that I have learned about the real God from you and Sarai, I think I will seek him out when we go past."

Abram's eyes brightened with curiosity. "What are you talking about, Aner?"

"There is a man, Abram, who lives somewhere on that hill," Aner pointed at the map as he explained. "He claims that God appointed him to be a priest. He offers animal sacrifices regularly to God on that hill and shares the meat of the offering with any who come by. Since he is the only one who lives there, he is called the king of Salem, the 'king of peace' or sometimes the 'king of righteousness.' In Canaanite, it is 'Melchizedek.' "

"I should like to meet him!" Abram said enthusiastically. "Praise the Lord, how I should like to meet such a man!"

Abram thanked his two new friends and gathered up his maps. "I must share what you have just told me with Sarai!" he said excitedly. "It will soon be time to travel!"

Two days later the entourage arrived at the place between Bethel and Ai. Abram had the tents pitched with Bethel on the west and the city of Ai on the east. After the meal and rest time were over, Abram called in some servants. Together they built an altar to the Lord. Then all of Abram's company came to the altar to worship. However, Salanna, her daughters and her people refused and stayed in their tents or tended their animals.

Abram's people were wearied from the long journey, and resentments had festered along the way, especially with the irritating Hurrians. Most of his people came to the worship reluctantly, wishing they, too, could be free to do as they wished. Abram sensed their growing defiance. For a moment, gripping fear and anxiety held him speechless. Then warm assurance came, and he knew what he must do.

Abram stood before the altar and called upon the name of the Lord, "My Lord God, Lord of heaven and earth, blessed be your holy name! Praise and glory are yours. Come, renew our strength and lift our burdens. Be known to us, O Lord!"

In the pause that followed, the holy reality and presence of the living God came and rested upon the people. For several hours they refreshed themselves together in praise. The flaming colors of the setting sun faded into rich pinks and darkening purples. Cares seemed to have disappeared as they departed with singing, merriment and friendly communion.

156

Following a day of rest, Salanna and some of her men bought supplies in Ai. When they returned to the encampment, they made arrangements to withdraw from Abram's people before the next dawn. They would take the Jericho road toward the mountains of Seir.

Lot had told Salanna of his love for her, but her mind was set upon leaving. She was hardly listening when he spoke to her.

"May I try to find you before the early rains, Salanna?" he implored. "Perhaps then you would need me as I need you."

"Lot," she replied irritably. "My beloved husband still fills my heart. I do not want to think of another man! No, I would not want to see you that soon! It would be . . . too soon!"

Lot was stung by the rejection, but her last sentence gave him some hope. "Perhaps a year, maybe two," he thought. "I will wait!"

Only in the darkness before she departed did Salanna allow Lot to embrace her in farewell. It was then that some of her rigidity broke. She felt his strong arms and with her head against his chest she sensed a security she had been missing.

"Perhaps in a few years. . . ," she faltered and then her body relaxed.

It was all the encouragement Lot needed. His arms tightened, and he eagerly kissed her. It became a long and passionate embrace as Salanna responded with restrained submission.

Lot walked beside her for several hours as the Hurrian company withdrew eastward.

Eshcol once counseled Abram, "The nearer Lake Gomorrah you travel, the less you will need to be concerned about Sarai's safety. You will have to worry more about your young men!"

Abram at the time thought Eshcol's words were exaggerated, but after his visit to Ai he found them sadly true. His young herders were sought after by many lusty eyed men of the city, whereas he noticed the women of his people were avoided and held in contempt. "They tire of petting themselves," Eshcol

157

explained with disgust as they rode watchduty the next day. "That is why they are so fond of strangers."

"And you say it is worse farther south?" Abram asked incredulously.

"The most sickening places on earth are probably Sodom and Gomorrah," Eshcol declared. "The men—there are few women living there—look like ordinary hard-working people. Their cities are prosperous, and they have done a good job of irrigation and farming. But their practices are unbelievable. Young boys are bought up at slave markets, used and abused by the men, and then offered as sacrifices to Baal."

Their camels loped on. Abram's heart was too heavy to talk further. His whole being cried out to God in the silence, "O my Lord! Is *this* the land of your promise? Do you tolerate these men in your holy land?"

Eshcol halted his riding camel abruptly, interrupting Abram's thoughts. "There is Aner! He has Melchizedek with him! Good for him! I was not certain he would be able to find him. Come, Abram, let us go join them!"

Eshcol raced his camel ahead as Abram paused to pray aloud, "O God Most High, Lord of all the worlds and ruler of all men! Thank you for sending me someone holy and righteous. O Lord, one good and righteous man redeems a land of evildoers!"

Abram soon joined Eshcol and Aner and the three dismounted. They stood before Melchizedek who was still astride his donkey. Abram bowed and spoke to him, "May we spread a place under those tamarisk trees? I have some bread and cheese. I welcome this opportunity to talk with you!"

Melchizedek was slightly shorter than Abram and his two friends. It was difficult to tell his age. His skin was tanned and like leather, his body lean of fat with the tight muscles of a mountain lion. Dark curly hair receded from his forehead and was cropped at the neckline, and his beard had been roughly trimmed close to his jaw. He wore a dark brown cassock and sandals. His eyes, the same brown as his cassock, were penetrating as he stared unanswering at Abram.

Finally, Melchizedek nodded affirmatively and slid from his donkey's back. He then led the way toward the clump of trees.

"What language does he speak?" Abram rushed to ask Aner, thinking he had not been understood.

"He understands the Canaanite dialect you spoke," Aner whisperingly replied. "He was very insistent on coming immediately to meet you!"

Eshcol had spread out his camel blanket and Abram brought the food, cups and an ale skin from his saddle bags.

Melchizedek knelt on the edge of the covering, tautly lifted up his arms and began praying in a dialect unknown to Abram. Then he shifted and prayed in the Canaanite language Abram had just used. Melchizedek thanked the Lord for their meeting together, the food provided, and the wisdom to be gained by their fellowship.

For the first time in many weeks, Abram felt a depth of peace in his heart. With even Sarai submitting to his spiritual leadership, he often felt alone in making decisions. His faith had many lives to uphold. Now he felt a confirmation in his spirit that he was indeed with a priest of God. He allowed the very presence of the holy man to minister to the aching questions of his heart and mind.

Melchizedek began to speak. His voice was soft but distinct and clear—like the distant bells of grazing oxen, Abram thought. The priest directed Abram's attention to the hill from which he, Melchizedek, and Aner had just come. "I have prayed many years on that holy hill. It is sanctified as this whole land is to be sanctified by the holy God. A man is to come, God has promised, whose offspring will bring this land true peace and righteousness!"

As the four partook of the meal, Melchizedek questioned Abram fully about his early life, his time in the Ararats, Sarai, and his long wait near Charran. Only when they were finished did Abram realize that he knew no more about Melchizedek than when he first sighted him on his donkey.

When Melchizedek rose to depart, his final words were, "It may be, Abram of Terah, that you are the man of the promise, the patriarch of this land and of all those who will believe in

159

the one holy God. For the most high God is preparing a land and a people for his coming!"

Abram watched Melchizedek and his donkey as they departed and wound up and through mountain pass. To Abram's senses, the words Melchizedek last spoke still vibrated in the air. They were almost tangible. ". . . man of the promise . . . patriarch of this land . . . the most high God is preparing a land . . . a people for his coming!"

Aner had returned the cups and ale skin to the saddle bags and brought Abram's camel to him. "Well, my friend," he said, sorry that he had to break in on Abram's meditations. "You have now met the king and priest of Salem. Tell me, do you feel he is a real prophet of God?"

Abram paused to look again at the disappearing figure of Melchizedek. Then he turned to Aner and answered with slow deliberation, "If I am a forerunner of the people that God is preparing to live in this land, surely Melchizedek is a forerunner of the order of priests for those people!"

It was the time of the early spring harvest. As Abram's large company passed by small towns and villages, Abram took his servants and the oxen to help work the farms. At first the townspeople were frightened and suspicious, but Abram and his men were pleasant and friendly toward them. Soon the farmers were begging Abram to stay longer.

The work was enjoyable, and it was good to feel the rich soil of Canaan. As Abram trod through the rows of grain, he claimed each cubit of the ground. Sarai worked beside him, and whenever their eyes met they could not keep from smiling. This was their land. This was the land their children would inherit!

Not since they had left Ur had Abram and Sarai felt so strong and healthy. Even Abram's foreskin infection had been healed shortly after his memorable meeting with Melchizedek. Since then the hope for a child kept them constantly expecting conception.

The long awns of the ripened barley seeds gave the grain heads a bearded look. After the spikelets were pulled off the shafts, the soft straw was gathered and cut and baled. It would be used for animal bedding or else chopped for livestock roughage.

The farmers gave Abram his share of the harvest at the end of his stay. The bales of straw were added to the oxen's loads. The valuable barley grain was dried in rotating jars over the fires and then stored in flax bags. Later, some would be malted for ale and the rest saved for winter feeding.

When the barley harvest was ended, Abram moved his people on toward the fields of Mamre, brother of Eshcol and Aner. When Mamre had heard his brothers' story and how Abram intervened, he called for his family and servants to prepare a feast. It turned out to be a joyous celebration for the wayworn travelers.

Abram immediately liked Mamre. Eschol and Aner's brother was a tall robust man with brawny muscles and a great expanse of chest. His face was large and jovial, and his eyes usually twinkled with amusement.

Mamre had built a home in a nearby village for his family, but he spent most of his time in tents near his fields. The land which he shared with Aner and Eshcol began some distance from the village, beyond a thicketed forest of oak trees. Mamre had dug several wells and had good pastureland for his animals.

"I will tell you, Abram," Mamre laughed heartily as the two of them toured through the young vineyards and the orchards that also belonged to the three brothers, "this is a fine life, but it is a life of chances. It's not just *if* the rain comes but *how* it comes and *when* it comes that makes the difference."

Abram nodded in concurrence remembering the days of waiting in Terrakki for the rains. He bent over and picked up a clod of soil and broke it in his hand. The dark gray dirt sifted through his fingers. "This is fertile soil," he commented, feeling the touch of the holy ground.

"By the end of summer no plow can break this earth," Mamre sighed, lifting his shoulders up and down in a gesture of resignation. "So we pray for the rains to come early and soften the ground. If they are late we get no winter harvest.

161

"But then," he grinned, "we must not pray too hard. If the rain comes and softens the ground, it may come again in torrents when the new grain is sprouting and destroy everything. The storms can be fierce with hail that breaks off tree limbs. Fortunately this has been a good year. But who knows about the next one?"

"What is your yearly harvest cycle?" Abram inquired.

"It is about the same as you probably had in the Charran area, although we may have more variety of vegetables here. Also, we rotate more land in flax. I sowed one small field this year with fine Kemian seed. It produced a soft, almost pure white linen."

"Sarai will enjoy hearing about that," Abram said as he thought how much Sarai appreciated working with good quality materials.

"We hoed up the flax fields over a month ago," Mamre related. "With the barley season over, the spring wheat will be ready soon. Then comes the dry season, and we have to spend all of our time irrigating the gardens and the orchards, and tend the vineyards. We have a very heavy dew that helps us grow excellent grapes, big luscious pink ones.

"Late summer," Mamre continued, "fruit is picked and dried." The two men walked through a grove of olive saplings as they talked together. Beyond them lay the ripening wheat fields with scattered mature olive trees making soft green blotches in the golden expanse. "Olives grow quite well here," Mamre explained. "I made graftings from some of the better wild trees. With regular water and fertilizing, I have been able to harvest every year rather than every other year."

All that Mamre said pleased Abram. Even the storms and unpredictable weather problems just convinced Abram that he would have to rely more on the Lord for help. Talking about the rich soil and the plentiful harvests warmed Abram's heart.

As they passed by one of the old olive trees, Abram stopped to examine a lower bough. Loose clusters of small whitish flowers hung from the axils of the silvery green leaves. Sarai once told Abram of a dove that bore a similar branch to Noah after the Flood as a sign of renewed life on the earth.

"God's promise is sure," he mused to himself. "It is proper that the olive tree should grow well in the land of the promise!"

Abram returned his mind to their conversation. "Have you gathered two harvests of wheat each year since you have been here?" he asked.

"All but that first year!" Mamre replied. "If it had not been for a terrible but wonderful first year, we never would have this land. There had been a long drought, and this part of the country was almost ruined. The farmers left in droves and never returned."

"You have done much since that time, Mamre," Abram complimented him.

"There is more land to the east of the oak forest that has not been touched. If you wish to settle there, Abram, we would be honored. If Chedorlaomer returns, he will not hesitate to burn our fields and destroy our wells. But with you, *Abram the Habiru,* here, I doubt if he would even come this way!"

A contingent of servants was left to help Mamre with his wheat harvest. They were also to build storage silos for Abram's grain, and malt enough of the barley to make a new supply of ale.

The rest of his people Abram led to the south toward Sheba. The color of the soil became a light gray, but it was still quite fertile. Villagers conserved water by use of terraces and cisterns. Wells were frequent and morning dews especially heavy. The animals could feed everywhere along the way, for the land was blanketed with prairie grasses.

The small city of Sheba lay in a gap between the hills. Fortunately, waters from the Sheba wells were abundant and fresh, for the grasses were beginning to dry out as summer set in.

The company crossed over the hills toward the coastal plains, following a gradually evaporating stream bed that wound from Sheba westward to the sea. There, better grass was found on the plain, but the nights were hot and oppressive. No sea winds blew until mid-morning. These

163

made the days pleasant, but when they stopped at sunset the hot land air drifted in from the east.

Abram met with Lot and Eliezer, and they determined to settle back by the oaks of Mamre until the rains began in late autumn. To avoid being ambushed by King Abimelech in the valleys of Gerar, they planned to travel a distance northward. Abram's good sense had to struggle with his curiosity in making that decision.

Abram had been warned by people in Sheba about Abimelech. The small kingdom of Abimelech was one of the original settlements in Canaan. The people by rote could trace their lineage back to Ham. The kingdom occupied the southern part of the Shephelah, the name for the red-soiled valleys and foothills above the coastal plains. The Amorites once lured Abimelech and his soldiers to battle on the sea plain while another Amorite tribe sacked Gerar and the other villages of the kingdom. The Hamite women were known to be attractive and most were taken captive by the Amorites, including the king's beloved wife.

Abimelech and his people feared and worshipped only the God of Noah, Abram was also told. This was the reason Abram and Sarai were so curious to meet him. But the king was wary, bitter and very suspicious of strangers. He seldom allowed anyone to enter his borders, and many who did never returned alive.

That autumn the rains came and gently softened the ground. Every available man, woman and child in Abram's camp took to the plows to prepare the fields. Because of the good weather, much of the land east of Mamre's oak forest was cleared, and was soon covered with green fringes of germinating winter wheat and barley.

A few days before the grain was ready for the sickle, the sky overhead grew black with clouds. Winds whipped up and a heavy rainstorm began. Large hailstones fell, beating down the burdening grain, crushing the tender flax seedlings and ripping away the leaves and fruit of the vineyards. One furious thunderstorm followed another and torrents of water rushed through the streams and river beds until they overflowed and swamped the lands.

Silos and other storage places were penetrated, and rot and mildew were the next destroyers.

Then the overabundant rains ceased suddenly. The latter rains that were needed for the second sowing were sparse, and hot air blowing in from the eastern deserts parched the ground. Yellowish dust filled the air, making visibility difficult, drying out nose cavities and causing painful throats. Tempers were edgy. A hard year lay ahead. Abram and Sarai often felt despair and had difficulty reassuring their people.

When the next autumn and winter repeated the disastrous storm cycle, a severe famine was imminent. The shepherds were forced to kill off many of the sheep and goats, not only for food but to conserve fodder for the remainder of the animals.

Reluctantly, Abram sent Lot with some of the servants and camels and donkeys to Sodom and Gomorrah to try to establish business relations there, trading supplies for copper from the mines south of the cities. The plan was to form a caravan and go back through Damascus to Charran. Eliezer took his family along, intending to settle them permanently in Damascus.

Lot used the opportunity while in Sodom to leave his men with the trading and go to the mountains of Seir where he found Salanna. After much persuading, she agreed to marry him when he came back from Charran. Lot promised her he would take responsibility for her daughters and adopt them as his own.

Abram and Sarai after days of prayer made preparations and arrangements to take the rest of the people and their possessions to Kemi to wait out the famine. It was difficult to leave Canaan. They had waited so long to come, and now Abram and Sarai felt driven away, at least for a while.

It was said that the law was upheld in Kemi and that visitors were treated with respect, a respect granted perhaps because of the exorbitant surcharge made upon foreign sojourners. The weeks before they left, Abram and Sarai studied the Kemian language and reviewed the history of that unusual country.

Chapter IX
PHARAOHS AND PYRAMIDS

(The following is a summary of Egyptian history up to the time of Abram and Sarai's entry into that country. The source materials used include Egyptian records and documents compiled during that period, the ancient writings of Greek, Roman and Egyptian historians, biblical references and related documents, plus the great wealth of modern scholarship and archeological evidence that is available today.)

The name "Egypt" is a late Greek appellation. The Hamites and Shemites who first settled along the convolutions of the great north African Nile River affectionately called the place where they lived Ta-mery, the "Beloved Land," or just the "Land." In more formal and general use, however, was the name Kemi. The word meant the "Black Land," referring to the color of the alluvial soil which the river yearly deposited when it overflowed. The Nile River up to Greek and Roman times was called the Hapy.

Life was maintained in the Land by the awaited yearly flooding or inundation of the Hapy during the season of Akhet. This time of flooding was followed by the season of Peret when the waters receded and plowing, planting and harvesting were all done. The last and the longest season was called Shomer, a time when water was scarce and most well buckets hung idle. During Shomer the burning glare of the sun and the hot desert winds teamed to desiccate the once verdant fields. Only constant irrigation, usually by manually carrying and emptying large water jars, kept the gardens and orchards closest to the river productive.

The Kemian civilization by necessity followed the contour of the Hapy. On either side of the river valley lay deserts of sand and dry rocky plateaus. To the south were mountains and jungles, and to the north lay the Mediterranean, called simply the Sea or the Great Sea. At first the small settlements along the river had self-rule. Then like the cities of the Tigris and Euphrates, they grew and stretched out along the banks forming city-states which were called nomes.

The nomes were each distinctive in dialect and customs. The kings of the nomes of the Hapy delta area met together and confederated into what is still today called the Lower Land. Cooperatively they built canals and drained the marshes near the sea. Irrigation was less troublesome in the delta, and the people enjoyed more time for culture and education.

The other nomes were interspersed along the great length of the river from the apex of the delta to the Jeb (later named the Elephantine), a large river island in the far south of the Land that marked the border of Kush. These nomes, formed along the river banks, made up the more diverse Upper Land.

The communities in the Upper Land, surviving on the narrow borders of the coiling long river, felt that the waters belonged to them since they were closest to the river's source. They resented the broad delta where the river branched out in many directions allowing the floodwaters to soak large pastures for cattle grazing and fields for vineyards. In turn, the Lower Land people considered the Upper Landers provincial and uncouth. Rivalries grew fierce between the two Lands early in their history.

The current of the great river flows from the south, while the prevailing winds blow in from the north off the Sea. This

THE LAND OF KEMI (EGYPT)

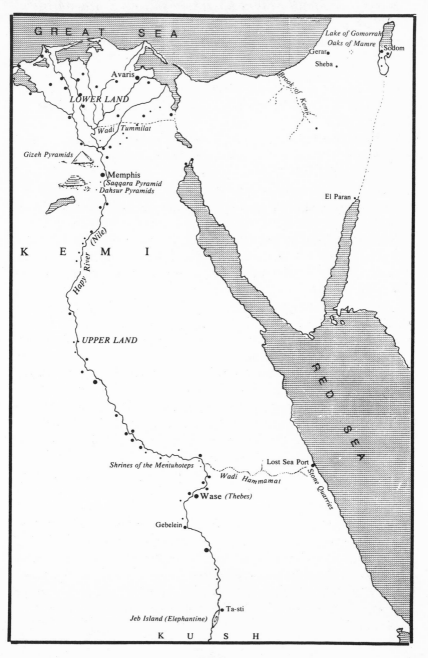

fortunate happening of nature allowed for easy down current travel and equally rapid upstream sailing. Caravan travel was only necessary to cross the deserts.

In the bickering that early occurred between the two parts of the Land, the delta Lower Landers refused to permit the Upper Landers access through their area to the Sea. In retaliation, the nomes of the Upper Land united under Menes, the king of one of the small mid-river nomes. Together the Upper Landers dammed up the river at a spot just before it reached the Lower Land, thereby succeeding in changing the course of the river and cutting off one of its main arteries. The act terrified the Lower Land people, and they became conciliatory.

With quick and astute wisdom Menes appointed a governor to rule over his own small nome and established himself as king over both Lands. He built a capital for the united country at the very place where the river's course had been changed. This was Memphis, the first capital of the united Land.

Menes reduced the kings of all the nomes to governors or nomarchs. Although Menes kept the authority to replace a nomarch, he gave them almost complete rule over their original territories.

Once a year the nomarchs met with the king in Memphis as an advisory council to help rule the entire country. To signify this new unity, Menes would alternately wear a white crown during the meetings representing the Lower Land and then a red crown for the Upper Land. Later kings combined the two into one symbolic head piece.

Menes knew only one God. He yearned for a divine order to come out of the chaos that he had seen, an order of righteousness and justice. Menes believed he needed, as king, to epitomize the maat (righteousness) and the akh (goodness) of God. With this first king's unique combination of humility, power, and desire for righteousness, the Land thrived with creativity and spontaneity. People were free to travel and to prosper. Justice was honored and legal courts were available to all citizens, men and women alike.

Boats no longer paid tolls and tariffs at each nome but had free access to any part of the Hapy River and to the Sea. A common language and a common script superseded all provincial dialects. Palaces, government buildings and private homes rose up in lavish style. Gold, ivory, precious stones and imported timbers commonly decorated the abodes of even the poorest farmers.

The reign of Menes lasted sixty-two years. It ended when the king and his small hunting canoe were smashed by the jaws of a large hippopotamus. His death occurred five hundred years before the time of King Akalamdu in Ur, about five thousand years ago, in 3100 BC.

Throughout the centuries that followed the union under Menes, tensions between the Upper and Lower Lands continued to surface. The royal line of Menes was usurped by a strong nomarch who in turn was ousted by others. Vying cults and superstitions grew and fed on the rivalries of the two Lands and the competition between the various nomarchs.

The early dynasties were brought to a close by the warlike nomarch Khasehemui who determined ruthlessly to destroy all traces of conspiracy and revolt. Khasehemui's reign initiated what Egyptologists call the Old Kingdom, 2686-2160 BC. Even though Khasehemui's immediate heirs were weak leaders, the nation held together. It was still united when the great Pharaoh (a title most kings preferred) Djoser ascended to the throne. Djoser united and strongly ruled Kemi at the time Akalamdu became King of Ur in Kamarina.

Imhotep was the brilliant son of Kanefer, the Director of Works for the Upper and Lower Lands. Kanefer was famous throughout Kemi and elsewhere as the first developer of the art of stone cutting. His son, Imhotep, became the protégé of Pharaoh Djoser, and, as was the custom, was sent away various places to study. Most certainly one of those places would have been Kamarina of Ur. And if so, it would have been during the time that Princess Puabi was a young girl being tutored by Gimil near the Academy.

Historians say that Imhotep was well versed in the wisdom of Menes and worshipped the same one God. His interests were broad-ranged and his active mind absorbed knowledge quickly. He would have been fascinated while in Ur by the buildings of the palace and the Academy at Kamarina. But the shape and construction of Akalamdu's Ziggurat especially would have appealed to him. Its symbolism easily fit into the beliefs and legends of his own country, for the Kemian people believed in the Great Flood but also believed that the world was originally a vast ocean called Nu, out of which a great primordial mountain arose. God came and rested on the mountain and life began.

However, if Imhotep thought of building a Ziggurat in Kemi similar to the one in Ur, he would not have considered using the easily destroyed mud bricks. Like his father, he would want to build a Ziggurat from precisely cut stones. If he built a "Mountain of God," it would last as long as the original one in the Ararats.

It is told that Imhotep as a young man presented the idea of building a step pyramid like a Ziggurat to the pharaoh. At the time Pharaoh Djoser was too interested in constructing his palace in Memphis to give the idea any consideration. The youthful Imhotep bided his time and set out to prove his worth and ability.

He began first by implementing a scheme to store grain in stone granaries, giant cone-shaped silos which he designed and had built and sealed onto stone platforms. These he filled during the years of good harvest when the grain was abundant and cheap. During years of famine Imhotep sold the grain back to the people for a reasonable profit.

As word of the storehouses spread abroad other peoples suffering from famine sought temporary refuge in Kemi. Those who could afford the high prices charged to foreigners paid willingly. To survive, others were forced to sell themselves for years of indentured service to the pharaoh.

Djoser granted Imhotep the right to engage these laborers to build a stone dam across the Hapy River. Imhotep's dam was the first to join together the natural stone outcroppings at a stretch of rapids in the far south. The dam and the lake that backed up behind it gave more even control over the river's yearly inundation.

As Imhotep's fame spread so did the pharaoh's trust in him. Imhotep was elevated to the position of Grand Vizier. Later the pharaoh recognized Imhotep's admirable moral and ethical beliefs and appointed him High Priest of the Land.

As High Priest, Imhotep wrote extraordinary and perceptive sacred texts that inspired many generations after him. "It is not the will of man which is realized but the plan of God," is attributed to him as one of his many proverbs. These also included advice for using restraint in speech and actions, decent conduct, good manners and proper etiquette.

As Pharaoh Djoser grew older Imhotep kept suggesting the building of the Ziggurat to bring the people back to the worship of the one holy God. Condescendingly Djoser agreed that the project could be started, but at Saqqara the limestone quarry and not at Memphis. The pharaoh wanted nothing to compete in beauty or stature with his palace and capital buildings.

Imhotep was pleased. He designed a beautiful six stepped pyramid, and planned it to face both north toward the Lower Land and south toward the Upper Land. Chapels where people could come to worship were clustered around the base. Animals, birds, flowers and plants, all symbols of the various nomes, were cut into the stones for decoration of the chapels.

Before the Ziggurat was completed Djoser saw its emerging beauty and magnitude. The pharaoh became consumed with jealousy. The Ziggurat would be more spectacular than anything he had built in Memphis. Furthermore it was built of stone and would outlast all else that had been constructed, even his beloved palace with its exquisite tiles, shining pillars of bound reeds, and roofs of imported timbers.

Driven by pride and vanity, Djoser demanded that Imhotep completely redesign the pyramid. It would be the pharaoh's tomb, a monument to his rule. Djoser even required Imhotep to have replicas of the palace and other capital buildings carved in the pyramid's stone walls.

The pharaoh stopped every other project and thought of nothing else. He enlisted all of the nomarchs for their support. Each was forced to collect revenues and supply stone cutting labor.

Imhotep lost all joy in his work on the project. Only his integrity forced him to complete what had been started. When the long-drawn-out project was finished, he retired to the small village of Gebelein south of the nome of Wase (later called Thebes by the Greeks) where he devoted the rest of his life to the study of medicine and to his writings. Never again, he vowed, would he design another building or hold public office. Other pharaohs and even nomarchs tried to duplicate the magnificent step pyramid of Djoser, but without Imhotep's skill they had little success.

Another dynasty of the Old Kingdom began after Djoser in the year 2613 BC. A commoner named Snefru came to power by marrying the princess, Hetepheres. The energetic new pharaoh spent much of his time boating up and down the Hapy River, visiting the nomes. As he learned to know the people, his popularity grew to momentous proportions. When Snefru suddenly dismissed every nomarch from his post and replaced each with appointments of his own relatives, not the slightest rebellion occurred. Snefru centralized the government by locating all the offices of the nomarchs in the capital at Memphis, making it a policy that no major decision affecting any nome could be made unless he gave his direct approval. Few people in Kemi realized at the time what great power had been transferred to Memphis.

Snefru wanted a pyramid erected for himself at Dahsur, a short distance south of Djoser's pyramid. He insisted that it not be a step pyramid but one with perfectly straight sides. His incompetent architect did not consider or know about certain weight phenomena. When the pyramid was completed it leaned and was referred to as the "bent pyramid."

Furious, Snefru engaged a different architect who supervised the building of still another pyramid at Dahsur. This straight-sided monument was an improvement over the "bent pyramid," but nothing as magnificent as the step pyramid of Djoser built by Imhotep.

The mathematical genius that finally designed still a third pyramid for Snefru was surpassed only by the methods that the same unknown engineers invented for executing the splendid creation. Precise construction and complicated engineering were developed that no architect then or since has been able to understand or copy.

This third pyramid's construction coincided with the time that the great scholarship in Ur was under attack. It could well have been the professors of the Kamarina Academy that King Akalamdu and Ipali had exiled who were the mysterious designers and architects. The historical timing would have been perfect.

When a model was completed for the third pyramid, Snefru was completely enamored with the result. Armed with promises of favors and rewards, the pharaoh directed his familial nomarchs to press grossly exorbitant taxes and labor upon the people. Then, just before the mammoth project was to begin, Pharaoh Snefru was mysteriously poisoned.

Queen Hetepheres quickly took control and announced that her son, Khufu (called Cheops by later historians), would be the new pharaoh. Hetepheres had her husband, Snefru, buried within the "bent pyramid." The other more perfect pyramid at Dahsur the queen designated for herself. Then Hetepheres demanded that the great pyramid to be constructed under the direction of the unknown scholars be dedicated to Khufu. A new location was chosen for its construction, just north of Memphis at Gizeh.

The pyramid became the young Pharaoh Khufu's obsession. The whole nation was coerced to accomplish the stupendous feat. When the southern nomes rebelled, Khufu organized an army and crushed the revolt, chaining the captive citizens into slave labor.

The brilliant pyramid engineers urged the young pharaoh to build a magnificent Temenos to surround the pyramid, also a great temple, and high walls for protection. The project required 2,300,000 stone blocks, each one weighing

*an average of 2½ tons. Soon Khufu had exhausted his funds
and more rebellion was simmering. If the engineers,
mathematicians and architects were from Kamarina of Ur,
they may have reminded Khufu of the strategy of King
Akalamdu. If Akalamdu could create a god of the moon in
one evening, why could not Khufu do something similar?
"Surely the sun is greater than the moon," one may have
expounded. "Declare the sun, Re, to be the god of Kemi.
You, most honored Pharaoh, be the incarnation of Re. Man
cannot bear to look at the sun, so we shall say that the sun
comes to the people as their pharaoh that they might behold
him and obey him."*

*However it happened, the youthful Khufu seized upon the
idea and found that it gave him the extra authority many
withheld from him because of his age. He placed the blazing
disk of the sun on all the emblems of his reign, combining it
with the Horus falcon which was the symbol of the Lower
Land, his birthplace.*

*Priests of the one holy God were dismissed, replaced by
the priests of Re. The Urians may have helped Khufu form a
paganism that nearly equaled the one that had ruined Ur
and caused their own exile.*

*When Khufu's spectacular pyramid was completed, its
beauty and magnificence so intoxicated the now aging
pharaoh that he began another one to honor his son and the
heir to the throne, Khafre. The second did not surpass the
first but was almost as glorious.*

*The pyramids of Khufu and Khafre were built on a rock
plateau. Many of the interior stones were cut out of nearby
limestone. The softer sandstone strata were left unused and
stood out in large crags, jutting up from the quarry pits. One
particular mass of sandstone bothered Khafre because he
felt it obstructed the view of his new pyramid. A clever
architect designed a statue of a lion to be carved out of the
sandstone. It would appear to guard the pharaoh's tomb.
Khafre was easily convinced of the idea when the architect
suggested that the lion's head be made in Khafre's image.
The great popularity of the statue, later called the Sphinx by*

176

the Greeks, soothed Khafre's concern over his pyramid's slight inferiority to Khufu's.

The inconceivable genius and skill that built the great pyramids at Gizeh lasted less than sixty years. After that the secrets of construction were lost and only poorly built imitations followed.

During the next five centuries the strong centralized government of the pharaohs decayed and the nomarchs once again fought among themselves for the lost power. The first to lay claim to the throne was from the Lower Land. While the Lower Landers ruled, the cult of the sun god, Re, continued. However, the cult's influence gradually diminished. Except during the time of the mysterious pyramid builders, temples were never built to the god Re.

As foreign traders brought stories of Ishtar and Baal, the people of Kemi adopted the gods, fitting the deities' personalities to their own culture and needs. The Upper Landers were quicker to incorporate the new superstitions and beliefs. Most nomes chose Baal, a male counterpart of Ishtar, whom they renamed Osiris. Others preferred the female Ishtar version called Hathor.

As the Upper and Lower Lands again sought control and power, Re and Osiris became rival cults and were used to unify each side against the other. The Horus falcon and the sun disk of Re continued to represent the Lower Land. The Upper Land used the symbol of their land, the hawk, combined with a bull representing Osiris or sometimes a cow for Hathor.

The only lasting tribute perhaps paid to the Urians, whose ingenuity may have brought forth the reason-defying pyramids, was a lesser god named Thoth. Thoth was the name for Nanner-Sin. In the land of Kemi, the moon god Thoth was the god of learning, the inventor of writing—and the lord of magic.

Near the beginning of the Middle Kingdom in Egyptian history, the Upper Land continually besieged the capital set up by

177

the Lower Landers. The city finally collapsed under a bold attack from the distant Upper Land nome of Wase. The general who led the Upper Land revolt became Pharaoh Mentuhotep. When Abram and Sarai left for Kemi, Mentuhotep IV ruled as pharaoh. The time was approximately 1998 BC.

Chapter X
SHETEPIBRE OF KEMI

Shetepibre paced impatiently through the intersecting walkways of the gardens of Meketre, nomarch of Wase. The familiar paths were protected from the hot sunlight by overarching trellises of leafy vines with occasional clusters of grapes hanging temptingly down from the branches. Rows of stately date palms bordered and interlaced the nomarch's estate, while smaller fruit and flowering trees stood in immaculate pruned groupings between beds of flowers and herbs. In the center of the garden, old olive trees portaled broad tiled steps that descended down toward a glimmering reflection pool. Graceful sprays of papyrus planted beside the pool mirrored themselves on the still water, and fragrant lotus blossoms grew in the pool itself amid the flat green circles of their leaf pads.

Shetepibre sat restlessly on a stone bench beside the pool but rose quickly when he heard footsteps arriving. Shetepibre was a tall, trim but strong looking, man with sharp clear-cut features and dark copper-colored skin. His black hair was set in intricate rows of tight curls. He wore a flowing white linen tunic with wide pleated sleeves and an ornate jeweled collar. Shetepibre's appearance was far different from the last time he met Nefer-Tachenen in that same garden.

179

His heart beat excitedly as he heard Nefer's gentle feminine voice questioning the servant, "But who is it that wished to see me, Messuwy?"

The aging manservant chuckled quietly, "You will see soon enough, my ladyship. It is an old friend."

As Nefer descended the steps that led toward the pool she hesitated, looking at Shetepibre a moment before she recognized him. "Tepi? Is it really you?" she cried out delightedly. "When did you arrive in Wase? Where have you been all these years?"

Shetepibre's eyes followed her as she approached him. When he had left Wase Nefer was already a pretty girl with a quick mind and a happy enthusiastic temperament. Tepi always felt joy and at peace when he was near her.

Nefer was dressed in a high-waisted pale blue sheath that alluringly left much of her graceful body bare. It was a traditional Wase costume during the heat of summer, but Tepi had forgotten how exciting a beautiful young woman like Nefer could look in that style. A soft brown semi-circular scarf wrapped around Nefer's forehead. It was pulled behind her gold ringed ears and fell in sculptured folds along her neck. She wore jeweled bracelets on each arm and ankle. Nefer's eyes were darkly outlined and her eyelids glistened with blue antimony. Vermillion was painted lightly on her lips.

Shetepibre spoke reservedly, "Nefer-Tachenen, daughter of Meketre, I salute you. You are indeed a more lovely lady than when I last saw you. I did not think that would be possible."

"Such elegant speech. You sound just like the courtiers of the Lower Land," she laughed as she studied the changes that had occurred in the one she had once known so well as a young girl.

Tepi had been the son of Nefer's handmaid, a woman from Ta-sti. Ta-sti was the first southern nome of Kemi. It bordered the land of Kush. Like Tepi's mother, many of its people were of mixed Kushite blood. Tepi worked as errand and chore boy for the nomarch. Nefer often followed him around, helping him finish his tasks so that they could play

180

together in the garden. She reminded him as they talked of the reed boat they had made and how they floated in it together in the pool.

"I have spent many years studying at Avaris in the Lower Land," Tepi told her proudly.

"The Academy of Avaris! Tepi, how did you get to study there?"

"When I left your father's employ, as you may remember, I applied to be a soldier with pharaoh's militia. I was sent to the Jeb in Ta-sti to help guard the frontier. Because of my Kushite background the people across the border accepted me easily. On furloughs I traveled far into the interior. Each time I brought back gifts for the pharaoh of ivory, ebony, ostrich feathers . . . sometimes leopard skins and live giraffes. One expedition led me to find the hidden gold mines of Kush in the Red Sea hill country east of the Kushite Hapy."

"*You* found the gold mines? I thought the pharaoh himself and an exploring party found them," Nefer said in amazement.

"With me leading them," Tepi smiled. "Nefer, in this country Pharaoh Mentuhotep must receive all the honor and the glory if one is to succeed in his government. But for my reward, he sent me as his personal protégé to the Avaris Academy."

"Have you returned now to serve in pharaoh's court?" she asked.

"I shall be in Wase for several months. If you are willing, I would like to ask for your father's permission to escort you to the palace banquets."

As Tepi waited for her response, he noticed the color rising on her face. "I do not know. . . ," Nefer murmured.

"You do not think you father would approve of a former houseboy from the Western Bank . . . with Kushite blood? Is that it?" he asked apprehensively.

"It is just that I am the youngest. All of my brothers and sisters have been carefully married into Eastern Bank families. You know how my father feels about even the pharaoh's Western Bank background."

Tepi remembered. Meketre, Nefer's father, continued in a family line of nomarchs at Wase. But Meketre's otherwise kindly nature had been warped through the traditions of his upbringing. He and his father before him rankled under the pharaohs of the Mentuhoteps.

Sixty years earlier, when the nome of Wase led the final rebellion against the Lower Landers that were then in power, the twin cities of Wase on both banks of the Hapy River united in the effort under separate leaders. The Western Bank army went by land and attacked the capital from the desert. The Eastern Bank battalion arrived at night on the river. The total victory they accomplished was unexpected, quick and brutal. In the fray, however, the Eastern Bank commander was killed. He was the nomarch of Wase at that time and Meketre's grandfather. Mentuhotep, the other leader of the coalition, seized authority and declared himself pharaoh of the Land. He took the added name of Smatowy, which means, "He who unites the Two Lands."

Smatowy Mentuhotep easily rallied support from the Lower and Upper Lands, for the people were weary of weak leadership and continuing revolution. Only the Eastern Bank of Wase held the new dynasty in contempt and was aghast at the power that had been wrenched from their hands. In conciliatory efforts, Smatowy Mentuhotep appointed the dead nomarch's son, Meketre's father, to assume the nomarchy of Wase. This might have been solace enough had Smatowy not decided to move the capital of the united Kemi to Wase and build a spectacular palace on the Eastern Bank, overshadowing all the other buildings of the city. Since then the nomarch's authority in Wase had been continually overruled by the pharaoh, who maintained his residence, his court, and his army at the new capital.

"I thought perhaps your father would approve of me now, Nefer," Tepi said hopefully. "I have as much education or more than anyone else in Wase. And the pharaoh has promised me a high commission in the militia."

"My father has become bitter and very defensive, Tepi. I am one of the few things over which he feels he has absolute control."

"Yes, I remember when he had such control over me! My mother and I were indentured for another five years at the time I left. He had plans to make me into a eunuch so that he would not have to worry about me around you and your sisters. My mother pleaded with him and sold herself to him for an additional five years so that he would not mutilate me. That was when I was released to join the militia."

Nefer looked puzzled and shocked. "You must be wrong, Tepi. I cannot believe he would do that. Besides your mother only stayed the five years of her first contract."

"After your mother died, Meketre took *other* favors from my mother!" he answered sharply.

Nefer could not look up at Tepi after his last words. "Perhaps you had better leave now. I will speak to my father of your request."

"Would *you* want to go with me?" he asked her earnestly.

When she did not respond, he lifted her face with his hand and pulled her gently close to him with his other arm about her waist. He tenderly kissed her cheek and whispered, "Ours could be a beautiful love, Nefer."

"An impossible love, Tepi," she replied, tears welling up in her eyes.

The next time Tepi called at the nomarch's villa to see Nefer, he was instead ushered in to Meketre. The nomarch greeted him warmly and asked the servant, Messuwy, to bring cups of wine.

"Sit down, Tepi," directed Meketre as he motioned toward several low chairs where they seated themselves and Messuwy served them.

"I felt it would be easier on Nefer if I talked to you," Meketre began.

"You do not want me to see her?" Tepi asked pointedly.

Meketre sat up in his chair and looked straight at Tepi. "I have always liked you. Your mother, too, is very dear to me."

The nomarch paused to sip his wine before he continued. "I am sure you will think I am wrong in my attitude, but I cannot allow you to be with Nefer," he stated flatly. "She is of marriageable age. Anyone who would escort her would be thought to have my approval for marriage as well. Ours is a proud family. We have suffered humiliation many times. I will not accept the jeers of those who would mock me if Nefer should marry a Westerner . . . or one of Kushite blood!"

Tepi could not suppress his rising anger. "You would deny her happiness because of your own vanity and pride?"

Meketre became flustered. "You will find, Tepi," he exclaimed tartly, "that keeping one's pride *is* happiness!"

Tepi put down his untouched wine cup and stood. Looking down at Meketre he replied, "I hope I never have such a narrow view!"

Tepi walked across the room to leave. Meketre called after him, "I really wish you well, my boy!"

Tepi turned, his anger now seething within him. "I warn you, Nomarch of Wase, you shall some day regret your precious pride!" he cried out defiantly.

Tepi returned to his quarters and for several days struggled with his depression and the rejection he had received. Attending the palace banquet alone, he saw Nefer at a distance. She was with a young man named Iperwer, one of Meketre's lesser officials.

The next day Tepi requested to see Pharaoh Mentuhotep. They met for the noon meal in the elegant palace garden. When Tepi arrived, the pharaoh was already seated on one of the low cushioned benches. Elaborate dishes of food were being brought before him and placed on the table. The air smelled of the rich delicacies and the sweet fragrance of the flowering trees and plants. Servants with tall red ostrich-plumes stood by the shaded eating area to fan away the flies.

Mentuhotep called out to Tepi as soon as he saw him, "Shetepibre! Good! I have been thinking of you a great deal lately. I am glad you wished to see me. Tell me, first, what is on your mind! Then I will tell you some of my new plans!"

"Your majesty, great pharaoh of the united lands of Kemi, master of the river Hapy, your humble servant desires only to bask in your golden friendship and do whatever you would bid him," Tepi said solemnly, bowing before the pharaoh.

"Perfectly said, Tepi! They taught you well the flattering lips of the Lower Land!" Mentuhotep laughed uproariously, his fat jowls and rolling belly bouncing and his gold and jeweled ornaments tinkling.

"Come, sit down, my son!" Mentu, as the pharaoh was addressed unofficially, smiled as he admired Tepi's fine appearance. "Yes, and how I wish I had a son like you!" he added affectionately.

Tepi looked at him sympathically. "No conception yet, my lord?" he asked quietly.

Mentu shook his head sadly. "I have annulled the marriage. Find me a woman that can excite this old body, Shetepibre. Then maybe I might still have an heir. Only my precious first wife could stimulate me. But all she bore were stillborn. Now she lies buried with them."

Mentu allowed his lonely heart to dwell a few fleeting moments on the woman he had adored for many years. "But now, tell me," the pharaoh resumed. "Why did you wish to see me?"

Tepi had not planned to tell the pharaoh about his experience with Meketre, but only to request a transfer of location. However, because Mentu had been frank in his own problems, Tepi told him about his encounter with Meketre and of his love for the nomarch's daughter, Nefer-Tachenen.

"Meketre is a noble and intelligent man," Mentu said as he offered the plates of food to Tepi. "He is also a ridiculous bigoted fool! That he would allow his daughter to be escorted by that meek, sickly Iperwer instead of you shows how insane he has become!"

Tepi grinned, "I am glad to see that we Western Bank men think alike!"

Mentu laughed heartily again and then stared curiously at Tepi. "You know," he mused, suddenly pensive, "what I was going to share with you might please you. You may never win Nefer's hand in marriage, but you may end up in authority over her father!"

"What do you mean?" Tepi asked curiously.

Mentu wiped his face with one of the steaming hot towels brought in by the servants. His voice grew serious as he

185

spoke. "Lately, the Kushites have ambushed every expedition I have sent into their country. They have even come down the Hapy and attacked our settlements below the Jeb. It is time that the land of Kush belonged to us. We should be one people!"

"I agree!" Tepi said emphatically. "I used to make plans how it might be done every time I travelled in Kush."

"I just thought you might be my answer!" Mentu exclaimed proudly. "What are your ideas?"

"After we finish our meal I will show you in more detail on your maps. But basically my plan would be to build a series of fortresses along the Hapy in Kushite territory with at least two fortresses at Semna, the place where the river can be easily forded by land caravans. Each fortress would be close enough to another to sound an alarm. Within minutes, an attacked fortress could call in a thousand reinforcements."

"How long would it take you and how many men?"

Tepi responded deliberately, "It will take every man under thirty . . . two, maybe three years."

"You would release them after the inundation for the plowing?" Mentu questioned.

"Of course," Tepi answered. "But I would need to keep a militia of several thousand."

Mentu pondered the idea. "If other pharaohs can pull men off their farms to build their cemeteries, I should be able to do it to conquer the land of Kush."

Then the pharaoh looked thoughtfully at Tepi. "Shetepibre, I trust you. If you are able to accomplish what you told me in that length of time, I shall reward you with great honor."

"I will need six months to do some scouting. Also I will need your best architects," Tepi explained enthusiastically, the new challenge sweeping away his past depression. "We should build the fortresses as we make advances, otherwise the Kushites will find ways to cut off our flank. Craftsmen and soldiers would need to fight together, then build together. Our hardest battles would be the first ones. Once we make the strongholds, the whole country will fall."

Mentu leaned back, enjoying the plan Tepi had presented. "You will have two major difficulties as I see it," the pharaoh responded. "You are young, and you have no position of authority. Perhaps I shall give you your reward before you begin!"

"What do you mean, my lord?"

"Tepi . . . I think I will make you the Grand Vizier of the Upper Land!"

Tepi sat in silence, astounded by what Mentu had suggested. His mouth agape and his eyes fixed on Mentu, he tried to speak. "But . . . but I thought Antefoker. . . ."

"Antefoker is a wise old counselor. But I need a wise young counselor as well as a wise old counselor. So, instead of only one grand vizier, I will have two. Antefoker is from the delta, so he can advise me on the Lower Land. You . . . you are perfect! You are part of Kemi and part of Kush. You shall advise me concerning the Upper Land and . . . the New Land we shall conquer together!"

Tepi could say nothing for a while. He smiled and thought of the strange paradox, "Shetepibre, Grand Vizier of the Upper Land! And if it had not been for my mother's sacrifice, I would forever be Tepi, the eunuch of Meketre."

Mentu and Tepi agreed that the announcement of his appointment should not be made until Tepi returned from his scouting in Kush. They went together to the palace to study the maps and make further plans.

Sometime after Tepi's return from Kush, the pharaoh proclaimed an appropriate celebration to honor the appointment of Shetepibre as Grand Vizier of the Upper Land. Hoping that the announcement would have impressed Meketre, Tepi went to the nomarch's home and requested to see Nefer. Meketre sent Messuwy to the gate with a message. The old servant looked apologetic as he repeated his master's words, "Nomarch Meketre wishes me to inform you that marriage papers have been filed for Nefer-Tachenen and Iperwer. They are legally married. Their celebration has been delayed only because of the new husband's illness."

Messuwy waited. "Do you wish to respond?" he asked softly.

187

"Yes," Tepi replied caustically. "Tell Nomarch Meketre that I shall not bother him again!"

Tepi left abruptly, a lonely stinging pain in his heart. He vowed that would be the last time in his life he would allow anyone to humiliate him without receiving vengeance.

During the next few months of preparation, Tepi's bitterness turned into a ruthless perfectionism. He drove those under him with an exactness that brought fear and obedience—and, surprisingly, an intense loyalty.

His ambition to complete what he had set out to do consumed him. Only on the day of Nefer's marriage celebration did he leave his planning tables. That day he went to his rooms where he drank strong wine until he was thoroughly drunk.

By the end of two years, the campaigns led by Tepi into Kush were successful. Fourteen fortresses were established, one at every key point on the Hapy River in Kushite territory. The forts were built of mud bricks with walls twelve cubits thick. Since the Kushite warriors usually attacked by land, deep dry moat-like ditches were dug around each fortress.

The Kushites admired strength. They were almost proud of the great fortresses built to subject them. When they learned that the grand vizier who led the fight against their armies was part Kushite, their readiness to do battle lost much of its fervor. Many of the Kushite warriors deserted and sought to serve under the great Shetepibre.

Tepi necessarily returned often during the Kushite offense to consult with Pharaoh Mentuhotep. Each time he endured seeing Nefer with her husband Iperwer who had risen in rank to be Meketre's treasurer.

At a banquet celebrating the final victory over Kush, Tepi inquired of the Pharaoh, "I do not recall that Iperwer, the nomarch's treasurer, was ever sent to duty in Kush. Did you excuse him?"

"No, not that I remember. Everyone under thirty was to serve at least one of the two years, regardless of his position," declared Mentu. "Meketre probably worked up some scheme to keep him from going."

"May I pursue it?" Tepi asked firmly.

Mentu studied his vizier and smiled, "I would say it was your noble duty to do so!"

"Good!" Tepi nodded. "I think I know just the duty that will give the Treasurer of Wase some excitement!"

The next week the pharaoh and Tepi embarked on the royal armada toward Memphis to have important consultations with Antefoker, now officially appointed the Grand Vizier of the Lower Land. The pharaoh's barge was surrounded by a fleet of smaller craft carrying guards, servants and supplies. Soon after the royal boats oared north from Wase, another long craft lifted its sails and departed to the south. It was a militia boat filled with new recruits to replace the frequent casualties at Semna in Kush. A frightened Iperwer, Treasurer of Wase, sat among the recently summoned men.

Chapter XI
EXILE IN AVARIS

The night before entering Kemi, Abram's company camped within sight of the green pastures of the Lower Land of Kemi. The journey had been difficult, for the route from Canaan was dry and barren. All the travelers were weak from the journey and the short food rations. Other refugees suffering the same plight were also crowding to Kemi to find sanctuary.

That night, as Abram and Sarai slept in their tent, Abram awoke from a dream. In the dream he saw a cedar tree and a palm tree. Suddenly some men came and began to cut down the cedar and leave the palm to stand alone. The palm tree cried out to them, "Do not cut down the cedar tree. For whoever cuts it down will suffer a curse." So the men spared the cedar because of the words of the palm.

Arising from his sleep, Abram pondered and prayed about the dream. Then he awakened Sarai. "It may not sound like it, Sarai, but it was terrifying," he recalled after relating the dream to her. "It was a portent from God, Sarai, a warning! I felt that *I* was that cedar, and *you* were the palm. The men in the dream were seeking to cut me down that they might have you! I fear both of our promises, our land and our heir, will be lost!"

"What should we do, Abram?"

"Sarai, if anyone in Kemi ever asks you about our relationship, tell them I am your brother, that Terah is our common father. Let them assume you have a husband still in Canaan. For if once they think I am your husband they will kill me so that you might become a widow and be free for their taking!"

The rest of the dark night, Sarai wept and prayed because of the dream and Abram's words.[12]

The surcharge on foreigners coming into Kemi was excessive. Those who could not pay were required to sign indenture contracts for two to five years of service for the pharaoh. Anyone captured attempting to enter illegally was forced to sign longer contracts or be executed.

As Abram's group approached the border, men of the militia directed them to herd their greatly diminished flocks into mud brick corrals and to report for inspection. They joined other travelers in a large detention room. There, men and women were separated and made to strip themselves of their clothing and bathe. Those destined for indenture were given specially dyed immigrant clothing. Their own garments, as well as those they carried with them, were burned. Inspection officials, bored by their duties, often watched the women unclothe. Sarai's beautiful body did not escape their attention.

When Abram and Sarai came for interrogation, the officials kept bestowing compliments on her. To amuse themselves they asked her far more questions than were routine. In the process they were astounded at her breadth of wisdom and knowledge. Abram did his best to interrupt and try to hasten the inspection, but he only succeeded in irritating the questioners.

"What relationship is this man to you?" one of them asked pointedly. "Did you not say he was just a kinsman?"

Sarai remained calm, her inner prayers giving her assurance. "He is my brother. I was adopted through the courts of Ur by Terah, his father."

Abram spoke up, "We are only here for a short time because of the famine! We have paid the entry tax!"

191

"Silence!" snapped the official. "If we want answers from you, we will get them later!"

"Now, my dear lady," he said pleasantly to Sarai. "We have found you well trained in the speaking and writing of languages, skilled in the textile arts, a teacher of young women in many fields of study, and perhaps the loveliest foreigner to ever pass through the gates of Kemi!"

Abram was incensed. "You have no reason to detain us further," he complained. "Release my sister that we might join our people and be on our way!"

The official eyed Abram suspiciously. "You seem unduly alarmed for just a brother of this woman," he said bitingly. "If she is only under a brother's protection, any man has a right to pursue her!"

Sarai smiled shyly at the man and explained, "This man *is* my brother. But I am also a married woman. I have a living husband."

"And where is your 'living husband'?" the official demanded.

Sarai looked down and paused before she answered. "God knows," she affirmed softly.

The official looked sympathic. "So you are married to one of those who took off and left you with your brother when times were hard! Well, if you remain in Kemi five years and he does not come for you, you are a free woman. The courts will declare him dead!"

Guards then ushered Abram and Sarai out of the room. They rejoined the others and began leading the flocks toward Avaris.

The drought and famine continued in the land of Canaan. High prices charged foreigners in Kemi for food and pasture-land soon depleted Abram's remaining funds. The animals had to be sold and his people were forced to sign five year indenture contracts. Once again Abram found himself humbled by the Lord. In his tent pitched outside of Avaris, he prayed fervently and desperately, "I have nothing, my God! Nothing left! Why must you test me again? Have I not been faithful, my Lord? How much longer must we wait?"

192

Although Abram heard no voice of the Lord, he did feel a comforting assurance that he was where God intended him to be. His weakened faith was strengthened, and he took courage once again.

Abram and Sarai applied at the Avaris Academy for teaching positions. The directors of the Academy heard their requests and interviewed them. Abram was immediately offered a position to instruct in astronomy and mathematics and was released from taxes and other burdens levied on foreigners. Sarai was asked to serve as an Academy scribe, translating literature of Kemi into Akkadian and Sumerian. Abram and Sarai lived quietly in Avaris for nearly five years. During all that time, they took care when in public to appear as brother and sister.

Except for the strain of this deception, their stay in Kemi was pleasant. Abram leased a large villa near the outskirts of the city and purchased cattle and other possessions as he had funds. One by one his people were released as their contracts expired, and they rejoined his household.

It was at this time that Antefoker, the grand vizier of the Lower Land, arrived in Avaris. He called together the Lower Land nomarchs, high militia officers, and the Avaris Academy directors for an urgent meeting. They gathered in a small but elaborate meeting hall in one of the Avaris nomarchy buildings. Antefoker requested the doors to be shut for privacy and signaled the men to come to order.

All eyes focused on the short, business-like figure of Antefoker. His position and his innate dignity commanded attention.

"Gentlemen! I have called this meeting to review the matters I will be laying before Pharaoh Mentuhotep," he began crisply. "The pharaoh and . . . the other grand vizier . . . are visiting nomes of the Upper Land enroute to Memphis. When I meet with them in a few days, we will be discussing my list of future projects.

"As you know," Antefoker went on, "our energies and our resources have recently been drained southward. For two years our people have been drafted to fight wars with Kush and build the fortresses. To this I have had no strong objections. Kush is a valuable asset!"

There were begrudging nods of agreement among the Lower Landers. Antefoker paused and then resumed his speech. "My problem, my friends, I am sure, is obvious. For several years, though the capital was in Wase, my offices were in Memphis. I could maintain a balance of emphasis. Now, with young Shetepibre's appointment, my influence is weakened. I fear the Lower Land will continue to suffer neglect unless we can do something to capture Mentuhotep's attention!"

"We dare not mention building his tomb monument," shuddered the nomarch of Avaris. "He would probably want that built near Wase as well!"

"Gifts are useless," another nomarch declared remorsefully. "With the long famine in Canaan, the pharaoh has become surfeited with wealth from the foreigners."

One of the militia officials seated at the meeting was Hirqnos. He had risen to his high rank during the past few years. When Abram and Sarai first entered Kemi, Hirqnos was the border official who was Sarai's persistent interrogator. After Antefoker had listened to the comments of most of the others, Hirqnos motioned to be heard.

"Yes, Captain," acknowledged the grand vizier.

"Your excellency, I believe it would be correct to say that since the annulment of the pharaoh's last marriage no other woman has been able to hold his interest. Am I right, sir?"

"That is my understanding," Antefoker agreed.

"If I may speak bluntly . . .?"

"You may, Captain Hirqnos. Do proceed."

"In my humble opinion, gentlemen, we need to present the pharaoh with a suitable queen . . . someone intelligent and ingenious enough to entertain the man, wise enough to keep him in line, and beautiful enough to excite his fading . . . virility!"

"Are you not suggesting an impossible combination?" joked another officer. "When a woman is young and alluring she is seldom wise. And when wise, seldom. . . ."

194

"But I know such a woman!" Hirqnos grinned slyly as he turned and looked at the Academy directors. "A beautiful foreigner. . . ."

"Not Sarai!" gasped the chief director. "She is too refined to be a palace ornament for that rustic Upper Lander!"

Antefoker's bead-like eyes shot toward the director. "*Is* she such a woman?" he demanded incisively.

The director was flustered. "She is all of that and more!" he said agitatedly. "She is also a foreigner and has a living husband!"

Hirqnos rose to his feet and thumped his fist sharply on the table. "This woman, Sarai, has lived here with her brother, Abram of Terrakki, over five years. No border records show that a husband has joined her in that time. By our laws and statutes she is a widow!"

There was silence in the room. Antefoker pulled at his chin, and his brows knitted tightly together as he contemplated. "What you say about the law is true, Hirqnos. But would she be willing?"

The distressed Academy directors shook their heads. The chief director spoke up, "Sarai and her brother Abram are very dear to us. Never have we had a more brilliant or able professor than Abram. Sarai, too, has opened classes for young women and has been an excellent scribe for us. We would not want to abuse them. Truly they have given much to the Land. Within the next month they plan to return to Canaan."

Antefoker listened carefully. "I have a suggestion," he announced. "Why do you not recommend, as chief director of the Academy, that I present this woman and her brother to the pharaoh for special honor and recognition. I will inform the pharaoh of the woman's widowhood. If he seems interested in her, we might pursue the matter. If not, the woman would be free to return with her brother."

The directors reluctantly consented.

"Hirqnos," Antefoker called. "Since you know the legal details of this case, will you and a small company of men escort the woman and her brother to Memphis? I should like to call on you to inform the pharaoh of their accomplishments."

Abram and Sarai were honored by the request to be presented to the pharaoh. They arrived in Memphis with Hirqnos and were lodged in the city not far from the palace to await Antefoker's summons. Lot was also with them. He had recently arrived in Avaris to accompany Abram and Sarai back to Canaan. Their thoughts and conversations were centered on their soon departure, and the trip to Memphis was regarded only as a happy climax to their stay in Kemi.

Chapter XII
THE ABDUCTION

Pharaoh Mentuhotep's armada passed by the scenic farmlands of the Upper Land, pausing just north of Wase. The boats slowly drifted by the site of the unfinished tomb project of Mentu's father. A short distance further on, the entire armada pulled to shore at the gleaming temple and shrine of Smatowy Mentuhotep, the first Mentuhotep and Mentu's grandfather. Both memorial locations held prominent positions on the west bank.

The royal party including the pharaoh and Shetepibre disembarked and walked through the lovely tree-shaded tiered courtyards. They then paid homage to the statues of Osiris and Smatowy Mentuhotep in the magnificent colonnaded temple that bore a pyramid replica as its capstone. The tomb shrine had been built on a natural rock plateau. It was secluded high above the river, cupped around by protecting high cliffs.

As they descended the flights of stone steps to return to the boats, Mentu lamented to Tepi, "My father wanted his burial place to equal this. But it is difficult to gather enthusiasm to build for the dead."

"Have you considered using your father's unfinished site for your own?" Tepi inquired. "You could remove his remains and place them here with the first Mentuhotep."

Mentu shrugged. "If I thought I did not have to spend the rest of my reign erecting my grave, I might be interested."

"It is wise to keep the people occupied in service to their pharaoh," Tepi reasoned convincingly. "The young men of the Land are well disciplined to forfeit part of their time for your concerns. To have an ongoing project would keep the country organized. Then should forces be needed elsewhere, they would be ready for deployment."

Mentu looked wistful. "The only thing I have ever desired at my death," he professed slowly, "is to be entombed in a pure white sarcophagus. I have envisioned a great statue of my body as part of the lid. I would like the whole top of the sarcophagus to be carved from a single solid block of the purest alabaster."

"My pharaoh, you shall have your dream," vowed Tepi impetuously. "You shall have your sarcophagus in less time than it took to conquer Kush!"

"Only the graywacke quarries on the Red Sea have produced such stone," Mentu commented. "But the route through the Wadi Hammamat from the Hapy River to the Red Sea is now impossible."

"The able Henu, steward of Samatowy Mentuhotep, your grandfather, used only three thousand men to quarry the white limestone and alabaster needed for his temple statues," Tepi countered. "We had over twenty thousand men each year in Kush."

"To clear the desert of the wild bedouin tribes and redig the wells is a high price to pay for a slab of alabaster, Tepi," Mentu opined as they reboarded the barge.

The pharaoh's words gave Tepi an opportunity later to present a plan he had been carefully nurturing. He had hoped to be able to discuss it at length before the scheduled meetings with Antefoker. Tepi rightly suspected that the grand vizier of the Lower Land would be well armed with many of his own designs and projects when they gathered together in Memphis.

After the voyage was reinitiated and food was being served, Tepi confidently began. "Concerning the desert route through the Wadi Hammamat, my pharaoh, I have another reason for reopening that access."

"Other than stone?" Mentu questioned, his interest quickening.

"Isn't it time that we have a port on the Red Sea that would serve the Upper Land?"

"You mean for large ocean craft? Yes, Tepi, it would be good, not just for the Upper Land but the whole country. But no one has ever found the harbor that was once on those shores."

"But I have heard that the secret harbor *has* been located," Tepi responded eagerly. "Some of my men came across one of the desert bedouins a while back. The man had evidently been thrown out of the tribal community for stealing. Both his right hand and his tongue were cut off.

"He was full of revenge," Tepi continued. "With signals he let my men know that he wanted to tell them something very important. He was brought to me. After he drew many pictures I began to understand his message."

"Yes . . . go on!" Mentu urged him.

"As you know, histories of Kemi by Imhotep spoke of a Red Sea port. In those days people of the Upper Land sailed directly from their own port to Kamarina of Ur, Tilmun and India."

Mentu's eyes widened. "Are you telling me that this bedouin has knowledge of the lost port?"

"I do believe so," Tepi declared earnestly. "The man drew pictures of a mountainous cove that would be very difficult to detect from the Red Sea because of an extended shore of protruding rocks. However, he showed me that there was a deep channel that wove between the rocks and entered the cove. Also, by his signs I learned that the bedouins are negotiating in Avaris for boats."

"Boats? . . . bedouins?" Mentu gasped, suddenly realizing the implications. "Pirating?"

"Exactly!" Tepi injected. "If we should open up the Wadi Hammamat route they will put up quite a fight to keep us out."

Mentu nodded in agreement. Then he smiled warmly at his young friend and vizier. "You have been leading up to this all day, haven't you, Tepi? Let me hear your plan!"

Tepi looked directly into Mentu's eyes as he spoke. "What if I led the militia of twenty thousand men across the desert, cleared the bedouins out, found the lost port . . . and brought back your stone!"

"It couldn't be done!" Mentu interrupted with astonishment. "The men would die of thirst before you reached the Red Sea. Those wells, even when they were active, would not water men and animals of more than six regiments at the most!"

"We would not be dependent on the wells," Tepi assured him.

"How then?"

"The water could be carried in jars . . . enough to last to the Red Sea. There is a great cistern at the quarries that is fed by an underground river. Once we have found it, our jars can be refilled for the return trip."

"It is risky, Tepi," Mentu cautioned. "Would you be willing to command such a march?"

"I would only be disappointed if I were *not* allowed to do so," he replied sincerely.

"We will discuss it further with Antefoker, Tepi. I am *very* interested in your proposal," Mentu reflected, ". . . *very* interested!"

The armada with the pharaoh and his grand vizier of the Upper Land arrived at the canal entrance to Memphis a day later. It was nearing sunset as the boats were hitched to the oxen that waited in paired teams along the canal bank. The old white walled city lay far in the distance. To the north, the mammoth pyramids of Khufu and Khafre rose up on the rock plateau of Gizeh, flawlessly profiled by the burning late afternoon sun. The panorama was mysteriously hypnotic.

Mentu's eyes were fixed on the pyramids. Tepi too looked toward Gizeh. "Do you want one of those erected?" he asked the pharaoh, carefully trying not to reveal any emotion in his voice.

"No, I am afraid that kind of monument is a lost talent," Mentu smilingly replied. "Nor do I want a country of slaves for years to come. Whatever you and Antefoker can build for me in the next few years, I will accept."

Antefoker and a full honor guard met the royal barge at the palace quay. The pinched-faced grand vizier of the Lower Land had every detail of the reception in immaculate order. No point of courtly etiquette was overlooked. The urbane Antefoker welcomed Mentuhotep with profuse compliments and an array of gifts. He was coldly reserved with Tepi, although he allowed no aspect of protocol to be forgotten.

The three walked between the honor guard to the nearby gardens of the ancient but well restored palace—Tepi, tall and erect, his new office and experiences of command giving him assurance and maturity; Mentu, once strong and athletic, now heavy from the rich food and sedentary life of his royal position; and short, bald, tense and alert Antefoker—a thin man except for a round pouchy stomach. All three were dressed in gold trimmed white tunics with brilliant red capes that hung down their backs from gold shoulder rings. Mentu wore the high red and white crown that symbolized his reign over the united Land. Antefoker and Tepi wore smaller headpieces adorned with symbols of both the Upper and Lower Lands.

During several days of conferences, banqueting and entertainment, Tepi noticed Antefoker's persistent attempts to regain his former power. Before Tepi's appointment, Antefoker was grand vizier pro tempore. He had held the position for over five years and enjoyed the full privileges the high rank afforded. But Mentu had been loath to have a Lower Lander be his chief consultant. He held back a final appointment, especially when Antefoker insisted that the duties of the grand vizier could only properly be executed from a central location such as Memphis.

Tepi admired Antefoker, even though he realized the older man's ambitions. Antefoker's knowledge of Kemi, its past and present, was unequalled. To his credit, being a Lower Lander, Antefoker did not want to see the country divided again. His single devotion was to make the Land, during his own lifetime, achieve its highest glory. That he must labor for this goal under a provincial pharaoh was frustrating. That he must share his grand vizier's power with a son of nobody was almost intolerable. Tepi sympathized with Antefoker's position, but had no intention of taking a subordinate role.

As the meetings continued, the discussions between the pharaoh, his two viziers, and other consultants followed an agenda prepared by Antefoker. Each time a project required any immediate action, Mentu approved the proposal but asked that it be postponed. Antefoker's patience finally could stand no more. "Why, good Pharaoh, possessor of all wisdom and honor, do you persist in vetoing these pressing matters until a later date?"

Mentu was tolerant of the outburst. "I have met with you all of these days, Antefoker. I have listened, and I approve of all of your suggestions . . . except the one to move the capital back here to Memphis."

"It was only a suggestion, my lord," Antefoker nervously replied.

"A good suggestion," Mentu agreed. "But I do not want to live in Memphis. Nor do I want to die here."

"Memphis is the departing place of the great pharaohs of Kemi," Antefoker quietly reminded him.

"Then it is time that we pharaohs spread our dust in other parts of our great Land!" Mentu exclaimed. "Tepi, tell Antefoker the plans we discussed on the barge!"

Antefoker's spirit was inwardly crushed as Tepi told him about opening up the Wadi Hammamat route, the building of Mentu's monument, and the hope of at last discovering the lost port. The grand vizier of the Lower Land knew he dare not resist the venture. Instead, in courtly manner, the little man feigned animated excitement and interest.

"What a glorious project, Shetepibre," he praised the young man. "We shall need men and supplies for the desert clearing, ships to transport the stones should you find the port, and the finest architects in the Land for Mentuhotep's monument. What superlative ideas, my pharaoh! I am in agreement! We should not do anything else until this effort is begun!"

Mentu was elated at Antefoker's unexpected enthusiasm. Tepi watched his counterpart with amazement. "Shrewd," he thought. No better word to describe Antefoker could come to his mind.

The aggressive competition between the two viziers, however, did not stop. It was still obvious that night during a late banquet. With one on either side, the pharaoh lightheartedly mentioned to Antefoker that Tepi was going to search for a woman beautiful enough to arouse Mentu's enfeebled desires.

"I should like to assist in this worthy venture," Antefoker said drily, but there was an insistence in his tone.

Mentu laughed, partly from amusement and partly from an excess of wine. He put his arm around Antefoker's shoulders, saying, "I know you are wise about my government, Antefoker, but surely Tepi would be a better judge of women!"

"We shall see, my lord," Antefoker replied, smiling to hide his irritation.

Abruptly, Antefoker excused himself from the pharaoh and went to one of the lower tables where Hirqnos and his men were dining. "Would you and perhaps two of your men be so kind, Captain Hirqnos, to speak before the pharaoh," he said softly, the intensity of the look in his eyes communicating more than the words of his voice. "I should like him to hear every detail of the . . . *physical* attractions of the woman Sarai!"

"Of course, my lord," Hirqnos answered as he rose quickly.

Then when only Hirqnos could hear, the grand vizier whispered, "Could you get her here tonight if he becomes interested . . . by force if necessary?"

"Within minutes!" Hirqnos responded assuredly.

Antefoker led Hirqnos and two of his companions before the pharaoh and Tepi. "There is a woman whom I was going to present to you in the morning. I should like these men to speak in her behalf. She and her brother are foreigners, educated in Ur. They have been recommended for honor by the Avaris Academy. The woman's husband has been declared legally dead, since he has not appeared in the Land during five years. Presumably he died in the famine. The dear lady must return with her brother to the desolate land of Canaan unless she can be spared such a fate!"

Mentuhotep waved for Antefoker to stop. "Must we discuss business this late? Put her on a pension if you like and award her citizenship. Come now, Antefoker, enjoy the rest of your meal!"

"But my good pharaoh, listen to these men describe the woman," Antefoker pleaded.

Before the pharaoh could resist, Hirqnos and his companions each in turn began extolling in vivid descriptive terms the fascinating beauty of Sarai. Mentu became slowly excited as he heard them out, and a desire to see Sarai for himself began to sweep over him. "I must see such a woman!" he commanded. "I must see her immediately!"

With a detectable glint of victory, Antefoker cast a glance at Tepi then curtly ordered Hirqnos, "Fetch her!"

Hirqnos signaled his other men at the table and the band of soldiers wove their way out of the banqueting hall, through the dark paths of the palace gardens, and out into the city. Soon Hirqnos was pounding at the door of Abram and Sarai's lodging.

When Abram opened the door, the light from the oil lamp he was carrying revealed the soldiers and their unsheathed swords. The dream of the cedar and the palm trees flashed before him. Abram suddenly knew that his latent fears were now being realized.

"The pharaoh is calling for your sister," Hirqnos spoke frankly. "We have described her great beauty to him. He wishes to see if all that we have said is true."

"We are to come before him in the morning! Can he not wait until a proper hour?" Abram answered evasively.

"The man is Pharaoh Mentuhotep!" shouted Hirqnos. "If he has desire for the woman tonight, then tonight *is* the 'proper hour'!"

"But she has retired. . . ."

"We have garments for her at the palace. Bring her here as she is at once," Hirqnos commanded, his voice becoming harsh and angry. "Or I shall run you through with this sword . . . perhaps the woman as well if she resists!"

Abram mounted the steps to the upper hallway. Sarai and Lot had heard the conversation and were waiting for him. Tears were streaming down Sarai's face. "I cannot, Abram. I cannot go!" she cried.

Abram's eyes stared blankly. "I want to destroy those men and rescue you from this, Sarai. But such heroics will not save you. This is not a test for *us,* it is a *test for God!*"

He embraced her and held her tightly as sobbing emotions shook his body. "God!" he cried out. "Curse those who curse us! God! God! Help us!"

Hirqnos, hearing the loud cry, brandished his sword and clambered up the long flight of stairs, his men following behind him. The sight of Sarai calmly pulling her cloak about her stopped him. "I am ready to accompany you," she said quietly, as Abram and Lot stood dejectedly to one side.

When Sarai was brought before Mentuhotep, his heart was moved with love for her and passion mounted in his body. Sarai's mature beauty surpassed that which he had so loved in his first wife. Wine inebriated Mentuhotep's inhibitions, and he ordered that she be prepared to be brought to his bedchamber.

"Should you not wait, my pharaoh," Tepi vainly cautioned him. "If she is a refined and wise woman as Antefoker says, you will offend her!"

Tepi's interference in front of Sarai annoyed Mentu. "That the pharaoh of Kemi wishes to sleep with her should be a *privilege* not an offense!" Mentu blurted indignantly. "You have other business to be about, Grand Vizier Shetepibre. I want you to leave, no later than dawn, for Wase. Organize the desert campaign immediately!"

Antefoker sat a short distance away, his fingers tapping lightly on the table. A well-pleased and satisfied smile traced his lips.

Then forgetting Tepi, Mentu turned to Hirqnos, "Her brother? Did he object?"

"Not when I threatened to cut him through!" Hirqnos joked, his companions all laughing with him.

Mentu stared again at Sarai's beauty as she stood before him, a sheer gown covering her body. Her eyes were downcast, but she refused to be ashamed. Mentu's thoughts grew possessive. "I want no man to take her away from me! Perhaps he lied? Perhaps he is her husband? I want no charge of adultery to mar my reign!"

"Then we shall return and kill him, also the nephew that is with him," Hirqnos offered.

Sarai controlled her fears and apprehensions as she overheard the conversation. Holding her head erect with dignity, she smiled and said gently, "Pharaoh Mentuhotep! I will go willingly to your bedchamber. But if you bereave me of my good brother and nephew, I cannot be anything but a sorrowful companion."

Mentu's heart melted with adoration at her unexpected words. Tepi saw the opportunity to regain the pharaoh's favor. "I shall be glad to enlist the services of the woman's brother and nephew for the desert march. Rest assured, my pharaoh, they shall be with me and out of your way by sun-up!" he promised.

The pharaoh was unsteady as he stood and leaned across the table, his eyes beholding Sarai. "Does that please you?"

Sarai looked at Tepi, her dark eyes meeting his. "You will not harm them?" she asked.

Tepi answered lightly, "As the pharaoh is my witness, I will treat them with the honor they deserve!"

Sarai's questioning eyes remained fixed upon him. Tepi saw that the double meaning of his words had not escaped her. He felt suddenly as if a great judge was demanding, almost extracting, a true answer from him. Before he could refrain himself, he found himself promising, "I vow before all these witnesses and the pharaoh that no harm shall befall your brother or nephew!"

No one else could recall that Sarai even responded. But Tepi heard her say to him, "Your vow was before the one holy God. You will know great blessing, Shetepibre!"

Abram and Lot spent the night in bitter weeping and prayer. Abram cried out his anguish and supplications before God hour after hour. As the faint light of dawn filtered through the shutters of his room, guards from Shetepibre's militia came and arrested both Abram and Lot. They were bound and put on one of the armada's boats. At the end of the Memphis canal, sails were hoisted and the fleet was on its way to Wase.

Two days passed before Tepi ordered that Abram and Lot be transferred to his boat for questioning, for he had reports that the two prisoners had refused food. But no sooner had Abram and Lot presented themselves than a rapidly oared dispatch boat pulled alongside the grand vizier's barge. A messenger quickly boarded and rushed to bow before Tepi. "I have an urgent message from Grand Vizier Antefoker," he spoke breathlessly.

"Yes, go on!" Tepi urged him.

"A plague has struck the palace at Memphis! It was thought to be contaminated food or perhaps poison in the wine!"

"What are the symptoms?" Tepi questioned the messenger anxiously.

"Mainly nausea, vomiting and diarrhea," he related. "Physicians say that the liver is poisoned and swollen. Many are developing jaundice. All of the men are affected. But few of the women at the palace are ill."

"The pharaoh? In what condition is he?"

"He languishes in his bed. He was struck immediately after he left the banquet . . . the night before you departed. He has not dared to wander far from his toilet since that time!" the messenger answered frankly.

"Did other orders come for me?" Tepi asked.

"No, sir. You were only to be informed of the plague and that a quarantine has been issued for the Memphis area. Although the plague has distressing effects, the pharaoh said it would not incapacitate him or Antefoker from taking care of necessary duties. The government will be conducted from Memphis, however, until the plague runs its course."

"You have a written copy of this communication?"

The messenger nodded and handed Tepi an official scroll with Mentu's seal.

Tepi motioned for his scribe who came running from his work at the far end of the boat. "Take this document," Tepi told him. "Write an appropriate response with my expressions of concern for the pharaoh and Antefoker's health. Then let me seal it so this man may return."

The messenger followed the scribe back to his station to await his scroll. Tepi turned once again to Abram and Lot. In his preoccupation, Tepi had almost forgotten their presence. When he turned to them he noticed the astonished and relieved countenances of his two prisoners.

"You have been charged with resisting Captain Hirqnos when he came to escort your sister to the pharaoh," Tepi said deliberately. "For a foreigner such an offense carries a minimum two year indenture sentence or death."

"With no trial or judge?" Lot asked.

"Not for an offense against the pharaoh," Tepi replied.

"Offense against the pharaoh?" Abram retorted.

"Gentlemen," Tepi spoke apologetically, "I tried to reason with the pharaoh. He was drunk, both with wine and desire for your sister. To arrest you was to save your lives!"

"Perhaps we should be grateful," Abram replied. "But we came to Memphis to be honored for our service to Kemi . . . not to be humiliated by its pharaoh!"

"Pharaoh Mentuhotep is a good man," Tepi affirmed. "He needs a queen as lovely and as wise as your sister. Except for his drunken behavior that night, I am sure he will be considerate of Sarai.

"Come now," Tepi invited them. "Let us talk and dine together. I would like to hear of your work in Avaris. I spent many years at the Academy." Tepi ordered food served and the three sat and discoursed at length. Tepi was delighted when Abram explained new mathematical formulations and theories of astronomy that he had been teaching in Avaris. Lot told of the conditions in Canaan and about the cities along his caravan route to Charran.

During the meal—the first that Abram and Lot had eaten since Sarai's abduction—the discussion turned to surveying.

Tepi became aware of Abram's broad experience in the field. "If only the ancient rulers of Kemi had left us decent maps!" Tepi deplored, going on to explain the lost sea port and the projects that lay ahead.

After several hours had elapsed Tepi leaned back in his chair and said, "Strange, I called you here to explain your arrest charge and find myself wanting to turn to you as advisors! The Upper Land does not abound in scholars, and I am afraid my Avaris training has tainted me with Lower Land interests and sensitivities!"

"Could you dismiss the charges against us?" Lot asked impetuously. "You know that we have done nothing!"

"It is for your safety that I must keep you with me," Tepi said sincerely. "Besides, if you had not been arrested, what would have kept the pharaoh from suspecting you of causing the plague? Fortunately Hirqnos left guards around your lodging after he took your sister away. They testified to me that you remained there throughout the night. Otherwise I am afraid I would be suspicious of you myself!"

"The grand vizier is right, Lot," Abram conceded. "We know that God has intervened. We must wait now for the next sign."

"Of what god and sign do you speak, Abram?" Tepi inquired curiously, remembering the words Sarai had spoken. "Is it Thoth the moon god or Osiris? Or do you say Nannar-Sin and Baal? Or do you worship the female Ishtar that we call Hathor?"

"I worship the one holy God, Shetepibre. The God of Menes and the God of Imhotep . . . the God of Noah!" Abram declared boldly but quietly.

"Noah?" Tepi asked, his mind tracing back over the stories and legends he had studied at Avaris.

A servant interrupted to say that the guards were asking if the two prisoners were to be returned to sleep in the boats or given leave to stay on shore for the night.

"I should like to trust you, Abram, and you, Lot. Would you consent to be in my employ rather than in my prison?" Tepi offered.

Abram looked at Lot who nodded his assent. "We gladly accept," Abram replied.

"Good! I want to question you further about Noah and your God. Go now. You may stay at the inn with the oarsmen."

Chapter XIII
THE MIRACLES OF
THE WADI HAMMAMAT

Immediately upon arriving back at Wase, Shetepibre issued a proclamation for a national conscription to reopen the Wadi Hammamat Pass to the lost port on the Red Sea and to find alabaster for the future tomb of Pharaoh Mentuhotep.

Because of the pharaoh's absence from Wase, palace banquets and social affairs were cancelled. Tepi thereby had no opportunity to see Nefer. He did learn, however, that her husband, Iperwer, was still at the fortress at Semna, reportedly in better health than when he was in Wase.

Within a few months the desert expedition to the Red Sea was ready to depart from a small village north of Wase. The place was situated at the opening of the Wadi Hammamat Pass.

Tepi reviewed his troops to see that all was in order. Each man carried a tall spear, which he could also use for a walking stick, and a skin of water. Divided by twos the men were given shoulder poles. Cords laced between the poles formed a litter for carrying personal supplies, twenty loaves of bread for each man, plus bows and arrows. Four large water jars hung from each set of poles as well. Camels were loaded with tents and other equipment.

The Wadi Hammamat was a dry stream bed except during the brief rainy season. The Hammamat valley pass cut through the desert plateau and wove between high serrated mountains to the coast. The journey was a four to five day trek if all went well. Tepi planned to locate the twelve wells along the route and mark them for future excavation. On this trip they would have to depend on their own water supply and the cistern at the quarries.

Abram and Lot rode camels for the journey since they were put in charge of surveying and mapping. By riding at the front of the march they also served as part of the watch guards.

Though everyone was in readiness, not a single bedouin was seen from the time the troops left the Hapy River valley to the sighting of the stone quarries. The trip had been tiring and uneventful, except for the finding of each desecrated well.

When they arrived at the quarries, a large encampment was set up. After several days, Tepi requested to talk with Abram. Tepi was seated and completing his meal; Abram came and stood in deference before him. "You have had no difficulty with your work, Abram?" the grand vizier inquired.

"No," Abram replied quietly. "It has been hot but not difficult work."

"Sit down, Abram," Tepi invited him. "I need to talk with someone. Since that time on the boat I have not had the opportunity to continue our discussions. Tell me, do you think it is unusual that we have seen no bedouins?"

"They are out there!" Abram said prudently.

"What do you mean?"

"Desert tribes are always independent. Even twenty thousand men would not frighten them away," he replied advisedly. "They never hide from anyone except as, an offensive measure!"

"I am just waiting for them to try something, Abram. Once they let me know their location, I want to bring those nomads into line!"

"Try, they will!" assured Abram. "Even if the ratio is twenty to twenty thousand. They like the desert to themselves!"

Without warning Tepi looked searchingly at Abram and requested, "Explain to me your belief in the God of Noah. On the boat you referred to him as the God of Imhotep and Menes."

Abram did not outwardly show the surprise he felt at the change of topic. "Perhaps Imhotep and Menes did not worship him purely, Shetepibre, but they did worship one God, the creator and sustainer of everything that is made. They must have known God as a friend as Noah did. Such righteousness and wisdom could never come from the pagan deities that are now in Kemi."

"Yes," agreed Tepi. "Our gods are even more evil than we are! When a man considers himself more virtuous than the god he worships, either the man is vain or the god must be false."

"The real God *is* a God of righteousness, as Menes confirmed, but he is also a God who wants to be known by his people."

Tepi looked pensive. "He is the hidden God—your God of Noah and my God of Menes. . . ."

"Have you ever tried to know him, Shetepibre?"

"No, Abram. I have only contemplated what He must be like . . . like light . . . or wind."

"Do you acknowledge the pagan gods of Kemi?" Abram asked directly.

"Abram, as grand vizier of the Upper Land," he smiled, "I should have you chastised for such a question! . . . But, yes, I do pay my tributes. It takes care of my sense of religious duty, while doing nothing for the emptiness of my soul!"

They talked on for some time. Then Abram asked Tepi if they might pray together. Tepi agreed although he was embarrassed. "I do not know how to begin, Abram."

"We will *praise* God. We will praise him for being holy and righteous. Then you can thank him for caring for you and ask for his help."

"You mean I might ask for his help to find the alabaster for Mentuhotep? We have searched three days for that pure white

213

vein. I cannot believe it has all been quarried. And we haven't discovered the great cistern. I'm very concerned about both."

As they bowed together Abram was reminded of his own awkwardness when he first heard Hosani and Sarai pray. When he looked at the young grand vizier he saw the tenseness begin to leave his face and a faint smile appear. Abram felt the presence of the Lord fill the tent. He knew that Tepi felt it too.

The next day some workmen were resting from their fruitless search for the alabaster gypsum. As they sat under shade tents a heavily pregnant gazelle suddenly approached their work area. It was not unusual to see a desert gazelle. The soldiers had shot several recently from fast fleeting herds while hunting in the mountains. What was strange about this gazelle was that the frightened creature should walk into the quarry within cubits of the men.

They watched in silence as the doe gingerly stepped among the hot rocks. Under the shade of an overhanging cliff she paused and hunched herself on a flat block of stone. She began heaving in birth labor.

The extraordinary happening brought many onlookers. One of the stone cutters brought a wide bowl of water and knelt by the doe. As he placed the water beside her, his trained eyes were alerted by the block of stone on which the animal and her newborn lay. Quickly he pulled his knife. Several of the men in the audience objected and called out, thinking he intended to harm the gazelle. Instead the workman scratched away at the surface stone.

"This is it!" he shouted excitedly. "This whole slab is pure white alabaster! Call Grand Vizier Shetepibre! We have found it!"

Other workmen gently lifted the gazelle and her fawn to a comfortable spot where she could easily retreat into the mountains when she desired.

Chippings revealed that the alabaster block was the whitest and most translucent that had ever been quarried in Kemi. Tepi watched the workmen from the cliff as they carefully chiseled the slab. Staring incredulously he murmured, "You are a God who comes and answers prayer—and leaves a miracle as your footprint!"

The next day, as the workmen quarried the stone, most of the battalions of militia fanned out over the area to look for any hostile bedouins. Others went with Tepi and Abram to make a search for the lost sea port. Time wore on. The water shortage became acute. Tepi ordered all men to halt their assignments and do nothing but look for the quarry cistern. Water was cautiously rationed.

After a whole day of searching availed nothing, Tepi became discouraged. That night he called in his officers and head workmen. Abram and Lot were also requested to appear.

It was dark outside and the moon was at the quarter. The chilled night air was penetrating after the intense heat of the daytime sun. The men gathered and were seated in the large tent. Oil lamps were lit, their light revealing tired and apprehensive faces.

Tepi began gravely, "My friends, I have struggled with the problem. I find we have no alternative. If we leave on the morrow our water supply will barely last to get us back to Wase. We dare not complete the stone cutting or search for the harbor any longer. It will have to wait until we can return with fresh water and supplies."

"You mean we must come back as soon as we get more water and supplies?" one of the officers complained. "The sun will be scorching by then!"

"I cannot return to the pharaoh without anything!" Tepi raised his voice nervously. "Twenty thousand men are here! Do you think Mentuhotep will allow me to use this many troops and come back empty handed?"

One of the older officers stood up belligerently. "Why, your excellency, in the name of the gods, was not a scouting party sent ahead?" he spoke sharply. "Why did you enlist twenty thousand men without proper advance troops?"

Shame burned within Tepi. "Perhaps you are correct!" he answered defensively. "I felt my strategy was wise at the time . . . a large deployment of men to clear the desert of the

215

bedouins, find the lost harbor, and return with pharaoh's white stone. It seemed highly possible!"

The officer was not appeased and continued his attack. "You did not mention that all those plans depended on finding the quarry cistern! Nor have we seen a single bedouin for our twenty thousand men to go chasing!" he cried out impatiently.

"I think you have said enough!" Tepi warned him. "Our campaign may have been poorly executed, but I will not admit it was a total mistake. At least we found the alabaster!"

"Thanks to the gods," another officer mumbled.

Tepi glanced over at Abram and then turning to the men said plainly, "Thanks to *the* God!"

When the meeting was ended most of the men were still disgruntled. Their anger had been vented, but no solution other than returning was possible.

The following morning the men at the encampment awakened before dawn to get an early march on the day. Because of the darkness a short time elapsed before anyone noticed that the camp had been invaded during the night.

"The water is gone!" came the first yell of discovery. "Our last supply! It's all been poured out on the ground!"

Tepi was just putting on his tunic when he heard the cries. Gripping fear overcame him. There would not be a man in the desert encampment that would not know what that cry meant. Twenty thousand men would die! They would die after first going crazy with the heat and the thirst. "They will tear me to pieces!" Tepi thought inwardly. "In their madness, they will tear me to pieces!"

His mind raced to Abram. He must find him! As he grabbed his spear and ran to the tent entrance, Abram met him abruptly. Abram carried a plain soldier's blanket. "Here," he said quickly. "Cover yourself with this so you will not be recognized. These men will soon go wild!"

The confusion was growing as Tepi and Abram mounted two camels and rode away from the settlement. "We cannot go too far, Shetepibre," Abram warned. "You can rest assured the bedouins are waiting for us!"

216

They stopped and dismounted in an open space where they could see all approaches. "Thank you for trying to protect me. It is no use, however. We will all die one way or another!"

"Shetepibre!" Abram said sternly. "Do you think God answered your prayer by sending that gazelle, and now he is going to let you die?"

"I need a *miracle,* Abram!"

"Then pray for one!"

For a moment the two men just stared at each other. Then Tepi knelt and Abram joined him.

"O God of Noah, God of Abram, God of Imhotep. O one holy God! I do not want to pray for myself but for these men and for our Land. O hidden God, direct me to the water. Please, O God. Show me the water!"

Almost the instant the prayer was said distant thunder rumbled. Abram and Tepi stood up and looked about them. The morning sun was rising in the east over the Red Sea. The sky was clear and blue in that direction. But to the northwest, dark storm clouds loomed over the desert mountains. Fast moving winds swept down the rugged slopes, whipping up a thick haze of dust. Large drops of rain began to splatter on the dry sands. Tepi and Abram watched, still holding their camels by tethers. The thick clouds moved overhead and for a few moments rain fell down in torrents.

But no sooner had the unseasonal storm come than it quietly dissipated and passed. "Does your God tease me, Abram!" Tepi cried out desperately.

Abram was not listening. Instead his eyes were fastened on a sand dune a short distance away. "Shetepibre!" he called out jubilantly. "See how the waters drain off! Instead of flowing away from that mound they flow toward it. Of course! The bedouins must have made a sand hill over the cistern! We have searched only for filled-in depressions!"

The two men pulled at their camels and ran toward the dune. The fast falling rain had cut fresh miniature canyons in the sand seeking the familiar water trough of the underground river. The little gullies pointed like long stringy fingers to the sand dune that camouflaged the great reservoir.

217

It did not take much digging in the loose sand to uncover a part of the great stone lid of the cistern. "Abram! Abram!" Tepi cried out, overwhelmed by the almighty power and divine action. "*Our* God . . . now I know he is real!"

"We must get to the encampment immediately, Shetepibre. The bedouins will have all their men stationed along the pass. If our men break out and leave in small numbers they will be picked off around every bend of the Wadi!" Abram warned.

"The men may be enraged by now, Abram. Will they listen to me?"

"Let me precede you," Abram counseled him. "And keep that blanket around you and over your head!"

With that, the two hurriedly mounted and raced their camels around to the west side of the encampment. The workmen and soldiers had grabbed their swords and belongings and had begun to leave in sporadic groups. Some were already out of sight beyond the bends of the mountain pass. Abram and Shetepibre knew too well what their fate would be.

They headed off as many as they could while Abram shouted out, "The cistern is found! Stay! The bedouins will kill you if you go farther! There is water now! The cistern has been found!"

The word spread quickly, and the frenzied terror of the troops turned to joy and relief. Before noon teams of men removed the sand hill and the great cistern was reopened. As jars were filled, the subterranean waters rapidly replenished the large vat. The supply was limitless, cold and refreshing.[13]

The bedouin tribes had gambled on hiding the cistern and attacking Tepi's weakened returning army. In their delight over outsmarting such enormous odds, the bedouins had been too sure of themselves. They left many tracks to follow after their night raid on the water supply. Their secret mountain camps were found, surrounded and routed out. Many were killed as they fiercely tried to escape capture, and some were taken prisoner. The rest elusively hid in mountain crevices or fled, disappearing amid the desert dunes.

A bribe of gold and a promise of release brought forth information from one of the captives about the location of the lost sea port. A regiment was sent up the coast, and the port was discovered in a far different place than the maimed informant had advised Tepi back in Wase.[14]

There was little loot to be found after the struggle. Valuable possessions had been quickly buried by the bedouins in caches beneath the sands. A few desert women were found hiding in a deep cave in the mountains. They were bound and taken to the encampment. One pretty girl fought particularly hard to avoid capture. She was the daughter of the leading shakana, Heka-nakht, who had been slain. Her name was Hagar.

Tepi returned to Wase with his large army and workmen. Immediately he sent back new detachments to clear the twelve wells along the Wadi Hammamat and to continue the stone quarrying. Messengers were dispatched to Memphis describing the victories. Accompanying the messenger's scrolls were Abram's maps showing details of the route to the Red Sea and the exact location of the port.

The Grand Vizier Shetepibre became the hero of the Land even on the Eastern Bank of Wase. His victories in Kush and the recent exploits in the desert won him unbounded adulation. Also, with the pharaoh and Antefoker becoming more ill and a stricter quarantine kept in Memphis, the name of Shetepibre sealed every important document of Kemi.

Although Abram as a foreigner could carry no official rank he nevertheless functioned as Tepi's main advisor. The two prayed together, and Tepi listened as Abram taught him the mysteries of the holy God.

One morning, several weeks after their return from the desert, Tepi was hearing the reports from the Kushite fortresses. Iperwer's name was listed among those killed in a recent ambush. Tepi's first inward reaction was elation. As the scribe read on, however, Tepi felt waves of guilt overcome him.

"Call in Abram the surveyor," he directed a servant, interrupting the scribe's recitation.

"I am sorry," Tepi apologized to the scribe. "Return later, and we will continue the reports. I have something else I must attend to at this time."

When Abram arrived, Tepi excused the others who were attending him. Then privately he related to Abram his past—his servanthood, his love for the nomarch's daughter, and his part in sending Iperwer to Semna.

"I know I have ordered many men to places where they have met their death," he admitted with sorrow. "But I have never before or since deliberately sent out a man in the hope that he would die. Before knowing you and having those experiences with God in the desert, I would have taken pleasure from this news. It was to be my revenge against Meketre."

"What about Nefer?" Abram inquired. "Did she love her husband?"

"I would not let myself believe that she could love Iperwer. He was a weak, frail man, always living with his widowed mother and seemingly dominated by her."

"Does Nefer know of her husband's death?"

"No, the report just arrived. Do you think I should be the one to tell her?" Tepi asked, earnestly seeking Abram's advice.

"Shetepibre, I know that God's hand is now upon your life. You have confessed your sin. Accept God's action in your life as his sign of forgiveness."

"But Nefer, do you think she will forgive me?"

"Knowing the heart of a woman is beyond my capabilities," Abram smiled. Putting his hand on Tepi's shoulder he advised, "We always punish ourselves when we sin against another. Perhaps your time of chastening is over."

When Nefer arrived at the palace following Tepi's summons, she was accompanied by her mother-in-law and her father. They firmly refused to allow her to see Tepi without their being present. Tepi responded by sending a courier to the palace waiting rooms with an indignant

220

message: "Shetepibre, Grand Vizier of the Upper Land and acting in the authority of Mentuhotep requests the presence of the wife of Iperwer in the court. Anyone protesting or interfering with this summons shall be detained in the palace prison."

The courier returned and fearfully reported, "The mother of Iperwer is furious, sir. Dare we arrest her and the nomarch? Meketre demands that you come to him in the waiting rooms."

Tepi laughed, "He does, does he! Go tell the Nomarch of Wase that I am considering a reappointment for his office. After I have delivered my information to his daughter, I shall be glad to discuss with him whom the new nomarch of Wase should be. You might add that I am thinking about finding someone from the Western Bank!"

The next time the courier entered Tepi's court he brought Nefer with him. "Nefer-Tachenen, wife of Iperwer," he announced formally.

"Come in, Nefer," Tepi smiled and rose to greet her. This time he found that it was he who was calm and she who appeared quite nervous. "I am sorry I had to deal that way with your father. But unless he learns to respect me and my position, he cannot retain his post as nomarch."

"It is difficult for all of us to realize how important you have become in the Land," Nefer said respectfully, sounding almost frightened. "I do not know if I could ever call you . . . Tepi . . . again."

He stared intently at her. She looked pale and fragile, and her happy spirit was subdued. "Nefer, I am sorry but I must bring you sad news," he said genuinely. "At one time I would have actually enjoyed saying what I must say. Now I have only deep regrets."

"Iperwer?" she asked.

"He is dead," Tepi answered. Nefer's eyes widened. Tepi detected shock but saw no tears form.

"How did it happen?" she asked softly.

"He volunteered for a dangerous sortie to clear out some Kushite rebels. He and those who were with him accomplished

221

the mission bravely. Unfortunately another band of rebels ambushed the group on their return."

"Iperwer would have been proud to have heard what you just said, Tepi," Nefer murmured.

"How do you mean?"

"My husband was sickly as you know. And his mother ruled his every action. Iperwer never knew what it was to be a man until he arrived at Semna."

"He *liked* being there?" Tepi asked incredulously.

"He was never happier!" she answered, a faint smile forming on her lips. "He sent letters telling of his exploits . . . even the Kushite women he had slept with!"

"What?"

"It's true," she laughed, the tears now rolling down her cheeks. "The poor boy did not know what freedom and manhood were until you sent him to do duty. His sickness disappeared and his last letters talked only of his desire for a life career in the militia."

"Could you pardon me for what I did then?" Tepi entreated her seriously. He did not resist the tears that welled up in his own eyes as he earnestly sought her forgiveness.

Nefer looked perplexed and said, "Tepi, you are the grand vizier. You do not need to ask for pardon."

"There are many things I wish to share with you at a more proper time. They would help you understand how important your pardon is to me."

"You have my pardon. And I know you would have had Iperwer's pardon as well. To my father's distress, Iperwer often wrote of his admiration for you, especially all that you accomplished in Kush."

Tepi shook his head in unbelief. "This miracle is even greater than the others," he thought aloud.

"Miracles?"

He smiled and went to her, embracing her gently in his arms. "I hope to have many hours with you and tell you about them!"

"Oh, Tepi . . . could it be possible?" Nefer leaned her head against his shoulder and wept. "I have thought of you so often since you came that day in our garden. But I never allowed myself to even dream we could be together."

"We shall be together . . . as often as you will let me see you," Tepi promised.

"My father," she cried. "He has become obsessed with his resentments. He will never allow me. . . ."

"As a widow, Nefer, no one has authority over you except the pharaoh."

"I don't know if I have the strength to resist my father . . . or Iperwer's mother. They both dominate me very much," she said hesitantly.

"Nefer, after your months of mourning, I want you to become my wife!"

While Nefer and Tepi were together, Abram, who knew of her coming, went to the palace waiting room. Approaching Meketre he introduced himself and asked the nomarch if they might talk privately. Meketre agreed and followed Abram through the palace halls and up the stairs to the map rooms.

"I really did not know we must go this far," Meketre complained. "If my daughter calls for me I want to be available."

"The visitors' guard knows you are here," Abram assured him as they entered the rooms. "I only wish to detain you a few moments."

"Well. . . ?" Meketre said impatiently, seating himself on a stool.

Abram drew up another stool and sat opposite him. "I am a friend and an advisor to the grand vizier," Abram told him. "He has informed me of the personal relationships he has with your family."

"Tepi has no personal relationships with my family!" Meketre declared. "Tepi is a nobody! His mother is a half breed and his father was a worthless laborer!"

Abram felt his own temper rising. "There is no man created by God that is a nobody!"

"Of what god do you speak?" Meketre asked bluntly. "One of your despicable river cities deities?"

Abram stopped and examined Meketre. He perceived something more in the man than just an angry prejudiced father bent on thwarting his daughter. "What god do you worship, Meketre?" he asked pointedly.

"As Nomarch of Wase, I serve. . . ."

"No," Abram interrupted, "as Meketre the man, in whom do you believe?"

Meketre hesitated. "As a young man I read the writings of Menes and Imhotep. Their God of righteousness is the only god I find worthy of worship. But in Wase it is not good politics to be sincerely religious!"

"What if the pharaoh were 'sincerely religious'?" Abram inquired.

Meketre laughed scornfully.

Abram added, "Shetepibre believes in and worships the one holy God! His victory in the desert was not his doing but due to direct miracles of God. He even had the stone cutters inscribe on the entrance walls of the quarry the story of the miracles that took place. He wanted everyone in Kemi both now, and for thousands of years to come, to know what his God had done!"

Meketre was quiet. Abram could feel God's presence in the room. Meketre must have sensed it too, for he said slowly, "I have not talked of the God of Imhotep in many years. You say Tepi believes? . . . I wish I were young again and believed the way I once did . . . before I became . . . so bitter. But Tepi is not the pharaoh, and Mentuhotep demands honor to be paid to Osiris."

"Mentuhotep has no heir," Abram commented, pronouncing each word distinctly. "If he died at this moment, who would be the next pharaoh?"

Meketre thought on the question. Without answering he asked, "Abram, could I see Shetepibre? He was once like a son to me. I am weary with my own anger and judgment. I see myself in Iperwer's mother, and I do not like what I see. If I had not stood in Tepi's way he would be married to Nefer. Instead. . . ."

"Iperwer is dead, Meketre!"

Meketre's eyes filled with tears. "Please, Abram, take me to see Tepi!"

When they arrived at the doors of the court chambers, Tepi was just escorting Nefer out. Tepi's reactions on seeing Meketre were tense. Before he could say anything Meketre announced hurriedly, "Abram has told me of Iperwer's death. Nefer will stay with me during her mourning period. You may visit her at any time, Tepi!"

Tepi looked into Meketre's eyes and saw the kindness and love that he had once known as a boy. Tepi could only recover enough from his surprise to stammer, "I would be honored. . . ."

Abram returned to the place in Wase where he and his nephew Lot were staying. Lot was restless. He spoke of wanting to return to Sodom where he had left Salanna, Minusa and Puluki. He was also irritated with Abram.

"I cannot see how you can speak of a God of righteousness to Shetepibre and others and yet live a lie before them!" he berated Abram. "You have the grand vizier's complete respect! Why do you not tell him about Sarai? How can you be here in Wase while she . . . she sleeps with Mentuhotep?"

Abram's face flushed from the rebuke. "You do not know, Lot, how many times I have said those same words to myself! But you were there when they took Sarai. You know how I said it was *God's* test. And he *did* save her! The plague hit the pharaoh first and then every man in the palace later that next day. A man having the runs of diarrhea and vomiting does not think about taking a woman to bed with him . . . even one as beautiful as Sarai. The plague has continued and the men grow weaker each day!"

"But what if it suddenly stops?" Lot asked impatiently. "How will you ever get Sarai back once the pharaoh is well?"

"According to logic the whole thing is wrong. But God warned me first in that dream. He also sent the plague!" Abram related. "If Sarai had not been taken we would never have known Shetepibre! Can you imagine, Lot, what would happen to this country if Shetepibre were the next pharaoh? No one comes close to him in popularity. With Antefoker also ill, who would resist him?"

"But Mentuhotep is determined to have an heir," Lot reminded him.

To which Abram replied, "Mentuhotep will recover from the plague when God releases it, but I do not believe he will ever be strong again. Certainly if he were impotent before the plague, he will still be so after such a long illness."

"But I cannot see why you have not told Shetepibre," Lot strongly reacted.

"I know what I have done is of God!" Abram exclaimed boldly. "To tell the grand vizier that the woman taken by the pharaoh is my wife would force Shetepibre to do one of two things: Tell the pharaoh . . . and probably lose his favor by the insult, or have me killed to protect the pharaoh's honor."

"He would do the first!" Lot said quickly. "And he should!"

"And this land would lose a future pharaoh that could lead it to worship the holy God!" Abram cried out. "Oh, Lot, do you not see how the Lord has worked? How he performed those miracles? The gazelle, the cistern, Nefer, and Meketre? God is using us to bring a whole country to himself!"

An intense stillness followed. Lot's eyes were wet with tears as his mind and heart were finally convinced. "I am sorry, Abram. That the God of Noah who created all things would use people like you and me to change the course of history is hard to believe. But I want to believe it . . . I *do* believe it!"

Abram's heart beat fervently for joy on hearing Lot's confirmation.

The months passed. Abram and Lot spent many evenings talking and praying with Meketre while Tepi visited with Nefer in the nomarch's gardens.

One night, as the four were at dinner, Tepi and Nefer asked Meketre if they might be married at the end of the inundation season of Akhet and just before the plowing season of Peret began. "Assuming that the plague continues, I must attend to the government until the season of Peret," Tepi reasoned. "My duties should be lighter while the people are busy on their farms. A later date would be difficult, for I must supervise the cutting of the stones for Mentuhotep's monument. The slab of alabaster will be here by that time." Almost unconsciously he added, "Oh, how I wish we could use that stone of the miracle for something else!"

"You have my permission to marry at any time, Tepi," Meketre smiled as he rose and walked over to his daughter. "And you are pleased?" he asked, gently kissing her cheek.

Nefer did not have to answer. Her face glowed with the joy of a woman well loved. In the past weeks she had known not only the love of Tepi but the love of his God as well.

Chapter XIV
THE PALACE PLAGUE

Before his coming marriage, Shetepibre decided it would be wise to make a tour of the Land. He was especially needed in Avaris where the Lower Land had been without leadership for over a year. Servants, wealth in gold, silver, turquoise and other precious stones, and livestock surfeited the pharaoh's armies, storehouses, and corrals. There were suspicions and accusations of graft, theft and mismanagement. Also Tepi wanted to spend time near Memphis where he could communicate quickly through a messenger with the pharaoh.

"I am having a difficult time securing courier volunteers," Tepi informed Abram one day as they were laying plans for the trip to Memphis and Avaris. "No one wants to go near the palace or even into Memphis. I dare not take the chance of going to see the pharaoh directly myself. If I come down with the plague, there might be anarchy in the Land!"

"Lot and I shall deliver the messages for you," Abram astonished him by saying. "It would give me opportunity to see my sister once again. Sarai is very dear to me."

Tepi was embarrassed by the mention of Sarai's name. He knew Abram had forgiven him for his part in her abduction, but Tepi wished that he could do something about the situation. Yet he felt helpless.

"Do you not fear the disease?" he asked Abram with concern.

"It is the curse of God that has struck the pharaoh and his men," was Abram's only reply.

Tepi stared at Abram intently. "Did you pray for God to curse the pharaoh this way?" he asked, his words spoken haltingly. "Do you have the power to curse with the plague, Abram?"

"God promised to bless those who blessed me, Shetepibre, as he has blessed you. God also promised to curse those who curse me," Abram added forcefully.

Tepi sensed that there was more that Abram could tell him. With a slight smile and a nod of understanding Tepi said, "I accept your generous offer to be my courier to the palace at Memphis. Once again, Abram, blessed of the holy hidden God, I am in your debt!"

They did not take the royal barge or the fleet that usually accompanied it. Instead Tepi chose to take two fast-oared clippers. Since he planned to visit the Upper Land nomes on his return trip, he directed the boats to go immediately to Memphis. They then headquartered at a small village just south of the Memphis canal.

The local inn of the town had been made ready for the grand vizier's use. After they had settled themselves and had eaten, Tepi prepared documents for Abram and Lot to deliver to Mentuhotep.

Abram and Lot took a small craft and paddled and punted it down the Hapy and into the Memphis canal. When they arrived at the palace quay, they were taken aback by the unkempt appearance of the docking area. Abram left Lot there and walked through the palace gardens. He found them uncared for and overgrown. The guards on duty looked emaciated and listless. Abram showed them his official papers and was directed toward the palace steps.

"One of the women will have to help you," mumbled a guard to him. "You are a fool to be here!"

As he entered the palace gates a maid greeted him. "May I help you?" she asked tiredly. "Are you another one of the magicians?"

"No," Abram replied with a tone of dignity and authority. "I have documents from Grand Vizier Shetepibre for Pharaoh Mentuhotep. But first, I would like to visit my sister, Sarai. She is the one betrothed to the pharaoh."

"You are Abram?" exclaimed the girl as her eyes brightened with interest. "Sarai has spoken often about you! Your wonderful sister has saved the men here at the palace! We maids could not have stayed with all this terrible sickness if she had not been here. Why, she even has classes for us, and we have times of singing. Master Abram, she has taught everyone in the palace about the one God! Come, I will take you to her!"

"Is she well?" he asked as he followed the girl.

"She gets weary like the rest of us," she responded. "There is much work to do, and the men are of little help. She does all of the pharaoh's correspondence and tends to anything that is official for him. She must also do the scribe work for Antefoker, although of late he has been too ill to be about."

"You spoke of magicians. Are there no physicians to care for the sick?"

"They are sick themselves!" she declared with a shrug. "The pharaoh has offered a great reward for anyone who has a cure. At first the announcement brought in many soothsayers and magicians. But they too fell ill. You are the first visitor in over a week!"

They walked down a corridor until the girl stopped before a large entryway. The carved wooden doors were heavily gilded with pure gold leaf.

"Where are we?" Abram inquired curiously.

"We are at the queen's suite," the girl answered innocently.

"The queen's ... suite?" Abram asked, catching his breath. "The pharaoh and Sarai. . . ?"

"Pharaoh Mentuhotep has sealed the marriage papers but has not yet publicly proclaimed Sarai as his queen. He says that he wants to wait until he recovers so that they might hold a proper ceremony. However, he wanted her to stay in the queen's rooms. The poor man has been too sick to think of anything but tending to himself!"

The girl opened one of the doors slightly and peered in. "My lady, your good brother is here to visit with you!" she announced sweetly. Then to Abram she whispered, "I will leave you two to be by yourselves."

When the maid moved aside Abram saw Sarai coming towards him. The door closed behind him, and he leaned back against it. "Is it really you, Sarai?" he could barely say the words.

"I am glad you are here," she responded quietly, the quivering of her lips the only noticeable sign of any lack of poise.

Abram could only stare at her. She did not look at all like the frightened wife he last saw leaving with Hirqnos. She now stood before him dressed as only the queen of the wealthiest country in the world could afford to appear. Sarai wore a flowing gown of the finest and costliest linen. A broad round collar encircled her neck, embossed with gleaming stones of cornelian, turquoise and lazuli in symmetrical patterns of gold settings. Her shining black hair was coiffed in elaborate curls, held in place by a sparkling gold diadem. The perfect features of Sarai's face were artistically painted in the Kemian style. Green malchite and dark galena boldly accented her lovely eyes, rouge warmed her cheeks and glistening red ochre colored her lips. Jewels hung from her ears. She was exotically beautiful.

"I feel like I am back in that canoe in the marsh swamp, looking at your loveliness for the first time," he said, somewhat gaining his composure. When she did not respond he became flinchingly aware that she was holding herself aloof from him.

"Sarai?"

She smiled but did not move closer to him. "Grand Vizier Shetepibre has written the pharaoh at great length about you," she said coolly. "Mentuhotep and Antefoker both regret sending you away as they did but are glad you were there to be helpful to Shetepibre."

"Sarai, what is wrong?" Abram exclaimed in alarm as he went to her and tried to embrace her.

Sarai pulled back. "He also wrote that you seemed very happy in Wase . . . that he hoped you would soon marry and continue to live in the Land!"

"Sarai, when you hear what has happened you will understand! God has used this terrible separation to do many mighty acts," he tried vainly to make her listen.

"God has also closed my womb during the time! Perhaps he wants us to be separated, Abram. Then you can find another woman . . . one who can still bear you children! And I . . . I can remain here and be the queen of Kemi!"

"Sarai. . . ," he tried to interrupt.

"Since you do not want me, and God has closed my womb . . . I will not go back with you! Mentu is terribly sick, but he has been very kind to me," she said, holding her beautiful face high. "And he is not ashamed to be called my husband!"

"I am not ashamed either, Sarai! But I wanted to live so that I could always *be* your husband! No one else will be mother to my heir but you! And I want no other man to sire your child but me! And you are *going to have a child!*" Abram was becoming angry. "Sit down, my wife. I want to talk to you, and I want you to listen!"

Reluctantly Sarai obeyed. Then Abram related the events that had occurred. Sarai's countenance softened. Her eyes revealed the wonder and awe she was feeling as Abram told of the gazelle giving birth on the precious block of alabaster and about the divine storm whose waters flowed through the sands and pointed out the cistern. Tears welled up when she heard of Tepi's faith, his growing acclaim and power, and how in time he might rule the entire land.

"It was indeed the hand of God," she said softly as she wept and fell into Abram's arms. "I was so alone here, Abram. I felt God was separating us forever! I felt he was telling me I was unworthy to bear your child! If he can do those miracles, and even cause this plague to keep me from being taken by another man, then maybe he will still have mercy."

232

The embrace was long and comforting, but as he released her Abram asked carefully, "Do you always look like this for Mentuhotep?" There was a bit of jealousy in his voice which he could not hide.

Sarai glanced hesitantly down at her resplendent attire. "Mentuhotep begged me to dress this way when visitors were expected," she explained shyly. "With the palace neglected and sickness everywhere, he wanted someone to bear an official appearance. Besides, I knew it was *you* who were coming today! I was waiting for you!"

Realizing what she meant Abram began to laugh. "I think I remember you said that once before! Only then it was the women in the swamp and their drums who warned you I was coming, not a pharaoh's courier!"

For several days Abram brought documents and messages and took them in to Mentuhotep. Afterward he would go with Sarai to her suite. The fourth day, Mentu was watching from his balcony as Abram left. Abram in his joy from being with Sarai bounded down the palace steps, lightly humming a tune as he went. Seeing him so full of energy and health, the pharaoh summoned Hirqnos to ask him more about Abram.

A few moments later Hirqnos entered the pharaoh's rooms. Mentu had slumped back in his bed. "You sent for me?" Hirqnos asked weakly, the long sickness having aged the soldier considerably.

"Sarai's brother has been coming here to the palace for four days delivering Shetepibre's messages to me. He comes and goes and the disease does not strike him! Do you know anything about him that would give him immunity over this horrible curse?" Mentu asked.

Hirqnos thought back, trying to remember his first encounter with Abram. "No, only that Sarai and her brother both believe strongly in one God, like the hidden God of our ancient fathers, Menes and Imhotep," he offered.

"Yes, Sarai talks often to me about her God," Mentu acknowledged wistfully. Suddenly the pharaoh rose up from his bed. "Hirqnos, go, see if you can stop Abram. See if he

233

will come and touch me and pray for me! Please, Hirqnos, go quickly! Ask him to pray to his God for me!"

Hirqnos left the pharaoh's bedside and went as fast as he could force his tired legs to move. He found Abram talking with a guard and about ready to depart in his boat with Lot.

"Wait!" Hirqnos called from the palace gardens. "Abram, brother of Sarai, wait, please!"

The strain of his effort caused Hirqnos to collapse heavily on the quay. Abram quickly climbed out of the boat and lifted him up. Hirqnos could wear only a loose fitting kilt. Like others inflicted with the disease, his jaundiced body was covered with itching welts. With fetid breaths he gasped, "I beg you, Abram, believer in a great God, go pray for the pharaoh. Pray that this curse be lifted off of us! You alone of the men who have come here have escaped this evil!"

Before Abram could answer, and to his surprise, Lot suddenly shouted angrily from the boat, "So long as his wife Sarai remains with the pharaoh, my uncle Abram will not be able to pray for him! Tell the pharaoh to give Sarai back to her husband! Then he will pray for him and he will get well!"

Just hearing Lot's words, Hirqnos felt strength come into his body. He pulled himself up, looked dumbfoundedly for a moment at Abram, then rushed to tell Mentuhotep.

"My lord pharaoh!" he cried out as he burst into Mentu's bedchamber. "All of these plagues and sicknesses have come on account of Sarai! She is the *wife* of the man Abram! Let Sarai be restored to her husband, Abram, and this plague will go from you and depart from all of us!"

"Abram is Sarai's husband?" the pharaoh shouted the question. "Then the plague *is* a curse!"

Mentu staggered to the balcony and called down to the guards. "Bring Abram, the messenger of Shetepibre, to me! Stop him! I must see him!"

When Abram came before the pharaoh, Mentu screamed at him, "What have you done to me on account of Sarai? She told me she was merely your sister, but she is really *your* wife! I took her while she was *your* wife!"

234

The pharaoh was breathing convulsively and was forced to stop to rest. When he could continue his voice was rasping, "You must take her and depart! Leave Kemi forever! But first, pray for me and the men of this place that the evil spirit may release us of this plague!"

"And if I pray for you and you recover, do I have your word as pharaoh of Kemi that you will not harm us?" Abram asked determinedly, the fearful dream of the cedar and the palm trees still in his mind.

"Would I want to suffer the return of such a curse?" Mentu exclaimed in exasperation. "You have my word!"

Abram went to Mentuhotep. He began to pray and placed his hand on Mentu's feverishly sweating forehead. The plague symptoms began to diminish. Although he was still weak, Mentu knew the disease was gone.

The pharaoh called for Sarai. When she stood before him in her queenly attire, he stared at her lovingly. "Only a divine power could make me give you up, my queen. But your God is stronger than I, and I give you back to him and to your rightful husband!"

The glow that appeared on Sarai's face in that darkened room was of such radiant lustre that she seemed to be standing in sunlight. Still longingly looking at her, Mentu asked her to get her ink sticks and scrolls. When she returned Mentu dictated a message to her for Shetepibre, telling him to reward Abram abundantly and escort him with his wife Sarai and his nephew and their people out of the Land. The pharaoh told Hirqnos, whose health continued to improve after Abram's prayer, to accompany Abram and convey Mentuhotep's scroll to the grand vizier.

Later at the inn of the small village near Memphis, Abram met with Tepi alone to explain what had happened. "At first I was offended when I read the message," Tepi admitted. "I thought you mistrusted me, Abram, by not telling me about Sarai. But you were right! Had I known, I would have insisted on doing something to get Sarai back for you. Now the whole Land will hear about the miracle of healing from your prayers!"

"All these miracles are for a reason, Shetepibre," Abram replied seriously. "God has prepared *you,* and he will prepare the people of Kemi to worship him. If the opportunity comes in the years ahead for you to be the next pharaoh . . . grasp it!"

"I will, Abram," he promised. "With Nefer for my wife and Meketre behind me, I will seek it! And should I become pharaoh, I will declare the hidden God of Menes and Imhotep, the same God of Noah and Abram, to be the one and only God of Kemi!"

When the boats arrived in Avaris, Tepi went to the pharaoh's treasuries for gold. Then he brought out the finest flocks and herds from the corrals. Carefully he selected servants and chose gifts of fine linen, dyes and precious stones. He added to these all the things he thought Abram could use for his journey and for his sojourn in Canaan. Lot also received gifts and flocks and herds.

Meanwhile Abram collected his own people, and Lot located those who were originally Salanna's herdsmen. Tepi cancelled any indenture contracts remaining for those servants.

When they were ready to leave the border of Kemi, Abram found himself to be a very wealthy man.

"I shall miss you, Abram," Tepi said as he embraced his friend. "You have changed my life!"

"We shall pray for you, Shetepibre, always!" Abram said in farewell.

As a special parting gift to Sarai, Tepi gave her Hagar, the attractive daughter of the desert chieftain who died in the Wadi Hammamat battle. The young woman had come with them on the boat from Wase and had served them. "She too is a princess, Sarai, a desert princess!" he explained. "She will be happier with you in Canaan than in Kemi. She is used to living in tents and being free to roam."

Seeing Hagar's perplexed look, Sarai gently put her arm around the girl. "We are going to a place chosen for us by God. It will be your home too, Hagar. And the one holy God will be your father now and will take care of you."

Hagar appreciated the unexpected affection. She followed Sarai at every moment, trying to find things to do to please her.

Rebounding in driving energy after his prolonged illness, Pharaoh Mentuhotep overexerted himself. He was found dead in his bed only weeks after Abram left Kemi. Shetepibre called a meeting in Memphis of all the nomarchs of the Upper and Lower Lands. Since there was no heir and the Land had grown dependent on his leadership, the nomarchs, led by Meketre, asked Shetepibre to assume the throne. Tepi immediately appointed Antefoker as his grand vizier. It was a peaceable transition for such a significant change of dynasties.

Mentuhotep was buried in the pure white alabaster sarcophagus, as Tepi had promised. The other stones, however, that were intended for Mentuhotep's monument were shipped to Wase. There Shetepibre and Meketre designed and erected the great temple to the one holy God.

Shetepibre added to his formal name the word "Amenemhet" which means "God of the reborn," taken from the the word "Amon" which in Kemian means "hidden God." As Shetepibre Amenemhet I, he became the initiator of the great twelfth dynasty of the Land, a dynasty that abolished the worship of pagan gods and turned the people's hearts to their creator, the one God.[15]

Chapter XV
LOT AND SALANNA

As watchmen led the way, shepherds slowly edged the flocks and herds along, and servants prodded the ladened camels and asses. Children kept their places behind the animals, their dung baskets slung over their shoulders, flopping on their backs as they ran. Women servants tended to the needs of the company, taking water and ale to the thirsty, caring for the very young, and preparing the meals.

On leaving Kemi, Abram pitched camp by the sea as he travelled along the northern coastal route. At the Brook of Kemi he led his people inland, following the road of that wadi valley and stopping for several days rest at the pastures and springs of Kadesh. Again the company paused at the wells of Sheba before continuing to the green valley plain of Sodom and Gomorrah.

The fertile lands of the Sodom and Gomorrah valley stretched out to the south of a placid lake, a lake glistening brightly from the hot overhead sun. Rough desert wilderness mountains bordered the long valley on the west, while softer, often grass covered, hills and mountains rose to the east. To the north the winding Jordan poured the waters of its river into the lake. The smaller towns of the valley, Admah, Zeboiim and Zoar, were located on narrow canals where they could draw from the fresh clear waters of the lake for irrigation.

The Lake of Gomorrah was large, oval and deep, with a floor depth of nearly a thousand cubits. Far down the southern side of its submerged basin was the mouth of an underground tunnel. Salts and impurities settling to that level drained off into an underground river that coursed far beneath the ground surface. These subterranean waters flowed on under the land plate of the Negeb toward the gulf reefs where they emptied into the deep ocean trench of the Red Sea.

The warm climate, the protective mountains and the abundant fresh waters meant the cities of the Sodom valley could raise crops year around and were not dependent on the erratic rainfall patterns of the rest of Canaan. The area was also blessed with tar pits of bitumen which surfaced in the low vale near Zeboiim.

The recent drought-caused famine had made the land around the Lake of Gomorrah very desirable. The five kings of the cities of the Sodom valley united in order to isolate themselves from the refugees who tried to settle permanently in their midst. Only people such as Lot and Salanna who were financially independent were allowed to take residence. Exceptions were also made for acceptable young men who wished to come, providing they submitted to and participated in the practices of the inhabitants.

Two such young Hurrian men had come to Sodom and had fallen in love with Salanna's daughters. Although they had to serve a year as male prostitutes at the Sodom temple, their plans were to marry Minusa and Pukuli as soon as the term expired.

When Lot entered his house in Sodom with Abram and Sarai, Salanna received them with uneasiness. With Lot's long absence in Kemi, Salanna had been forced to use nearly all of their resources. She was pleased to have Lot return, for she had grown to respect and love him, and she was overjoyed to know of his new herds and flocks and that all of her herdsmen were back with him. But she knew before he suggested it that Lot would want to stay on with Abram and live in tents away from the valley cities.

At first, Salanna did not display her strong feelings about leaving her home in Sodom. Instead she welcomed her husband lovingly and showed warm and polite hospitality to Abram and Sarai. She and her daughters with the few remaining servants prepared a simple but savory meal for them.

"Salanna, you are a wonderful wife for Lot," Abram complimented her as they finished the repast. "I see now why he was so anxious to return to you. And Minusa and Pukuli are lovely women. I am only surprised that they have not married yet."

Salanna smiled graciously and said, "There are few men in these cities with desire for women. Until Tul-tesup and Pai-tesup came here from Nuzu, our homeland, the girls despaired of ever marrying. Even now I am worried. Tul-tesup and Pai-tesup are beginning to change. . . ."

Lot turned to her, his face reddening and reflecting his concern. "What do you mean?" he asked.

Salanna looked from Lot to Abram and then to Sarai. She had not planned to say what she had, and she was apprehensive of going further. With resumed poise she replied, "I simply mean it would be best if we stayed in Sodom so that Minusa and Pukuli could be near their betrothed."

"Salanna, you are my wife now," Lot spoke gently but firmly. "I want us to go with Abram!"

"Of course, Lot," she tried to answer brightly. "Only let us keep this house so that we and the girls may return often."

Lot glanced at Abram for advice but saw that his uncle was determined not to intervene. He turned next to Sarai, "Do you think it would be wise?"

Sarai reached over and took Salanna's hand. "You will never be able to worship God freely or purely here, Salanna. It is an evil city! Please break away from it and be part of our family!"

"I do not *think* like you do, Sarai," Salanna responded defensively. "I believe there is a God . . . somewhere. But I do not want to spend my life believing in promises that are never fulfilled. I once gave up everything that I enjoyed for

Arnawar's dream. All I ask now is that we keep our house so that I may live at least some months in the city each year."

"I want you with me!" Lot spoke to her determinedly. "With my caravaning and the two years away from you in Kemi, I don't want you to be away from me again at any time!"

"But Lot," Salanna replied with anguish, "if you would sell the herds you would have more than enough to establish the caravans again. You would not have to go on them but just supervise them from here. We could always be together!"

Lot thought on what she had said. "We will keep the house for a while," he relented. "But I want you and Minusa and Pukuli ready to leave with us in the morning."

"In the morning. . . ?" she questioned, blinking back her tears.

"The flocks will be ready to move," Abram interjected. "We want to go back to Bethel once again. Remember, Salanna, that is where we built an altar and claimed the promise of the land. It will be as if we were beginning again!"

Salanna stared at Abram. His lean body was strong and agile and his voice still had the enthusiasm of a young man. But his hair had become almost white and his face deeply lined. She looked then at Sarai. Salanna had always liked Sarai, but could never understand her strong convictions.

"How can you two go on this way?" Salanna cried out. "You claim God has given you the whole land of Canaan, but the best you can do is live in tents and wander about.

"And you, Sarai," she continued in her frustration, "waiting to bear a child! It is ridiculous! I have little hope to ever bear Lot a son, but *you* . . . you are almost twice my age! I know you do not appear so . . . but you are!"

Lot felt hurt and confused by the conversation. He rose abruptly from the table. "Go, make your preparations, Salanna. We must return to the camp soon, and I want you to be with me! We can come back for the servants and other things."

Lot motioned for Abram and Sarai to go with him into the courtyard. They left the room without further words.

"That was probably the right thing to do," Abram tried to console his nephew as the three of them sat together in the garden.

"I have waited nearly two years to be with my wife, and I have left her in anger after a few hours!" Lot anguished bitterly. "Perhaps she is right. I could become very wealthy if I stayed and organized my own caravans. I know all the connections now in each city both south to Kemi and north to Charran."

Lot suddenly rose and left them, going back into the house and up the inner court stairs. Salanna was packing in her room. Lot entered, closing and bolting the door behind him. The strain and resignation had not left Salanna's face as he approached her and bent down and kissed her forehead. "I am miserable, my precious wife," he whispered, pulling her to him and caressing her. "Let us go with Abram and Sarai for a while. If it is unpleasant for you we will return to Sodom. I promise you!"

"Oh, Lot, would you?" Salanna pleaded.

"Will you try to like living with them first?" he asked.

"I will try," she answered quickly. "I will really try! Can we make a decision after Bethel?"

Lot smiled and just looked at her. Suddenly all thoughts but the desire to embrace her left his mind. He held her, kissing her ardently and then lifted her in his arms. "I want only one thing now, Salanna!" he said as he placed her on the soft cushions of the bed and loosened her robes. "I may have to live in the midst of the men of Sodom, but it is only my woman who excites me . . . excites me so unbearably!"

About an hour passed. Lot lay with his wife still enjoying the warmth of her body after their passion. A quiet knock sounded at the door. The two arose and dressed as Salanna talked to her daughter through the closed door.

"Yes, Pukuli! What do you wish!" Salanna asked.

"Tul-tesup and Pai-tesup will not go with us, Mother," Pukuli called out. "They are becoming just like the other men! If we leave they will lose all desire for us."

"No, my dear," Salanna tried to soothe her daughter. "It is just the temple duty. Now that they are free, they will return to natural feelings."

"Oh, Mother!" Pukuli cried out. "They said some older men want them. They plan to sell themselves for another year. They said that way they will have money enough to marry."

Lot opened the door. His tear-stained adopted daughter stood dejectedly before him. "We must go then without them, Pukuli," he said gently. "Go, get your sister. We will return to Sodom soon. Perhaps it will be different then."

Pukuli looked up at Lot. "Father Lot, do you know that Minusa and I could walk naked throughout the streets of Sodom and Gomorrah and no man would even notice us? Can you imagine what it is like to be a woman and be so rejected?" she complained bitterly.

"No, I cannot understand," Lot replied with sincere sympathy. "You and Minusa are so beautiful. . . ."

When Abram, Sarai and Lot had entered Sodom early that morning the streets had been almost devoid of people. Now, as they and Salanna and her daughters departed with a band of their watchmen and packed camels, large crowds mostly of men gathered.

Pushing their way toward the gates of the city, Abram, Lot and the watchmen found themselves leered at, pinched and clutched. "Leave us alone!" shouted Lot. "I am a legal sojourner here. By your laws, I and my guests are allowed freedom and protection!"

"Let them be!" a clear voice sounded over the noise. The crowd quieted and parted to let King Bera pass through.

The king of Sodom was an imposing and unusual looking man with smooth well-oiled skin, large pensive but mocking eyes, and sharp thin features. His dark hair was an intricate mass of carefully curled ringlets. He was immaculately clothed in embroidered fine linen and jewels and broad gold arm bracelets. Bright glittering rings adorned his fingers, even his toes.

"Well, my dear friend, Lot," Bera greeted him. "You have returned and are already leaving us so soon? We have missed the treasures of your caravans, and we have much copper and silver to be exported. Do not say that you depart from us. Have I not protected you? Has your wife not found safety with us? And isn't your house as you left it?"

"You have kept you word, King Bera," Lot concurred. "We may return. But for now I must find pastures for my flocks and herds. I brought up many from Kemi."

"But you may pasture them here in winter and let your herders take them to the mountains of Seir after the rains," the king persuaded. Then noticing Abram's stern look of disapproval the king turned to him. "And who is this?" Bera asked Lot tartly.

"This is my uncle Abram and his wife Sarai," Lot replied. Realizing Abram's growing irritation and desire to leave, Lot added, "We must go, King Bera."

"No, wait!" the king said in pleased surprise. "You mean this old man is 'Abram the Habiru?' *This* is the great black giant that strikes fear in the hearts of the Amorites?" The king and those about him began to laugh.

"If you do not let us out of this city," Abram yelled at Bera and the crowd, pulling out his sword as did his men who followed his action, "you may soon find out why we are called the black giants of the Habiru!"

Bera's smile quickly changed. "Why are you threatening us?" he demanded indignantly.

"I want your pawing men out of our way!" Abram declared emphatically.

Bera saw that his first impression of Abram was mistaken. The intelligence that showed on Abram's face and the fire that blazed in his eyes revealed a man who could well frighten Chedorlaomer and the other Amorite shakanas. "We mean you no harm," Bera apologized. He motioned to his guards to clear the street.

"Abram," Bera entreated him as Abram and his group turned to leave. "We need someone like you and your men! If you would stay in Sodom, I and the other kings of the valley cities would pay you well to defend us. You do not have to be *like* us! You could live outside the city. But just stay close enough to protect us from the Amorites. With you here we would never have to pay tribute! In fact, we will pay *you* the tribute! You could be the wealthiest man in Canaan!"

Abram spat on the ground to show his disgust. "I will never accept pay to protect what God calls an abomination!"

The next day as the thousands of sheep, goats, oxen, asses and camels pushed toward Bethel, Salanna and her daughters talked with the Hurrian herdsmen. Soon afterward, bickering and fighting broke out between Abram's men and those of Lot and Salanna's.

Abram found the spot where he had first built an altar. It had been torn down and its stones carried away. He assembled all the people of the company, asking them to help in the building of a new altar. But the Hurrians sullenly refused to participate, keeping to their tents as they had done once before.

When the altar was completed, two unblemished lambs were sacrificed and a large measure of fine grain was burned as an offering. Abram gathered all who would willingly come to pray before the Lord. Lifting praises, Abram gave thanks for the great wealth and blessings God had bestowed upon them and for the safe return to the promised land.

Abram and Lot had hoped to camp at Bethel for some time. The water supply was ample, but the pastureland soon became overgrazed. The feuding between the herdsmen intensified as each group sought out the heavier grasses.

At a noon meal Lot approached Abram and the two sat together under a hillside shade tent to discuss the problems. The strain and anxiety Lot was enduring was conspicuous on his face.

"My mind and heart are being torn apart, Abram," he agonized. "I love the Lord and his righteousness. And I am hoping Salanna's herdsmen are beginning to believe as well, in spite of their refusing to pray with the rest of us. They are not ignorant of the miracles that occurred in Kemi, and they have witnessed how God has blessed us. But they still hold to Arnawar's dream and yearn for the mountains of Seir."

Abram scanned the hills crowded with flocks and herds. "We cannot have strife between us or between our herdsmen," he conceded, inwardly tormented by the problem. "The whole land is before you, Lot. You may separate from me in any direction. If you go left, I will go right. If you go to the right, I shall go left."

Lot sadly surveyed the land around them. Then he looked back through the wadi that wound around the foot of the hillside where they were sitting, meandering until it merged with the Jordan River valley. In the far hazy distance lay the blue waters of the Lake of Gomorrah, the cities of the verdant Sodom plains, and the mountains of Seir. At last he made the fateful decision. "We will depart tomorrow. I will take the road east to Jericho, skirt the lake on the east and camp near Sodom once again."

The parting was difficult but happened quickly. After a farewell blessing from Abram and Sarai, Lot took all of his possessions plus extra servants and some of Abram's herdsmen that were Lot's close friends. They left before dawn and by the time the sun rose, Lot's people were but specks on the distant hillsides.

Abram remained in the valley near Bethel. The fall rains came early. They were gentle and steady. As the ground softened, Abram's people began the hard labor of breaking up the ground and plowing and sowing the nearby fields that had lain fallow and deserted during the famine. The shepherds led the flocks and herds into the hills and mountains for the new grasses. It was not long before the rested fields yielded a first and then a second harvest that were unexpectedly abundant.

Large groups of Canaanites began arriving in the spring seeking to find the homes they had left during the long drought. They eagerly bought up Abram's surplus grain. Many had come back from Kemi. It was from them that Abram and Sarai learned of Mentuhotep's death and the ascension to the throne of Shetepibre Amenemhet as pharaoh of the Land.

One night in early autumn Abram tossed restlessly on his bed. Sleep would not come. In his half wakefulness Abram saw God. He appeared to him in a lucid and commanding vision, saying:

"Go up to the high mountain of Hazor. See all the land to the east, the west, the south and the north. This is the land I give to you and your descendants forever!"

In compliance with the vision, Abram arranged for part of his watchmen and servants to remain at Bethel with the shepherds. Then with Sarai and a small army of forty watchmen and a few servants, he left for Hazor.

Each watchman rode a camel, as did Abram and Sarai. The servants walked behind, leading pack asses. The first night's camp was set up near the ruins of a city on the slope of a high hill. Only a few returning refugees from the famine lived among the deserted remains, using the stones from broken down structures to build small hovels for themselves. The city was marked on Abram's Sumerian maps as Shechem, although these refugees called it Sakmemi.

As the servants prepared their meal, Abram and Sarai walked further up the hill so that they could look down on the once heavily populated site. The shape of the city was outlined by its jagged and battered thick walls. The criss-crossing cobblestone streets were filled with debris and old bricks and stones. A fertile plain stretched east of the city, overgrown with weeds and brambles.

"A dangerous place to build," Abram commented. "They were not high enough up the slope. With two mountain-sized hills on either side, an enemy ambush would not be difficult to execute against them."

"That must be why they built such high thick walls," Sarai noticed. "It is hard to imagine a whole city of people just vanishing."

"I doubt that they vanished, my darling," he answered frankly. "I suspect that their blood and their bones lie in those ruins. This may have been the 'example' that the Amorites used when they raided Canaan over twelve years ago."

Sarai shuddered, "A whole city. . . ?"

"Men destroy for their own gain, Sarai. But God too sometimes destroys . . . for the sake of his own righteousness!"

Early the next morning they stopped for a time of prayer under the oak that Abram had named Moreh. Then they departed for Megiddo, a city where they could buy supplies. The tents were pitched some distance from the famous metropolis. The old city had survived a succession of inhabitants since the time of Menes in Kemi. Sometimes buildings were leveled by invaders, other times they were simply leveled for rebuilding. Over the centuries the natural plateau on which the original settlers had lived had become an elevated mound. Strategically the city was well located for its own defense. From the top of its eight cubit-thick walls guards could survey the entire plain north and east to the hills of Chinnereth. They could also view great lengths of the incoming trade routes, including the north-south pass through the coastal mountain chain.

As Abram and Sarai and several servants entered Megiddo the following day, they walked up a broad ramp on the north side of the city and through a guarded gate between two flanking towers. The cobbled entrance plaza was bustling with commercial activities. They moved through the crowded area to the heavy main gate that was used to close the massive walls of the city. The heavy bronze-plated portals had already been swung open on their stone hinge sockets. Scrutinizing guards stood in pilaster cells on either side of the gateway.

Once past the gates, the city seemed to be much like Damascus—busy, preoccupied and indifferent to strangers. Abram and Sarai and the servants who had accompanied them began buying supplies. They were unaware of a military detachment that brushed its way through the food stalls, the women with their produce baskets balanced securely on their heads, the laden asses and camels, and the chattering and bargaining customers of the market. As Abram was inspecting a collection of knives, the unit of twelve uniformed men approached him.

"Are you Abram of Terrakki?" the command captain inquired, nothing in his voice betraying his mission.

"Yes," Abram replied in astonishment. "How did you know of me?"

"With your consent, I have been requested to bring you before the ensi of Megiddo."

"With what charge?" Abram demanded obstinately.

"There is no charge, sir, simply a request. The matter has not been made known to me," the captain explained courteously. "I can guarantee you safety, however."

"Does the ensi request all of us?"

"No, sir. Only yourself, and your wife Sarai, if she wishes to accompany you."

Sarai looked up startled. "You know my name as well?"

The captain smiled and evading her question turned to lead the way. "If you will come with me, it is only a short distance," he replied.

Abram and Sarai left the servants and were escorted on either side by the soldiers. They were led through the streets of Megiddo until they entered a large open plaza. There, the center of the gardened square was dominated by a large and obviously ancient round altar. From three directions, temples faced toward the plaza altar with the main rooms of the temples and porches open to adherents.

Within one of the open temples stood a statue of Ishtar, an unclothed body of stone with grossly exaggerated female features. A large phallic pillar of Baal-Hadad was centered in the second temple. Noisily beckoning male and female prostitutes hung from the balconies of the side rooms of the Ishtar and Baal-Hadad temples. Most were gaudily but scantily costumed, and many had open sores of the diseases common to their business festering on their bodies. In the third rather run-down temple was a statue of Nannar-Sin, a distant copy of the one that King Akalamdu had placed hundreds of years before in the upper rooms of the Ziggurat of Ur. An inverted crescent pendant hung on the coarsely made image. Below the moon god, a young woman's figure was depicted holding snakes in her uplifted hands.

An imposing civic building also faced on the square. Abram and Sarai were led through its entryway, down a long corridor and into the ensi's antechamber. As the door of the main court of the ensi opened, Abram and Sarai were completely struck by surprise. One of the two persons who stood before them they knew immediately.

"Welcome, Abram and Sarai of Terrakki. I am Ensi Ibnamalik, Prince of Megiddo. I believe you already know this gentleman, Captain Hirqnos."

Chapter XVI
VIEW FROM HAZOR

"Abram, good friend, and Sarai! Only yesterday the guards at the gate were given your descriptions and told to watch for you. Your God of miracles has surely brought you here!" greeted Hirqnos as he stepped forward and embraced them with genuine enthusiasm.

"Hirqnos!" Abram exclaimed in astonishment. "Why are *you* in Megiddo?"

"By orders of his majesty, the great pharaoh of the Land, Shetepibre Amenemhet!" he beamed proudly.

Ensi Ibnamalik smiled and acknowledged, "Captain Hirqnos has come to discuss unification of the great trade cities in Canaan with the Land of Kemi to ward off Chedorlaomer and his Amorites."

Abram was immediately concerned. "Does Shetepibre fear an attack?"

"May we sit down, my lord Ibnamalik?" Hirqnos requested of the ensi. "I have never been healthier since the prayer of this man, Abram. With words to his God he released me from the plague. But I have much to tell him."

"Certainly, let us go into a smaller, more private, room," the ensi suggested, motioning to a servant to bring wine.

"Mentuhotep?" Sarai inquired of Hirqnos as they seated themselves around a low table. "Did he suffer much pain in his death?"

"No, my lady Sarai," Hirqnos replied kindly. "He enjoyed every day as if it were a gift, and he might not have another. But he tried too soon to make up for his lost work, his lost play, and his lost eating and drinking. After a long night of banqueting his heart just stopped. It was soon after he had fallen asleep in his bed."

Hirqnos then went on to explain his mission. "During the famine many Amorites from the four tribes of the shakanas, Chedorlaomer, Amraphel, Arioch and Tidal, were sent to Kemi. They did not come out of necessity but to infiltrate our country. Shetepibre learned of this when he investigated the deteriorating state of affairs in the Lower Land. As you know, the plague kept both Antefoker and myself away from our duties for nearly two years."

"You mean that many of the indentured refugees were really Chedorlaomer's and the other shakanas' men? What has Shetepibre done to root them out? What are his plans?" Abram questioned him.

"He has enlisted every indentured Asiatic in the Land to build a fortified wall along the lower eastern border of the delta, following the Wadi Tummilat. As you may remember, that wadi forms a natural boundary. By the excellent way the wall is being constructed, it should hold back invaders coming by land from the east for centuries," Hirqnos informed them.

"A wall? To keep out the Amorites? What a remarkable plan!" Abram exclaimed with pleasure and excitement over Shetepibre's maneuver. "He will keep the infiltrators out of mischief by building a wall against their own allies! Magnificent!"

Hirqnos nodded enthusiastically in agreement, "The Asiatics will be fenced in but will not be suffering. Shetepibre has provided tents, plenty of water and food, as well as ample bonuses for good workers."

"The term 'Asiatics,' whom does that include?" Abram asked.

252

"Any person without proof of citizenship from a recognized government. You left just in time, Abram. You might now be mixing straw and mud and making bricks!" Hirqnos laughed and then added respectfully, "Although it is my opinion that you would be grand vizier of the Land had you remained. There is no man the new pharaoh honors more than Abram, the friend of the one hidden God!"

Abram and Sarai both felt a warm inner response as Hirqnos spoke his last words. "You are a believer, Hirqnos?" Sarai asked softly.

The ensi was confused by the strange interruption, but he kept silent. He, like Abram and Sarai, waited for the embarrassed captain to respond.

"How could I not be a believer," Hirqnos said gratefully. "I was there . . . and I knew the touch of the finger of God!"

The poignant and intense interlude quickly passed.

Hirqnos resumed the conversation, his face and voice serious, "It is still a very dangerous time for Kemi and also for Canaan."

"You have knowledge of Chedorlaomer's plans of attack?" Abram inquired.

"Yes," Hirqnos replied affirmatively. "Part of my assignment was to locate you and warn you. The ranks of the Amorite leagues have swollen with all the refugees from Canaan. The total number of men in the combined tribes is more than any single standing army from the river cities to Kemi. King Shulgi of Ur has united the Sumerian cities, and they have held Chedorlaomer and the other three off . . . but Akkad has been almost annihilated, I have been told."

"Where are the Amorites now?" Abram pressed him.

They are encamped and in training somewhere east of Akkad. Our spies have confirmed that they plan to march next spring and attack the cities of the Sodom valley."

"Down the trade routes?" the ensi interjected anxiously.

"No," Hirqnos answered quickly. "My information is that they will come directly across the desert."

"They cannot take camels across the desert without first going north near Damascus," Abram countered strongly. "There is a basalt barrier lying northwest to southeast! A camel will not set foot on it. By Kemi reckoning, the strip is a day's journey wide, perhaps seven days in length. It begins south of Damascus with its southern tip opposite but far east of Sodom."

"They have both camels and asses, we are told, thousands upon thousands of them," Hirqnos unfolded.

"Then they must be dividing accordingly," Abram projected, his mind intensely trying to conceptualize the Amorite battle tactics. "They will probably launch an attack with the camel battalions on smaller cities south of Damascus, probably beginning with Karnaim, Ashtaroth, Ham . . . then hit Kiriathaim near the Lake of Gomorrah. They will be sure to let the news of their coming unite the Sodom cities to expect attack from the north, in that case. Or perhaps they will avoid the Sodom valley at first and raid farther south. If they did that, the camel troops would probably return to the west side of Lake Gomorrah. Meanwhile their ass-mounted troops will have made a straight cross over the desert and the basalt, attack the Hurrians in the mountains of Seir, and fall on the Sodomites from the south."

There was silence while the others thought on Abram's logic. The ensi spoke first. "You do not think they will try to attack our trade cities . . . or Kemi?"

"Not when they learn of Shetepibre's wall and hear that the trade cities are uniting with Kemi," Abram answered readily. "But give them a few more years, when you are not alerted, and they will attempt to sack your cities. Even Shetepibre's wall may not stop them in time."

As the discussion drew to a close, the ensi invited the three to join him and the citizens of Megiddo that evening for an annual celebration. The feast, he told them, marked the beginning of the "season of entreaty." The worshippers of Baal-Hadad performed rites and offered sacrifices to revive the yearly slain deity. The roasted meat from the sacrifices would be served at the all night affair.

"We worship a holy and jealous God," Abram declared to the ensi. "Baal is a mockery of the real God's purity and righteousness!"

Ibnamalik shrugged and smiled, "You should not take your religion so seriously, Abram. The real God is big enough to have many names and personalities. Baal is the sporting nature of the gods, taking pleasure in man. My dear friend, as it is with our lovely goddess Astarte whom your people called Ishtar, whenever you receive pleasure Baal receives pleasure. When enough men become carnally excited this time of year, the god Baal awakens and rises. He returns to the earth causing it to bring forth its fruits and animals to mate and bear young. . . ."

"Stop!" shouted Abram angrily, his patience exhausted. "Such lies pollute every good and pure gift that God has given his people! God is holy and he is righteous! He destroyed a whole evil world with the Great Flood except Noah and his family."

The ensi twitted, *"You,* the brilliant Abram, the great soldier of Damascus, the counselor of the pharaoh of Kemi . . . *you* believe in the Great Flood?"

Abram refused to answer. "We must return to our camp. You are welcome, Hirqnos, to join us for the evening meal if this city's orgy does not please you. We would like to hear more about Shetepibre and Kemi, for tomorrow we will depart for Hazor."

Hirqnos apologized to the ensi, "Forgive me, but I too am now a worshipper of the one hidden God. After we complete our business I should like to join Abram and Sarai."

"As you wish," Ibnamalik retorted brusquely. Then turning to Abram he said, "If you are going to Hazor, let me assure you that the celebrations of Megiddo are mild compared to Hazor's. Almost all of the temple priestesses from Akkad have fled to Hazor. It is a very . . . 'open' city!"

The next morning Abram sent five of his men back to Bethel with the supplies purchased in Megiddo. The five were instructed to continue on after their journey to Bethel until they found Lot and to warn him about the planned invasion of Chedorlaomer.

Abram gathered the rest of his company and went north toward Hazor, pitching camp not far from that city. Leaving

255

his tents in the early afternoon, Abram climbed alone up the nearby high mountain. He carried food, an ale skin and a blanket for sleeping.

As he reached the mountain's summit, Abram saw the higher mountains of Hermon and dark forests of cedar to the north. Turning toward the south, he could see as far as the distant Brook of Kemi. From the height of the Hazor mountain and in the clearness of the autumn air, the whole land of Canaan stretched out before him. He suddenly yearned to know and to pace out every cubit that he saw, to explore the winding, twisting Jordan River, to walk the coastline shores of the Great Sea, to climb each mountain and hilltop, to camp in each valley.

The assurance of the promises kept coming back to him over and over. Then the Lord spoke to Abram, "Just as the dust of the earth, so shall your descendants be in number. Go, walk the land that you see. It will be yours and your seed for ever." Abram spent the night watching over the land in the starlight, rejoicing in thanksgiving and prayer.[16]

Coming down from the mountain at daybreak, Abram walked to the city of Hazor. He was able to enter unnoticed as the gate guards had left their posts to help quell a mass of drunken fighting men. The city was in its second day of entreaty fertility rites. Business was at a standstill. People walked about in the streets either loud and boisterous or in a dull stupor.

The center of the city was much like Megiddo. In the opened temples, gyrating priests and priestesses danced around the phallic symbol of Baal and a vulgarly squatting nude image of Astarte, their form of Ishtar. A round altar about twenty cubits wide stood in the middle of the plaza. A fire blazed in the center of the altar where sacrifices were burned. Couples, men and women, lay naked around the fire, publicly and grotesquely copulating. A frenzied looking father carrying a newborn baby tore himself away from a screeching woman and tossed his son into the smoking flames. "Awaken, O Baal!" he yelled as his wife moaned and collapsed behind him. The man shoved her away and went in search of one of the priestesses.

The activity was not confined to the square. As Abram sought to find his way back out of the city he witnessed every form of ugly debasement. Leaving the walls of Hazor he saw the mountain where he had felt so close to God only hours earlier and his heart ached.

Later in the day Abram discussed with Sarai his experiences of his twenty-four hour period away from her. "The time before the Great Flood could be no more evil, Sarai, than what I beheld in Hazor. Why does God say that this is the holy and promised land and yet the people are saturated in vileness?"

"We can't cleanse the land ourselves, Abram," Sarai comforted him, putting her hands in his. Abram knew from the way Sarai spoke that she had been long hours in prayer herself while he was gone. Everything about her expression was soft and glowing.

"Has God been speaking to you, Sarai?"

"I think I am beginning to understand the uncompromising . . . and divine way of our God," she said slowly.

"Please go on, Sarai," he urged her as they seated themselves on the bedding in the tent.

"God keeps promising us a great multitude of descendants?"

"Yes."

"Then possession of the land can never be in our lifetime," she rejoined. "Our offspring would be too few against the iniquity that is growing in this land."

"There are still many righteous in Canaan, Sarai. We have heard of Abimelech. There is Melchizedek, Mamre and his brothers, and surely some righteous people in every city."

"But the abominations will become more evil, Abram . . . as they did before the Great Flood. There will be no one righteous!"

"No righteous, Sarai?" Abram objected.

"I believe our children will leave Canaan for many years . . . they will stay in a land where they can multiply and where God can be worshipped," her words rang with the vibrancy of prophecy.

A long silence followed. The idea churned within Abram's mind, and he felt an inner confirmation. "Kemi!" he whispered loudly. "The Land of Shetepibre, *a womb to hold our descendants captive until they have multiplied into a nation for God!*"[17]

"Yes, Abram. A nation for God mighty enough to return to Canaan and cleanse the whole land of its depravity, to burn Hazor to the ground!" Sarai's voice had become triumphant and almost harsh. "Like you said, Abram. God too sometimes destroys for the sake of his own righteousness!"

"Sarai, do you think that would be necessary?" Abram said. He resisted the thought, for he saw wrath in Sarai's eyes which had replaced the glow that only moments before he had been admiring.

Sarai's answer was oblique but definite, "Only eight persons survived the Great Flood!"

For four months Abram, Sarai and the band of watchmen and servants travelled together, surveying the lands that Abram had seen from the high mountain near Hazor. Abram made sketches of new maps and corrected his old ones, while Sarai helped him keep an accurate journal of his findings.

They returned to Bethel in late winter. Many difficulties had arisen during the months they had been gone, problems coming from the influx of returning Canaanites and Hurrian Perizzites. As the impoverished refugees poured into the towns of Ai and Bethel or passed through the Bethel valley en route to the Sodomite cities, they did not hesitate to contemptuously raid and steal from Abram's possessions.

Abram immediately gathered his people together at the altar of Bethel. After they had prayed, a decision was made to migrate quickly toward Sheba and settle the families and servants beside the oaks of Mamre.

One other thing constantly disturbed and worried Abram. The men he had sent to warn Lot had not been able to find him, and Salanna had refused to tell them where he was. She said that Lot would be returning soon and that she would give him the message herself.

When Abram and Sarai arrived with all their people and possessions at the village of Mamre, they found the place deserted. No one had remained during the long famine.

Abram's large company set up camp on the lands beside the oak forest, and the flocks and herds were led off to graze on the nearby pastures and hillsides. With the watchmen and servants Abram erected an altar and placed offerings on it.

It was cold and bleak that night as the weary and discouraged people came and knelt to worship. With the women and the young ones, there were nearly three thousand around the altar. Gradually, as they began singing and lifting praises, the joy and blessedness of the Lord's presence gently removed their feelings of loneliness and despair. Even when it became late, the fires of the camp were kept blazing, for no one wanted to leave. They felt close to God and close to each other, though the desolate farmlands and withered orchards lay in the dark shadows all around them.

As Abram walked with Sarai back to their tent after the time of prayer, he confessed the depression he had felt earlier. "We have many riches, my lovely wife, and God has brought us back to claim our land, but I miss the fellowship of Lot and my brother Nahor, and men like Shetepibre and Meketre. Now even Mamre and his brothers are gone. . . ."

A few days later, as if the Lord had heard and answered his desire, a loud familiar voice boomed outside their quarters. "Look who beat us back, my brothers!" Mamre shouted. "The king of the promised land!"

When Abram ran from his tent to welcome the three brothers, he took one glance at their sorry appearance and fell on their shoulders weeping.

"We are really not as poor as we look," Aner laughed, his friendly smile a bright contrast to his emaciated body and tattered clothing.

"At least we are alive," Eshcol joined in jokingly. "Our families are still in Mari, but we have returned to our weeds and stubble!"

Sarai greeted the brothers and rushed to get the servants to help prepare for a celebration. The good news spread all over the camp, and the banquet later that evening was a very special occasion.

Although Mamre, Eshcol and Aner had lost all their possessions during the famine, they were eager to begin again. However, the days that followed the welcoming celebration were difficult ones for the three brothers. Mamre found that what the storms and the drought had not destroyed, wandering refugees had stolen. His young olive trees had been ruthlessly chopped down and only stumps remained of all the fruit trees. The wells were polluted and Mamre's house in the village had been sacked and burned.

Eshcol and Aner had left their wives, Yadida and Tasuba, in Mari. Both young women had given birth. Yadida, Eshcol's wife, had a son, and Tasuba, Aner's wife, a daughter. Mamre's wife and their five children also waited in Mari with the other two women in crowded conditions, hoping for good news from their husbands.

Disheartened, the brothers went to Abram. "We must return to Mari, my friend," Mamre announced sadly. "I don't think I shall ever come back again."

"But I have wealth and servants to help you," Abram offered. "Remain until the rains come. We shall plow together. Everything can be restored in a few years."

Eshcol smiled appreciatively. "You wish to be free to move your people about in the land, Abram. We wanted to build our homes here."

"We are fools, Abram!" Aner cried out. "That is what we are saying! Proud fools! With no wealth, no servants, we can't begin again! Never!"

"There are hundreds of Canaanites that will return when the rains come," Abram tried to console them. "They will be looking for indentured work. You will have as many as you wish."

"And pay and feed them with what?" Mamre questioned. "Your provisions?"

"At least until the rains, come work for me," Abram suggested. "I want to train my watchmen during these months. You know this land and have had military experience. I have picked over three hundred men. I would like to place one of you over each battalion."

A flicker of hope lighted the eyes of the discouraged brothers. A broad smile broke across Mamre's face. "How I would enjoy doing something like that again!" he beamed.

"I will pay you well," Abram rejoined. "It will be a beginning!"

Chapter XVII
ASSAULT OF THE AMORITES

Through success of his battles and the fierceness of his warriors, Chedorlaomer had maintained preeminence over the other shakanas of the lawless roaming tribes of the Amorites. As Chedorlaomer grew older he demanded an even tighter reign.

Reducing Arioch, Tidal and Amraphel to commanders under his authority, Chedorlaomer ordered them to bring all of their troops to the land of Elam east of Akkad. There for many months the hardened fighters and renegades of the four tribes trained as one army.

When spring came, Chedorlaomer sent out Arioch and Tidal with ten camel battalions of one hundred men each. True to Abram's prediction the camel troops avoided the desert basalt and preyed upon the small villages east and south of Damascus.

Years before when Chedorlaomer and the three shakanas had attacked and raided they had frightened the smaller towns and cities into paying yearly tribute. The famine had halted much of this revenue as fleeing villagers left their communities unoccupied. Now that people were resettling, violence from the extortioners was planned to reactivate the payments.

The southern Canaanite towns of the Sodom valley had been the Amorite's largest source of tribute. When King Bera heard that other towns were no longer paying, he and the other kings of the valley refused as well, although in their case it was not due to the famine. For this insolence, the Amorite shakanas planned not to destroy the wealthy Sodom cities but to chastise them severely. Chedorlaomer was also interested in securing a good supply of copper from the Sodomite mines for his weapon makers.

After Arioch and Tidal's men had sacked Astaroth, Karnaim and the small village of Ham which was a short distance southeast of the Lake of Chinnereth, they kept a fast pace to Kiriathaim, northeast of the Lake of Gomorrah. Avoiding the Sodomite valley by way of a circuitous forest and mountain route, the two commanders led attacks on the unwalled Hurrian settlements of Seir before travelling south to pillage the gulf port of El Paran. Next they swung northwest, wreaking destruction in Kadesh and upon scattered independent Amorites who, like Mamre and his brothers, had settled in small farming villages. The last of these was an Amorite community named Hazazon-Tamar. It lay in a wadi not far from the northwest shores of the Lake of Gomorrah.

Tidal and Arioch were eager to force any strong looking Amorites of Canaan to join their league, and they gave such men little choice but death if they refused. With these enlistments and the booty from their raids, the camel troops of Arioch and Tidal appeared in view before the waiting armies of the five kings of the Sodom valley.

Bera, the king of Sodom; Birsha, king of Gomorrah; Shinab, king of Admah; Shemeber, king of Zeboiim; and the ruler of the small village of Zoar had joined their forces at the southeastern shores of the lake. Lot was among the thousands of men recruited to defend the cities. There was a nonchalant almost arrogant attitude among the kings and their soldiers.

"The barbarian Chedorlaomer may terrorize villages with those camel riders," King Bera claimed, proudly enjoying pacing in front of the other kings in his decorative armor. "But he certainly won't bring us down with so few men!"

"Perhaps we should lead in the attack tomorrow against them," Shemeber exclaimed, his deep set piercing eyes darting from one ruler to the other to see if they agreed. "Why

THE LAND OF THE PROMISE

should we wait here? They may fear us and turn away. I say let's go after them!"

The kings of the Sodom valley had been receiving continuous information about the camel raiders' activities from scouts as well as from persons who had escaped from the assailed villages. In preparation for an attack, the kings had closed within the cities' walls the rest of their people, their animals and their riches. Only the leaders and the armies stirred outside.

From her rooftop Salanna could see the panorama. Fearful premonitions bothered her even though she knew the small Amorite horde she saw in the distance would be no match for the armies of the Sodomite cities. She tried desperately to forget the message from Abram that Chedorlaomer might be sending two separate divisions against the valley cities. She had never shared the warning with Lot, thinking the message was a ploy by Abram to get her husband to leave Sodom. As the sun was going down she watched nervously as fires of the opposing warriors were lit on both ends of the lake—the small elite group of camelmen on the north and the armies of the five kings to the south.

At dawn Sodomite lookouts shouted out that the Amorites were giving fire signals from their camp. When the kings and their soldiers heard the word, they looked about and then stared terrified at the mountain tops that lined their valley to the east. Sparkling like innumerable flaming stars were thousands upon thousands of fire beacons flashing in the still grayness. The unexpected ass-mounted division of Chedorlaomer and Amraphel had arrived, and their heavily armed men were ready to descend upon the valley.

The camel mounted warriors raced around the lake toward the Sodomite encampment to close the trap. In panic the army discipline of the Sodomites disintegrated and each man fled to reach the safety of his own city. But before the gates of the cities could be opened the Amorites swarmed down from the mountains, surrounding and herding the confused soldiers toward the plain of the valley. King Bera and King Birsha along with many of their men were captured when they became mired in the tar pits of the bitumen fields as they tried

265

to escape. Others broke ranks and ran for refuge to the mountains where they were cut down by constantly advancing raiders.

The Amorites sacked the five cities and brought out all valuable possessions—fat lambs, bread, fine ale and wines, oil, honey, garden fruits, shining linens, precious and costly stones, perfumed oils, barley seed and ground malt, and the cities' vast store of smelted copper.

The five kings prostrated themselves before Chedorlaomer, Amraphel, Arioch and Tidal, kissing their feet and moaning before them.

"Enough!" shouted Chedorlaomer, his large heavy frame looming over them. "*You!* Bera! You are the one who first stopped paying my tribute! It shall be *you* who will suffer!"

"Have mercy, O great king and master of all the lands! Spare me and I shall give you anything you ask!" Bera pleaded, kissing again and again the dusty, dirty feet of his oppressor.

Chedorlaomer laughed derisively, roughly cuffing the face of the groveling Bera with the side of his foot and sending the king sprawling backwards. "And what does the king of Sodom have to offer me that I haven't taken?" Chedorlaomer asked with contempt.

The bruised king pulled himself to his feet. "There is a wealthy man in Canaan," Bera called out. "More wealthy than anyone in the whole land. I can tell you how to strip him of his wealth, and he shall even beg for the honor!"

"And why should a wealthy man leave his walled city and give me his possessions?"

"If I tell you . . . and if you desire to do as I suggest . . . will you grant me my life?" Bera pleaded.

"You have my word!" the big Amorite nodded. "You also have my word that my sword will slice you through if what you say gives me no pleasure!"

Bera looked distrustingly at Chedorlaomer and the other three shakanas. He knew he had to chance their interest.

"Abram, the Habiru, the man whose company stopped your people at Carchemish!" Bera blurted out. "He is back from Kemi with all the richest gifts the pharaoh could give him."

Chedorlaomer glowered critically at Arioch. "Is he the one who shamed you at Carchemish?"

"I was not there!" Arioch complained defensively. "Besides, the man had thousands of giant warriors! A whole hillside of them came upon my men. They said the land grew black with their great number and size!"

"What if he has rearmed since the famine," Amraphel asked cautiously. "Perhaps the new pharaoh is sponsoring him to keep us from attacking Kemi?"

Chedorlaomer thought on Amraphel's words. "You might be right!" he admitted, thinking to himself how Shetepibre Amenemhet had found out about the Amorite plot to invade the Lower Land, and how the new pharaoh had arrested all of the men Chedorlaomer had carefully infiltrated into the delta and forced them to build the defense wall the whole length of the Wadi Tummilat.

Chedorlaomer turned back to Bera, "Tell us what you know about the Habiru, Abram!"

"I do not know how many men he has. He brought only a detachment of watchmen with him when he was here," Bera explained, his voice now shaking with fear.

Arioch jolted. "He was here! When! Where is he now?"

Bera replied, "His nephew's family waited out the famine here in Sodom. Abram and Lot, the nephew, came for them, but the nephew's wife did not want to go. Recently the nephew and his family returned. The women are in the city, and Lot is one of the men you released to help with the burying of the dead."

Malicious smiles spread across the faces of the Amorite shakanas. They quickly understood the usefulness of Bera's information.

"It is important that no word of this reach the Habiru until we are far away from here," charged Chedorlaomer. "I want to see him come all the way to Elam if he wants to get his nephew back—with his weapons, camels, and silver and gold for ransom!"

Motioning to Amraphel, the big Amorite then said in an aside, "Find this man, Lot. See that he has no opportunity to escape! And get his women and all he owns as well! When we get to the back side of Damascus, I will send a messenger to find and inform the great Abram."

A young shepherd was nearby. One of his legs was bandaged, and he leaned on a forked stick for a crutch. He had been forced by the Amorites to watch the choice lambs that were being taken as booty. His back had been turned from King Bera and the shakanas, but the boy's keen ears had heard every word of the conversation.

With a pretext of seeking a bleating lamb's mother for milk, the boy hobbled to the Amorite guards and gained permission to go after the big sheep. Once hidden in the brush, the lad left his crutch and raced to the Jericho road. Avoiding the caravan route, the shepherd boy, Ammiel, took a sheep's path toward the village and oaks of Mamre.

Ammiel had been born in Terrakki, the son of Elisur, one of the shepherds over Abram's flocks. On the long trip to the land of Canaan the small boy Ammiel had walked behind the sheep picking up dung droppings. In Kemi he and his mother had been separated from his father and placed in a wealthy home in Avaris to work as servants. Elisur was detached to the pharaoh's famous cattle breeding farm in the delta. Ammiel had yearned for the life in Canaan. He remembered how the mighty Abram had prayed at the altar at Bethel. During those seven years in Kemi, Ammiel too prayed and knew what it was to walk with his God.

When Elisur came to the house in Avaris with release papers for his mother and Ammiel, signed by the Grand Vizier Shetepibre, the boy was ecstatic. His joy had continued until the return to Bethel. Then the bickering between Abram and Lot's shepherds began, and his father chose to go with his long time friend and companion, Lot.

Since coming to Sodom the boy had suffered many abuses and attacks from the men of the city. So much so that his father kept him always in the sheepfolds outside the city walls whenever the boy was not away grazing the flocks.

It was mid-morning of the next day. Approaching the fields that Mamre had once sown each year, Ammiel saw large clouds of dust sweeping toward him. Suddenly before his eyes racing camels dashed by him no more than a hundred cubits away. Mounted on the camels were tall black cloaked men, their bows drawn and flashing swords clashing at their sides. The boy's eyes sparkled with joy and excitement as he watched what to him was a familiar scene.

No sooner had the noisome cavalry passed than one charging rider broke from the drill practice and came to the boy. As the tall warrior pulled away his black hood the boy recognized the austere but kindly face and sharp dark eyes of Abram. "Ammiel! What are you doing here?" Abram called out with concern.

The boy quickly told about the Amorite attack on the cities of the Sodom valley and of the plans to take Lot as hostage.

Abram queried the young shepherd, "They said that they planned to go as far as Damascus?"

"Yes, sir," Ammiel answered quickly. "They said the 'back side' of Damascus."

Abram lifted the boy up on his camel and rode to find Mamre, Eshcol and Aner. Urgently signalling the three brothers away from the watchmen, Abram went with them and Ammiel into his tent.

"We must get word to Damascus," Abram stated emphatically, after relating Ammiel's story to the brothers.

"You think Chedorlaomer would dare attack Damascus?" Aner questioned.

"He might threaten, but he is too smart to try," Abram said in response. "If under siege Damascus can put fifty thousand men in each of the high mounded garrison villages of Hobah and Habieh and still have plenty of soldiers on their walls."

"Did you plan that defense system, Abram?" Eshcol asked with obvious admiration for his friend. "No other city I know is so well protected."

Abram smiled. "I was there at the time," he confirmed abruptly, his mind concentrating on a way to rescue his nephew. "If I could get word to Eliezer and the Ensi Akhiezer. . . ."

"Could I help?" Ammiel inquired hopefully.

The four men turned to the boy. Ammiel's short tunic was dusty and still wet with perspiration from his bolting escape from Sodom.

"He is brave enough," Mamre declared. "What would be required of him?"

Abram studied the boy's intent face and said, "We could escort him to the caravan route. He would have to get to Damascus alone and find some excuse for the guards to let him in. If they know Chedorlaomer is anywhere nearby they will have fortified and secured all gates. He would have to be lifted over the wall."

"I could break my leg!" Ammiel suggested eagerly. "I mean I could pretend . . . as I did in Sodom with the Amorites! Otherwise they would have taken me for slavery with the other boys."

"That was clever, Ammiel," Abram mused, his thoughts somehow slipping back to the time he first heard Terah tell about Sarai's pretended leprosy.

An expeditious plan was developed. Knowing that the Amorites would be sending out scouts, it was decided to travel after them by night. Ammiel would be sent ahead to Damascus to notify Eliezer and Ensi Akhiezer.

Abram suspected that the Amorites would corral their captives near Damascus and rest for a few days before crossing back through the desert. Or else the four shakanas had plans to divide their booty and separate at Damascus to their own territories. In either case a period of time would be spent at one location. If they mentioned the 'back side' of Damascus as their destination that could only mean the valley that the Sea People used many years earlier for their encampments.

If the ensi of Damascus alerted his soldiers at Hobah and Habieh to advance at the signal around both sides of Mount Ube, Abram's men would attack from the south. It would be up to Eliezer to bring weapons through the crevice pass of Mount Ube and arm Lot and the other prisoners. When the battle horns sounded the captives would know to break out and fight from within the Amorite camp.

"So much depends on you, Ammiel," Abram said gravely to the boy. "The ensi must be sure that no soldier moves from the garrisons until the battle has begun and the first horn blown! If the Amorites have any forewarning they will scatter, probably killing the captives and hostages, and disappear into the desert."

The Amorites moved steadily north through the land of Canaan. Bethel was spared, but Ai was looted as were most of the villages in their path. During the day Abram and his men hid on the west sides of the hills. They caught up with their enemy each night, watching the hilltops as they journeyed. There, the Amorite night scouts were posted above their sleeping camp. The scouts communicated with one another through the flashing fire beacons. Knowing their code, Aner and Eshcol could tell that Abram's troops had not been discovered and that the Amorites were unaware of their pursuers.

After many nights of cautiously following after the slow moving Amorites, Abram, Mamre, Eshcol, Aner and three hundred and eighteen watchmen and servants approached the hills on the "back side" of Damascus. There they leashed their camels and proceeded on foot, creeping toward the Amorite camp. To their amazement no Amorite guards were stationed on the hills that sheltered and embraced the broad valley.

The Amorite campsite was illumined by thousands of cressets, oil pots mounted on tall stakes which had been driven into the ground. Tents were spread throughout the valley and rested in the firelight like a host of giant night moths. Burly men clustered about glowing braziers feasting on roasted meats, fresh bread and free-flowing wines and ale.

"There is something strange here," Eshcol whispered suspiciously to Abram and his brothers, as they looked down upon the camp from behind a rock shelter. "They are obviously enjoying a victory celebration, but they have no guards!"

"I am going down there and find out!" Aner said, his voice hushed but determined.

"No, Aner," Abram protested. "You might expose our whole attack!"

"Ammiel is not the only actor on this stage, my friend," Aner smiled wryly. "Remember, we brothers once travelled with these tribes of Amorites. My left buttock is still marked with the brand of Amraphel!"

Abram was still cautious. "What are you suggesting?"

"That I come into the camp as if I'm sick and returning from a time of vomiting in the trees. It will give me an excuse for covering my head and will keep others at a distance. Then I will try to find a place near a fire where I can listen."

"How will you retreat?" Mamre asked worriedly.

Aner laughed quietly. "No one ever stops a vomiting man on his way to the woods!"

Aner's plan worked smoothly, and he was soon in the midst of the enemy's camp. He learned that this was the first long rest that the Amorite shakanas had allowed. They were giving their men a great feast and all the ale and wine they desired. The male captives had been bound tightly and tied to trees so that they would not have to be watched. The women were forced to prepare the meal and serve the food. After listening for some time, Aner groaned, coughed, and heaved as if he were sick. No one even looked up as he ran away from the campsite into the darkness. Stumbling up the hillside he found his way back to his brothers and Abram.

"There is some good news," he whispered. "And there is some very frightening news!"

His three listeners waited tensely while Aner caught his breath. "The captives are bound, and no man is required to serve guard duty."

"That is insane!" Abram retorted. "Not even one guard? And none on these hills?"

"They think they have no need!" Aner replied. "Damascus refuses to pay them any tribute, as it has always refused, but Ensi Akhiezer agreed to furnish food, wines, and ale to the Amorites and to allow them safe passage past the garrisons. The Amorites on their part will pay the road toll and not threaten the city or any who come to trade there."

"Why should the ensi compromise with those bandits!"
Abram objected as terrifying fears began to grip him. "Aner!
Do you know what this means? Our three hundred and
twenty-two men against. . . ." Abram's eyes scanned the
valley. So many thousands of tents and men were arrayed
before him that their number staggered him.

Mamre said gravely, "We have no assurance either that
Ammiel entered Damascus. Without the captives' release . . .
we have no chance."

"Shall we retreat, Abram?" Eshcol asked.

The four men sat on the ground, their backs against the
hard rocks. In front of them were their own sparsely scattered
troops. The forms of the black cloaked warriors blended in
with the strewn volcanic rocks and the high grasses of the
hillside.

It was a beautiful night for death to seem so imminent. A
half moon had risen. The white snows of Mount Hermon
were gleaming as they caught its light. The dark tall forest of
trees below Abram's position stood in peaceful quietness.
Drunken cries, shouts and whoops drifted up from the valley
on the other side as did smoke and the sweet smells of
roasting meat and baking bread.

Abram silently walked among his men calling them
together for prayer. After an hour of beseeching the Lord,
Abram felt a great surge of courage and boldness flow through
him. Although he informed his men that they could expect no
help from Damascus, Abram could tell from the peace and
excitement on their faces that they too had been emboldened
by divine strength. Not one man desired to turn back.

"God met the test in Kemi, Master Abram," one of his
faithful watchmen spoke out. "He will not put us to shame!"

With that reassurance Abram set a plan of attack in
motion. Quickly the three hundred and twenty-two crept
down the forested hillside, dividing off in different directions
to surround the multitude of the enemy. Abram had so few
men that when they encircled the Amorites they were spread
great distances apart from one another.

The din of the Amorite camp had become unusually quiet.
As Abram's men slowly advanced, sounds of loud snoring

273

and low moans and belches of over-indulgence could be heard.

Abram blew loudly on his shofar. The others followed with blasts that echoed and re-echoed throughout the valley. Mamre and his brothers led their commands toward the Amorite tents from the south, east and west. Abram led his men to the far side where the captives were held.

To his welcome relief Abram saw Eliezer, his four sons and young Ammiel frantically cutting the bonds of the prisoners. Abram's men quickly went to their aid.

"Eliezer!" Abram cried out, reaching to embrace his adopted son. "God is good to let me see you before this terrible trial! Have you found Lot?"

Eliezer was breathing hard and sweat beaded his forehead. A wide smile of joy crossed his face as he looked at Abram, "Lot was one of the first released. He and the others have gone for the weapons and the black cloaks."

"Black cloaks?"

"The Habiru of Abram always wear black cloaks!" Eliezer called out proudly. "I brought all that could be found in Damascus."

Suddenly Lot and hundreds of black cloaked men appeared out of the darkness. "Abram, praise be to our God!" Lot shouted as he clasped his uncle's shoulders. "Thank you, Abram! You risk everything to do this!"

Because the women were in the camp, bows and arrows were left and only swords were drawn. Abram now had over two thousand men added to his first number.

The captives dispersed and joined the attack. Everywhere could be heard the Amorite cry, "Habiru! It is the Habiru of Abram!"

The Amorites that had been asleep were slain before they could become aware of what was happening. Others who were drunk but still awake staggered and ran, pushing and shoving to find their swords. The horns kept blowing. In dizziness and fear the Amorites soon forsook the fight and in haste sought escape. Of those that fled, many were slaughtered as Abram's men chased them north of the Hobah garrison.

When daylight came the Amorite camp was in complete disarray. Thin smoke wisps streaked upward from the ashes of the fire pits. Fallen tents, dead bodies and rubbish covered the ground.

Abram and his comrades stretched out in exhaustion. Lot had found Salanna and her daughters. They were unharmed and were helping the other women prepare a breakfast from the food that could be found.

"With all four shakanas killed, do you think the Amorites who got away will return?" Eliezer asked as he rested near Abram on the soft heavy grass.

"They might if they realize how small an army drove them out of this valley," Abram said, his heart and mind still marveling that God had allowed him such a great and complete victory.

"The wine will be out of their systems by now," Eliezer noted. "The ensi sent out the strongest wines available. Even the ale was potent. He wanted to do more to help, Abram, but his council would not allow it. They feared retaliation. Chedorlaomer threatened to ambush all trade caravans coming to Damascus if the ensi's men shot a single arrow."

"Did the ensi give you the weapons?" Abram asked.

"Yes . . . and most of the black cloaks!" Eliezer smiled. "He also sent a crew to clear the overgrowth in the pass so we could get through."

"And you, Ammiel," Abram called to the boy who was walking about restlessly. "Did you have any difficulty?"

Ammiel bounded toward Abram, happy to find that he wanted to speak to him.

"No, sir," the boy replied. "I was more sorrowful looking than a wounded bird." With lively animation Ammiel rendered an act of the performance he had given when he had approached the Damascus wall.

"And what did you say caused your broken leg?" Aner laughed.

"I never had to say," Ammiel chuckled. "A wall guard made a joke of me and asked if my ass had hoofed me. When I told them that Eliezer would pay them handsomely if they took me to him, they lowered a basket and hoisted me up!"

275

"It is a good thing the boy looks like his father, Elisur," Eliezer joined in. "Or I would not have believed the story. Those guards demanded a costly sum for their small efforts!" Abram glanced over at the corrals of asses and camels left by the Amorites. Next to them were piles of baggage wrapped in tent cloth and heavily roped. "I think from all that booty we can reimburse you, Eliezer," Abram assured him warmly.

Ensi Akhiezer of Damascus led several battalions from his city to meet with Abram. The two men conversed as the Damascene soldiers helped to bury the dead and clean up the camp.

The ensi's voice revealed his sincere admiration. "I never thought I would see you alive again, Abram. Once again you have honored our city with your valor. I am only sorry that we did so little to help you."

"In God's plan, you did more to aid us than if you had sent all your men into the battle," Abram disclosed, his appreciative smile relieving the ensi's misgivings.

"My scouts have learned that the Amorites who escaped have separated, each going on foot to his home territory," the ensi reported. "It will be safe for you to rest here a few days."

"No," Abram politely resisted. "We only need time to praise and thank our God for the great act he performed last night. Then we must pack and leave."

"May I help you in any other way?" Akhiezer offered.

"If you can get a reasonable trade exchange for all the extra camels and asses and for the copper in the booty, I would be grateful," Abram replied.

"I shall attend to it immediately," the ensi said as he bowed and departed.

When the ensi returned sometime later, he brought with him fresh food supplies, and a great fortune in gold and silver.

As the large company of men and captives returned, they crossed the bridge over the headwaters of the Jordan. The bridge was a low dam built of basalt boulders and rocks. The upper cracks had been filled with gravel and the top of the expanse paved with smooth flat stones for a roadway.

On the right side of the dam was a clear cold lake fed by the melting snows of Mount Hermon and the other high mountains that loomed behind the sparkling waters. The lake was surrounded by thick papyrus marshes.

To the left, rushing through the cracks of the lower boulders beneath the bridge, began the Jordan River. The surging water formed cascading rapids as it steeply descended between the high walls of a rocky basalt gorge.

Chapter XVIII
THE SEAL OF THE BLOOD

Along the route from Hazor to Bethel, supplies and food were purchased for Abram's men and the former captives. When camp was set up each night Abram required everyone to gather for prayer.

For most of the captives it was their first experience to worship the one holy God. The experience was an alarming one, for their lives had been enmeshed in the hedonistic paganism of their cities. To stand before the real God demanded from them not lust, but a desire for purity and righteousness. The exaction either intensely attracted or violently repelled them.

Many sought God and asked Abram to pray for them. Others slipped away in the darkness to return to their defiling practices, indiscriminately satisfying themselves with the bodies of one another.

When Abram heard of the clandestine behavior he became greatly annoyed. Day after day as the company marched southward he expressed his incensed feelings to Lot and Salanna. He also pleaded with them not to go back to Sodom.

Salanna resented the discussions. One day when she felt Lot was about persuaded to rejoin Abram she lashed out. "Stop it, Abram! Stop trying to dominate our lives! Lot is not your young nephew anymore, always there to do your bidding. He is a man in his own right! He has a prosperous business in Sodom! And we live in a nice home, not in bedouin tents!"

Salanna's face was determined. Her accusing eyes were opened wide and were unblinking as she continued to defy Abram. "The men of Sodom do peculiar things, yes! That is their own problem! They leave us alone, and we do not cast judgment on them! I only wish *you* would leave us alone as well!"

Before Abram could respond, Salanna turned her wrath on Lot and upbraided him with the words, "Choose one of us! Either go whimpering back to your uncle *alone* or take me back to the city of Sodom!"

Abram and Lot knew that once again they must separate. Abram spent hours each night praying before God for Lot's welfare and safety.

Shortly after the abrasive conversation, Abram along with Mamre, Eshcol and Aner led the people to a path that crossed the mountains and into the valley of Shaveh.

The valley of Shaveh was the beginning of a wadi that poured off the winter rains into the distant Lake of Gomorrah. Other times during the year the stream bed served as the shortest route from the west to the Sodom valley. The broad valley of Shaveh lay just north of the holy hill of Melchizedek.

Abram and the three brothers scanned the area as they approached, hoping to locate Melchizedek. They did see him. To their inexpressible amazement, the priest was leading his ass and behind him trailed a long line of men and women carrying skins of wine and baskets of bread. The bearers dispersed among the tired travellers, serving the refreshment. Melchizedek walked stoically until he stood before Abram.

"Blessed be Abram by God Most High, the maker of heaven and earth!" the priest declared solemnly. "And blessed be God Most High who has given your enemies into your hand!"

When Abram heard the words he dismounted and fell prostrate before the priest. Melchizedek knelt and placed his

279

hands on Abram's shoulders. The two men of God prayed and cried out thanksgivings and praises to God.

For a few moments the onlookers were hushed. Then a stir went among the crowd as other sounds and voices could be heard in the distance. From around the bend in the wadi came the recognizable figure of King Bera and a legion of his troops.

The bowed Melchizedek looked up sharply. "As I have prayed for your safety and victory, so also have I prayed against that man and his wicked city!"

"Has he done you harm?" Abram asked, his hand on his sword ready to defend the priest if necessary.

"Look at the men and women who are serving your people," Melchizedek directed, waving his hand back toward the bread and wine bearers.

Abram noticed for the first time that those who served the bread and wine were limping and most appeared in pain. Melchizedek told Abram of the sadistic tortures, whippings, and mutilations these people had suffered under the Sodomites. "Many come to me just to die in peace," he continued. "Every day I cry out to God against those evil cities, for they have become more base than any animal!"

As Bera came closer into view Abram called to his watchmen to bring the camels that were packed with gold and silver. There were ten of them. Abram took the rein of the first camel and said to Melchizedek, "This is a tenth of the gold and silver from our victory. Accept it as a tithe to God for our deliverance. May it be useful to you in providing for those who seek your help."

Melchizedek accepted the offering. He goaded the camel to kneel and then silently transferred the heavy packs to his ass. Meanwhile Abram spread out his camel blanket and the priest joined him. The two ate of the bread and wine, ignoring Bera until the king stood immediately before them. Abram's men, aware of the king's arrival, had cautiously stationed themselves on the hillside, bows and arrows held tautly and aimed at Bera's men.

"My good Abram," the king of Sodom spoke out haughtily. "I see you decided to accept my offer to protect our cities from the Amorites!"

Bera warily glanced up at Abram's watchmen. "You may dismiss your mercenaries!" he added. "I do not want the goods or possessions you have retrieved. Only let me have the people that are mine. You may keep the loot as payment for your services."

Abram stood and faced the king. His eyes stared coldly at Bera. Raising his right hand Abram vowed, "I have sworn to the Lord God Most High, the maker of heaven and earth, that I would not take anything that is yours, in case you should say, 'I have made Abram rich.' I will take nothing but what my people have eaten, and a share each for the three men who helped me lead the attack."

Abram went to the nine remaining camels laden with gold and silver. He divided them and gave three to Mamre, three to Eshcol, and three to Aner. Then he went to King Bera of Sodom and said, "Mamre, Eshcol and Aner have their share. The rest is yours!"

Bera directed his soldiers to herd all the animals and possessions, except Abram's riding camels, toward Sodom. Captives that were returning to the Sodom valley followed behind. Lot, Salanna and their daughters walked sadly with the others, not waiting to pause or look up as they passed. Abram's heart ached and heavy sorrow weighed upon him after they had departed.

"You need time to pray," Melchizedek advised, observing Abram's grief. "Have your people rest in the valley. You may seek the Lord here on the holy hill, the sacred Zion of the Holy God."

Abram willingly agreed. He left others in charge and climbed with Melchizedek to the priest's altar on top of the broad mountain's crest. Olive trees surrounded the low walls of the marked area giving seclusion from the cluster of huts built on the slopes and from the tents now being pitched in the valley.

281

Shaded from the late spring sun by the awning of a small tent, Abram stayed alone at the place and sought God's presence. Later he rose and walked about the enclosure. Pacing to and fro he began to recall vividly the details of the battle with the Amorites. As he wondered at his very survival, debilitating fears swept over him.

He leaned against the walls that encompassed the sanctuary. Looking down he saw his meager troops. Haunting and unnerving thoughts obsessed him. By all rights he and all those who went with him should be dead, torn in sunder by the Amorites.

When it became night Abram felt God very near. Sensing the holiness around him, Abram took off his sandals and knelt. In a vision of the Lord he heard God say to him, "Do not be afraid, Abram, I am your protector; your reward from me shall be very great."

Abram cried out to the Lord in the darkness, "O Lord God, what will you give me? I remain childless, and the heir of my house is Eliezer of Damascus. You have given me no son; and a man born as a servant in my house will be my heir."

"Eliezer shall not be your heir," Abram heard the Lord answer. "Your own son shall be your heir. Look at the heavens and number the stars, if you are able to count them. So will your descendants be."

Abram searched the skies about him. The stars shone brilliantly in splendored limitless myriads. As he beheld them, belief surged into his being, slowly but completely dissipating his fears.

The next day Abram spent meditating on what the Lord had said. Against all reason, belief that he was to have a son had been restored. He felt peace as he prayed before the Lord, not because of anything he had done but because of the renewed faith in his heart.

As late afternoon approached, Abram's mind struggled with the unfulfillment of the second promise concerning the land. The land that was promised to him—*his land*—was a place with evil cities like those of the Sodom valley and fortified centers of trade like calloused Megiddo and Damascus. It was a land of vileness and paganism such as he witnessed in Hazor, raiding murderous Amorites, and thieving and lawless Canaanites.

The joy he had in believing for a son faded. Despair and uselessness overwhelmed him. The confirming words of the Lord came again, "I am the Lord who called you and brought you out of Ur to give you this land as your possession."

"O Lord God!" Abram shouted plaintively. "How am I to know that I will ever possess it?"

The answer came in the form of a command: "Go and lay before me a heifer three years old, a she-goat three years old, a ram three years old, a turtledove, and a young pigeon."

Descending the hill to the level of Melchizedek's huts, Abram asked the priest for the offering animals. Melchizedek took Abram to his corrals and cages and Abram chose the animals he needed. The priest called a young man to help, giving him a rack of hot coals in a rope-bailed pot and placing a pile of brushwood on his back.

Abram slung the bag with two fluttering birds over his shoulder and with an unlit torch in his hand he began leading the animals up to the Zion altar.

When the two reached the summit the servant placed the brushwood on the flat stones, put the smoking pot nearby and returned down the hill. After the young man had left, Abram took a knife and slit the throats of the offerings, cutting all but the birds in halves.

As he exposed the bleeding bodies on the kindling, high soaring vultures quickly fell in charging swoops from the sky. Hungrily they circled the freshly killed meat. As the birds of prey dove toward the altar Abram fought to drive them away. Flapping and gliding, the scavengers persistently returned to tear at the carcasses.

Only when the sun began to set did the thwarted vultures depart. Exhausted, Abram fell by the tent into a deep sleep. As he slept, a heaviness of dread and darkness fell on him and he heard the Lord say, "Know of a certainty that your descendants will sojourn in a land that is not theirs, and will become slaves there. For four hundred years they will be oppressed. Then I will bring judgment on the people that they serve, and afterward they shall come out with great possessions. As for you, you will die here and go to your fathers in peace. You will live many years before you shall be buried. Your descendants shall come back here in the fourth generation. Then shall the sins of the Amorites be complete."

In the darkness of the night Abram suddenly saw the torch he had brought up from Melchizedek burst into flames and puffs of smoke waft up from the glowing fire pot. As he watched, the torch and the pot began to move in the blackness, passing between the pieces of the slain animals on the altar.

The flames and coals ignited the brushwood and the offerings roasted in the fire until they were burned. In the midst of the sacrifice the Lord came and made the covenant with Abram: "To your descendants I will give this land, from the river of Kemi to the great river Euphrates." It was a promise sealed with blood.

Chapter XIX
THE CHARM OF HAGAR

Abram had not consulted with Sarai before he made the decision to pursue Chedorlaomer. Ammiel's coming with the message from Sodom, the discussions with Aner, Eshcol and Mamre, the plans and the packing—all had happened while Sarai was in a distant part of the camp, weaving materials with other women. When she arrived at their tent there was only time for a brief explanation and a quick embrace.

After watching the three hundred and twenty-two men disappear into the darkness, the rest of the people along with Sarai apprehensively returned to their quarters, few to sleep peacefully. Sarai lit a lamp. Folding her legs under her, she sat on a deep cushion and stared at the steady undisturbed flame. The shadows grew large in the tent, magnifying its furnishings.

Fear and loneliness swelled up inside Sarai like a pushing internal force. Waves of heat rushed through her and, as happened so often, her body became wet with perspiration. These physical menopause reactions heightened her fears and dulled her faith. She could not make herself pray. She repeated the promises God had given, but they brought no relief. She tried to play her harp and to sing praises to the Lord. Instead, the test of her faith left her feeling forsaken and alone. Finally she released herself to her tears and wept bitterly, questioning why God would send Abram out into such a hopeless battle.

"My lady," Hagar whispered softly as she almost skipped into the tent. "I brought you wine. Do not fear for Master Abram. It will be a great victory!"

Hagar was no more than sixteen. Her bright eyes danced as she talked, and an irrepressible smile parted her pretty lips. Sarai looked up at the refreshing face. She tried to control her hurting emotions as she responded, "Hagar? Oh, Hagar, I am so glad you have come. I need someone to talk to...."

"But my lady, it is a night to celebrate! Oh, how my father and my brothers would love to be riding with Master Abram tonight. If I were but a man I, too, would race to join him!"

Sarai smiled faintly as Hagar gave her the wine. The girl grabbed up one of Abram's swords, swiping and parrying it in the air. "Why, why did I have to be born a woman?" she raised the question merrily. "I would have made such an excellent bedouin chieftain!"

Sarai watched appreciatively, the distraction somewhat easing her distress. She was very fond of Hagar. The young girl was one who could not tolerate confinement and routine; therefore, Sarai had permitted her to run errands and deliver messages and to accompany her on trips.

"I didn't think that I really liked Master Abram," Hagar announced boldly, her bright twinkling eyes beaming. "I thought he was an old man, too educated and full of the city to know how to fight. But did you see him, my lady Sarai, as he led his Habiru? He was as fierce and as brave as any desert man I have ever seen!"

"Is that how you remember your own father, Hagar?" Sarai inquired as she sipped the comforting wine.

"My father, too, was brave and fierce!" Hagar asserted eagerly. "Did you know that we had fewer than two hundred men against Shetepibre's twenty thousand?"

Sarai encouraged her to tell more. "There are nine tribes in the eastern desert of Kemi," Hagar began. "Some are small, only one family, like the Wentewuats. They will have nothing to do with the other eight except steal from them. They are like the black beetles, the Wentewuats, the way they can disappear in the sand with their loot!"

"Did they not all unite against Shetepibre?"

"Oh, yes," Hagar admitted. "All united at first. My father was the strongest of the shakanas. He was taller, and he could talk faster than the rest!" She laughed and giggled at the memory of her father.

Hagar went on to tell Sarai about the whims of bedouin loyalty and how quickly their enthusiasm waned. "At first as we waited in the mountains, watching Shetepibre's men search for the quarry well, it was great sport. But the fighters soon grew bored. For a while my father bribed many to stay. Other times he threatened them. Finally it was decided to slip into the camp and break the water jars. He had to give the men some action and excitement . . . or else they would run away!"

"But it also led Shetepibre to your hiding place," Sarai reminded her.

Hagar shrugged her shoulders. "It is very hard to cover your tracks in the sand at night, my lady. Besides, if your God had not pointed the way to the well we would have won the honor of defeating the great Shetepibre and the army of Kemi all by ourselves! Twenty thousand men to our two hundred! It is still a victory . . . the fact that we *almost* did it!"

"You hated Shetepibre?" Sarai asked her.

"The great Shetepibre! No, never! Who could have a more exciting enemy? But he was our enemy! He would open up the Wadi Hammamat and the desert would no longer be free. *We* would no longer be free!"

"A single pass in the whole desert?"

"Right across the middle!" Hagar exclaimed indignantly. "There are few oases in the eastern desert. The date palms and the water are not enough for even the nine tribes. The desert pastures wither soon after the spring rain. In the summer the heat destroys everything. Only the giant quarry well does not go dry."

"Summers must have been difficult for you," Sarai sympathized, her own anguish subsiding as she imagined the hard life Hagar had endured.

287

Hagar grinned coyly, "I loved them best of all! All the tribes had to come together then, except the Wentewuats who hide water jars in the sand all year like squirrels here bury acorns. We camped in the mountain caves near the quarry well. There was much fighting and drinking, but there were also times at night, after we had eaten, when long and wonderful stories were told. And the *poems,* the beautiful poems, were said. Every bedouin is a poet, my lady Sarai. I have heard my father recite verse after verse describing the loveliness of an acacia tree or the song of the bulbul."

On many of the nights that followed, Hagar came to Sarai's tent after the evening meal and talked of her life in the desert, sharing some of the bedouin stories and reciting long eloquent poems.

Sarai in turn held Hagar entranced by the stories she told the girl about Noah, the way life was before and after the Great Flood, and the years she and Abram had waited for the land and the promise of a child.

"But are you not too old to bear a child, my lady?" Hagar asked bluntly. "If your God wanted you to have a child, would he have closed your womb? You are so beautiful . . . I have never seen anyone so beautiful! Perhaps your God did not want you to be fat and ugly and to give milk like a cow!"

Sarai was amused by the girlish frankness, but Hagar's questions also hurt like hot brands. So often in her prayers God had confirmed his promise that she would indeed bear a son by Abram. But now no one could deny that her change in life had come. Belief in the promise had to be re-evaluated.

Hagar interrupted Sarai's thoughts. Putting her hand in Sarai's, Hagar looked earnestly at her mistress. "I am able to bear a child for you, my lady," she suggested unblenchingly. "I am strong and have many years to bear other children for myself. Give me to your husband until I conceive. When the child is born, it will be yours. I shall bear it on your knees. As it leaves my womb, it shall be in your hands to do with as you like."

Sarai looked at Hagar's young and vigorous figure. She felt envy for the girl's youth. "Have you borne a child yet, Hagar?" she inquired tentatively.

"No, my lady. By the threat of my father's sword and the protection given me by the great Shetepibre when I was taken prisoner, I am still a virgin," she replied, not knowing whether she should be ashamed or proud of such an admission. "But I have excited men! I know that I have! Master Abram is old, but I could warm his bed . . . enough."

"My husband is still very much a man," Sarai affirmed, her eyes growing distant and misty as she thought about him. She had to rebuke the moments of terror that came upon her as her mind dwelled on Abram and his small contingent stalking after the unknown thousands of Amorites. Almost forgetting Hagar and their conversation, Sarai lamented, tears coursing down her face and falling on her gown, "If only he had left me a child . . . some part of him before he died! Oh, Hagar, I fear I shall never see him again! He has left no heir to inherit his promised land and no son for me to teach the mysteries of the God of Noah!"

Before she gave way completely to her fears Sarai checked herself. "Hagar is but a girl," Sarai told herself. "She cannot be expected to understand."

"I am burdening you," Sarai said kindly, gently lifting the girl's long dark braids, and patting her head lovingly. "You are very kind in your willingness. If my husband is saved by a miracle of God then perhaps he should have sons by those whom God has made fruitful. Go now, Hagar. It is quite late."

But that night, like most nights for Sarai, brought only restless sleep, disturbing dreams, and hours of wakeful hopelessness.

The balmy spring days were beautiful around the oaks of Mamre. The ewes stood in serenity and contentment as the woolly newborn lambs wiggled to pull at their teats or pranced in circles about them. Singing birds, fragrant piles of barley sheaves, dazzlingly colored wildflowers, pure blue skies, and luxuriant green grasses coalesced into a vernal fantasia.

But oblivious to such splendor were the dazed survivors of the raided and destroyed villages who walked and staggered down the nearby road. Some had overloaded asses. Others carried their few belongings. They often stopped by Abram's settlement to inquire after lost family members and friends, or to steal when a guard was not watching. They told graphic tales of horror and viciousness at the hands of the Amorites.

The most difficult news came from a caravan that stopped to draw water. Damascus, they said, had capitulated to the Amorites, allowing them to rest on the backside of the city and receive safe passage by the garrisons. Agreement had been made that the Amorites would not attack the city or any who were passing through Ube. In return no Damascene would shoot a single arrow against the marauders.

The unmistakable portent of the message was not missed by any of Abram's people. Without help from Damascus, they all knew that there was little hope of seeing the brave watchmen and their four leaders alive again.

It was as if God withheld his presence and comfort during this time of trial. Though Sarai insisted on hours of prayer and fasting, a heaviness of futility and listlessness fell upon the camp. For the first time many talked of running away and finding work in the villages.

Sarai knew what was happening. All she could do was to cry out to God, "Why, O Lord, do you test me again and again? Giving in abundance and then taking away? Promising such wondrous things but denying their fulfillment. Why, my God? Why? Why should Shetepibre receive miracle after miracle, and I must wait year after year? Why must I stand ashamed before these who believe in you because of my words?

"Of what value is beauty in a wife if another woman must lie with her husband to bear him children? But now . . . would that I even had a husband! I would gladly give him my maid!"

Such despairing cries and prayers continued until one day they were suddenly dispelled by the soft rumble of many camel feet. Men servants, women and children ran, danced and yelled out screams of delight as the black camels and their riders came in view. Everyone in the camp raced to welcome the unexpected joyous return of Abram, the three brothers, and the three hundred and eighteen proud watchmen.

So convinced was she that Abram would never return that Sarai alone remained by the tent door stunned. "O my God," she murmured. "Once again you have preserved us!" As she prayed, a decision was made in Sarai's mind. She would not chance losing the seed of Abram again. He *must* have a son to inherit the land promised to his descendants, and she must have a son to pass on the sacred history. Since she could no longer bear a child, he must conceive a son by Hagar.

The dreadful experience of separation made Sarai anxious to do what must be done. Even amidst the rejoicing as she heard Abram call for her, she resolved that, come evening, he must take Hagar as a wife. Sarai knew he would desire to lie with her, after many weeks away. It need only take a few moments, at most an hour, for him to lie with Hagar first instead.

With the act confirmed in her mind Sarai ran out of the tent and was caught up immediately in Abram's arms. "Sarai, my beautiful, beautiful wife! There you are! I thought I might never see your lovely face again!" he cried out, holding her body close and warmly kissing her over and over. "What miracles our God performed! Our little group of watchmen, Sarai! We routed out the whole combined Amorite tribes! It will be years before they dare sack Canaan again!"

That evening after feasting and much wine and ale had been served, details of the victory were told with many of the men adding different stories about the attack. It was difficult to end the happy celebration. The miracle that all returned alive was still hard to believe. The others, especially the children and the young girls, just wanted to stare and listen to the leaders and the watchmen.

Eventually Abram nodded to Sarai and the two rose and walked to their tent. "Enough of the stories," he smiled down at her, the light from an oil lamp he was carrying lighting their way. "It is time to enjoy my wife! My body has longed for you, Sarai!"

"And I yearn to lie beside you, my husband," Sarai said nervously. "But. ..."

"I will not force you, my dear," he assured her, knowing that in the past few years tenderness and much affection were needed to arouse her. "If it takes all night we will not rush. But I do want to come to you. ..."

"My concern was for something else," Sarai faltered and broke off.

"Tell me, my dearest one," he said lovingly, passion and desire for her rising within him.

Sarai hung her head. She could not look at him and say what she must say. "Abram, for eight years my monthly flow of blood has been . . . irregular. Now it has ceased altogether. At night I find myself burning with heat or shaking with chills. I often grow despondent and fretful. These are not uncommon signs. They happen to all women when the time of child bearing is over and the female body changes. I know that.

"But because I cannot bear a child," she continued gravely, "does not mean we cannot have a son. You must father him through another woman."

"Sarai. . . ?"

"If something should happen to you, Abram, all would be lost!" she pleaded. "You would have no offspring! God has promised you children . . . and I cannot give them to you!"

"I do not want to know another woman," Abram objected firmly.

Ignoring his words Sarai said tersely, "My maid, Hagar. She waits for you in her tent. Go to her, Abram. Lie with her, now while you feel passion for me. Should she conceive she will bear us a strong son."

"She is but a young girl, Sarai."

"She has a woman's body," Sarai cried tearfully, biting her lip as she braved looking at Abram. "I do not want you to *love* her."

As they entered their tent they were surprised to see Hagar waiting for them. No longer was her dark hair braided. It was well brushed and fell long and silky down and around her. She had put on Sarai's loveliest sheer linen gown and adorned herself with her mistress's jewels, ones Sarai had not worn since she was in Mentuhotep's palace. Hagar had also found cosmetics Sarai had brought from Kemi and had applied them artistically to her lovely face. The fragrance of a soft perfume filled the air about her.

"Forgive me, my lady Sarai," Hagar spoke happily. "But if I am to lie with Abram, the fierce and brave Habiru, I wanted to dress worthily of the occasion. I thought it proper to borrow your things for this special night!"

Before either Abram or Sarai could protest, Hagar took the lamp from Abram and pulled him teasingly toward the tent opening. "Come, my master. We will hurry. You may return to my lady Sarai soon. Come! I will lead you to my bed!"

Sarai remained alone. It had happened so quickly. She wondered why Abram did not resist. He had not said one word, but merely went with the girl. For many hours Sarai sat alert and awake, waiting. When dawn came she rose from her bed, dressed and moved through the camp to Hagar's tent. Pulling aside the flap she saw her own gown thrown carelessly on the carpets of the tent floor. In the darkness she could see the nude young form of Hagar, lying in the sleeping embrace of her own husband.

She went to Abram and shook him. "You did not need to stay all night," she whispered, her voice expressing her hurt feelings.

Abram pulled himself up on his elbows and tried to wake from the heavy sleep. "It was the long ride . . . and the wine, Sarai," he mumbled apologetically. "I must have fallen asleep right away."

Hagar had wakened, but instead of rising she clung tightly to Abram. "Do not leave without kissing me, my lord! Like you did so many times last night!"

Abram struggled away from her and reached for his clothing. Hagar's words before Sarai filled him with embarrassment. "It was not as it seemed, Hagar. In my thoughts you were my wife, Sarai," he tried to explain.

"But you did not call me Sarai!" the girl pretended to pout, laughing and falling back in her bed. "You called me Hagar! Hagar, your sweet little desert princess! And how violently you came in to me, Abram! Surely I shall conceive and be the

293

mother of your son, the son you have desired so long! *My* son will inherit this promised land, won't he, my husband?"

Sarai ran from the tent, confused and humiliated. Abram caught up with her, and together they walked in silence, Abram's arm around her shoulders. Sarai stared blankly ahead.

"Sarai," Abram pleaded. "I only did what you asked. A man is not capable of going to a woman without some feeling. I did try to think only of you, but Hagar would not keep still. She was very . . . aggressive."

Sarai turned on him sharply and indignantly. "May my shame be on you! I gave you my maid to embrace, but now that she thinks she may have conceived she holds me in contempt! May the Lord judge between you and me!"

"She is *your* maid, Sarai," Abram shrugged. "She is in your power. Do as you wish with her."

Jealous fire burned in Sarai's eyes as she answered, "I *will* tend to her!"

When Sarai found Hagar later that day the girl smiled impudently. "I did not come to work for you today, my lady Sarai," she said, breaking into giggles. "I stayed awake too long working for you last night!"

"You do not need to work today," Sarai answered sternly. "I want you to pack your things. Tomorrow you will leave with the shepherds. You will be under the authority of Tamarelli, the wife of the head shepherd. You will help with the cooking and gather dung with the children!"

"I will *not* gather dung!" Hagar shouted hotly. "As daughter of a shakana I never touched a dropping. As a wife of the leader of this tribe I shall do as I please!"

"Abram has disowned you! You are still a maid, Hagar. *My* maid!" Sarai reproached her emphatically.

Sarai called in two large strong women who had been waiting outside. "See that this girl is whipped and bound without food or water," Sarai commanded harshly. "When the shepherds leave, she is to serve Tamarelli. She is never to be allowed in the main camp again!"

Hagar thought like a true bedouin. When she saw victory she could be deceitful and competitive. But in defeat she knew only to run and flee to the desert.

After the thrashing, Hagar was tied in her tent. She managed to escape her bonds by tricks she had mastered years before under her father's tutelage. Quickly packing Sarai's dress and jewels in with her own belongings, Hagar slipped away late that night. Quietly she stole one of the best riding camels from the grazing pasture. Passing by the storage tents she took skins of water and ale, stacks of bread, cheese rounds and links of sausage. With saddle packs bulging she noiselessly departed.

Following the stars she headed southwest toward the main caravan route to Kemi, "the way of Shur." When guards tried to halt her she shouted indignantly, "Tamarelli sends me to deliver these to the shepherds! They are scouting for some lost lambs." Tamarelli's commands were law among the shepherds and watchmen. The big cook did not like her word disputed. The guards let Hagar pass without comment.

Any fears that she had were overshadowed by the excitement of escaping from her captivity. As she rode, Hagar enjoyed the memory of the intimate hours spent with Abram. The old man had responded with much more passion than Hagar had expected. She had found it a delightful adventure in spite of Sarai's jealousy. "What if I do carry his child, even now," she mused with a mischievous smile crossing her face. "It was a good night for conception. My woman's blood was many days ago. Perhaps I shall return in a few years and bring Abram his son. I could demand a great inheritance!" The ideas pleased her, and her mind continued to scheme as she journeyed.

The sultry early morning heat was oppressive after the long night's ride, and Hagar stopped. The path was descending through a valley between two high hills and would soon merge into the Shur road.

Tethering her camel to forage behind a thicket, Hagar stayed out of sight of travelers on the road. It was nearly an hour before a long caravan of pack asses and ox carts carrying wood beams passed before her. It was a well guarded shipment, and Hagar quickly decided to ride behind it. Should thieves be about she could take a chance and race for the protection of the caravan.

After a brief meal of bread and cheese she left her lookout and slowly followed the caravan at a safe distance. The light sea breeze cooled her warm face and she threw back her cloak to allow the refreshing air to flow through her long hair.

"I am a woman," she thought to herself proudly as she kept the rein of her camel securely held in a slow walk position. Her only companion plodded beneath her, his hump rhythmically swaying and rocking. "I have known a man . . . and a man has known me! What a son I could have!"

Hagar's eyes sparkled in the sunlight as her thoughts turned within her. "He would be like Abram . . . wise, respected and brave. Or he would be like my father, Hekanakht . . . wild, fierce and strong, and a lover of the desert! Or perhaps *she* would be like me!" she laughed, patting the camel's neck as if he too had enjoyed the joke.

The days became long and tedious. Hagar wished that she had chosen to follow a camel caravan, and would have done so if one passed by. Since the Amorite raids when all travel had stopped, few caravans had gotten through this far. This shipment she followed was probably loaded at Megiddo since its wood was cedar.

When the caravan camped for the night near a spring ahead of her, Hagar found a place behind a low bare rock hill to hide from their view. Soaking a disk of dried bread in ale she rolled it around a chunk of sausage for her dinner and then stretched out on her blanket. The setting sun still glowed in her eyes as she watched the darkening clear blue sky above her. One by one the stars made their appearance in the twilight. Suddenly the whole host twinkled brightly overhead. "Only a desert sky can look like that," she uttered aloud.

Thinking about the desert, her mind began to dwell on what she must face when she returned to the Eastern Desert of Kemi. She had many brothers in her tribe. Several had been killed by Shetepibre's men, but most had escaped. "Surely they were together again. But who would be the new leader? If it is Kedar," she thought pleasantly, "I shall be held in honor and be free to do as I wish. But Kedar is kind and not very

296

bold. If Heti becomes the shakana he would stop at nothing! Heti may even murder Kedar."

The morbid thought upset her. "If Heti is the shakana, how would he use me? He might even sell me back to Shetepibre for a reward. Or, no! He would probably marry me off to another shakana. I could not stand to live in the Eastern Desert and be married to someone of a lesser tribe!"

Hagar twisted her face into a frown of disgust. "Heti was the one who talked Father into joining the tribes together at Hammamat. A terrible idea! Bedouins do not fight well alongside strangers! You fight for your father, your mother or your sister . . . maybe a brother. No desert man fights for just 'somebody,' " Hagar pondered indignantly. "Why should we fight Shetepibre together and then turn around and fight each other the next day.

"But it might have been a victory!" she thought happily to herself, shifting effortlessly to weigh the other side. "Perhaps then I would have become the Queen of Kemi!" The idea made her think immediately of Sarai.

She felt a twinge of remorse. "Sarai always understood me before that night with Abram. She was kind, and she let me be free. But what did she expect? If Abram was to be the one to break open my womb I did not want him thinking about *her* while he did it! I am not a whore or a woman born in his house!"

Once again she pictured Abram as he kissed her and remembered how warm it felt when he pulled her body on his. She drifted off to sleep and her memories became dreams.

The next morning when she awoke Hagar saw that the caravan had already left the spring. Fetching her camel she dragged her packs after her and led the beast down to the water.

The area around the small water hole was strewn with dung and cluttered with scraps of food, ashes and torn pieces of clothing. The sand was pocked with foot and hoof prints.

Hagar allowed the camel to take his fill of the spring first, while she sat on a rock ledge just above the waters.

Unexpectedly Hagar heard a voice calling her name. Instinctively she dropped off the rock and crouched near her camel. Grabbing a rock she looked warily about her.

Again the voice came. "Hagar, maid of Sarai, where have you come from? Where are you going?"

Hagar trembled. Her eyes darted in every direction seeking the person who was speaking.

Then she saw a vision of what appeared to be a man. She blinked and strained her eyes, for he was the angel of the Lord and unlike any man she had seen. Like a desert mirage he stood some distance from the spring almost glimmering in the bright sunlight.

Finally she found words to reply to his question. "I am fleeing from my mistress, Sarai," she replied haltingly.

A strange feeling came over the girl. Vividly she recalled the times of prayer at Abram's encampment. While others prayed with shouts and singing Hagar had always felt ill at ease. With any pretext she would seek to avoid the meetings. But whenever Sarai insisted that she stay, she did remember this same feeling, awesome but comforting, that would remain a few seconds and then fade away.

"Is this the voice of the God of Abram?" the thought burned in her mind. "Am I talking to a real and living God?"

The angel of the Lord said to her, "Return to your mistress and be submissive to what she says."

Hagar felt humbled and ashamed. She had harmed Sarai! She, Hagar, was the one who promised to bear a child for her mistress. So willingly had she offered. And she had meant it when she said it. But after seeing Abram come from the battle, such a hero among the people, she had relished giving herself to him.

She had betrayed her mistress! If God would send a plague in Kemi to curse those who intended harm to Sarai, will not this God now destroy her. Such thoughts flashed through Hagar's mind after the angel of the Lord's command. The girl could only nod in affirmation, so contrite had she suddenly become.

Then the angel spoke again. "I will greatly multiply your descendants so that they shall be too many to count."

Hagar did not understand. If she must return to serve Sarai, when would she ever be able to go back to her people and have so many children?

The voice of the Lord spoke compassionately to her. "Behold, Hagar, you are with child, and shall bear a son. You shall call his name Ishmael, 'he hears,' because the Lord has given heed to your affliction. Your son will be like a wild ass. His hand will be against everyone, and everyone's hand will be against him. And he will live to the east of all his brothers."

Hagar pondered the sacred words before she answered. Her mind grasped to understand what was told her. She was pregnant. Therefore she must be pregnant with Abram's child. She would bear a son to be named Ishmael.

An appreciative smile beamed on her face and her trembling ceased as she repeated the words to herself about the son to be born. Then aloud she cried out, "I shall bear a son to Abram, but he shall be *like* a son of Hekanakht!"

With joy and peace she knelt in the sand to worship the angel of the Lord who had been speaking to her. But as she did so he was gone.

"O God of Abram and God of my mistress, Sarai. Blessed be your name, O holy God. You are a God who knows all about me. And I have seen and heard you and have lived!"

When Hagar opened her eyes they fell upon the basin of the spring whose waters, surging and churning up from its sandy floor, flooded out ending in small mossy ponds. As she leaned over and cupped her hand to drink she saw her own reflection intermittently broken by smooth circling ripples. "This is the well of one who has seen God and yet lives," she uttered in unaccustomed awe and fear. Therefore she called the well Beer-lahai-roi.

Knowing that God's hand was upon her, Hagar mounted the camel and turned back to the road on which she had come.

In all of the lands about, punishment for runaways servants who were under indenture was death or recommitment to a lifetime of service. When Hagar returned to Abram's tents she went immediately to Sarai. In bedouin custom Hagar bowed low before her mistress, pulling her hair to the side of her face and baring the back of her neck. For one of the desert it was the ultimate act of submission.

Sarai was moved by the gesture, but she kept her voice severe. "You are guilty of theft and disobedience, Hagar."

"My neck is yours to cut, my mistress," the girl replied quietly.

"Why have you returned?" Sarai inquired. "As you may know, I sent no one to look for you. You were free to leave for your desert home."

Hagar lifted her head. There was assurance in her face. It was not the insolent pride she had shown before but something far different.

"I would be with my brothers even today, had I not met your God and heard his voice." The girl searched Sarai's eyes for understanding. "Because of the son I carry in my womb, I have seen and heard your God and have lived!"

"God told you that you have conceived? You are pregnant with Abram's child?" Sarai hastily questioned her, joy mixing with darts of hurting envy.

Hagar earnestly continued, "The child will be wild and free, like my father. He will be against his brothers, *your* children, Sarai. And they will be against him. His name shall be called Ishmael, and he will dwell not here nor in the deserts of Kemi. He will live to the east."

Sarai studied Hagar for a moment. Tears rolled down her face as she thought of the years of waiting she had endured. Now in one fateful night God had conceived a son for Abram in the womb of this girl. "You may bear your child here, Hagar. He shall be raised as our own son. I do not understand the full meaning of the words spoken to you about the child. But God in his wisdom will be faithful to what he has said to you."

"As I promised, I will bear the child on your knees, my lady. He shall be your son if that is what you wish," Hagar vowed. Her eyes, so dark brown they appeared black, did not leave Sarai's face.

"Go now to the shepherds, Hagar," Sarai told her. "Help the women but do not strain yourself. You do not need to gather . . . fuel," she added, smiling.

300

Those words were enough for Hagar to know that forgiveness had been granted. Without another word she left Sarai's presence and spritely skipped and ran to the far side of the encampment.

Chapter XX
ISHMAEL AND THE SIGN

In early spring of the next year Sarai was called to Hagar's tent by a servant midwife. Hagar was about to deliver her child. Sarai placed herself between Hagar's legs as the girl's body pushed in hard contractions. Hagar breathed heavily but did not once cry out. She was wet and exhausted from the ordeal when the baby was finally ejected.

Sarai lifted the bloody infant while the midwife cared for the cord and the afterbirth. With a sharp back pat Sarai caused the small baby boy's lungs to clear, and he cried out loudly. The excess blood was gently wiped away before the birth cloths were wrapped firmly around him.

The infant's hair was dark and heavy, growing far down his little forehead. His reddened face flushed as his squalling continued. When Hagar was rested enough to nurse, Ishmael was laid beside her, and the baby stretched open his wide mouth and closed it tightly on her milk-swollen breast.

While Hagar was alone and nursing, Abram came to her tent and sat beside her. A gentle breeze drifted in through the open tent flap and the bright sunlight outside reflected in on the young mother and her child.

"I have prayed for you, Hagar," Abram spoke gently. Carefully he stroked the small head and felt the new born body beneath its wrappings. "He looks healthy and strong like his lovely mother."

"He is *your* child, my master," Hagar ventured. "And my lady Sarai's."

"You are his mother," Abram broke in. "You shall not be separated from the one you have borne."

"When the holy God spoke to me he said I would have a son and to name him Ishmael, 'he hears.' "

"He *does* hear, Hagar," Abram said tenderly.

The babe had finished sucking and lay asleep. Abram lifted the small bundle in his arms. "I name you Ishmael," he declared proudly. "As God has commanded, Ishmael is your name!"

After Ishmael was weaned, Hagar left the child for long intervals and helped with the shepherds. Sarai took over the care of the baby boy as she would her own son.

As the child grew Abram and Sarai began to teach him the ways of God and tried to instruct him in scholarly subjects as well. Ishmael was bright, but he could not concentrate long. His impatience to play and be outdoors made him restless and exasperating.

The boy yearned to be with the shepherds and near Hagar, his real mother. With her he felt free to chase after the lambs like a shepherd dog or throw with his sling and shoot arrows at birds and hares. Hagar would often race across the fields with her son, enjoying the play as much as he.

When Ishmael was ten years old, Hagar taught him to ride his first camel. The beast, Kazibu, was old and cantankerous. "If you can learn the ways of this mean one," Hagar encouraged Ishmael, "no other camel will ever concern you. A true bedouin must know the ways of the camel. It is as important as knowing the ways of men!"

For days the training went on. Ishmael never tired of these studies. Over and over he practiced mounting and riding Kazibu. After several weeks the old buck grew weary with the child's constant drill. Swinging his long neck the camel bit at Ishmael's leg. The boy impulsively lashed back with his prod, hitting the animal's sensitive long nose. There were indignant snorts and grunts, but Kazibu did not retaliate—until the next day.

When Hagar woke the boy in their tent, she cautioned him, "Kazibu may be angry with you for hitting him the way you did yesterday. Better take him some dates when you go to fetch him."

"Would Abram the Habiru take dates to a mean old camel?" Ishmael snapped obstinately. "I shall hit him even harder if he bites at me again!"

"Be ready to throw him your coat and tunic if he comes at you," his mother warned.

No sooner had Ishmael approached the camel range than Kazibu spotted him. Coughing and uttering loud deep growls the camel impatiently pawed the ground and then suddenly charged toward the boy.

Terrified, Ishmael tore off his coat and tunic and threw them at the camel. The old buck halted and noisily sniffed the heap of clothes. Biting at them and using his head, Kazibu tossed coat and tunic up into the air. Angrily the camel pawed and tore the clothes and stamped his padded front feet and then his back feet on them, spitting on them and finally urinating on the ground where they lay.

Hagar came to Ishmael laughing and bringing other clothes. "That will teach you to respect the great one of the desert! Now, here, give him his dates!" she said as she handed her son a bag of the fruit.

Ishmael put on the fresh clothes and took the dates to Kazibu who still sulked aimlessly around the small pile of ragged clothes. The camel spied the dates and as if greeting an old friend ambled over to the boy, nuzzling him first lightly on the neck and then digging playfully with his long nose into Ishmael's bag for the treat. All was forgiven.

After that, being near the camel herds was the only thing that pleased the boy. Ishmael begged Abram to let him help care for the riding camels. This elite black herd, that Abram had developed from mares given to him by Shetepibre, were much lighter weight than the usual draft camels. They were extremely agile and fast pacers with long endurance.

But Abram insisted that his son first learn to work with the draft herd, gathering their valuable hair as it was shed and milking the mares. This also kept Ishmael nearer to Hagar.

During the next three years peace continued in Canaan. Shetepibre Amenemhet's alliances with the trading cities and his fortifications of smaller towns along the "way of Shur" had prospered trade and commerce.

The Amorites, so decisively defeated by Abram's men, returned to Canaan, but this time they settled as individuals and families in the villages and cities. Only the wildest and youngest continued in the raiding, plundering bands, blustering about the great days of Chedorlaomer. Their forays were usually ill conceived, sporadic and brutal, many of their own men being lost with each venture; however, the raids were sufficient to keep people on guard.

Abram's community remained about the same in number as when they returned from Kemi. Some of the servants left when their indenture contracts were completed. Others stayed. During the late spring and the summer the tents were pitched near Mamre's oaks. The rest of the year Abram led his people, and they camped throughout Canaan. The herders would fan out from wherever the main tents settled.

One warm night when it was nearing summer, Abram became restless. He was by then ninety-nine years old. He walked out through the dry fields of stubble and past the rows of servant tents. The guards greeted him silently as he passed their stations.

He wandered to a tent by the camel range where Ishmael often stayed. The boy lay asleep outside the tent, stretched out on his riding blanket. Abram smiled at the scene. "Even a tent is too civilized, my brave wild son?" Abram asked lovingly, not expecting a response.

As Ishmael turned in his sleep the moonlight fell on his handsome young face. He had become a tall strong youth and muscularly built. Abram prayed over the boy. Then mounting one of the camels he slowly rode out to the countryside. As the camel loped almost noiselessly on the dusty path, Abram analyzed his restive spirit.

Although he had aged, his body was still vigorous. God had blessed him in that no infirmity bothered him, except one. That one was the recurrence of his foreskin disease. In that he was not alone, as it had spread among many of the males of

305

the camp. No one cared to discuss it, but it was causing irritability among both men and women.

Sarai, though nearly ninety, was to everyone physically amazing. Her beautiful figure was still shapely and her round breasts firm. Streaks of gray highlighted the soft waves of her hair which fell gracefully down her back as it did in her youth. Only light lines etched her face near her eyes, lines like other women might have at the age of forty or fifty.

Yet Abram and Sarai no longer slept together. Part of Sarai's reluctance was still due to her agony in knowing that Abram had found pleasure with Hagar and that a son had so easily come from that brief union. The other problem lay in Abram. As he grew older, sexual desire became less frequent and when it did stir him the sharp pain from the disease quickly quelled the hunger. Although neither suggested it, both Abram and Sarai suspected that he had become impotent. Somehow it was easier to find excuses to sleep separately than to face this seemingly final denial of God's promise for an heir through the two of them. As Abram's romantic advances grew fewer, Sarai also assumed herself inadequate and drew away from close contact. Their relationship became very formal.

Abram paused in these recollections at a small wayside well. Already the water level was low, and there was no jar or rope with which to draw. Frustrated but amused Abram could not help but compare himself to the old hewn rock well.

As he leaned against its walls he looked up into the beautiful heavens and beheld the stars. They reminded him vividly of the night on the Zion mountain. He remembered the torch and the pot of coals, how strangely they moved over the animal sacrifices, igniting the brushwood beneath. At that time God had told Abram to count the stars if he would know the number of his descendants. It was only three nights later that Sarai had encouraged him to lie with Hagar. "Was Ishmael the answer?" Abram thought. "Is Hagar's child the child promised in that covenant?"

Abram fell to his knees by the well and sought the Lord. When the presence of the Lord came, God said to Abram: "I am God Almighty. Walk before me and be blameless, and I will give you the promise made between me and you. I will multiply you exceedingly."

Abram could no longer kneel in the awesome presence and power that encompassed him. He fell on his face, and God continued to speak.

"Behold, my covenant is with you, and you shall be the father of a multitude of nations. No longer shall your name be Abram, but your name shall be Abraham, father of a multitude. For I will make you the father of a multitude of nations.

"And you will be fruitful, exceedingly fruitful. I will make nations of you, and kings shall come forth from you.

"I will establish my covenant between me and you and your descendants after you throughout their generations for an everlasting covenant. I promise to be God to you and to your descendants after you.

"And I will give to you, and to your descendants after you, the land of your sojournings, all the land of Canaan, for an everlasting possession. And I will be their God.

"This is my covenant, which you shall keep, between me and you and your descendants after you: Every male among you shall be circumcised."

As the words of the Lord flowed, Abraham, as he knew he must now and forever be called, could not stir from his prostrate position. He felt transported as if to some heavenly realm. Yet the earth was poignantly near. He could smell the sweet dry dust beneath him and feel the small stones under the palms of his hands. The lofty words of the covenant had held him spellbound until the Lord's command, "Every male among you shall be circumcised." Suddenly the Lord's words were very much a part of his life—his body.

"You shall be circumcised in the flesh of your foreskin," the voice of the Lord resumed. "It shall be a sign of the covenant between me and you. He that is eight days old among you shall be circumcised. Every male throughout your generations, whether born in your house, or bought with your money from any foreigner who is not of your offspring, both he that is born in your house and any man bought with your money, shall be circumcised.

"So shall my covenant be in your flesh an everlasting covenant. Any uncircumcised male who is not circumcised in the flesh of his foreskin shall be cut off from his people. He has broken my covenant."

The words of the Lord reminded Abraham of Sarai's advice years before when they were still in Terrakki. She too had spoken of circumcision as a sign. Abraham rose and once again leaned against the stones of the well.

As he thought of his wife the Lord spoke concerning her: "As for Sarai your wife, you shall not call her name Sarai, but Sarah shall be her name. I will bless her, and moreover I will give you a son by her. I will bless her, and she shall be a mother of nations. Kings of peoples shall come from her."

Abraham slumped as he heard the words. Then he began to chuckle at the thought of his barren post-menopause wife giving birth to nations and to kings. He knew how others had joked and ridiculed him and his wife for their obstinate beliefs. He considered the years he had been married to Sarai. How many thousand nights had he lain with her, entered her, and prayed with her to conceive? He thought of his own aging body and his exhausted male organ, shriveled and diseased. Falling on his face again, he covered his head with his arms to hide his reaction to the ludicrousness of the situation. No longer feeling guilty or ashamed but only frustrated and hopeless, he rolled about on the ground, convulsed with laughter. "Shall a child be born to a man who is a hundred years old? Shall my ninety year old wife bear a son?" he cried hilariously, tears streaming from his eyes.

At last Abraham stood and reached his arms up beseechingly. "O that Ishmael might live in your sight!"

"No," God declared, "but Sarah your wife shall bear you a son, and you shall call his name *'he laughs,' Isaac!*"

Fear slowly permeated Abraham. Had he so dishonored God by his laughter? He thought of other times when he had laughed in the presence of the Lord, not out of despair but from the sheer joy and ecstasy of knowing the one holy God. He smiled in relief as he thought again of the name Isaac. It was as if the Lord were adding a bit of divine humor to lighten the long wait of faith.

But the Lord had not finished, for the words proceeded: "I will establish my covenant with Isaac as an everlasting covenant for his descendants after him. As for Ishmael, I have heard you. Behold, I will bless him. He too shall be fruitful, and I will multiply him exceedingly. He shall be the father of twelve princes, and I will make him a great nation.

"But I will establish my covenant with Isaac, whom Sarah shall bear to you at this season next year."

Suddenly Abraham realized that he no longer felt the presence of the Lord. Soberly he left the well and searched about for his camel. The animal was still tied by the long leash, contentedly munching at tufts of dry grass. The camel's obliviousness to the magnificence of the moonlight theophany caused Abraham to caution himself against what he had heard. *Had it really happened?*

Then he remembered what a wonderful sensation it was to be in the presence of the holy God, how alive he felt as he listened to the Lord.

Abram rubbed the camel's neck and ruffled its hair between his fingers. As the coarse outer hairs parted Abraham touched the soft thick downy coat beneath. His fingers felt with the sensitivity of touch like one who is blind. He was aware of the camel's heartbeat, the warmth of its body, the slight dampness of its skin.

As Abraham mounted, his alert and enlivened senses were nearly intoxicated by the spring night's enchantment, fragrances, and symphonies of sounds. Reverence and joy swept over him as the dark camel retraced the path back to the camp.

On the way Abraham rehearsed for himself the words the Lord had spoken. He determined that the next day all males under his authority would be circumcised. Also, regardless of how anyone might scoff privately he would insist on being called Abraham. He was *Abraham,* father of a multitude. And Sarai? Sarai would be called *Sarah,* no longer daughter and princess, but *mother* and *queen!*

It was then that Abraham recalled the final words of the prophecy: ". . . I will establish my covenant with Isaac, whom Sarah shall bear to you at this season next year." Of all the times the Lord had reiterated the promise of a son, never had a time been set for the birth. It was difficult for Abraham to conceive of the promise having a terminus, "at this season next year."

Abraham went to Sarah's tent. She was lying awake. "Sarah, mother and queen of the land of promise!" he called excitedly to her.

Sarah thought he was jesting. For hours that night, as happened many times, she could find no sleep. The still frequent hot flashes and dizziness had aroused her, unremitting signs that always mocked her. "Do you wish something?" she asked vaguely.

"I have been with the Lord!"

"And he told you I was to be called Sarah?"

"Yes."

"And you, did he give you a new name as well?"

"Abraham, father of a multitude!"

Sarah lifted herself up slightly. She could barely see the form of her husband in the grayness of the dawn. She began to laugh at him.

"Sarah, please do not laugh," he pleaded. "I too laughed when God spoke to me. I begged him to consider Ishmael. But I was told that, although God will greatly bless Hagar's son, you, Sarah, will bear a son. You will bear a son at this season next year! When I laughed at the idea I was told the name of the son would be Isaac, 'he laughs.'"

Sarah reached out and put her arms around Abraham. "Isaac?" she repeated softly. Her interest quickened and all self pity was gone from her voice. "That reminds me of the first time you knew the Lord. Remember how you laughed when you knew God in the Ararats after we came back from seeing the ark? And how you laughed on the rooftop of Terah's villa in Kamarina when God spoke to you?"

Abraham nodded. "Sarah, do you also remember the time in Terrakki when you suggested to me that I should circumcise myself to stop my constant irritation? You said the cutting away of my flesh would be a sign of my belonging to God and a cutting away of the past."

"I have thought of it many times. Especially these past years that we . . . we have been separated," Sarah answered shyly.

"God confirmed your word tonight. As a sign of the covenant, God has commanded that every male in our camp must be circumcised . . . today!"

"Every male in the camp?" Sarah wondered in surprise.

"Any male over eight days old, just as soon as I can gather them together," he affirmed.

Abraham kissed her and held her closely. "Already I have stirrings of desire for you, my darling. But if I stay longer it will only cause pain and disappointment. When I am healed from the circumcision ... we shall ... try again!"

Sarah could only smile and look at him, bewildered from the renewed hope and promise.

After the morning chores were completed the men who belonged to Abraham's house assembled at his bidding, some carrying male infants no more than eight days old. Younger men and boys joined them as they gathered in a large shaded clearing in the forest.

The hot sun illumined the vaulted meeting place penetrating the overarching leaves and dabbling the area with irregular blotches of bright golden light. A soft wind drifted between the tall erect trees, spreading the delicate woody perfume of the oaks.

Abraham gave an explanation of his intention. With prayers and singing the circumcisions began. Forty servants who were adept at animal butchering were appointed to perform the operations. They sat on the ground and the men and boys lined up in front of them.

Abraham was the first. He removed his clothing and leaned back against one of his strong watchmen who gripped Abraham's arms. Using a sharp flint knife the servant cut away the hanging foreskin. The pain was biting and blood fell profusely. A tourniquet of linen was firmly wrapped around the wound and Abraham stood back to allow Ishmael to take his turn. The boy barely winced as he was cut.

After many hours the command of God was fulfilled. The men and boys left the forest. A few collapsed and fainted. All felt the pain of the sign.

Chapter XXI
DESTRUCTION OF
THE CITIES

The healing time varied for those who were circumcised. Some recovered in a few days, others felt very tender for months. The psychological and spiritual effects were indelible. A blood relationship had been established between all the believers who had participated and between their families as well.

One day, toward the end of summer, Abraham sat at the door of his tent. The heat of the brilliant sunlight was tempered by soft winds that crept over the western hills from the sea. A large oak shaded Abraham's tent and the ground about it.

With dry chaff and twigs they had gathered, the women of the camp were starting charcoal fires for the mid-day meal. Menservants prepared meat to be grilled, and young girls had begun pounding out grain for flat bread. It was a tranquil time.

Abraham allowed himself to doze. When he awoke he looked up and saw three men before him.

He was immediately alerted. No alarm had sounded. No guard had ushered these men to his tent. Abraham's watchmen were skillfully trained. No strangers were allowed to enter his camp as these had obviously done. It was as if no one else were aware of the three intruders.

Then the awesome presence of the Lord came upon Abraham. He ran from the tent to meet the men, bowing low before them. "My Lord, if I have found favor in your sight do not pass by your servant," Abraham appealed prayerfully. "Let water be brought to wash your feet, and rest a while under the tree while I get bread for you. Since you have come to your servant, please refresh yourselves before you leave."

"Do as you wish," they said to him.

Abraham spread mats and cushions under the tree, and the three men seated themselves in silence.

Sarah had just risen from her rest in the tent when Abraham hurriedly entered and called to her, "Quickly, take three portions of fine meal, knead it and have bread made for my guests!"

Without explaining further, Abraham left and went to the cattle corrals. He called to one of the men servants who was butchering the day's meat allotment. Selecting a young well-shaped calf, Abraham directed the servant to prepare it before any other.

When the tender meat was grilled and the bread baked, Abraham took yogurt and milk as well and set the food before his three guests, standing to wait upon them as they ate.

"Where is Sarah your wife?" they asked him.

"She is in the tent," he answered wonderingly.

"I will surely return to you in the spring," one of them said, "and Sarah your wife shall have a son." The man, Abraham knew without doubt, spoke the words of the Lord.

Sarah had entered the rear of the tent after returning from the bread ovens. She was curious about the sudden visitors and walked softly to the opened front door of the tent. As she stood listening under the awning that covered the porchway, she heard only the last few words, ". . . in the spring, and Sarah your wife shall have a son."

Sarah thought back over the many years of her barrenness. Although her heart sensed that it was the Lord who had spoken the words, Sarah could not resist laughing to herself with inward embarrassment and resignation. "Now that I am old and my husband is old shall I indeed bear a child?" she thought to herself.

The man spoke again and Sarah strained to hear.

313

"Why did Sarah laugh and say, 'Now that I am old, shall I indeed bear a child?' Is anything impossible for the Lord to do?"

Abraham did not attempt to reply.

The man repeated his prophecy. "At the time I set I will return to you, in the spring, and Sarah shall have a son."

Still out of their sight Sarah flushed with guilt. Stubbornly, relentlessly, she had always defied unbelief. Now she had given expression to it by her own unuttered laughter. It was as if Noah had stopped to laugh at himself for building the ark when he was almost five hundred years old and he saw no rain. Her ridicule of God's promise meant she had truly given up hope.

Sarah ran from the tent and wept before the men, denying what she had done. "I did not laugh!" she cried.

"No, Sarah, you did laugh," came the response. They were compassionate and understanding words.

Her heart stinging with contriteness, Sarah could not bear to stay in the Lord's presence. She left the men and returned, ashamed, to the tent.

The three arose, and Abraham followed them toward the road. The Lord spoke to the other two, "Shall I hide from Abraham what I am about to do, seeing that Abraham is to become a great and mighty nation, and in him all the nations shall be blessed? For I have chosen him, that he may charge his children and his household after him to keep the way of the Lord by doing righteousness and justice, that the Lord may bring to Abraham all that has been promised to him."

The voice of the Lord called back to Abraham, "Because the outcry against Sodom and Gomorrah is great and their sin is exceedingly grave, I will go down to see whether they have done altogether according to the outcry which has come to me. If not, I will know."

The two men departed taking the way that branched toward Sodom, but the man who spoke as the Lord remained and Abraham ran up to him. "Will you destroy the righteous with the wicked?" Abraham questioned with fearful concern for Lot and Lot's family. "Suppose there are fifty who are righteous in the city? Would you destroy the place and not spare it for the fifty?"

When there was no answer Abraham came closer and beseeched the Lord in anguish, "Far be it from you, my Lord, to slay the righteous with the wicked! Far be that from you! Shall not the judge of all the earth do right?" Abraham was appalled by his own boldness, but his love for his nephew constrained him.

At last, the Lord answered, "If I find at Sodom fifty righteous in the city, I will spare the whole place for their sake."

Hastily Abraham replied, "Behold, I have dared to speak this way to the Lord, I who am but dust and ashes. But suppose . . . five of the fifty are lacking. Will you destroy the whole city for lack of five?"

"I will not destroy it if I find forty-five are there," was the answer.

Again Abraham asked nervously, "Suppose forty are found there?"

"For the sake of forty I will not do it," the Lord promised.

"Oh, please do not be angry, my Lord, and I will speak once again. Suppose thirty are found there?"

"I will no do it, if I find thirty," came the reply.

"But wait, since I have taken upon myself to speak in this way to you, suppose . . . twenty are found there?"

"For the sake of twenty I will not destroy it."

"Oh, let not the Lord be angry," Abraham begged. "I will speak again but this one more time. Suppose *ten* are found there?"

"For the sake of ten I will not destroy it."

Then the Lord left him, and Abraham returned, worried, to his encampment.

When Lot had returned to Sodom with Salanna, Pukuli and Minusa, King Bera restored his house and possessions and insisted that Lot be a member of the city's elders. This Lot did only because it gave him opportunity to voice his bitterness. He detested the ways of the people of the city and became quick and sharp in his criticism.

Lot did not hesitate to condemn the perverseness of the Sodomites. He told them of the holiness of God and his demand for righteousness. He warned of God's wrath against

315

them, and how God destroyed the earth once before because of its wickedness.

In condescending ways the council of elders listened to Lot's attacks, often would pretend contriteness, but did nothing to change. The council of Sodom and the other city councils and kings of the valley felt the need to humor Lot because of the lucrative trade business he operated. Lot alone of the Sodom valley traders handled the personal contracts with the pharaoh of Kemi. Shetepibre Amenemhet had little respect for the Sodomites and would deal with no one else but Lot. Therefore, it was very much to King Bera's interests that Lot be sometimes pacified.

Lot and Salanna also kept a small home in one of the Hurrian villages in the Seir mountains. Their herders were settled in the place, pasturing the flocks along the sides of the mountains as far north as Damascus and back.

Salanna was Lot's solace and joy. Because she knew his restlessness in Sodom, Salanna carefully planned to keep her husband as happy as possible. She did all she could to provide for his pleasure and diversion.

The only time Salanna would become aggravated and distant would be at the mention of Abraham and Sarah. At first this did not keep Lot from visiting his uncle, especially when Abraham was settled by the oaks of Mamre. But gradually the visits became farther apart and then ceased.

Twenty-four years had passed since Lot first met Salanna near the bridge at Carchemish. Pukuli and Minusa, who were only sixteen at that time, were now mature women. They looked even more like their mother than when they were younger.

The two sisters had married the young men from Nuzu, Pai-tesup and Tul-tesup. Through the daughters' insistence, Lot had forced Pai-tesup and Tul-tesup into the marriages because of the debts they owed him. It was not a happy situation in either daughter's case. To be rid of their debts and to be able to bribe future favors from Lot, the two men entered into the marriages. But never once did either man lie with his wife.

Instead each night Pai-tesup and Tul-tesup left together to sleep with each other or join a city-wide orgy. Usually they

316

walked wantonly through the streets finding partners for their lust in the darkness or else went to the feasts and hot baths at the temple. It was at the temple where young boys could be bought for the night. Some were publicly mutilated before the lascivious crowds, their torture sadistically tantalizing the desires of the onlookers.

During the daylight hours the inhabitants of the cities went about their work. Guards were posted to see that strangers were not bothered, especially any who came to trade. But caravaners had long learned to stop only at mid-day. They hurried quickly away after their business was over.

Lot made it a practice to sit by the main gate of Sodom when evening approached. There he tried to keep unknowing travellers from entering to find lodging.

It was almost dark. Lot was preparing to leave his post at the gate when the two men of the Lord came toward the city. Lot ran to meet them to prevent their entering. When he sensed that the men were holy, Lot bowed low, his face touching the earth before them.

"My lords," he cried out. "Turn aside from this place, I beg you, or else come to my house to spend the night. Come to your servant's house and let me wash your feet. Then you may rise up early and go on your way."

"No," they both said. "We will spend the night in the streets."

"But it is not safe for you!" Lot implored, knowing full well how the men of the city would abuse them. "The men of Sodom have given up natural relations with women. They are shamelessly consumed with passion for one another. If you stay in the streets they will surely dishonor your bodies!"

The men assented to go with Lot and entered his house. Lot called to Salanna and his servants and soon a meal and unleavened bread were set before the visitors.

As the men ate, Lot served their needs in silence. He wondered as he watched them who they were and what was their mission. Abraham had told him years ago about the servant girl Hagar's experience with a messenger from God. Abraham himself had seen and heard God speak through visions and angels. "Are these wise looking men at my table angels?" he pondered, his heart humbled by the thought that God would ever bless him in such a way.

Lot had always believed all that Abraham and Sarah had taught him. He had seen God's provisions and his mighty miraculous hand at work. But Lot had never had the holy God speak to him or come to him in any way.

Lot ceased his thoughts. Seeing that the men had completed the meal, he led them through the enclosed courtyard to their room.

No sooner had he left them than he heard clamoring noises and loud poundings on his door. The tumult increased until shouts bellowed all around his house, fists hitting against the walls and the shutter locks clanging as the windows were being forced to open.

"Where are the men who came to your house tonight?" came the screams and jeers. "Bring them out to us! Let us know them!"

Lot could feel no fear for himself so concerned did he become for his guests. If they were men or angels of God, he must protect them.

Boldly he opened the door. The men of the city, even the youngest and the oldest, were all there before him. Lot quickly pulled the door shut, and it bolted behind him leaving him to face the mob alone.

Lot lifted up his lamp, and the sight he beheld was sickening. The bodies before him were heated with lust. He saw his own sons-in-law leading the men, and his heart was pained when he thought of Pukuli and Minusa. He could only shake his head when he remembered how they longed to be loved by their husbands.

"I beg you, my brothers," he entreated them, agony straining his words. "Do not act so wickedly!"

There were hisses, catcalls and mockings of response and contemptuous demands for Lot to bring out the two strangers.

Lot stretched out his arms to block the door as the crowd pushed in closer. "Wait," he cried out to them. "I have two daughters who have not known a man. Let me bring them out to you. Do with them as you please. Only do nothing to these men, for they are men who have come under my roof!"

"Stand back!" shouted those in front.

318

"This fellow of his own will came to live among us and now he wants to judge us!" shrieked an old bearded man, his eyes even more lecherous and evil looking than the younger men around him. "Now we will deal worse with you than with them!"

With that the crowd began to maul Lot and tear off his clothes while others fought to pull him away from the door. Suddenly the door gave way, and Lot found himself pulled to safety inside by the two strangers.

As hands continued to beat against the door outside and flail the walls of the house, a new furor of hysteria and confusion arose. The men of Sodom had been stricken with blindness. The moon and the many lamps no longer gave them light, and the crazed men groped to find their way.

Salanna came down the steps, her robe pulled about her. She said nothing but her eyes revealed her fear as she beheld the two strangers supporting Lot. She saw her husband scratched and bleeding, much of his beard and hair pulled out, and nearly all of his clothes ripped off of him.

"Do you have anyone else here?" the men asked Lot and Salanna. "Sons-in-law, sons, daughters, or anyone else you have in the city? You must bring them out of this place. We are about to destroy it because the outcry against its people has become great before the Lord."

Those who had pressed against Lot's door had by now stumbled away to the temple or to find other activities. Reclothing himself, Lot left his house and lifting his lamp went to search for his sons-in-law. He soon found them crawling about on their hands and knees, giggling and poking at one another.

"Where are all the blasted lamps!" screeched Pai-tesup. "Did dreary old Lot blow them out?"

"Did you see him squirm?" Tul-tesup asked drunkenly. "We may make him one of us yet!"

Lot shook them both roughly and ordered, "Up, get up and get out of this place! For the Lord is about to destroy the city!"

"Hee-hee-hee," laughed Tul-tesup derisively. "He is back for more, Pai-tesup!"

319

"Did you not hear me?" Lot shouted impatiently. "The Lord is going to destroy the city of Sodom! Those men in my house are messengers of the holy God!"

"You turn on the lights, dear father-in-law," Pai-tesup smirked scornfully. "If you do not turn on the lights, how can we see your Lord destroy our city. Yes, Lot, turn on the lights! We want to watch!"

The two had had much to drink, and their ridiculing caused them to convulse with cackling laughter. They slapped and clawed at the air to reach for Lot, then rolled about on the ground and crawled away. Lot had no desire to pursue them further.

He returned to the house and found Salanna and the daughters packing. "Didn't you warn the servants?" Lot queried her.

"The two men did not say to get the servants," Salanna replied tartly.

Lot went to her and grabbing her arms turned her strongly toward him. "Salanna! Do you not believe those are angels of God? Do you not realize the seriousness of what they say?"

"Lot, I *am* packing," she replied stonily. "But I do not want anyone besides our family to think we are running away because some 'angels' came and told us they were going to destroy the city and even the whole Sodom valley for no reason!"

"No reason!" he exclaimed aghast.

"As far as the servants and others will know," she continued adamantly, ignoring his remark, "we have decided to go down the valley to visit Zoar. If you think these men are not out of their minds, so be it. We will do as they ask. But we need not *look* like fools!"

Dawn was coming, and the men insistently summoned Lot from below. "Arise, hurry! Take your wife and your two daughters who are here, lest you be consumed in the punishment of the city!"

Salanna had not finished packing. "Hmph," she sniffed and her contempt of the situation began to weaken Lot's conviction.

"Perhaps you are right, Salanna," he said lamely, sitting on the bed and watching her. "How could they destroy the cities?"

Before Salanna could reply, one of the two men broke into the room. He seized Lot and Salanna and with unusual strength forced them down the stairs. The other man came bringing the protesting daughters, Pukuli and Minusa.

Handing each one their clothing pouches the men commanded sternly, "Flee for your life! Do not look back or stop anywhere in the valley. Flee to the hills lest you be consumed!"

Reluctantly but frightened, the four left the house leading several pack asses of food supplies. The two men followed and urged them on.

Salanna drew near to her husband. "Lot!" she whispered. "They want us to go up into the hills of the wilderness! Only a madman would go there now! This is the heat of summer! Besides I brought little water and mostly wine thinking we were going to the wells of Zoar. We will die!"

They were nearing the gates of the city. The streets were strewn with sleeping men who had been unable to find their way. The gate guards had evidently left their posts to join the blind revelry, for the stations were empty.

The two men easily opened the heavy bronzed portals and pressed Lot to move quickly, warning him, "Remember, do not look back! Flee to the hills!"

Lot hesitated. Then imploring them he cried, "Oh, no, my lords. I know that I, your servant, have found favor in your sight, and you show me great kindness in saving our lives. But please, I cannot flee to the hills. It is desolate, and the heat will overtake us, and we will die. Look, the far city! We could make it there. It is but a small place. Let me escape there."

Lot pointed south down the valley to the village of Zoar. "See! Is it not a little one? Let me flee there, and my life will be in no danger."

"All right," agreed the man. "We will not overthrow the city of which you have spoken. But make haste! Escape, for nothing can be done until you arrive there!"

Lot led the asses to the south, away from Sodom. Salanna and the daughters walked sulking behind. They took a path that bordered the main irrigation canal. The waterway drained off from the Lake of Gomorrah to the farmlands of the

321

valley. Green gardens grew near the canal with rows of vegetables, but the grain fields beyond were dry and left idle for the summer.

When the canal narrowed at Zeboiim the road circled the city and led through the lower valley. There water came more from deep-bored artesian wells that overflowed in gushing fountains and into little gullies leading to the beautiful date palm forests and vast vineyards. Glimmering clusters of heavy grapes that produced the famous sweet wines of the Sodom valley hung temptingly in the sunlight as the weary foursome passed.

The breezes that fanned in all directions off the lake in the daytime were but slight relief as the late summer sun grew hotter and they walked between the sections of thickly planted palms. The soft winds waved the high rustling fronds overhead exposing the drooping bunches of ripened dates. Nowhere except in the Sodom valley did so many varieties of date palms flourish.

Salanna grew bitter as she trudged along with Pukuli and Minusa. She did not care for the men of Sodom, but she loved this beautiful valley. Her mind could not reason why Lot was doing what he was doing. "How could he be so deceived by those two men?" she thought, and fearful suspicions entered her mind. "What if they forced us to leave so that they could rob us of all we own while we are gone?"

As they arrived in Zoar the bright burning morning sun was high in the sky. The small city's gates were flung open and the market sellers were noisily calling from their booths.

Lot was well known in Zoar. His unusual appearance, travelling unescorted by servants or caravan, was immediately reported to the king.

While Lot sought to find accommodations the king approached him. "Lot, my friend! Welcome to our humble city! Why is it you come bringing only your women? Surely our markets have nothing to offer them that they could not find better in Sodom!"

The peaceful ordinariness of the village of Zoar and the blunt curiosity of the king made Lot feel ashamed and ridiculous. He hesitated and admitted confusedly, "I was warned by my God to flee."

"Flee? Why should you flee?" asked the king. He would have said more but Lot threw back the linen cloth that had been wrapped around his head and face as protection against the sun.

The king of Zoar stared at Lot's scratched and battered face and was alarmed. "The men of Sodom have abused you! Why? Why? King Bera puts high value on your being in the valley! He has threatened to fight any of us if we should offend you or allow stealing from your servants or tax your caravans!"

"Because," Salanna broke in sarcastically, "Lot and his uncle and that priest, Melchizedek, think you are all perverse and detestible people! They spend their days and nights praying to their God to destroy you! Two insane men came to Sodom last night. They said they were sent by God to bring judgment and punishment on all the cities of the valley."

Becoming anxious and twitching with nervousness, the king of Zoar scrutinized Lot. "We have heard that the plague of the former pharaoh of Kemi was a curse put upon him by your uncle. If Abram the Habiru has dared to curse our valley, I must hold *you* responsible!" he declared with growing vehemence.

Salanna quickly realized what she had done by her outburst. She tried to cover over the remarks. "It is but foolishness, your honor," she said soothingly. "The men of Sodom know the two strangers are there. They came after them last night, but my hospitable husband protested. Lot was beaten up while his guests did nothing but hide inside the house. Guards will have arrested the two troublemakers by now. Melchizedek probably sent them to stir up fear. You *know* King Bera will take care of them!"

With her words the king of Zoar relaxed somewhat. "Very well, then," he said more cordially. "May your stay in our city be pleasant."

The king turned to leave but then came back. Overlooking the former conversation, he spoke to Lot concerning lowering caravan prices for the products of Zoar. Lot tried to discuss the business affairs, but his mind was stirring feverishly with apprehension. The angels of the Lord had told him they would not destroy the cities of the valley until Lot reached Zoar. It was half an hour since they had arrived. If the destruction did begin, the king of Zoar and his people would surely turn on Lot and his family.

With great effort to remain calm, Lot agreed on several fees with the king, giving ample discount in order more quickly to extricate himself. Leaving the king and moving through the market and back outside the walls, Lot led Salanna, Pukuli and Minusa to the place where their donkeys were being held by the entry guards.

"We have completed our business," Lot commented as matter-of-factly as possible to the attendant.

Salanna's expressive eyes looked at her husband. "We are returning to Sodom?" she asked questioningly, with a faint happy smile.

Lot replied slowly, still in the hearing of the guards. "It will be a hot walk, but we will journey before the breezes stop. Come, my wife and daughters!"

They had left Zoar a short distance when Lot said resolutely to his wife, "We are *not* returning to Sodom, Salanna!"

"What? Why then did we not stay in the village?"

"We could not stay in Zoar. They would kill us for being responsible for what is going to happen!"

"Lot! You *are* crazy!" Salanna gasped and in desperation and fury began to beat against him with her fists.

Lot grabbed her arms and held them firmly. "We are going to take the road to the Seir mountains," he said determinedly.

"That is another two days' journey!" Pukuli chimed in, sounding exactly like Salanna.

Before Lot could reply the ground beneath them jolted and swayed.

"It is happening!" Lot yelled in terror. "Come Salanna! We cannot make it! We must return to Zoar!"

Minusa pulled two of the asses while Lot plunged ahead dragging the others back toward the city. The brief quake had excited the animals, and they had to be goaded to keep moving.

"It is but a small quake shock, Lot!" Salanna protested, refusing to follow him. "You know they happen nearly every week!" Then Salanna whispered to Pukuli, "I am going back to Sodom! I fear those two men are only there to steal our possessions. I will get the servants and join you later. Take care of your . . . your deranged father!"

"Mother, let me come with you!" Pukuli begged. "I do not want to spend the night in Zoar!"

"No, Pukuli," Salanna refused. "Lot needs you. When this dream of his is over he will feel foolish. You two stay and tend to his needs."

Lot and Minusa were nearly to the city gates when Pukuli ran to catch up with them. The frightened king of Zoar had ordered the gates closed after the tremor. Pukuli was the last person to enter them before they were shut.

Salanna looked back at Sodom. She decided to take a low mountain path that paralleled the valley to keep Lot from finding her and preventing her retreat.

The byway gave Salanna a clear view of the valley. The brilliant sun shone on the cities that lay like hubs of four giant flat cultivated wheels in the broad expanse with little Zoar squatted at the southern end. The large glistening Lake of Gomorrah was shrouded with a misty cloud formed by rapid evaporation in the summer heat. The serenity relieved her and arrested the qualms of uncertainty and guilt that she had from deserting Lot.

Then the earth trembled again. Before her eyes, Salanna saw the whole valley sway and rock. The fields rippled like ocean waves. Screams and cries poured out of the cities as mud bricks houses and walls crumbled and collapsed in clouds of dust.

Salanna stood terrorized as a gaping crater opened at the end of the lake and a spray of fiery rocks and steaming water hissed and thundered out to form a towering spout. The burning cinders fell like flaming hail on the people who fled to the fields.

The earth shook violently and a ghastly wrenching sound reverberated and echoed throughout the valley. Unbelievingly Salanna saw the whole floor of the Sodom valley drop as if a great weight has been pressed upon it. Rips in the ground opened up and scalding geysers of water and molten salts and sand shot up. The spewing waters trapped Salanna so that she could not retreat. The heat blistered and stiffened her body. She stood rigid and dying for torturous seconds as the scorching belching spray continually dumped its brackish mélange. The crystalizing white-hot sand and salts encased and entombed all they covered. Salanna became a haunting looking mass of siliceous rock, a pillar of salt.

In a final wave of tremors the bitumen tar pits erupted and leaping flames burst upward into the sky. Nothing remained in the valley of Sodom but scorching charred earth and the dismayed village of Zoar with its surrounding undisturbed palm trees and vineyards.

As the quakes lessened, the darkening sky over Sodom became a red blazonry of fire. The heat and smoke drove the panic-stricken people of Zoar out of the city. The pitiful survivors fled madly southward.

Though it would soon be dark Lot knew he must go to the mountains. He led Pukuli and Minusa and the asses. They entered a dry river wadi that cut a wide gorge through the towering sandstone escarpment. The ascent was contorted with bends and turns as the narrowing wadi scaled up into the mountains.

Lot found a wide-mouthed cave for shelter. They all knew there was no hope for Salanna. While Pukuli and Minusa wept with grief, Lot mechanically unburdened the asses and spread out mats. There were skins of wine, ale and water, bread and dried meat, and bags of dates—enough supplies to last several days.

Lot poured a ration of the water for the asses and allowed them to feed from leather pouches of provender and to forage the brittle grasses that had found root near the cave.

Even summer nights were usually chillingly cold in the mountains. But this night the broiling heat from the valley belched hot smoky winds up the wadi courseway. The outside air became stifling. Lot, the two women and the asses moved farther into the cave.

All of Canaan had felt the violent shock waves of the quakes. As soon as dawn came Abraham left his tent and made his way toward Sodom. When he reached the point where he had interceded with the Lord for the valley cities, he saw the whole eastern horizon darkened by massive thunderhead clouds of black smoke. Like a smoldering furnace, the Sodom valley lay beyond the mountains ahead of him. Acrid fumes pungently infiltrated the fresh morning air as the desert winds blew them westward. Coughing and choking, Abraham was forced to turn back, his nose and throat smarting with pain.

The comforting and familiar oil lamps lit up the blackness of the cave. Lot sat tearless. His whole body ached from the suffering loss of Salanna. He had not slept since the terrible destruction.

"Drink, my father," Pukuli implored him as she lay a skin of the sweet wine before him. "It may be the only way we can endure another horrible night."

Lot looked at her tenderly and then at Minusa, seeing his beloved wife in their forms and movements and words. His heart gripped with painful spasms of despair. "Would not these reminders of his wife's love and beauty forever keep him in remorse?" he cried out inwardly.

He took the wine and drank of it freely. As Pukuli watched, she whispered to Minusa, "Lot is old, but there may be no other man left on earth to come in to us."

"What are you saying, Pukuli?" Minusa blinked, guessing the intent of her sister's words but still shocked that she had said them.

"Come, help me," Pukuli answered resolvedly. "Encourage him to drink more wine. We will lie with him and have children by him, at last, for ourselves . . . and for Mother."

Minusa sadly agreed and took another wineskin to her father, replacing it for the one he had emptied by his side.

"Keep drinking, my father," she said sweetly. "Come, let me lift it to your lips." Minusa lightly tipped the full skin into Lot's mouth, encouraging him to forget his miseries.

When Lot was quite drunk, the women stretched out his body on his mat and disrobed him. Minusa retired to the far side of the cave while her sister lay beside Lot.

As Pukuli embraced Lot, his arms felt the warm nudeness of her body and his hands searched for her breasts. "Oh, Salanna, my lovely wife," he mumbled in his stupor. "Come to me, come to me. . . ."

Awaking the next morning, Lot knew nothing but that he had dreamed of his wife. Slowly, he rose to face his lonely reality.

The soot-laden smoke outside the cave forced the three to remain in their dark sanctuary another day. After the evening meal Pukuli and Minusa once again insisted that Lot drink to ease his sorrows. He did so willingly.

That night Minusa lay with her father.

Chapter XXII
ABIMELECH

The hazy smoke still drifted in from the Sodom valley, but Abraham was restless to go and see what had happened. Three days had passed since the calamity. He met with Mamre, Eshcol and Aner and the four decided to take a band of watchmen and leave the next day before dawn.

Mamre and his brothers had established their own village since the Amorite battle. The little town was developed with farmlands and orchards on all sides. The area beyond the oaks was kept in pasture for Abraham and his people who settled there each year for the summer months.

When Abraham came to his own tent to gather his things for the trip, he found Sarah despondent.

"What is the matter, my wife?" he asked tenderly.

She turned away from him and did not answer.

"Will you not tell me why you are crying?" he asked. "I must leave soon. I don't want to go if something is wrong." Abraham gently stroked her hair as he spoke.

Sarah's tearful eyes were hurt and angry. "How can you ask questions like that?" she cried bitterly. "You should know why I am offended!"

"*I* have offended you?" Abraham responded innocently. "How have I offended you, Sarah?"

"Are you not leaving with Mamre and his brothers? Did you not say you planned to go on to the Seir mountains and look for Lot?" Sarah asked emotionally. "Did you not say you would be gone several weeks?"

"Yes . . . but it may or may not take that long," Abraham said, still confused by her distress.

"And did you not tell some of the watchmen that if Lot were safe that you might go to Sheba and do some surveying?" Sarah's tears were now streaming down her face.

Abraham realized that he had made such arrangements and had not even mentioned them to Sarah. He was not quite sure why he had not told her, for they usually planned together.

"I could see no reason why you would object," he said weakly. "I would not be gone more than a few more weeks. I have never mapped the area of Gerar. Abimelech keeps it tightly guarded. I thought if I went alone I might make peace with the man as well."

"Do you not know that the time of summer fruit is almost over and the olives are ripening on the trees?" she wept and sobbed.

"Sarah? What do you mean?" he asked, completely perplexed and bewildered by her behavior.

Sarah could only look at him and grieve, her heart was so heavy. Nonplussed, Abraham began to walk away.

As he left the tent he heard her cry disconsolately after him, "If I do bear a child by next spring, *it shall not be fathered by you!*"

Her words smote him. Immediately Abraham realized what he had done. He had unconsciously planned to be away from her during the month that she must conceive if she were to have a son by next spring.

Going ruefully to her bedside he said contritely, "Forgive me, Sarah."

"You no longer enjoy loving me, do you, Abraham?"

"That is not so, Sarah. You know that if I have any desires left in this old body they are for you!" he answered.

Sarah's eyes alone questioned him in silence.

After a long pause, Abraham confessed, "I fear I planned the trips not to avoid you, my precious wife, but to avoid

330

admitting my own failure as a husband. In younger days my love for you could overcome those thoughts. Now an urgency to 'perform' is placed upon me. It makes me impotent."

Sarah cried dejectedly, "And how then do I conceive the child God has promised? *God Himself* said that the child would be born! It was not a vague promise this time, my husband! He said I would bear a son *next* spring!"

Abraham's remorseful face brightened. "Perhaps, Sarah, if you went with me! It would be a change for both of us. Besides, you are still the best survey helper I have ever had!"

Sarah smiled tearfully. Abraham took her in his arms, warmly embracing her until all the inner hurts they both felt disappeared.

So it was that Sarah went with Abraham the next day to Sodom. It was not long before they got their first distant view of the devastation. It was a strange and unexpected sight. The mountains on either side were blackened by tarry soot. The beautiful valley had sunk two to four cubits and the waters from the Lake of Gomorrah and the pushed-up subsurface reservoirs flooded the burned out fields. At the farthest end of the valley remained the buildings of Zoar. Outside its walls the vineyards and palm trees stood submerged in a cubit or more of water. The palm fronds and the leaves of the vines were brown and dead. Nothing was green or growing.

Abraham's company skirted the valley and entered Zoar. Its streets were deserted and, except for the haunting winds, noiseless.

Aner called their attention to the water that lapped the sands outside Zoar's gates, the place where the road once led into the city. "No wonder the trees and the vines are dead. Taste the water!" he exclaimed, wrinkling up his face as his tongue touched his wet fingers. "Salt! Whatever underground river tunnel that carried away the Lake of Gomorrah's silt must have collapsed in the quakes."

"And its stored up deposits probably erupted to the surface," Abraham surmised, as he picked up and examined one of the innumerable chunks of tar that washed up in the murky water.

331

Through the forest of dead palm trunks, the isolated group could see four dark flat mounds in the expanded lake, resting above the water like giant black lily pads. They were all that remained of the cities of Sodom, Gomorrah, Zeboiim and Admah.[18]

"This place is nothing but a sea of death," Eshcol sighed and those about him nodded in accord as their eyes stayed fixed on the frightening scene.

The group picked its way around the strange new eastern shoreline. The desolation was eerie and forbidding. Abraham chose the same path that Salanna had used after leaving Lot. As they passed the pillar that enclosed Salanna's body, one of the watchmen shrieked. "Look, master!" the man yelled. "It looks like a hand! There is a ring upon it!" They gathered to see the charred black fingers that extended from the glassy rock. It was an unpleasant sight, and Abraham shielded Sarah from viewing it.

The watchman brought the ring, and Abraham beheld it in horror as it rested in the palm of his hand. "It is a Hurrian ring, sir," the watchman said.

"I know, my son," Abraham replied faintly, closing his hand around it and praying.

"Salanna's?" Sarah asked quietly.

Abraham shook his head in affirmation. "If Lot is still alive, I could never bear to tell him of this."

Abraham and Sarah and their watchmen departed to the south, and Mamre, his brothers, and their watchmen returned to their village.

On the road to Kadesh, Abraham met the king of Zoar and his citizens fearfully trekking back to their city. When the king of Zoar recognized Abraham he screamed out irritably, "Abram the Habiru! Have you been looting our city!"

"Why should I loot your city?" Abraham shouted indignantly from his high camel mount. "Was it not I who brought back your filthy riches from the Amorites?"

"Then why are you here? I suppose you look for your nephew?" the king asked hoarsely.

"Do you know if he escaped?" Abraham asked quickly.

The king sniffed and said brusquely, "We are poor, but you are rich. I will receive pay for my information!"

Before the king's guards could draw their swords, Abraham's watchmen instantly had their arrows tautly against their bows, aimed at the king and those around him.

"Where is Lot?" Abraham pressed the king.

The king shrugged his shoulders, forsaking his bribery. "We all fled when the earth began to shake. He and his daughters went up one of the wadis into the mountains. I never saw his wife leave. They had four or five pack asses of supplies with them."

Abraham glared at the king and back at the sad line of refugees trailing behind him. "The holy God spared you, king of Zoar. Lot is a righteous man. Because he came to your city you were not destroyed. Remember, it was that one righteous man that saved your city!"

The king tossed his head in defiance. He signaled his people and grumbling they moved between Abraham's camels and on to Zoar.

Concerned about Sarah in the extreme heat, Abraham divided his watchmen, sending some to search for Lot and taking the others on with him to the springs of Kadesh. They camped beyond the city on the way to Shur.

Abraham needed to correct his maps of the area, but most of the time he and Sarah spent in prayer. Awe and fear after seeing the devastation and annihilation of the Sodom valley made them seek the Lord's presence.

The prayer times were rewarding and reassuring. But at night in their tent when they lay beside each other, Abraham once again became tense and impotent and Sarah hurt and confused.

"If I could conceive even now, Abraham, it would be late spring before a child would be born. But if you cannot impregnate me, how . . . can I? Oh, why did not the Lord bless us with children when we were young? Why, now that we are old?" she remonstrated.

"We are to be an example, Sarah. If we are to be the parents of those who have faith in this land, then we must have the greater faith," he said unconvincingly, his eyes downcast to avoid hers. "Let us rest now."

The next day, a watchman who had been in Kadesh reported to Abraham, "The people say that Abimelech has recently allowed travellers and visitors into his territory as long as they come in families. There is an inn in his village of Gerar."

"They don't think he would allow even our small group of watchmen in, however," added another one of the men.

"Perhaps Sarah and I shall go and tell him our desires," Abraham replied thoughtfully. "Meanwhile, you men could continue to camp here, should I need you."

"Will not Sarah, your wife, be in danger, my master?" a watchman objected.

"Abimelech has a wife and many concubines, I am told," laughed Abraham. "I do not think someone of Sarah's age would interest him."

"She is still a beautiful woman, sir," the man persisted, remembering the experience in Kemi. "Would it not be safer to say again that she is your sister?"

"You speak well!" Abraham agreed. "As a precaution we shall do so."

Abimelech's black hair and beard, his dark deep-set eyes, and his tall erect stature would hardly seem to be that of a man over one hundred and fifty years old. When Abraham had been invited to the king's residence, he had somehow not anticipated the king to be such a strikingly handsome man.

"You do me great honor, Abram of Terrakki, or should I say, Abram the Habiru," the king greeted him genuinely. "I have often desired to meet the man who saved all of Canaan from the cursed Amorites. My kingdom is yours to enjoy!"

"May all praise be to the holy God of Noah!" Abraham replied enthusiastically. "If you would, I prefer to be called Abraham, a name given to me by my God."

"Ah, it is good to hear a man speak of the holy God of Noah, Abraham," Abimelech exclaimed. "We are Hamites, as you may know. My fathers have lived in Gerar since the

334

dispersion from Shinar. I am but six generations removed from the Great Flood!"

"And your people worship as you do?"

"If they serve me, they must serve my God!" the king answered strongly. "I keep my borders free of any who bow to Nannar-Sin, Baal or Ashtar, or who practice the ways of the Sodomites!"

Abraham was refreshed by Abimelech's faith. He liked the tall melancholy man and the two began to talk of many things. Although Abraham was tempted to tell the king about Sarah and her background in the Ararats, he hesitated to admit their true relationship. His watchman's warning held him back. "It is foolishness, though," he thought to himself. "Sarah is old. Why should Abimelech desire her? She could bear him no. . . ."

Abraham's inner discourse stopped when he remember the prophecy of the Lord, ". . . in the spring . . . Sarah your wife shall have a son."

Instead Abraham told Abimelech that he had brought his aged sister, Sarah, with him to assist in surveying the land. At first the king was suspicious about Abraham's reasons for mapping his land. But Abraham brought out his writings and other maps of Canaan, Kemi, and the land of the rivers.

"Your area is the only section I am missing, Abimelech," he explained as he spread out the papyrus rolls. "I shall be glad to make copies of any of these for you if you like. To my knowledge, they are more accurate than any done previously."

Abimelech was obviously pleased. "You will surely need more than an elderly sister to help you. Let me send servants to care for your needs and assist you. Would four men be enough? I will also send two women to cook and market with your sister."

"You are indeed most hospitable, my friend," Abraham accepted pleasantly. "That would satisfy my needs completely. Tomorrow I will have my sister order the supplies, and I shall train the men outside the city as soon as the winds rise."

"Excellent," Abimelech agreed and the two separated congenially.

Although years before, the Amorites had taken almost all of the women in Abimelech's small kingdom, many now lived in his land. They had come after the famine when the king offered indentured servanthood to unmarried females. They were freed from their indenture if they married, which most were pleased to do. Abimelech himself had recently taken one young woman as his wife and kept many as servant concubines. His previous wife who was stolen by the Amorites was reported to have been killed when she tried to escape not long after her capture. The king mourned for her many years before he could find interest in another woman.

Abimelech sent the servants to Abraham's lodging the morning following their conversation. As soon as they arrived, Abraham took the young men to fields beyond the city and taught them the use of some of his surveying equipment. While they worked with levels, protractor rods and measuring cords, Sarah directed the buying with the two women servants in the city market.

"Sarah, sister of Abraham?" a man called out in the market.

Sarah whirled about at the sound of an unfamiliar voice saying her name. She looked up into the face of a tall impressive man standing very close to her. His dark eyes did not leave her as he grinned and said, "An aged sister indeed! Your brother did not tell me you were the most beautiful woman ever to enter my kingdom!"

"And you are . . . Abimelech, king of Gerar?" Sarah replied, regaining her composure.

The king studied her features intensely, pleasurably examining her face. Standing back a pace he silently inspected her stature. "Your loveliness is unlike other women, Sarah," he slowly declared, his smile widening with obvious appreciation. "You have the beauty of the earlier age!"

It had been a long time since Sarah had been looked upon with such admiration. That morning in his excitement to be surveying the last section of Canaan, Abraham had left Sarah abruptly. She had been concerned about their safety in what had always before been a hostile kingdom. But Abraham did not seem to mind leaving her alone with the strange servant women that Abimelech had sent. This compounded her basic feeling of rejection; that since they left the oaks of Mamre, Abraham had not once attempted to make love to her. Sarah had tried to hide her feelings from Abraham and even from herself.

"You are very kind to flatter an old woman, King Abimelech," Sarah replied uncomfortably. She was fearful of this man, but she was also very much attracted by him. She longed for Abraham to be protectively by her side, only to remember how carelessly he had left her.

"Let the servants finish your buying, my sweet woman. Come to my palace. It is a humble place, but there we can talk and enjoy the mid-day meal together. Your brother will not miss you, I am sure. He seemed very anxious to spend the day with his work."

The king could not realize how much his words pricked Sarah's heart. "You are gracious to me, but it would not be right in the Lord's sight for me to do such a thing," she answered him.

The smile left Abimelech's face. "The man, Abraham, told me he was your brother!"

"Abraham *is* my brother," Sarah put forth quickly. "He is truly my brother."

"Are you not a widow? Only widows seek a brother's protection. No husband would allow a wife as beautiful as you to go about even in a market alone."

"My brother and I have surveyed many years together. I am helpful to him and adept at computations," Sarah related as she tried to pull away.

Then unexpectedly Abimelech began speaking to her not in Canaanite but in another language. As Sarah heard each resonant syllable, she felt a far away happiness of her childhood sweep over her. Abimelech was telling the story of the Great Flood in the original tongue of Noah, saying the same words that Hosani used when she told Sarah the story by the shores of Lake Aratta.

337

"How is it that you know the tongue of Noah, Sarah?" Abimelech demanded. "I can see by your face that you understood me. I spoke as I did to test you."

Sarah forgot that she stood in the middle of a busy market place or that guards of the king of the city stood near her. She only rejoiced that she had heard the sweet words that Abimelech spoke. It had been so long since she had heard the simple dynamic language, the same tongue of Methuselah, Enoch and Adam. She closed her eyes and could see the cold, clear waters of the lake, the old moss-covered cottages and the radiant lined face of Hosani.

"I am descended but four generations from Noah. Shem was my father's grandfather," Sarah admitted softly. "I was the last to leave Noah's vineyards on Lake Aratta."

"Come, Sarah," Abimelech said tenderly as his guards grasped her arms gently but firmly to compel her to go with him. "Let us talk of these things together."

"Please," Sarah protested. "Do not dishonor me!"

"I shall not dishonor you," he pledged, his sad eyes for the first time sparkling.

"But . . . my brother!"

Abimelech's face hardened. "It is good that he *is* your brother. I swear before the holy God I would slay any other man who would take a woman I wanted away from me in my own kingdom!"

The people in the market were aware of the encounter between their king and Sarah. Carefully they kept their backs turned and engaged in loud continuous chatter. The two women servants sent to help Sarah stayed at a discreet distance, pretending to be oblivious to the scene. When Abimelech had Sarah led away, the two women shrugged and went on with their buying.

The guards escorted her with the king back to the low-built rambling palace and through its narrow gate.

The spacious entry courtyard was shaded by ancient sprawling oak trees. Worn flat cobbestones made broad paths around brilliant flowering garden plots. A sunlit old walled well squatted in the center covered by a tightly thatched pointed roof which was held up by stone pillars.

"We believe that Ham himself dug that well, Sarah," Abimelech said as he led her to it.

Sarah ran her hand over the smooth stones along the top of the waist-high round wall. Bucket ropes had worn grooves into the sides of the stones, and feet had hollowed polished furrows in the slabs of limestone pavement that encircled the well.

For all the anxiety of her situation, Sarah felt at home and at peace in the centuries-old courtyard. Perhaps her own distant uncle had hewn this well and nursed these trees. Her heart ached from the years of living in tents, of never having a home or children.

"This can be your home, Sarah," Abimelech whispered close to her ear. "The God of Noah is worshipped in my kingdom. He has blessed us, and we know long life in this land."

Sarah tried to look away, but she found it difficult in herself to resist Abimelech.

Abimelech smiled at her affectionately. "You have not been thoroughly loved in some time, have you, Sarah? A woman of such voluptuous beauty should not be so long a widow!"

That he knew she felt desire for him embarrassed her. "Do not feel shame," the king chided her gently. "Come with me, Sarah."

He motioned to the guards who led her up the courtyard stairs to the balcony and into his bedchamber. The pleasant darkness of the thick walled room was a cool contrast from the bright sunlight by the well. Sarah saw that the carpeted room was dominated by a massive linen-covered bed. She grew frightened and tried to break away. The men took off her outer cloak and unfastened the shoulder brooch of her gown. Abimelech dismissed the guards, and they released her, closing the heavy door behind them.

"I want to lie with you, Sarah!" Abimelech said firmly. "This is my land, and I am king. You looked at me in the courtyard as if you would enjoy my love. Why should you resist me now? I shall take you by force if I must. But I would rather spend the hours of this day caressing you and making love to you."

Abimelech had taken off his tunic, and his tall muscular body was lean and darkly tan. Sarah tried not to look at him. Desperately she fought off the strong magnetic stimulation he aroused in her.

"You promised you would not dishonor me," she pleaded weakly.

Sarah's gown had fallen away from her full and pointed breasts. "I am the law in this land. You are now *my* wife!" he said as he gazed at her. "Your breasts give you away, Sarah. They, at least, want me to love them!"

As Abimelech reached to embrace her, he suddenly drew back, his hands clutching over his heart. In excruciating pain he doubled over, his breathing becoming short and gasping. "Help . . . help me, Sarah!" he struggled to say, his face becoming ashen and his eyes filled with fear.

"Lean on me!" Sarah directed him as she braced her shoulder under his and led him staggering to his bed.

Abimelech clenched his fists as the stabbing pains gripped him. He lay tensely on the bed, striving to get air. Sarah pulled a covering over his body.

Refastening her gown, she left the room to search for help. Running down the stairs and out of the courtyard she found the same guards who had escorted her. "The king is quite ill," she said urgently. "He needs someone to attend him immediately!"

The guard in charge was suspicious and nodded to two others to hold her. To a third he commanded, "Go quickly! Bring Commander Phicol!"

"The king should not be alone like this!" Sarah screamed as she struggled to get away from those who held her.

"How do we know you did not do him harm?" the man shouted at her as heavy pounding footsteps approached. The other guard returned through a dark doorway and behind him came Phicol, a towering brawny giant of a man.

"Where is King Abimelech?" Commander Phicol roared to Sarah, his sharp accusing eyes glaring down on her. "What did you do to him, woman?"

"It is his heart!" she said defiantly as Phicol threateningly lifted his arm as if to strike her.

"Take her to the rooms of the other women," the commander ordered. "And do not allow her to escape! If necessary tie her down until we know what has happened!"

The big man lunged through the courtyard gate, and every step he took could be heard as he and the other guards climbed their way up the steps to Abimelech's chambers.

While Sarah was led through the courtyard, the commander came out of the king's room and his booming voice sounded from the balcony of the upper floor.

"Water, bring fresh water!"

One guard let Sarah go and dashed to the well, dropping in the bucket and allowing the rope to burn his hands as it slipped through his fingers. There was a deep, distant splash, and the young man began feverishly retrieving the pail. He was mounting the steps with the filled bucket when Sarah was taken through a doorway and into a connecting corridor. The hallway opened into another smaller courtyard enclosed by the rooms of the king's women.

Sarah stayed in the smaller courtyard during the rest of the day, meeting Abimelech's young wife, Intaluanza, and his five concubines. Servant girls were sent in to care for their needs.

Intaluanza was a Hurrian. She had been traded to Abimelech for several hostages who had entered the small private kingdom without permission. Intaluanza was a frail young woman with delicate sensitive features and doleful, frightened eyes.

When Sarah spoke to the girl in Hurrian, she relaxed for the first time. It was as if the Canaanite language imprisoned her more than Abimelech or his guards. As they talked, Sarai found that Intaluanza was with child by Abimelech, as were the five concubines. Sarah could see that each was in a different stage of pregnancy.

These other women drew near to talk with Sarah. They were servant girls who, at one or more times, had been taken to lie with the king. When they reported their pregnancy, the king released them from their duties during their waiting time

341

and allowed them to do lighter chores and sewing. Some had had several children already by the king, and their toddlers and infants crawled about and played in the courtyard under their supervision.

"The king had only one son by his first wife, the woman taken by the Amorites," Intaluanza related. "The son was a cripple and died shortly after his mother left. They say it was pitiful. The loss of his mother and seeing his father's grief made him kill himself. He threw himself over a cliff, although they tried to tell the king he had fallen."

Looking quizzically at Sarah, Intaluanza asked, "Are you to be a wife to Abimelech? Or did Phicol steal you from your husband?"

"What do you mean?"

Phicol is very devoted to the king, Sarah. But he has a cruel heart. He has killed many travellers to take their wives as gifts for Abimelech."

"I should think the king would not need such violent assistance," Sarah replied pensively.

"He would not even look at the women! They stayed here weeping and mourning until Phicol dragged them out and made them marry any man who would take them!"

"Are you happy here, Intaluanza?" Sarah asked the young woman compassionately.

Intaluanza blushed and held her swollen stomach. "At first I was very afraid. One of the hostages was my brother. When Abimelech agreed that I would be called his wife and not a servant, my family was pleased for me to come in exchange for the others."

"But are you happy?"

Intaluanza smiled shyly. "I love King Abimelech with all my heart!" she said wanly. "But I do not please him, Sarah. He worships a god I do not know. He always prays after we lie together. Then he becomes upset with me and asks me to leave. For many weeks he will not ask for me again."

It was time for the children to be fed, and Sarah joined in helping with the chores and cooking. The time passed quickly, and when darkness began to fall Sarah retired to a small unoccupied room. She bathed with water she had drawn and knelt to give herself to prayer.

A timid knock at her door jarred her. Sarah called to find out who it was. "It is I, Intaluanza," came a whispered cry. Sarah took her lamp and opened the door. She saw Intaluanza holding a blood-soaked towel between her legs. "Sarah, please, tell me what to do! The physicians are all with the king. I fear I will lose my child."

Sarah led the weak girl back to her room and cleaned her bed. "Lie flat, Intaluanza," Sarah ordered with authority. "We must elevate you!"

Sarah placed a soft cushion and cloths under the girl's hips and cleansed her. Gently and soothingly she rubbed oil on her abdomen. Intaluanza wept and shook. "You must remain quiet and calm," Sarah warned her softly.

As she spoke, a face peered around the door of Intaluanza's room. It was one of the pregnant servant girls. "What is it, Samida?" Sarah asked.

The frightened girl looked from Sarah to Intaluanza. "I too am passing much blood, my lady. All of us are! What terrible plague has hit our palace today?"

Sarah felt her heart leap within her at the mention of a plague.

The young men that Abimelech had sent to help Abraham were bright and quick to learn their duties. They were also helpful in that they had grown up in the area of the Shephelah as shepherds and knew the terrain well. Abraham had thoroughly enjoyed the day and felt when he arrived back late at the inn that it had been a profitable beginning.

The woman servants greeted him with an inventory of their purchases. When he brought gold to pay them they refused laughingly. "No, sir," the elder one replied. "The good king, Abimelech, has paid for everything. You are to be his guest while you stay in our kingdom."

Abraham smiled warmly. "Your king is gracious."

The younger servant said tartly, "It was a good bargain for the king, sir. He has abducted your sister! He said to tell you not to be concerned for her. He does not plan to dishonor her, but to take her for wife!"

The women left, and Abraham was speechless. He sat down weakly on a low stool as a weighing heaviness overcame

343

him. Anxious self-recriminations began to embattle his mind. "Why did I bring Sarah here?" he thought. "Why did I endanger her again! There was no need . . . I did not have to map this area . . . not at this particular time!

"Why have I thought because of her age that she would no longer attract a man, especially a man like Abimelech—he who is fifty years older than I but looks young enough to be my son!

"And Sarah, still so beautiful! But I have not seen her beauty," he lamented. "I have only seen her as my barren wife, almost demanding my physical attentions!"

Abraham left the crowded courtyard of the inn and entered his rooms. He knelt by his pallet and wept,crying out to the Lord.

In the midst of his pleadings, he was sharply struck with a paralyzing fear. "The promise! O God, the promise that Sarah should have a son next spring! By him, O my God? Is it to be by Abimelech?"

Abraham beat his hands against his head and chest in agony. "No, my God! Please! No! Let my wife be returned to me! Do not give her into his arms!"

Jealousy raged within him. Abraham bolted to the door, but he stopped short. "How can I go madly to Abimelech and demand my wife? It was I who disclaimed her and called her my sister. If I do not keep up this deception, he will surely kill me and perhaps punish Sarah as well!" Once again he collapsed to the floor. "Perhaps I *am* impotent, and God has chosen another who is closer than I am to Noah, to be father to Sarah's son. She wanted a son to teach the wisdom of Noah. Has God found Abimelech more worthy than I?"

His jealousy and anger dissolved into panic and despair. Abraham did all he could think to do. He pleaded and prayed to God, but found no comfort.

The physicians of the king tried all the remedies they knew, for death seemed certain. When Abimelech fell into a deep sleep, they retired to let him rest, fearful that they would not see their king alive again. The hulking form of Phicol sat disconsolately outside the bedchamber.

"Will he live?" Phicol demanded, rising to stand a full cubit taller than the three doctors.

The physicians shook their heads gravely. "It is not likely," answered one. "The pain did not leave him even when he fell asleep."

"I and my men will watch here the entire night," Phicol announced. "We will call for you if there is any change." The doctors agreed and went to nearby quarters.

The hours of the fateful night wore on. As Abimelech slept, God came to him in a dream, saying, "Behold, you are a dead man, Abimelech! You are a dead man because the woman you have taken is another man's wife. She is the wife of Abraham."

In his dream Abimelech answered defensively, "Lord, do you slay the innocent? Did not the man himself say to me, 'She is my sister'? And she said herself, 'He is my brother.' In the integrity of my heart and the innocence of my hands I have done this!"

The king heard the Lord respond, "Yes, I know you acted in the integrity of your heart. It was I who kept you from sinning against me. It was I who did not allow you to touch her.

"Now then," said the Lord, "restore to the man his wife. He is a prophet, and he will pray for you, and you shall live. But if you do not restore her, know that you shall surely die, you, and all that are yours!"

When Abimelech awoke from the dream it was early morning. The pain still ached deeply inside his breast and radiated down his left arm. Slowly he climbed from the bed and dragged himself toward the door.

Phicol, hearing the movement, opened the door and rushed to support him. "You should not be up, my lord," Phicol declared, his face lined with concern.

"Go, Phicol," Abimelech whispered desperately. "Call together all the soldiers and male servants. And send for that man, Abraham! Bring him here immediately to this courtyard."

Phicol edged Abimelech onto the bench outside his bedchamber, the same one that Phicol had rested on throughout the night. Hastily the commander called out

345

instructions over the balcony to the servants below. Then the big man clumsily tried to make the king comfortable. Phicol knew about the hemorrhaging of the king's women, but he did not tell Abimelech for fear of upsetting him.

"Phicol, leave me be!" Abimelech told him, the agony and the shortness of breath making speech difficult. "Go for me and bring into the courtyard lambs and oxen and male and female slaves, the proper number for a sin vindication. And have the treasurer release for me one thousand pieces of silver."

When the courtyard was filled below and the animals herded near the well, King Abimelech stood weakly above the crowd and looked down at Abraham who had been set there before him.

Speaking so that all could hear, Abimelech disclosed the dream that he had just suffered. The people were greatly afraid.

Pointing a long arm and finger at Abraham, the king cried out harshly, "What have you done to us? And how have I sinned against you, that you have brought on me and my kingdom a great sin? You have done to me things that ought not to be done!"

A muffled uproar against Abraham rose. The men began to shout and crowded around him. Abimelech's broken voice mounted over the din, "What were you thinking of, that you did this thing?"

Abraham tore himself away from the guards and ran up the steps. Phicol grabbed him and kept the others from ascending.

"Let him speak!" demanded Abimelech.

"I did it because I thought there is no fear of God in this place, and they will kill me because of my wife. Besides she *is* my sister, the daughter of my father but not the daughter of my mother, and she became my wife. And when God caused me to leave the home of my father, I said to her, 'This is the kindness you must do me. At every place to which we come, say of me, he is my brother.'"

Abimelech called to the shepherds to bring the sheep and oxen to Abraham. "Get the woman Sarah," he demanded, and Phicol sent a man running for her. The commander then told the king and the people about the plague of the women. "Their wombs are shutting out the young. All of them are weak and have lost much blood." Abimelech did not respond but stared in awe at Abraham.

When Sarah came, she stood by Abraham. Abimelech, pain distorting his face, said to both of them, "Behold, my land is before you. Dwell wherever it pleases you."

To Sarah the king said, "Behold, I give to your brother a thousand pieces of silver. It is your vindication in the eyes of all who are with you. Before everyone you are righted!"

Leaning against the balcony wall for support the king pleaded breathlessly to Abraham, "Prophet of the holy God, pray for me! Pray for me and the women of my house!"

Abraham rushed past Phicol to the king. Laying his hands upon Abimelech, Abraham lifted up prayers for the king's healing. As he did so, Abimelech straightened himself and breathed deeply. A healthy color came to his face, and he began praising God with shouts of thanksgiving.

The astonished men were wide-eyed and still. They made no objection as Sarah and Abraham descended the steps and went through the crowd to the women's rooms. She took him first to the bedside of Intaluanza, and then each of the other young women. As he prayed for them, the bleeding stopped and the aborting spasms ceased.

When they returned to the outer courtyard, Abraham and Sarah found Abimelech and all of his men kneeling in prayer. "God has healed the women as he had healed you, King of Gerar," Abraham announced loudly.

Abimelech rose and went to him. The king's health had completely returned, and his step was spritely and determined. "Will you be staying with us to do your work?" Abimelech inquired, his voice steady and appreciative. "You know you may dwell safely here!"

"My watchmen are camped just outside your kingdom. I will send for them, and we will pitch our tents in your land," Abraham agreed.

Abimelech had avoided Sarah, but as Abraham turned to leave, the king looked longingly at her. In the Noachian language he bid her farewell. Their eyes met, and Sarah felt again a haunting attraction for the man.

"If our God had not prevented me," Abimelech smiled down at her, "I would have loved and adored you and made you my queen. Perhaps like our fathers, we would have lived together for centuries!"

As Abraham overheard the words, he felt tired and old. He had not slept, and his body ached and his head throbbed.

Chapter XXIII
THE SON OF LAUGHTER

Abraham had left the animals and slaves with Abimelech until he had opportunity to set up camp. He and Sarah walked to the inn as the villagers were waking and beginning their morning activities.

The innkeeper had been aroused early when the soldiers had come to get Abraham. The burly pot-bellied man blocked the entrance of his inn as Abraham and Sarah approached. "Go away!" he remonstrated gruffly. "I want no one staying here who is in disfavor with my king!"

Abraham was in no mood to argue with an ill-tempered man. Instead he turned wearily to the stables to get his camels.

"Wait, my husband!" Sarah objected.

Abraham looked back to see his wife obstinately challenging the innkeeper. "Do you dare insult the man who by the power of the holy God healed King Abimelech and stopped the plague that attacked the women of his household?" she said defiantly. "Do you not know that the king paid the vindication offering for his sin in taking me from my husband? The king himself told us we may dwell safely anywhere in his kingdom! Shall we return to him and tell him *you* have not shown us hospitality?"

As the astonished innkeeper listened, he was appreciating the fiery beauty of Sarah in anger. His mood changed, and he apologized. "Forgive me. What you say must be true. I cannot imagine King Abimelech allowing a woman of your loveliness to go free! Nor can I believe that Phicol would allow your husband to live if he thought the king desired you."

He backed away from the entrance and beckoned them to enter. "I shall have food sent to your rooms. Please, please do not mention my rudeness to the king!"

Abraham was stunned by her boldness, and he also did not miss seeing the innkeeper's wandering glances at Sarah. They entered the inn's courtyard, and Abraham watched Sarah as she walked in front of him. Her cloak hung in loose folds that swayed gracefully as she moved. She too was tired from the long night, but she held her head erect.

Hardly had they reached their rooms when three young servant girls came scampering after them, one with a pitcher of hot milk, one with a tray of fresh bread and curds, and another with a basket of summer fruits. The bright-eyed youngsters quickly arranged the meal on a low table and left.

Abraham and Sarah spoke little as they ate, finding the meal comforting and strengthening. Abraham wanted to talk of many things to Sarah, but he was too exhausted. Falling back on the bed, intending to rest but a moment, he fell into a deep sleep.

Sarah lay on the other pallet. She tried to blank out the events of the past hours so that sleep would come. A feeling of peace came over her as she closed her eyes. "Why should I worry about whether or not my husband lies with me? God has proved by his mighty hand that he wants no other man to know me. If the holy God wants a son to be born by me, then *he* must do the miracles: open my womb, and cause my husband to desire me!"

It was past noon when they both awoke. Abraham turned away from Sarah fearing that she might wish him to pursue her. He thought miserably to himself, "Why is it that Abimelech and even the innkeeper are excited by Sarah? But I, who love my wife and have her to hold, feel . . . nothing?"

Sarah rose and dressed. "There are still many hours of daylight, Abraham," she called to him gaily. "If you feel rested, let us forget all that happened and begin working on the measurements! This kingdom is part of the land that God promised! When the maps of the Shephelah are completed, you will have paced every cubit that God showed you from the mountain near Hazor!"

That Sarah did not expect him to embrace her surprised him. It made him want to reach for her which he did, but she pulled back.

Smiling wistfully she related, "I would really enjoy helping you survey the land today. Do you think the lads who assisted you yesterday will still be waiting for you?"

Abraham was delighted at her interest. "They spread a tent in the fields last night in order to wake early today and practice," he answered enthusiastically. "I am sure we can locate them!"

"I would like to camp tonight in those tents," Sarah replied with a whimsical frown. "I am tired of these musty rooms and walled-in courtyards. I miss our big black tent that moves like the bedouin about our land!"

"Sarah. . . ?" Abraham called to her tenderly. "You really want to be back in a tent after being offered the love of a king and another palace?"

"What palace, my wonderful husband, has a view of the Great Sea, the snow-capped mountain of Hermon, the sparkling waters of the Lake Chinnereth, the endless dunes and drifting sands of the desert, and the peaceful oaks of Mamre? Our tent has them all!"

"Then tonight we shall set the threshold of our tent in one of the charming valleys of the Shephelah under a canopy of sycamore trees," Abraham said, his eyes twinkling and his heart warm with affection for his wife.

Abraham and Sarah left instructions for the women servants to bring out the supplies on pack asses the next morning. Then taking enough food for the evening, they mounted their riding camels to join the young men in the fields. Immediately upon their arrival, they divided duties and began the survey.

There was a thrill of excitement each time an angle was measured, a line corded, or a distance computed. Abraham eagerly made notations and diagrams in his journal as he

351

began to enter the last maps of the promised land into his records.

After the evening meal the young men returned to Gerar leaving the tent and equipment for Abraham and Sarah to use. The sea breezes had stopped and the pleasant stillness of the night surrounded them. Having slept so late in the day, neither was ready for sleep again. Abraham brought their pallets outside, and they lay back together to look at the sky. The stars were brilliant, resting like countless diamonds above the graceful limbs and leafy tree tops of the sycamores. A distant star fell, and its comet train made a quickly disappearing arc in the glistening heavens.

Sarah began lightly singing praises to the Lord. As she did so, Abraham began to pray. Both of them felt the presence of the holy God close at hand, his Spirit everywhere around them.

"Abraham?" Sarah sat up suddenly. "I feel strange! . . . Touch me here, over my womb!"

Sarah slipped off her sleeping gown and placed his hand below her navel. Abraham moved his hand gently back and forth feeling hard contracted muscles under her smooth skin.

Sarah rose and went in the darkness into the tent, bringing back a burning lamp. Holding it so that she could see, she examined her gown. "There is blood," she uttered in wonder. "Abraham, do you suppose God has opened my womb?"

He asked her to lie down once more, and methodically he felt her body again. The tension had begun to ease. "How do you feel now, Sarah? Are you in any pain?"

"No," she said and hesitated. "I feel . . . moist and . . . open. . . ."

The lamplight made flattering shadows and highlights on Sarah's bare figure. Abraham allowed his hand to glide over her hips and down and around her thighs.

Sarah lay back, her arms and hands pillowing her head. With eyes fixed blankly at the stars, her mind searched intensely to comprehend the mystery. She knew the Lord had visited her. Somehow her womb had been miraculously opened.

Only vaguely did she realize that Abraham was fondling her. She felt him lie over her, kissing her in a way he had not

352

done in many years. Then came pleasurable tingling waves of erotic ecstasy as he entered her, his seed miraculously merging to form life in her womb.

The watchmen joined Abraham and Sarah in Gerar, bringing with them the other watchmen who had gone to search for Lot. Rather shamefacedly these men related that Lot had refused to return with them. "He told us he had taken his two daughters to wife and would live in his house in the Seir mountains," said one of the watchmen. "He seemed... almost happy!"

The surveying of Gerar was completed before the rains came. Abraham's people had come with the flocks, pitching camp in Abimelech's kingdom and along the greener coastal plains.

It came as a surprise to the shepherds and watchmen when Abraham announced that this year he wanted to continue to camp near Gerar and later on move to the oaks of Mamre. At the time only he and Sarah knew that under her flowing gowns was beginning to develop the child they had conceived.

Sarah found herself wandering by the tents of the younger women, holding their babies and playing with their little ones. In many cases the young mothers were great-great-grand-daughters of friends Sarah had known when she was first adopted by Terah. Sarah was proud of the child she was bearing, but humiliated to admit to anyone she was pregnant. If she and Abraham had laughed at the thought of their having a child, how would these servant girls and others react?

But the time came when the whisperings and twitterings began. Young and old, men and women, were amused and many astonished that Abraham and Sarah still had intimate relations and that anyone as old as Sarah should be carrying a baby. The knowledge that Abimelech had taken Sarah to his bedchamber raised speculations by some as to who really fathered the child.

It was a final test and much more difficult to endure than either Abraham or Sarah could have imagined. To do the will of God and to wait for his promises proved less demanding than to have people scorn and laugh when those promises were at last being fulfilled.

"The compensation for the ridicule," Abraham consoled her as she drew near to her time of delivery, "is that we know it is *unnatural* for us to have a child. But what better way to know that it is also a *pure miracle of God!*"

That day was warm, and Sarah felt the heat more than she usually did as she rested outside the tent. The strain of the pregnancy had aged her, and she had little energy. "I pray the holy God will allow me to live to see the baby. That too would be a miracle!"

Abraham's eyes grew sad. They had discussed the danger of the birth, but as the time came closer neither had wanted to mention it further. "The Lord is a merciful God, Sarah," he said to reassure her and to fight off his own fears. "What can we do but trust him?"

"I do not have the strength of Noah from my mother's side," Sarah reminded him in one of the few instances she ever mentioned her mother. "Nor was my mother a strong woman. Though she was still quite young, she died the first winter in the Ararats after giving birth to me."

"You have trusted in the one holy God for all these years, my wife. Be at peace and trust him now."

Sarah nodded slightly and lay back against the cushions, closing her eyes. She folded her hands over her greatly distended stomach. Abraham kissed her lightly and rose to leave.

Sharply the first birth pain began, and Sarah's eyes opened wide as she experienced the exquisite wrenching contraction. "Abraham! Abraham!" she shouted, all apprehension dispelled by a delirious joy and expectation. "It is happening! Oh, my husband, it is happening!"

Abraham raced back to her side and then nervously left once again to seek the midwives. When all was in order, he called his people to prayer and interceded for Sarah and the babe to be born.

Hours went by. The people fasted and prayed throughout the night, while Sarah's contractions grew stronger and became slowly closer together. There was a glorious sense in the camp that the holy God was present and acting.

Abraham went and stayed in the tent while Sarah brought forth their son. He held the promised child as it came from Sarah's womb. All the while Abraham was praising the Lord and calling the boy by the name the Lord had given, Isaac. The baby was perfectly formed and beautiful. After wrapping young Isaac in birth cloths, the midwives put the child to Sarah's breast and left the tent, taking the soiled linens and water pots with them.

Sarah looked up sleepily at her husband and down at the wet ringlets of dark hair on the small head resting on her arm. Tears streamed down her cheeks as she smiled in grateful wonder and happiness.

New vigor entered Abraham as he watched his new son suckle from Sarah. Kneeling beside them he felt renewed as if the strength of his youth had been returned to him. He began buoyantly quoting the words of the Lord.

"I am God Almighty. Walk before me and be blameless, and I will give you the promise made between me and you. I will multiply you exceedingly.

"Behold, my covenant is with you, and you shall be the father of a multitude of nations.

"And I will give to you, and to your descendants after you, the land of your sojournings, all the land of Canaan, for an everlasting possession. And I will be their God!"

Tears now filled his eyes. "Sarah, my wife, Isaac, my son. . . ." He wanted to say more, but the Lord's reality and power were too present in the tent. As Sarah sang softly, Abraham lifted his arms to praise his God—and to laugh for joy.

APPENDIX

Cover quotation from *Abraham: Recent Discoveries and Hebrew Origins* (Faber and Faber, London, 1936), p. 19.

1. For those who question the association of Shem with the Sumerians, Samuel N. Kramer offers this explanation: "The equation of 'Shem' and 'Shumer' . . . presented two difficulties: the interchange of the vowels *e* and *u* and the omission of the final *er*. Now the first of these presents no difficulty at all; the cuneiform *u* often becomes *e* in Hebrew—a particularly pertinent example is the Akkadian *shumu,* 'name,' and the Hebrew *shem*. As for the second difficulty— the omission of the final *er* of 'Shumer' in its Hebrew counterpart 'Shem'—this can now be explained by applying the Sumerian law of amissibility of final consonants. For the word 'Shumer' was pronounced *Shumi* or, even more probably, *Shum* (the final *i* is a very short, *shewa*-like vowel), and the Hebrews thus took it over from Sumerian as 'Shem.' " From *The Sumerians* (University of Chicago Press, 1963), pp. 297-298.

2. When Sir C. Leonard Woolley excavated Puabi's tomb in 1924, he discovered it amazingly intact. The twenty-five attendants still placidly surrounded the wooden bier, their festive apparel, insignia and jewels in place. "It is most probable that the victims walked to their places," wrote Woolley, "took some kind of drug . . . and lay down in

order. . . . There does not seem to have been anything brutal in the manner of their deaths." From *Ur of the Chaldees* (Norton Co., NYC, 1965), p. 60.

"The tomb was identified by a lapis-lazuli cylinder seal bearing the name and title of Shub-ad [British Museum experts have recently claimed that the word *Shub-ad* was a title and that the young woman's name should be translated *Puabi*]. At the southwest end of the shaft there lay a harp and the bodies of two women. The harp stood against the pit wall and one woman lay right against it with the bones of her hands actually in the place of the strings; she must have been the harpist and was playing almost to the last." From *Discovering the Royal Tombs at Ur* edited by Shirley Glubok (Macmillan, NYC, 1969), p. 71.

"For there was treachery—at least, that is how it would appear. Excavators found that the Lady Shub-ad's [Puabi's] wardrobe box had been placed in such a way as to cover a gaping hole in . . . her tomb chamber and the hole led into another . . . tomb, a king's tomb." From *Abraham: His Heritage and Ours* by Dorothy B. Hill (Beacon Press, Boston, 1957), pp. 36, 39.

Note: The beautiful gold, lapis-lazuli and carnelian headpiece, earrings and necklace of Princess Puabi are on display at the University Museum in Philadelphia.

3. Charran, Harran or Haran. The first spelling is preferred by many scholars because it more accurately follows the original pronunciation. The other two, however, are commonly found on maps and references and are often confused with Abram's brother's name, Haran, which is a completely different word in the original languages.

4. ". . . it would seem reasonable that any substantial change in the earth's climate must somehow be related to changes in the water vapor content of the atmosphere. More water vapor would create a warmer and more uniform climate; less vapor would cause a colder and more sharply zoned climate." From *The Genesis Flood* by Whitcomb and Morris (Baker Book House, Grand Rapids, 1961), p. 225.

5. "Since the Pliocene and Pleistocene are supposed to represent the most recent geographical epochs, except that of the present, and since nearly all the mountains of the world have been found to have fossils from these times near their summits . . . all have been uplifted essentially simultaneously and quite recently." From *The Genesis Flood,* p. 128.

6. Woolley's excavations of Ur found evidence of the Great Flood. This is the way he described it:
"We had long before seen the meaning of our discovery. The bed of water-laid clay deposited against the sloping face of the mound, which extended from the town to the stream or canal at the north-east end, could only have been the result of a flood, no other agency could possibly account for it. Inundations are of normal occurrence in Lower Mesopotamia, but no ordinary rising of the rivers would leave behind it anything approaching the bulk of this clay bank: 8 feet of sediment imply a very great depth of water, and the flood which deposited it must have been of a magnitude unparalleled in local history. That it was so is further proved by the fact that the clay bank marks a definite break in the continuity of the local culture; a whole civilisation which existed before it is lacking above it and seems to have been submerged by the waters.
"Taking into consideration all the facts, there could be no doubt that the flood of which we had thus found the only possible evidence was the Flood of Sumerian history and legend, the Flood on which is based the story of Noah." From *Ur of the Chaldees,* pp. 28-29.

7. "And Nicolaus of Damascus, in the fourth book of his history, says thus: 'Abram reigned at Damascus, being a foreigner, who came with an army out of the land above Babylon. . . . Now the name of Abram is even still famous in the country of Damascus; and there is showed a village named from him, *the habitation of Abram.'*" From *Josephus,* translated by William Whiston (Kregel, Grand Rapids, 1974), p. 32.

8. In a book describing present day life in the marshes of Iraq, Wilfred Thesiger writes: "Before the first palaces were built at Ur, men had stepped out into the dawn from such a [reed] house, launched a canoe like this, and gone hunting. Woolley had unearthed their dwellings and models of their boats buried deep under the relics of Sumeria, deeper even than the evidence of the Flood. Five thousand years of history were here and the pattern was still unchanged . . . canoes moving in procession down a waterway . . . narrow waterways that wound deeper into the Marshes. A naked man in a canoe with a trident in his hand, reed houses built upon the water, black, dripping buffaloes . . ." From *The Marsh Arabs* (E. P. Dutton, NYC, 1964), pp. 9-10.

9. This description of Sarai follows the details given in Abram's Journal as it was recently translated from the Dead Sea Scrolls. The Journal of Abram was composed or else copied from other manuscripts sometime between 250 B.C. and 68 A.D. The part about Sarai concludes, "Her beauty is greater than all other women's and she excels them all. What is more, along with all this beauty she has great wisdom. . . ." From "Memoirs of the Patriarchs" in *The Dead Sea Scriptures,* translated by Theodor H. Gaster (Anchor Books, Doubleday and Co., Garden City, NY, 1964), p. 259.

10. The Great Flood is included in Mesopotamian legends about a king named Gilgamesh and his friend Enkidu. After many daring exploits together, Enkidu is killed. Gilgamesh is terrified to realize that he too must someday die. The hero sets out to find his ancestor Utnapishtim to whom the gods had granted eternal life. It was said that Utnapishtim would never die because he along with his wife had saved human and animal life during the Great Flood. After a dangerous journey, Utnapishtim is finally located. Gilgamesh hears the story of the Flood and is told of a special plant that will renew his youth. Gilgamesh finds the plant, but the plant is later seized by a snake while Gilgamesh is taking a swim. The story has many obvious biblical parallels.

11. "[Abram] was a person of great sagacity, both for understanding all things, and persuading his hearers. . . . He communicated to them arithmetic, and delivered to them the science of astronomy. . . ." *Josephus,* pp. 32-33.

"Eupolemus, an Alexandrian historian, says that 'in the city Kamarina of Babylon, which some call the city of Urie (that is, being interpreted, city of the Chaldaeans), there was born in the thirteenth generation (after the Flood) Abraham, who surpassed all in birth and wisdom.' The so-called 'interpretation' of the name is no interpretation at all but an allusion to the Biblical phrase, but the name Kamarina, 'the Moon City,' faithfully recalls the religious significance of the ancient Ur whose patron was Nannar, the Moon-god, and the qualification 'of Babylon' defines its whereabouts." From *Abraham: Recent Discoveries and Hebrew Origins* by Sir C. Leonard Woolley (Faber and Faber, London, 1936), p. 19.

12. The dream of Abram concerning the palm and the cedar trees is vividly described in part of his Journal found in *The Dead Sea Scriptures,* p. 258-259.

13. "Much more interesting is a group of rock inscriptions in the already often mentioned graywacke quarries of the Wady Hammamat. Hither . . . [he] sent his vizier . . . to fetch him a great sarcophagus. It may well be doubted whether as many as 20,000 men really accompanied the expedition, but there is no need for skepticism as regards two miraculous happenings which attended their short stay. The graphic story is told of a gazelle advancing fearlessly in full sight of the workpeople to drop its young upon the very stone intended for the lid of the sarcophagus. Eight days later there was a great rain-storm which disclosed a well 10 cubits by 10 cubits across full of water to the brim. To the prosaically minded historian the personality of the vizier . . . is of greater interest, for it seems well-nigh certain that he was none other than the future Ammenemes [Amenemhet] I." From *Egypt of the Pharaohs* by Sir Alan Gardiner (Oxford University Press, 1961), p. 125.

The exact translation of the quarry inscriptions describing the miracles that occurred to Shetepibre may be found in *Ancient Records of Egypt,* Volume I, by James H. Breasted (University of Chicago Press, 1906-7), pp. 439-450.

14. The difficulty in finding the historical Red Sea port is still with us today. "The location of the Red Sea landing ports is one of the problems to be solved by future archaeology." From *The Ancient Kingdoms of the Nile* by Walter A. Fairservis (Crowell, NYC, 1962), p. 115.

15. "Amenemhet I had been a vizier under the last of the Eleventh Dynasty pharaohs. Just how he won the throne is not known, but his reign brought into prominence a god who had been practically unknown before this time, or at any rate, had been no political force in Egypt. This was the god Amon, after whom Amenemhet took his name.

"Amon was a force which could easily be extended toward wider dominion—ultimately to universal dominion. The name Amon meant 'Hidden,' so that Amon was an unseen being, a god who might be immanent everywhere. . . . He came to supersede the gods who had formerly stood for Thebes [Wase] and to function as the god of the nation. . . . As the God of the Egyptian nation, he was to become the great imperial god under the Empire and thus to assume a universal nature. Toward the end of the Empire he came to be the wealthiest force in the world, and the power of his high priest rivaled that of the pharaoh. Now, at the beginning of the Twelfth Dynasty, he was being dragged out of cosmic obscurity to begin this tremendous career." From *The Culture of Ancient Egypt* by John A. Wilson (University of Chicago Press, 1951), pp. 130-31.

Many dates are suggested for the birth of Abraham. With the most recent archaeological discoveries, however, more and more scholars agree that he lived in the twenty-first and twentieth centuries (2075-1900), entering Canaan in 2000 B.C. and leaving for Egypt in 1998. Abraham's journal discovered in the Dead Sea Scrolls claims that Abram and Sarai stayed seven years in Egypt (The Dead Sea Scriptures, pp. 259-260). Amenemhet was the Grand Vizier at that time and became the pharaoh in 1991 BC, the probable year Abram and Sarai returned to Canaan.

16. The account of Abram going to Hazor is found in *The Dead Sea Scriptures,* p. 263, and the *Book of Jubilees* 13:20-21. The mountain Abram climbed is the modern Jebel el-'Asur, near Hazor. It is the highest spot in central Palestine. See footnote 25 in above reference.

17. At no time in Egypt's long history was it ever more blessed than in the two hundred years of the dynasty of Amenemhet I. Nor was there ever another period of time when the Land of Kemi could have been a more suitable nurturing place for the sons of Abraham:
"We have seen that under the vigourous and skillful leadership of Amenemhet I the rights and privileges attained by the powerful landed nobles were for the first time properly adjusted and subjected to the centralized authority of the kingship, thus enabling the country, after a long interval, again to enjoy the inestimable advantages accruing from a uniform control of the nation's affairs. This difficult and delicate task doubtless consumed a large part of Amenemhet I's reign, but when it was once thoroughly accomplished his house was able to rule the country for over two centuries. It is probable that at no other time in the history of Egypt did the land enjoy such widespread and bountiful prosperity as now ensued." From *A History of Egypt* by James H. Breasted (Chas. Scribner's Sons, NYC, 1909), p. 177.

18. "The part of the Dead Sea south of the Lisan peninsula is really a large shallow bay, never more than three feet deep, and it has been suggested that it is of fairly recent formation, having been created by an earthquake which lowered the level of this section of the Rift by several feet, and thus caused the waters of the Dead Sea to flood over into what is now the southern basin. It is held that if this did happen, it would explain the destruction of the . . . cities of the plain. . . ."

From *The Geography of the Bible* by Denis Baly (Harper Bros., NYC, 1957), p. 205.